# Critical Acclaim for Janet Dailey's
## THE PRIDE OF HANNAH WADE . . .

"Readers who love Janet Dailey will no doubt love *THE PRIDE OF HANNAH WADE.* Dailey's novels have always been marked by strong stories that barrel along at full throttle. . . . An atmospherically charged, action-filled story."

—*Chicago Sun-Times*

"Janet Dailey weaves a wonderfully romantic tale, and *THE PRIDE OF HANNAH WADE* is no exception. . . . A spellbinding story."

—*Chattanooga Times*

"A double-barrelled melodrama. . . . The reader . . . is in for a galloping adventure."

—*The New York Times Book Review*

"Janet Dailey's ability to recreate the West is enhanced by a courageous heroine and a ruggedly appealing hero. . . . *THE PRIDE OF HANNAH WADE IS JANET DAILEY AT HER BEST.*"

—*Publishers Weekly*

**Books by Janet Dailey**

The Pride of Hannah Wade
Silver Wings, Santiago Blue
Calder Born, Calder Bred
Stands a Calder Man
This Calder Range
This Calder Sky
Foxfire Light
The Hostage Bride
The Lancaster Men
For the Love of God
Separate Cabins
Terms of Surrender
Night Way
Ride the Thunder
The Rogue
Touch the Wind

Published by POCKET BOOKS

Most Pocket Books are available at special quantity discounts for bulk purchases for sales promotions, premiums or fund raising. Special books or book excerpts can also be created to fit specific needs.

For details write the office of the Vice President of Special Markets, Pocket Books, 1230 Avenue of the Americas, New York, New York 10020.

# Janet Dailey

# The Pride of Hannah Wade

PUBLISHED BY POCKET BOOKS NEW YORK

Another *Original* publication of POCKET BOOKS

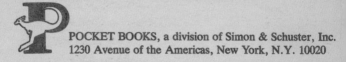

POCKET BOOKS, a division of Simon & Schuster, Inc.
1230 Avenue of the Americas, New York, N.Y. 10020

ISBN: 0-671-49801-0

First Pocket Books Mass Market printing November, 1985

10 9 8 7 6 5 4 3 2 1

POCKET and colophon are registered trademarks of Simon & Schuster, Inc.

Printed in the U.S.A.

# CHAPTER 1

*March 1876,*
*Apacheria Country*
*Near Fort Bayard,*
*New Mexico*
*Territory*

"Out here, a lady has to survive the best way she can," Hannah Wade offered in droll sympathy to the young woman showing her dismay as she looked about the huddle of adobe buildings, stacked with pottery and wares inside and out. "Sometimes that means enduring unladylike conditions."

Suddenly the hot stillness was broken by the clatter of unshod hooves pounding across the hard desert floor. One minute the only dust that stirred in the nameless, half-Mexican settlement of straw-and-mud-brick adobe buildings was raised by the trailing hems of the fashionably bustled dresses worn by the three army officers' wives—and in the next dust swirled in a low-hanging haze around the scrawny piebald ponies and their Apache riders.

Hannah Wade stiffened at the sight of the Indians charging toward them. No shouts or war cries shattered the air; that was not the Apache way, which was a practice of stealth, silence, and surprise. Two long years of watching her husband ride out at the head of cavalry companies had taught her that much.

In the seconds they had before the Apaches were on them, Hannah glanced at their escorting officer, whose rough features were shaded by the brim of his campaign hat. "Captain?" The thread of alarm in her low voice demanded his instruction and guidance, but her poise remained as smooth as the coil of mahogany hair at the nape of her neck.

His hand was already lifted, forestalling any action by the black sergeant and the two black troopers waiting by the army ambulance, the military conveyance that had brought the women to this trading settlement. "Be at ease, ladies." Captain Jake Cutter raised a long, thin cigar to his mouth, his narrowed and keen blue eyes showing a watchful calm. The gauntlet-style gloves were tucked through his belt, leaving his large hands bare.

The Apaches halted their ponies in the small clearing, filling it with billowing alkali dust. Four of them dismounted and advanced toward the brush-roofed *ramada* where Hannah stood. Lieutenant Sloane's young wife was at her side and somewhere behind her was Ophelia Bettendorf, wife of the commanding officer at Fort Bayard.

Mrs. Sloane, who was new to the territory, gave a little cry of fear at the approach of the unkempt-looking savages. At the same instant, Hannah noticed the small band had isolated them from the army ambulance and the soldiers—and any protection they might lend. Captain Jake Cutter continued to occupy a corner of her side vision, the pungent smell of his cigar mixing with the raised dust in the air.

No war paint adorned the blunt-featured faces of the Apaches, and the weapons they carried were held in loose readiness, not brandished in a threatening manner. Some of the high tension left Hannah as she recognized that the captain's split-second reading of the situation had been accurate; they were not being attacked.

With an effort, Hannah ignored the silent menace of the Apaches' presence and turned from the stare of the flat black eyes to the young wife of the recently transferred Lieutenant Richard Sloane. "Do you suppose the Apaches guessed you are a new arrival, Mrs. Sloane, and staged all this for your benefit?" The lightness of her voice assured the newcomer that she had nothing to fear.

"Wh—what do they want?" Rebecca Sloane shrank against Hannah as a lithely muscled Apache brave walked toward them.

His shoulders were wide and his chest deep. Bared to the waist, his dark copper skin was covered with a fine, dulling film of dust. A breechcloth was wrapped around his waist, the front hanging to his knees and extending over the buckskin leggings of his high moccasins. His ageless, heavy-boned features had a brutal quality, their harsh composition aggravated by a knife scar across the right cheek.

For a brief instant, contempt showed in his expression as he noted the fear in Rebecca Sloane's voice and eyes; then he rudely shouldered his way past the women to enter the trader's small store. Two other braves followed, pushing their way past as well. The rank odor of their bodies was so strong that Hannah pressed a lavender-scented handkerchief to her nose to block out the smell. She was barely able to disguise her disgust for these vile, filthy savages, who bore no

3

resemblance to the "noble red man" that she'd read about in the eastern newspapers before coming west.

"After all these years on the frontier with the colonel," the matriarchal Mrs. Bettendorf murmured, "I still find the manners of these heathens insufferable."

Fear continued to edge Rebecca Sloane's expression, but it was overcome by an uneasy worry that she might not have acquitted herself well in the eyes of the commander's wife. "I . . . I've never seen a wild Indian before," she stammered out in her defense. "Only the scouts at the fort. It was rather frightening when they rode up like that."

"It gave us all a start," Mrs. Bettendorf assured her, although Hannah personally doubted if anything was capable of shocking this iron woman, a staunch supporter of her husband and his career and the occupant of the female side of the fort's throne, ruling over the officers' wives. "As long as those Indians are in that store, I don't intend to go inside." With a regal swish of her skirts, the commander's wife turned and marched to a corner of the shady brush arbor, her amply rounded figure emphasizing the wig-wag of her swagged bustle. "You'll need some of these clay jars, Mrs. Sloane."

Ollas were suspended from a corner post of the *ramada*. Hannah drifted after her companions, not listening to the lecture about the dual use of the containers, which kept water cool by evaporation and also provided a cooling effect on the surroundings by the same method. Her attention remained with the Apache warriors left on guard in the clearing. She was curiously repelled and fascinated by them at the same time.

Short of stature and honed to a tough leanness, they wore a ragtag collection of clothing. Two were dressed in the loose-fitting shirts and pants of white men's attire, and a third wore buckskin pants and a plaid shirt. One of them, Hannah noticed, was quite heavy for an Apache. Lank black hair hung to their shoulders and below, faded sweatbands around their foreheads. Except for the lizardlike awareness of the eyes catching every movement about them, the Apaches appeared indifferent.

The dust had settled, although the smell of it remained in the still air . . . the smell of dust and cigar smoke. She glanced at the holder of the long brown cigar, skimming briefly that hawkish face leathered to a smooth shade of brown by constant exposure to the harsh desert elements. Small seams showed around his features, lines of experience drawn out from the corners of eyes that were as dry and blue as the desert sky—quick eyes that missed nothing, including her glance.

"Are they Chiricahuas?" Although Hannah's husband's regiment, the Ninth Cavalry, had only been transferred from Texas to the District of New Mexico six months ago, she had quickly become familiar with the local Indian problems. Since the death of Cochise a year and a half ago, more and more Chiricahua had become discontented with reservation life and left the agency land in neighboring southern Arizona.

"They're Chiricahuas, but not from Cochise's band." From his position in the *ramada*'s shade, Captain Cutter had an unobstructed view of both the clearing and the crudely built adobe store. "More likely, the *Nde-nda-i* group."

For many newcomers to the Southwest, the Apache tribe was a confusion of smaller bands: the Lipan-Apache, the Kiowa-Apache, the Mescalero, the Jicarilla, the Chiricahua, and the Western Apache. And each band was made up of groups that shared hunting grounds and cooperated in certain undertakings such as war and religious ceremonies. The groups were composed of scattered, extended families, the lineage reck-oned through both parents although the culture was essentially matriarchal. Each group had leaders, but no chief could make commitments for the whole tribe.

When Cochise made peace, he had spoken only for himself and promised to urge the rest of his group to agree to the terms. No treaty was made with the other Chiricahua bands, leaving them free to raid and war as they were wont to do, as evidenced by the frequent sorties they made against the miners in the Silver City area.

Hannah had heard the frustration caused by the too-democratic system discussed too many times. The army didn't know how to deal with it. But it wasn't that knowledge that brought her attention to the captain now. He'd spoken with certainty rather than suspicion in naming the band. More than once her husband, Stephen, had complained about the difficulty of telling one Indian from another, yet the captain was claiming to distinguish one Apache band from a host of others.

"How do you know this, Captain?" she challenged. He absently rolled the cigar along his lips, taking his time in answering. The action showed the angles and hollows of his jaw and cheek. Of all the officers at Fort Bayard, Captain Jake Cutter alone remained clean-shaven, growing neither whiskers nor mustache. It set him apart from the other men, as did many things about him.

"See that dumpy, mean-looking one on the glass-eyed roan?" He spoke around his cigar, his lips barely moving while he clamped the butt between his teeth. "He fits the description of Juh, a leader of the *Nde-nda-i* group." He pronounced the Apache's name as *Hwū*.

In her earlier perusal of the small band, Hannah had glossed over the fat one. This time her glance paused on him. Whether or not her impression was colored by Captain Cutter's words, she sensed a malevolence behind those devil-black eyes, a base cruelty that brought a shiver to her skin and prompted her to look away.

"What is he doing here?" She sought to dispel the sensation and rushed the question, giving it a tone of demand.

"Shopping, the same as you, Mrs. Wade." The dry reminder came with the hard gleam of a smile. "Although I expect they're wanting to trade for something other than odd pieces of pottery and baskets to pretty their wickiups."

His comment obviously revealed his skepticism about the importance of this trip. They'd come to purchase some inexpensive Mexican goods that would be utilitarian as well as decorative for Mrs. Sloane's quarters on Officers' Row. Without some attempt to brighten it, army housing could be as drab and barren as the desolate land surrounding it.

"Spoken like a jealous bachelor who has no woman to create a cheery corner where he can slip away from the army's hard existence," Hannah retorted, completely sure of her role and purpose in her husband's life, which was to provide beauty and grace and to alleviate loneliness.

"I knew I was missing something." His jesting comment mocked her sentiment, but not unkindly.

A flurry of movement distracted Hannah, checking her reply as the Apaches who'd been in the store came out. They moved swiftly, not appearing to hurry yet gliding across the ground. They swung onto the blanket-covered saddletrees strapped on their horses' backs and each gathered up the single braided rawhide strand looped around the horse's lower jaw that served as both bridle and rein. The shifting hooves dug up the dust layers, the horses snorting to clear their nostrils.

The first Apache, the bare-chested brave with the scarred cheek, faced his tan and white pony toward the store. The look he threw at Captain Cutter was a killing one, but the border Spanish he called out was intended for the trader inside the adobe building.

"He said he would be back when the 'yellow legs' and his 'buffalo soldiers' had gone," Hannah translated. "Yellow legs" referred to the yellow stripe down the legs of a cavalry officer's trousers, while "buffalo soldier" was the Indians' descriptive term for the Negro troopers whose kinky hair reminded them of the shaggy mane of a buffalo.

"I heard." But he couldn't guess the reason for a return visit—perhaps to complete a trade for illegal goods or to settle a score over some slight, or merely to talk big.

In a scurry of ponies, the Apaches swept out of the clearing and melted almost instantly into the desert scrub that grew thickly along the dry wash. Cutter watched until there was no more trace of them, then brought his attention back to the party of women.

A shaft of sunlight pierced the dried brush roofing the crude shelter and awakened fiery lights in the red-brown hair of Mrs. Wade. They caught his eye, causing his glance to linger on her. Slim and round-bodied, she had ivory-fair skin and heavily fringed brown eyes. Her smoothly refined features held a contented look, as of strong passions running a serene course. His attention centered briefly on the soft crease of her lips, a hint of will and pride at the corners. When her glance swung to him, it was full and direct.

"You speak Spanish." Cutter remembered the instant translation she'd made of the Apache's words only minutes ago.

"When we were stationed in Brownsville, I had a Mexican woman for a maid. And you, Captain, where did you learn?" The heat was already building, even in the shade beneath the *ramada*. She lifted a lace handkerchief to her face and delicately pressed it around her mouth to absorb the fine sheen of dampness.

"I guess I picked it up during all those years on the Texas border, too." Cutter observed her action, so indicative of breeding and refinement. The lavender fragrance drifted across the heated air to him, stirring up memories and an old bitterness. Those were behind him—and better left there.

So instead he considered the way the army could isolate a man. Even though he and Major Wade had served in the same regiment for the last four years, this was the first time they'd been assigned to the same post. Therefore he'd only recently become acquainted with the major's wife. At some of those Texas outposts, months would go by without Cutter ever seeing a white woman. Few officers permitted their wives to join them, not necessarily because they were bothered by the hardships of the post or the threat of hostiles, but because they were concerned about their women living in close proximity to all the enlisted colored soldiers. Exceptions were the forts near centers of civilization, like Brownsville.

The entire officer corps of the Ninth Cavalry Regiment was white. The Negro soldiers they commanded never advanced beyond the noncommissioned ranks. And few officers were happy about serving in a colored regiment, but Cutter had been with the Ninth since its inception after the War Between the States. Besides, he'd always had trouble fitting the mold.

At the outbreak of the Civil War, he'd enlisted in the Union army at the age of eighteen. He was a natural leader, and all his promotions had come in the field, catapulting him up through the ranks and earning him an officer's commission without the benefit of a West Point education, something the War Between the States had done with many a soldier.

But that need didn't exist after the war was won, and the army found itself with a surfeit of officers. Like many other officers, Mrs. Wade's husband among them, Cutter had been demoted at the close of the war. But unlike Major Wade with his West Point ring, he didn't insist on the observance of military courtesy that dictated his being addressed by his former rank. While the others scratched and clawed to regain their previous status, Cutter found no great difference between the major he'd been and the captain he now was. Having seen the army from both sides—officer and enlisted man—he was satisfied with the uniform and the job.

He was an officer, but he didn't fit in with them; Jake Cutter was a soldier, but he didn't belong in the ranks. At thirty-two, he was an outsider to both, and the years in between had calloused him with a hard self-sufficiency. So when he looked at the proud major's wife, she represented a class and lifestyle he didn't seek—the formal soirees and teas, the petty post intrigues and politics, and all their accompanying emptiness and greedy ambitions.

"Tell me, Captain Cutter"—the scented lace was lowered and smoothed by her slender white hands—"how did you know those Apaches intended us no harm when they rode in? You didn't even put a hand to your pistol."

Her observation produced a brief flicker of admiration in him. "A collection of things, but most notably their clothes," he answered, smiling as he held the cigar in his hand. "Only one of them was stripped to . . . his native gear; the rest were fully dressed. Nah-tay, the Apache scout at the fort, told me it's bad to wear clothes when fighting. If you're shot, a piece of material can get inside the wound and cause an infection. Don't ever underestimate the natural intelligence of an Apache, Mrs. Wade." He shifted to survey the clearing with its scatter of adobe huts. "Perhaps you should join the other ladies and finish your shopping. It might be best if we don't linger here too long."

A small question flared in the brown wells of her eyes, but she was too well-trained a military wife to ask it. Army discipline dictated that one accept orders without questioning the reasons for them.

"Of course, Captain." The long folds of her skirt made a swishing sound as she turned to rejoin her companions.

His gaze lingered on the gentle slope of her shoulders and the fashionably nipped-in waist of the black-and-green-striped dress top. A beautiful woman. Then his thoughts moved on to more pressing matters as he left the shade of the brush arbor and crossed to the army ambulance.

The driver, a tall, leanly muscled black sergeant named John T. Hooker, stood by the four hitch of long-eared mules. Sergeants were the officers' communication links to their troops; all orders were funneled through them. John T. Hooker was A Company's top sergeant. He'd served under Cutter during those long border years in Texas and had earned the chevrons on his sleeve through skill, courage, and intelligence. Unlike most of the black troops, where literacy was a problem, Hooker could read and write. He was officer material, but Cutter knew no black trooper would rise above a noncommissioned rank in this white man's army.

"Came outta nowhere, didn't they?" Hooker studied the brush.

"They usually do—if you're going to see them at all," Cutter replied.

"Think they'll be waitin' for us?" Hooker wondered. The two accompanying troopers stayed by the military ambulance where their horses were tied, standing at ease now that the threat was gone, yet remaining watchful and alert.

"They stopped here for one of two reasons—ammunition or supplies." A mule stamped its foot at a fly, its brace chains rattling. "Let's hope it was ammunition. They'll be less likely to waste what they've got left on us." A humorless smile lifted the corners of his mouth.

"That was a raidin' party on their way to Mexico, and I'd bet my stripes on it," the sergeant declared, perspiration from the desert heat giving a sheen to his brown-black skin and accenting his strong cheekbones and jaw.

"I don't think you'd lose." With an idle slap on the curried-slick neck of a mule, Cutter turned to bring the women into his view. They were still outside poking through the odds and ends stacked under the *ramada,* nicknamed the "squaw cooler" by some whites, in search of some house trinket.

The owner of the store emerged from the adobe building, a potbellied white man with a bushy mustache and long, flowing sideburns, slovenly dressed in baggy pants secured by dark suspenders over the faded red of his long johns. He was one of the early settlers of the area, drawn by the stories of Apache gold and then held by the money to be made selling supplies to miners, soldiers, and Apaches. Long ago he'd married a squaw from one of the Mimbres bands so he could have a foot in both camps, the white man's and the red. But he was never fully accepted in either; whites looked askance at a squaw man, and the Apache never forgot the white man's greed.

"'Lo, Captain." The locals called him "Apache Jack" Reynolds. As he approached Cutter, he showed a measure of discomfort, a nervous tic twitching the skin along the corner of his upper lip. "Sorry about that little incident. Hope it didn't scare the ladies much. They were just some of my wi—Little Dove's relatives come to visit." He checked the impulse to identify the heavy, plodding Apache woman as his wife, craving the respectability of his own kind and deprived of it by their prejudices against his copper-skinned wife, no longer the maiden he'd once desired. "They're comin' back. Like most of their kind, they get nervous when the army's around." He laughed, weakly trying to make a joke out of it while explaining the parting comment in case Cutter understood Spanish.

"Relatives." Cutter somehow doubted that. "I thought I recognized Juh. Who was the one that called to you?"

Beads of sweat broke out across the trader's forehead. He couldn't be sure whether the question was a trap and Cutter already knew the warrior's identity. He mopped his brow with a soiled bandanna and tried to hide his unease.

"Lutero." It was a tight, forced smile he offered with the name; then, in defense, he added, "You know how tangled these Apache relations get sometimes. I mean, even Cochise was related to Mangas Coloradas and that war shaman Geronimo."

Lutero. Cutter matched the name to the scar-cheeked image in his mind and filed it away. Such pieces of information were maybe important and maybe not. But it might be worth remembering that he had seen an Apache, believed to be Juh, in the area with a handful of warriors, among them a brave called Lutero. Maybe a raiding party? Blood always ran fast in the spring. It had been bold of them to show themselves to Cutter and the escorting troopers. There was no doubt in his mind that their little group had been thoroughly scouted before Juh and his band had ridden in.

"Is there anything I can do for you, Captain?" The inquiry had an edge to it; the questioning had put Apache Jack on the defensive and turned him slightly belligerent.

A mule snorted, ridding its nostrils of accumulated dust. "We'd like to water the team if you can spare it," Cutter replied.

"The well's there to the side. Ya can draw what ya need." The white trader gestured in the general direction of the desert well.

"Sergeant." Cutter, knowing Hooker had overheard the conversation, left the business of watering the mules to him.

"Grover!" Sergeant John T. Hooker called to one of the troopers, a strapping, ebony-skinned man named Angst Grover who was a six-year veteran with the Ninth.

"Yo!" he responded to the summons, and moved quickly toward his sergeant.

"Get some water from the well for these mules," Hooker ordered.

As the trooper drew abreast of Cutter, the trader pushed his chest out and adopted a surly stance. "You're welcome to water your animals, but I ain't got none to spare for them niggers of yours." A victim of prejudice himself, Apache Jack was still quick to turn the tables and look down on those he considered inferior.

Neither Private Grover nor Sergeant Hooker blinked an eye at the discriminatory remark. They were used to such bigotry, encountering it wherever they were stationed. A and C companies of the Ninth Cavalry Regiment had been assigned to Fort Bayard in southwestern New Mexico to provide protection for the miners and settlers around Silver City, but few were keen to be protected by colored soldiers—and they made no secret of their feelings.

Jake Cutter was a man slow to rile, but when pushed, he shoved back hard. "What's the matter, Reynolds? Do you think he might contaminate your water? Maybe you're afraid the black rubs off? Well, it doesn't!" He reached out and roughly wiped his hand across the trooper's sweat-shiny ebony cheek, then held it palm up toward the trader. "See," he challenged. "But don't worry. We won't drink your damned water."

Apache Jack Reynolds backed away from Cutter, wary of that cold temper. He looked over his shoulder as the women filed into his store. "Best see if I can help the ladies," he muttered, and left quickly.

Through it all, Grover had stood silently next to Cutter, his sergeant on his other side. As his rancor eased to a grim tolerance, Cutter glanced at the colored soldier. A flare of pride and deep resentment was in the answering looks of both men.

Cutter released a heavy breath. "Wiping your face like that embarrassed you, didn't it, trooper?" he guessed.

"Yes, suh." It was confirmed with defiant stiffness.

"I was trying to make a point—" Cutter began, then stopped and gave a small shake of his head.

"Water the mules, Grover," Sergeant Hooker inserted quietly, dismissing the soldier.

Cutter watched him walk away. When he spoke again, there was a hard edge to his voice. "I'm tired of hate, John T." He dropped the military formality. "I'm tired of Rebs hating Yanks, whites hating blacks, white men hating red men. Such unreasoning hatred . . . it makes no sense. It's like hating the desert because there's no water in it."

"Yes, suh," was the noncommittal response.

Across the clearing Cutter saw Mrs. Wade pause in the doorway of the store and look back in a questioning manner. He touched his fingers to the brim of his hat and feigned a slight bow, assuring her all was well.

# CHAPTER 2

LESS THAN AN HOUR LATER, HANNAH FELT THE STEELY strength of Cutter's gauntleted hand as he assisted her aboard the army ambulance and waited while she arranged her skirts to sit on the seat. When she was comfortably settled with Mrs. Bettendorf and Mrs. Sloane, he walked to the back of the wagon and untied his horse. She watched him swing onto his McClellan saddle and wished, for an instant, that she had ridden her blooded thoroughbred. Army ambulances did not provide the gentlest of rides.

"Do you ride, Mrs. Sloane?" she inquired with interest.

"I have," came the hesitant response from the young wife.

"I ride almost daily. There are some lovely trails close to the fort. You must have your husband find a gentle mount for you, and we'll ride together some morning," Hannah urged.

16

"Mrs. Wade is a most accomplished horsewoman," Mrs. Bettendorf volunteered in endorsement of Hannah's skill, although she herself had long since given up the pleasures of the sidesaddle for something a little more settled. "Naturally the colonel insists she never leave the fort unescorted, for her own protection."

"I don't let that stop me." Hannah's voice had a carefree, lilting sound to it. "Even when Stephen is on duty, there is never a lack of officers to ride with. An escort can always be arranged."

"I'll mention it to Dickie—Richard." Mrs. Sloane hastily corrected her usage of the familiar nickname.

The scrape of the brake being released was followed by the jangle of harness and bridle bits. Hannah gripped the seat for balance as the mules lunged into their collars. The wheels rattled over the stony ground, rolling and gathering momentum to sweep the wagon along.

The track led into the mountain-wrinkled desert and took a northerly course toward Fort Bayard, which lay at the foot of the Pinos Altos Mountains. The two troopers deployed to their respective positions, one ranging in advance of the ambulance to ride point and the other lagging to the rear to ride drag. On the right, the side opposite the drifting dust of the wheels, Captain Cutter sat astride his drab brown horse, rocking in an easy canter.

Hannah's attention lingered on him, noting his tight seat in the saddle. That was the army way, which she had learned from Stephen. No longer could she be ridiculed for "rising" when her horse trotted; her seat in the sidesaddle was firm and secure. This winter Stephen had been so pleased with her progress that he'd even begun letting her jump the cavalry hurdles and ditches. She was becoming quite good.

Idly she studied Jake Cutter's long-bodied form, muscled and erect. He did not dance attendance on the young women living on Officers' Row, as most of the bachelor officers did. Any attention he tendered was usually obligatory, such as this escort duty; the colonel had given him the assignment even though there were probably any number of volunteers for the task.

Conscious of his alertness, the restless sweep of his gaze along their path, Hannah found herself searching the brush and gullies for any glimpse of a hiding Apache. The winter had been relatively quiet, but many officers—her husband among them—expected the raiding to begin with the onset of spring.

Fort Bayard in the New Mexico Territory sat at the end of the rough and dusty ride. The frontier outpost was strategically situated where the desert and mountains met. To the south, the land prickled with cactus and thorny trees all the way to the Rio Grande and Mexico, and to the north lay the awesome canyon country of the Gila River area.

Outside the fort's perimeter there was a small encampment where the Apache scouts lived with their families. The head of the scouts, a white man named Amos Hill, lived there as well with his Apache squaw. As they passed, Hannah recognized her working outside the brush-covered *jacal,* her face whitened with rice powder.

They passed the guardhouse post, entering the fort. No outer wall protected the collection of military buildings that surrounded the parade ground. There was no stockade behind which the soldiers could hide. Their only protection at this fort was their own vigilance—and their guns. It resembled a small town with its barracks, barns, shops, and supply stores, its military "upper-crust" housing along Officers' Row, and the limited housing for the families of enlisted men on Suds Row, so named because the wives took in laundry to supplement their husbands' army pay.

The ambulance rolled down Officers' Row, with its

collection of squat, crudely built multifamily dwellings of adobe brick. Chimneys, constructed of the same mud-and-straw brick, poked from the tops of the brush-covered roofs. *Ramadas* jutted from the fronts of the structures, providing shade and a frontier-style galleried porch that faced the parade ground. When the ambulance stopped in front of one of the buildings, Captain Cutter dismounted to assist the ladies down from the wagon seats while the sergeant collected their purchases.

"We did so enjoy your company this afternoon, Captain," the commander's wife thanked him.

"My pleasure, Mrs. Bettendorf." But the response was merely words, spoken without sincerity or any attempt to feign it.

"The major and I are having a little get-together this evening to welcome Lieutenant and Mrs. Sloane to Fort Bayard. I do hope you'll come, Captain," Hannah invited, and saw the polite but definite refusal forming in his expression.

"Of course he'll be there, won't you, Captain?" Mrs. Bettendorf stated in the most positive manner.

"How can I possibly decline?" He bowed his head in a subservient manner, a resigned acceptance flattening his smile.

As the empty ambulance with its escort of riders rattled toward the stables, Cutter took his leave of the women and remounted his brown cavalry horse. Instead of heading toward the barns, he turned the heavy-headed animal in the direction of Suds Row. Cutter knew what tonight's party meant—formal military dress, so he'd be needing his clean laundry.

The long, rectangular parade ground was like a village square with everything built around it. Officers' Row was the "right" side of town, and Suds Row was the "wrong" side. The parade ground that separated them was as wide as the class distinction that separated them. Even if the Ninth hadn't been a colored regiment, there would have been no socializing between the families of the officers and those of the enlisted men, and almost no contact of any kind except for the laundress services or the occasional maid help.

The brown horse carried its rider across the parade ground at a shuffling trot and responded sluggishly to the pressure on the reins that turned it down the row of tent housing behind the adobe-walled barracks. A handful of young Negro children, pickaninnies, stopped their noisy play to stare at the white officer.

Halfway down the row Cutter saw the ripely curved black woman standing by a fire and stirring something in a big iron pot. He slowed his horse to a walk as he approached her, the sight of her lush body blotting the children out of his vision. Clothes boiled in the iron kettle. As she stirred them with the long, water-whitened stick, her body swayed from the hips with the rhythm of it. Hers was an earthy beauty, full pouting lips and knowing eyes that looked at a man and knew what he wanted.

Steam and perspiration had combined to plaster the cotton blouse to her torso. Her full, rounded breasts were clearly defined through the dampened fabric, even to the extent of showing the nubby points of her nipples. Cutter had trouble looking away from them. Cimmy Lou Hooker had a body that aroused a man, regardless of the color of her skin—and the fact that she was his sergeant's wife.

She stepped back from the heat for a moment's relief from the steam and smoke and pressed her hands to the small of her back, flexing her muscles and thrusting forward those tautly round breasts. When she caught sight of him sitting on his horse watching her, her pose became deliberately provocative.

"You likin' what you see, Cap'n Cutter?" She

grasped the long stick and slowly churned the clothes some more, making the action somehow suggestive.

"Is my laundry ready, Mrs. Hooker?" The saddle leather squeaked as he shifted his weight and settled deeper in the flat-shaped McClellan saddle.

"How come you always pick up yore clothes yo'self and don't nevah send that young striker of yores?" She continued to stir the boiling clothes, her coffee-brown face all shiny and her young earthy beauty powerful as sin. "What you afraid I'm gonna do to him?"

"I know what you'd do. It's what the sergeant might do that worries me," Cutter acknowledged dryly.

"I knows how to keep John T. happy," Cimmy Lou insisted softly, and laughed when he looked away. She rested the stick against the side of the big iron kettle and moved away from the fire, wiping her hands on her skirt. "Best be fetchin' yore laundry for you. That *is* what you came fo', ain't it, Cap'n?"

"Yes." He watched her start toward the large tent with its door flap tied open. She had a natural way of moving that always pulled a man's glance to her hips—the same way that, when she talked, his eyes were drawn to her lips.

Stopping short of the door, she turned to look back at him. "Ain't you gonna get off that horse and come with me?"

"I don't mind waiting." Cutter refused the invitation as she'd known he would. It was a game she played— she liked playing with men. Marriage hadn't changed that about her. She knew what she did to them, and she liked doing it. At times, Cutter wasn't sure whether he envied John T. or pitied him.

"Are you afraid of comin' inside this tent with me, Cap'n?" she taunted. "Maybe you think you might not be man enough?"

"Is any one man enough for you?" he countered, unsmiling.

Anger flashed in her eyes at the implied insult, and Cimmy Lou swept inside the tent. Cutter's horse stamped at the flies buzzing incessantly about its legs, the brown hide on its withers shuddering to shake them off. She was gone only a matter of seconds, then reappeared at the tent's opening with a bundle of fresh laundry in her arms. She crossed to him, her bandanna-wrapped head tilted at a proud angle. He took the clothes from her.

"Reckon yore goin' to that party Miz Wade's havin' tonight. I gotta go dress her hair fo' her—and Miz Bettendorf, too," she informed him importantly. "My mama taught me all 'bout such things. She used to be Miz Devereaux's personal maid. 'Course, that was b'fore the war." She lifted her hand, turning up her rose-brown palm. "You owe me five dollahs, Cap'n Cutter."

He reached inside his pocket for the money and flipped her a five-dollar gold piece. She caught it with one hand and slipped it inside her blouse, finding a place for it in the crevice between her full breasts. Those dark, knowing eyes watched him turn his horse away.

At sundown the bugle called retreat and the flag was lowered with all the accompanying pomp and ceremony the two meager companies of the Ninth could muster. Afterward the columns of mounted troops rode to the respective stables of their companies while orderlies collected the officers' horses and led them away. The day was at an end, and the white officers drifted toward their quarters.

In the Wades' bedroom, Hannah leaned close to the mirror to fasten her earbobs. She wore a brown dress, with sleeves and bodice streaked with gold thread that caught and reflected the light. Its shining darkness and the darkness of her hair drawn up on top of her head made the creamy white of her throat and neck appear all the more fragile. With the pair of glittering earbobs fastened, Hannah straightened away from the vanity mirror above the dressing table.

"I do admire that gown on you, Miz Wade," Cimmy Lou declared, and wistfully eyed the finery.

"Thank you, Cimmy Lou."

"Hannah?" The muffled summons was followed by a knock on the bedroom door. "Are you ready yet?"

"That will be all, Cimmy Lou," she said, dismissing the colored girl hovering behind her. Her skirts rustled as she turned to face the door the laundress-turned-maid opened.

Outside, Stephen Wade stood in the narrow hallway, garbed in his full-dress uniform complete with gold epaulets, sash, and regimental cord. Tall, nearly six feet, he cut a dashing figure, with his smoothly handsome features and brown-shaded mustache. The coiled energy and restlessness that were so much a part of him swept Stephen into the room. He barely noticed the young, dark-skinned woman who eyed him before she stepped past him to leave.

The dark pupils of his eyes were shot with flecks of gold. They glittered now with admiration as his encompassing glance took in his wife. "You look beautiful in that dress, Hannah," he said with force.

"You always say that." She held out her hands to him. He took them and drew her close, raising both of them to his lips in courtly adoration.

"That's because it's true," Stephen Wade insisted. "Brown is such a drab color, yet you make it come alive."

"Flattery comes too easily to your tongue." But Hannah loved it. "You are a handsome devil, and you know it."

His hands shifted to span her waist, leaving her fingers to rest on the front of his uniform. Pride and confidence settled onto his strongly chiseled features.

"Everyone talks about what a beautiful couple we make." Possession was in his face, mixed with love and passion—but not too much of the latter. It wouldn't be seemly for an officer and a gentleman to reveal such a coarse side to his lady.

"That's because I love you more than I did five years ago when we married." The instant the words were out, Hannah regretted them, wishing she hadn't emphasized the passage of time.

Five years. Stephen had hoped for so much to happen in that time. Hannah recalled their first meeting at her father's silversmith shop in Philadelphia, and the lifting of her heart at the sight of this dashingly handsome officer. She had learned he was on leave, visiting friends in the city. They had met again at a soiree given by the Van Camps, old and valued patrons of her father. His reputation as an artist in silver and the wealth he'd accumulated, plus her mother's socially prominent but impoverished family background, gave Hannah an entree into Philadelphia society. And on that night, they had gained her a formal introduction to Major Stephen Wade. The attraction between them had been instantaneous. Hannah had been drawn as much by his intelligence and sureness of purpose as she had been by the striking figure he made in his uniform. She had noted, too, the ambition-riddled restlessness that caused him to chafe at his martial duty in the Reconstructed South. He had applied for a transfer to another regiment, preferably one posted on the frontier.

His leave had been short, so their courtship had been fast. His orders, assigning him to the Ninth Cavalry in Texas, had arrived the day before their wedding. There had been no time for a honeymoon.

Initially Stephen had attempted to discourage her from accompanying him to the western outpost, but his warnings of adverse conditions, hardship, and danger had made Hannah all the more determined to go with him and provide a cultural oasis for him in the harsh environs of the frontier.

It had been a challenge from the beginning. Over the last five years, they had moved three times, sold and set up three households, but there had been no promotions, no advancements, no permanent assignments. Living in this uncertainty, never knowing where he might be posted next, to what dregs of the frontier outposts the army would assign the Ninth or when, they had postponed starting a family. Out here in these Godforsaken frontier outposts civilization was at its barest—few schools, even fewer churches and hospitals except what the army provided. Babies, a family, they had decided, would wait. Only time was slipping away.

Stephen's jaw hardened for an instant after her comment, that gnawing frustration surfacing briefly before he broke away from her, turning so she couldn't see his expression. But his reaction was evident in the tension that showed in his body, in the muscles held taut and stiff.

"Custer has been summoned to Washington to testify at the congressional hearings about all those accusations he made against Belknap this past winter in New York." W. W. Belknap was President Grant's secretary of war. "Some are speculating that he won't be back in time to lead the Seventh on its summer campaign."

"I hadn't heard." Hannah was careful not to comment on the news, aware that he was sensitive to any discussion of the Seventh Cavalry.

"I should have accepted that transfer to the Seventh four years ago and gotten away from these damn niggers. But the promotions were coming faster for the officers in the colored regiments," Stephen said, reiterating the arguments that had convinced him to stay with the Ninth. "And I didn't fancy serving under that glory-hunting boy general. Maybe I was wrong."

Wisely she said nothing, merely slipping her hand inside the grip of his fingers. "We need to check to be sure everything is in readiness for our guests."

The living quarters were austere, the lamp flames reflecting on the dull adobe walls. The drabness and severity of form were part of the army stricture that no habitation should be better than any other save that of the commanding officer. So all of them had colorless adobe walls, plank floors, and green shades at the windows.

Only Hannah's personal and prized possessions, brought with them from outpost to outpost, relieved the severity of their quarters. A green and gold Turkish carpet, a wedding gift that she had insisted on shipping all the way from Philadelphia with their china and silver service packed inside its roll, gave the parlor its color, and the hues were repeated in the sofa throw and finely embroidered pillows that Hannah had stitched by hand over the long, lonely hours when Stephen had been away from the fort on patrol. Lace curtains, remnants of an heirloom tablecloth from her mother's family that had been destroyed by bugs, relieved the starkness of the windows, while family pictures and framed samplers, more of Hannah's handiwork, adorned the blankness of the earth-bricked walls.

The dining room held a small buffet table with a punch bowl of lemonade as well as platters of canapés and dainty cakes. Hannah inspected every item. Everything had been prepared by their striker, the army term for a soldier hired to be an officer's servant. It was a coveted job, since it meant additional wages besides a soldier's regular pay, as well as relief from routine duty. The practice had been officially outlawed six years ago, but it continued. It was too difficult to find and keep good help. Private Delancy was a superb cook, trained in one of the finest New Orleans restaurants. Rumor said he'd killed a man over a beautiful octoroon. He was a very quiet man. Hannah would never have thought their excellent soldier-servant was capable of violence.

"Have you heard of an Apache called Juh?" she asked, repositioning the silverware to a more precise angle, her thoughts running back over the afternoon's incident and her subsequent conversation with Captain Jake Cutter.

"A leader of one of the Chiricahua bands," Stephen recalled. "Why?"

"Captain Cutter believed he was with those Apaches this afternoon." Hannah paused. "Do you think it means anything?"

"The bands are moving. I don't think the quiet is going to last," was the most he was willing to venture. "The Tucson ring has gotten too strong. Too many people—from government contractors to miners, ranchers, and lumbermen—want to see the Apaches concentrated on one reservation. In Arizona, they've already transferred all the Indians from the Camp Verde and White Mountain reservations to San Carlos. It's only a matter of time before they decide the Mimbres—the Warm Springs Apaches—have to be moved from their New Mexico reserve at Ojo Caliente, and the Chiricahuas from their desert mountains. The Apaches will fight." His lips thinned into a long, straight line. "And here we are—undermanned, at half company strength, mounted on inferior horses—and no one cares."

Hannah understood the bitterness Stephen felt. For five years, he had played the political games of currying favor to gain the attention of the right people, his company distinguishing itself in all its engagements with the enemy. During the Civil War, Stephen had legitimately possessed a major's title, and he would never be satisfied until he was no longer addressed as "major" out of courtesy, but because he had earned the title back.

"Then you expect there will be trouble." Hannah turned from the buffet table to study him fully.

"I hope there is. I'd hate to be stuck out here and forgotten." A wry smile slanted his mouth as he lifted his punch glass.

She picked up a glass and filled it, keeping her private fears out of her expression. "To the victor, Major Wade." She toasted him, inwardly knowing what his assertion meant. Making war on the Apaches meant taking chances—calculated risks, Stephen called them. It meant fighting and killing—things a soldier's wife should understand. But hers was the waiting game, the sitting at home and worrying while smiling bravely.

The hollow tramp of footsteps on the packed earth outside their door signaled the arrival of their first guest. "It must be poor Lieutenant Delvecchio," Stephen guessed in advance of the knock at the door. "I feel sorry for him."

"Why?" Hannah set down her lemonade glass.

"Because he's in love with you, and you're mine." He smiled as a hand rapped at the door, and she was charmed by his possessive affection and that sense of being so very special to him.

Together they went to answer the door. Lieutenant Delvecchio stood outside and the Sloanes, the guests of honor, were coming up the walk. The atmosphere took on a social air, one of flirtatious fun and good company.

Cimmy Lou strolled along the path that circled the parade ground, which was outlined with rocks. Oblivious to her surroundings, she daydreamed about all she had seen in the private quarters of Officers' Row: the beautiful clothes, the satins and laces, the bright baubles and beads, the gilded hairbrushes and combs, and the pretty food. She'd snitched one of the cakes and now she sucked at her fingers to get the last sugary bit of the icing's taste while her long skirts swayed with the sauntering rhythm of her walk. Molasses was about the sweetest thing she'd had lately.

Ahead of her, a trooper leaned against a rough cedar post that supported the *ramada* roof attached to the fort's bakery. Long and slim, he was half hidden by the purpling shadows of twilight. At Cimmy Lou's approach, he kicked leisurely away from the post and intercepted her. There was something catlike about him, with his small face and shiny-dark eyes, his pencil-thin mustache and pointy chin, and he had a cleverness about him, the scheming slyness of a cat, too.

"You shouldn't be walkin' by yo'self afteh dark, Miz Hooker. I'll make shore you get safely home."

She pulled her fingers from her mouth with a small, smacking sound and studied Private Leroy Bitterman with a considering look. Her strong sexual instincts made her always aware of the maneuverings between a man and a woman, the planned setting up of a seemingly happenstance meeting. And this man, who had long shown indifference to her, now was casually offering to walk her home.

"I don't need protection," Cimmy Lou asserted, losing interest in him now that he'd come around like all the others.

"I'll walk with you just the same." He smiled and matched his stride to her slow stroll.

"Do as you please."

"I'll always do that." He walked along. "You don't like me much, do you?"

"You ain't very nice." She eyed him. "I think you could be cruel sometimes."

"I'm a full-blooded tomcat. I sure as hell ain't as tame as the men you been toyin' with." He spoke with an arrogance and sureness that Cimmy Lou didn't like.

"You don't know what I do," she retorted.

"You like to get a man all hot an' excited, then throw cold water on him. Makes ya feel big."

"Then don't get excited."

"Cold water won't stop me."

"There ain't gonna be no startin', so there won't be no stoppin' neither." Cimmy Lou kept her voice down as they came to the tent housing of Suds Row, but her tone was firm.

"Then why you been walkin' with me and talkin' with me? Why you been watchin' me all these months?" Several yards short of her tent, his steps slowed. "You don't know me. But you will."

Bitterman left before she could order him to go, and that angered her. She liked to control such things. Like all men, he had eventually come sniffing after her, but he'd backed off on his own. First Captain Cutter, now Leroy Bitterman, two in one day. It worried her, made her restless and edgy as she entered the tent.

John T. was standing at the cookstove, stirring a pot. A pair of suspenders stretched up over his bare torso, his dark skin rippling with lean muscles. He was handsome, the handsomest man she'd ever seen, with his proudly ridged features and darkly brilliant eyes. Cimmy Lou knew he'd cooked supper for her. He was always doing kind things for her, she realized with a flash of irritation.

"What's that I smell?" she demanded, catching an odd scent mixed in with the familiar aroma of stew made from potatoes, onions, tinned tomatoes, and stringy beef.

"I put some of them Mexican peppers in it. Really livened up the taste." He held out a spoonful for her to test and watched her pouty lips graze the spoon's edge as she drank the tomato broth.

"It's hot," Cimmy Lou ventured hesitantly, and John T. smiled at her dubious response. "It's a change, that's for shore."

Later when the stew had been dished into metal bowls and they sat at the homemade table and spread butter made from suet on sour bread, Cimmy Lou reflected on the stark differences between the dainty repast at the Wades' quarters, the buffet arranged on china and silverware, and her own dinner. She described the bite-sized sandwiches and sweet cakes and the beautiful finery to her husband.

While she talked, John T. watched her. He could see the hunger in her face, the intense wanting, the great needs that never seemed to get filled. She'd always been a hungry woman. It troubled him.

"Maybe you shouldn't be goin' and workin' for the officers' ladies," he said at last.

"But they pay me. Look at all the extra money I make fixin' their hair an' doin' for 'em," Cimmy Lou protested.

"It ain't good to cross over and see how they live. Yore always upset when you come home. I see the wantin' in yore eyes." Many things he could give her—the prestige of his top rank, the status and respectability, and a sergeant's pay—and every ounce of his love. She was the kind of woman who drained a man dry. Even in bed, she kept coming back for more. God, how he loved her.

"Sometimes, John T. . . . sometimes I get to feelin' so hungry for things" —the intensity of her feelings was present in her voice and expression, a mixture of fierce impatience and frustration—"that I get to hurtin' inside." The admission turned her petulant and she pushed the half-empty bowl of stew away from her.

"An' sometimes I get to wishin' Lincoln'd never freed us. If I was a slave, I'd be livin' in the Devereaux's fine big house, wearin' nice dresses an' eatin' good food. I wouldn't be boilin' clothes an' ironin' all day, an' sweatin' like a field hand."

"Don't say that." John T. pushed himself angrily to his feet. "Don't ever say that. Yore momma's filled yore head with tales about those times, but it wasn't like that. An' yore too young to remember how it was to be a slave." The metal spoons clattered together in the tin bowls as he gathered up their eating utensils to clear the table. "If you was a slave in that house, one of them Devereaux men would be beddin' you—maybe all of 'em. An' there wouldn't be nothin' you could say about it."

Cimmy Lou wasn't unduly troubled by that thought. Her body had always gotten her what she wanted and she was not averse to using it, but she was wise enough not to say that to John T. Men tended to be jealous, possessive creatures, but that could be used too. Besides, she knew all about being sent up the back stairs at night to one of the masters' quarters. Her momma had told her about that—and about the little presents they sometimes gave if a girl was real good at pleasing them. And Cimmy Lou knew all about pleasing a man. The fact remained that if she was a slave now, she could have the Devereaux with their pretty gifts and John T. as well. Because John T. couldn't have done anything about her going up those stairs.

With the dirty dishes set aside in the metal basin, John T. turned up the coal oil light. "You need to practice yore readin'." His body cast a long shadow on the canvas wall as he crossed the tent to fetch the well-worn reading primer.

Reading and writing had always been such a mystery to her—and still were despite John T.'s sporadic attempts to teach her. Too often he was away from the fort on patrol for days, occasionally weeks at a time, and too much time passed between lessons. Now John T. sat close beside her at the table and held the primer open, watching over her shoulder while Cimmy Lou struggled to identify each simple word. John T. was always patiently correcting her.

She resented his superior knowledge. She disliked anything that made her feel small, and her inability to grasp the rudiments of reading made her feel foolish in front of him. Usually it was men who made fools of themselves around her, and she didn't like it the other way around.

Cimmy Lou pulled back and took her finger away from the printed words on the page. "Don't they ever write 'bout nothin' besides dogs and cats?"

"Sure, but this is for learnin'. Ya gotta start out with the easy ones. Come on," John T. urged her, pointing to the primer.

"Does anybody write books 'bout a man and woman lovin'?" She set out to distract him and make him forget that boring and frustrating primary reader. "Now, I'd like ta read 'bout that."

"There's books like that."

"Have you ever read any of 'em?"

"Sure." He eyed her with a downward glance, conscious of the heat of her warm flank along his thigh and the rounded point of her shoulder against his bare chest.

"Tell me about 'em." She slid an insinuating hand, fingers splayed, across his flat stomach and up to his chest. "Do they tell you how a woman feels when a man holds her an' touches her? What do they say 'bout lovin'? Do they talk 'bout different ways?"

The book was taken from his hands and laid aside. "Cimmy Lou, this ain't no way to learn to read." But his curiosity was stronger than the mild protest as she shifted, half-rising and hitched up her skirts to sit astraddle his lap. The heavy globes of her breasts were before him, straining against the confinement of her blouse. John T. had trouble looking higher.

"Then let's learn somethin' else." Her soft mound moved suggestively against his hardening shaft. "I nevah did know how to ride a cockhorse. Some kinda cavalry sergeant you are nevah to have teached me. Let's giddy-up, John T." She bit at his ear as he groaned and loosened the fly front of his uniform trousers. Their silhouettes on the canvas wall merged into a humped outline before he reached to turn the kerosene light down to a dim flicker. Then his hands were grasping her haunches, holding onto her as she rode the bucking horse.

# CHAPTER 3

A DESERT MOON REIGNED OVER THE VELVET-SOFT NIGHT, aglitter with stars arching high above the inky blackness of the parade ground. To the north the mountains stood, a high, black wall rife with a sense of danger and mystery and all that is ancient and wild.

From the guardposts around the fort's perimeter came the echoing call, "Nine o'clock and all's well," traveling from sentry to sentry. Jake Cutter stepped up to the wooden post supporting the *ramada* roof outside the Wades' quarters and angled his body against it, resting the point of his shoulder along a rough corner.

Light spilled out the window, cheerfully throwing itself into the shadows and reaching for the darkest corners. Cutter looked through the opening, seeing the officers and their ladies gathered inside, their warm voices and faint laughter drifting out to him. He'd put in his appearance, satisfied Colonel and Mrs. Bettendorf, and now he would leave, undoubtedly not missed by anyone there.

Yet something held him. Cutter felt the catch of loneliness and tried to shake it off. He was used to being alone. He was beyond these sentimental longings.

He straightened, intending to leave, but the soft sound of a footfall checked the impulse, staying him. He turned to see Mrs. Wade slip out of the house. He saw her hesitate when she recognized him; then she came forward, her manner relaxing.

"Captain Cutter, I should have guessed you'd be out here." She stopped beside the pillar where he stood, her head tipped back while her direct glance went over him. "No cigar?" she observed with some surprise. "I thought you'd come out to smoke."

Any explanation seemed pointless, so Cutter reached inside his uniform for a long, slim cigar that was tucked in one pocket. "Do you mind?" he asked, bringing it out.

"Not at all." Although the night air was mild, she wore a shawl around her shoulders. She faced the parade ground and the desert stars above it, showing him the clean, white line of her throat. Her eyes observed the flare of the match and, in a sideways study, watched him drag the flame into the cigar tip, puffing long and slow until it was burning well. "It's quiet out here," she said when he'd shaken the match dead.

His glance went to the window and its clear view of the people inside. "And not nearly as crowded," he added.

Her laugh was a small, soft sound. "You don't like being confined, do you, Captain? Not by walls or people . . . or what they might think."

"What makes you say that?" His head came up, watchful, though he made no attempt to deny it.

"An impression I have." A faint shake of her head seemed to dismiss the importance of it. Yet a second later, when he looked away, her eyes came back to study him. Hannah sensed the ease in him, the loose and relaxed feeling returning to him as his initial tension at her approach left.

It was odd how she could look into his face at this moment and see the thing that made him different. All evening she had watched Stephen, seen the intensity in his eyes when Apache strategy was discussed and observed the tightness around his mouth when he was in the presence of superior officers.

Cutter seemed to have shrugged off the ambitions and worries that whipped and exhausted other men. Some long-ago decision had settled the question of his future to his satisfaction, and tomorrow didn't trouble him.

"Everyone expects trouble from the Apaches." Inside, the men had talked of little else, hushing when a woman came by, Hannah had noticed.

"People usually get what they expect."

"What do you think Colonel Hatch will do? Put a force into the field?"

The cigar tip glowed red, then faded under a dulling accumulation of ash. Pungent smoke scented the still air. "He'll do what he's ordered to do. He's a soldier."

"And what will you do?"

"The same." After a short silence, he said, "I'm not good at small talk, Mrs. Wade."

"On the contrary, Captain Cutter, you are very good at it." Her voice had a sharp edge to it. "You just said precisely nothing."

"Idle speculation serves little purpose." But her frankness had thrown him off stride.

In the darkness he searched her moonlit face. Self-control was evident in her composure, and that flare of pride was unmistakable. A strong will was there, too, revealing itself sometimes at the corners of her lips and in the tone of conviction in her voice. A rather reluctant glint of admiration came to his eyes. He wondered if Wade knew what a lucky man he was.

"If I may be so bold as to say it, Mrs. Wade, you are a remarkable woman." The smile that gentled his hard mouth had warmth to it.

"More small talk, Captain?"

"No, ma'am."

"I must write my cousin in Memphis and invite her for a visit." Hannah spoke the thought aloud, then looked at him for a reaction. "I'll introduce the two of you."

"Is she southern?"

"Do you have a preference for southern ladies, Captain?"

"They do have soft white skins—smooth as a magnolia blossom." The musing recall was followed by a slow exhalation of cigar smoke.

"Yes, they have lovely complexions," she agreed, and his lidded glance concealed the wicked glint in his eyes. He could have told her that it wasn't their faces he was remembering, but the innocence of her expression reminded him that, despite her married state, she was sheltered from all things that did not bring out man's finer instincts. "What was her name?" Hannah asked unexpectedly.

"Whose?" His head came up slightly.

"The one whose skin you recall with such fondness. Were you very much in love with her?"

"That was long ago, Mrs. Wade." He listened to the night's sounds, hearing in his memory that softly drawling voice.

"What happened? Or would you prefer not to talk about it?" she asked.

"Not at all." Cutter shrugged to deny the suggestion.

"She was an unreconstructed Rebel who despised the blue uniform I wore. Eventually she got over that, but she couldn't forgive me for commanding a company of coloreds. She wanted me to resign my commission, and I refused."

"How unfortunate," she murmured.

"I have no regrets," he stated. "It wasn't her love I rejected. I simply didn't want her hates."

Laughter rang out loudly from inside the house, and its intrusion reminded Hannah of her duty. She caught back a sigh before it escaped. Her shawl slipped lower on her shoulders as she made a small movement in the direction of the door.

"I must see to my guests."

The gold braid on his dress uniform glinted as he bowed slightly, his hair heavy and black against the night's darkness. "The evening has been a pleasure, Mrs. Wade." His hard, tanned face was engrained with a roughness, presently tempered by an expression of respect.

"There is no reason to leave so early." Hannah was surprised into the protest.

"There is no reason to stay any later," he countered.

"But the party—" She looked over her shoulder to the window's view of her guests.

"I'm not their sort. We both know it, Mrs. Wade," he said without apology. "I enjoy a rougher kind of pleasure. This cigar needs a shot of whiskey and a good poker hand to make it taste good."

"Drinking and gambling. You disappoint me, Captain."

"They are honest sins."

"Indeed." A smile broke across her lips, creating a small dimple in her left cheek. It danced there an instant before she gave him her hand. "Good evening, Captain Cutter."

"Mrs. Wade." Briefly, he pressed his mouth to the smooth knuckles of her hand, inhaling the warm fragrance of her skin.

A moment later she was gliding through the door and Cutter was alone with the night. He paused to take a last drag on the cigar, then flipped the butt into the darkness. Down the steps he ran with a light tread and swung along Officers' Row to the bachelor quarters. A shot of whiskey was sounding better and better.

"Hayes. Hayes!" he called impatiently for his striker, tugging at the collar of his dress uniform the minute he entered his rooms.

A gangly Negro lad still in his teens tumbled into the room, all eagerness to serve his officer. "Yes, sir, Captain."

A city boy from Philadelphia, Hayes had never been west until two months ago. He couldn't ride, couldn't shoot, but he was pursuing the romance, glamour, and adventure of a soldier's life for all it was worth.

"Whiskey—and my blues." Cutter shed the jacket of the dress uniform and tossed it on a chair for the boy to pick up.

"Going out again, sir?" Hayes tried to do all the chores at once, carrying the regular uniform while juggling a whiskey bottle and a glass, and picking up the discarded suit. "Where?"

"To see if there isn't a game in progress in Grimshaw's back room—or to start one if there isn't." He rescued the bottle and glass from the young private's clutches before they shattered on the floor.

"Ya mean poker? Gosh, sir, you don't suppose I could come along and watch?"

There was the smallest break in the lift of the whiskey glass, the faintest hesitation of movement. Then Cutter threw the liquor down his throat, a hardness ridging his jaw and cheekbone.

"Not with me, Hayes." The denial was flat and unequivocal.

There was a line that existed between officers and enlisted men—a line that wasn't to be crossed. The delineation of rank had to be maintained for order and discipline. Nothing must ever interfere with the unquestioning obedience to an officer's command.

"Yes, sir." Hayes's glum, crestfallen response tugged at Cutter, but he poured himself another drink and finished changing uniforms.

Thirty minutes later he was seated at the poker table playing a game of seven card stud in the private room located in back of the fort's trading store. Oates Grimshaw, who held the trading franchise with the army, ran the store and reserved a separate room for officers, segregated from the enlisted men. An attempt had been made at giving it a decor befitting a gentleman's rank. Inexpensive reproductions of hunting scenes adorned the rough walls and water-filled ollas were suspended from the rafters to cool the room. The latest available newspapers and eastern publications were on the tables conveniently situated near the armchairs. Officially, gambling was against army regulations, but a friendly game between fellow officers was invariably overlooked.

With a snap and a flourish, cards were dealt to the players around the table, four besides Cutter. Two were fellow officers, second lieutenants in rank, and the one in the checked jacket and bowler hat was Hy Boler, owner and editor of the Silver City *Gazette*. The well-dressed fourth man was the proprietor, Oates Grimshaw.

One of Grimshaw's lackeys brought a round of drinks, then disappeared through the door, swallowed up in the smoky haze of the enlisted men's side. A pair of aces were showing among the cards in front of Cutter as he flipped a poker chip into the table's center without looking at his hole cards. "That pair is worth something." He waited to see who was going to stay.

There was a spilling of chips into the pot, each player matching the bet and remaining in the game to see the last card. "Down and dirty." Oates Grimshaw dealt it out. His bushy mustache swept into handlebars as if its thick profusion could make up for the receding hair on his head.

"Come on, Lady Luck," the newspaperman coaxed in a murmur as he dragged the final card close to the edge of the table to steal a look. He was a big man, his bulk solid, and he had a bulldog quality to his features. An easterner, he hadn't adapted to the western style of dress, clinging instead to his vests and gold watch chain.

"Speaking of ladies"—Grimshaw finished the deal with himself and set the deck aside—"you didn't stay long at the Wades' party for that new lieutenant and his wife, Captain." It was an idle observation, not requiring comment as he picked up his three hole cards to peruse them in cautious secrecy. "Mrs. Wade is a beautiful woman. I've always thought so."

"All women are beautiful," Cutter replied dryly, and sliced off the end of a new cigar with his knife, then placed it in his mouth to moisten the cut tobacco end.

"I've seen some that would disprove that claim," one of the lieutenants scoffed, a bachelor like most of the junior officers at the fort.

"That's because you got too close." Cutter smiled and made his bet, his pair of aces showing still commanding the table. "A thing of beauty can rarely withstand a close inspection for flaws."

"Yes. You are likely to find another man's fingerprints all over her." Hy Boler frowned over his cards. "I don't have any use for a woman who's been handled by others." He reached for his chips. "I'll see you, and raise you."

The second lieutenant took another look at his cards. "Handled or not, there's something to be said for taking down the hair of a beautiful woman." He matched the bet.

Cutter had an instant's vision of the deep mahogany tresses lying in a smooth pile atop Mrs. Wade's head when she'd stood with him on the porch. Just as quickly, he clicked it off.

As the betting came full circle to him, he matched the single raise and called the bets. He flipped over his downed cards. "Full house. Aces over sixes."

"Damn," the newspaperman swore at his luck as the winnings went to Cutter.

The cards were thrown into the center to be gathered by Grimshaw, the dealer. "Women," he shuffled the deck. "They are the root of many a man's troubles."

"I don't know." Cutter settled back in his chair to await the new deal. "A man's always running either from something or after it."

"Which would you be doing, Captain?" the trader asked curiously.

"Well, it depends"—a grin curved his mouth—"on whether the Apaches are chasing me or I'm chasing the Apaches."

Grimshaw pushed the cards to be cut, and asked the table, "How about a little five-card draw?"

It was late by the time the last of the guests had gone along to their own quarters on Officers' Row. After an initial clean-up, the striker was dismissed for the night, leaving the bulk of the work for the morning.

Seated on the small cushioned bench in front of her vanity mirror, Hannah stroked the bristled brush through the length of her deeply red-brown hair, its hidden fire cascading down her back onto the voluminous, lace-trimmed nightgown. Stephen lay in bed, his hands folded under his head as he watched her.

"It's late, Hannah. Turn out the lamp and come to bed." A low urgency vibrated through his husky, well-modulated voice.

She felt its invisible caress and gentle pull. Her lips softened. She found it sweet that Stephen disliked going to sleep unless she was at his side. He was so devoted to her.

A little knot of excitement tightened her stomach at the sight of him lying in bed waiting for her, his strong arms ready to hold her. The gilded hairbrush was returned to its place next to its companion comb and hand mirror as Hannah straightened to blow out the lamp flame.

The defused glow of the lamp momentarily back-lighted her, silhouetting the high roundness of her breasts, the concave flatness of her stomach, and the full curve of her bottom. Stephen's tongue seemed to thicken in his throat as he watched his wife, her cotton nightgown made diaphanous by the light. A stiffening heat burned in his loins. Then the room dissolved into darkness, lamp smoke briefly scenting the air.

In the ghostly light of varying shades of gray and black, she approached the bed, the white of her nightgown a mass against a darkened backdrop. With blood running fast through his veins, Stephen unclasped his hands and reached to encircle her shoulders with an arm as she joined him in the bed.

"Your hair . . ." His hand made a slow stroke down the rippling waves of red-brown hair that had fallen into the valley between her breasts. He curled the ends around his finger, using the motion as an excuse to leave his hand there, resting against the firm swell of one breast, the material of her nightgown interposing. "It reminds me of rose petals, all velvety and scented with a sweet, heady fragrance."

Her head turned on the pillow, her face tilting toward his, her body warm against him. In the paleness of the night's shadows, Stephen could see the pulse beating in her throat, confirmation that her emotions were stirred by his touch, his nearness.

"Do you ever tire of complimenting me, Stephen?" Her lips were smiling at him, but her tone was saying she loved it.

"No. I never tire of holding you and kissing you. My own sweet love." He leaned toward her and kissed her lips, lingering on their soft shape to nuzzle and tickle her with his mustache. "The evening was a success. Everyone enjoyed themselves, naturally. They always do when you entertain."

"It did turn out well," Hannah conceded modestly, and drew back slightly, her skin tingling from the contact with the soft bristle of his mustache. The dimness accentuated the proud and handsome features of her husband. "You looked so grand in your uniform tonight." Her slender fingers touched the collar of his nightshirt where it opened at the throat, a furry mat of chest hairs curling inches below the slit. "This nightshirt doesn't fit the image of a dashing officer. Perhaps I should sew you a new one with epaulets on the shoulders."

Hannah was conscious of the physical stimulation of his embrace, senses heightened, stomach fluttering with unnamed emotions. The pleasure she experienced during lovemaking was a very special thing.

"Epaulets? And a sash and braid, too?" Stephen laughed softly at the idea. "What did I do before you came into my life?" An answer wasn't required.

"Love me?" She asked in order to be told.

"Insanely," he insisted, his arm tightening around her, a barely perceptible movement. "I know I should send you east for the summer, out of this deadly heat."

"I wouldn't go," she returned evenly. "My place is here, with you."

"I wouldn't let you go anyway. I can barely stand to

let you out of my sight. This evening I nearly came out on the porch to bring an end to your dalliance with that officer. Who were you with?"

"Captain Cutter. Were you jealous?" She eyed him with fascination.

"Naturally. Half the men in this fort are at your feet, jumping to do your slightest bidding. Don't tell me you haven't noticed?" he mocked.

"I'm your wife. How do you expect them to treat me? It's kind of them to be so attentive to me and to allow me to feel important, just because I had the good fortune of marrying you." Hannah was sincere, certain it was her position more than her looks that gained her the attention of the men in the officer corps. Idle flirtation was a harmless game everyone played, an exercise in wordplay, a stimulant of sorts, and nothing more.

"What of young Lieutenant Delvecchio? He was a lovesick puppy, dogging your heels almost all evening."

"That isn't kind," she protested at the way he derided the young officer's gallant behavior. "He's promised to ride with me the day after tomorrow when you'll be on duty. Lieutenant Sloane is going to accompany us. I think he plans to obtain a gentle horse for his wife to ride, and he wants to check out the safe trails."

"Your idea, I'm sure," Stephen murmured.

"It would be pleasant to have another woman with whom I can go horseback riding," Hannah admitted. "Especially when you're on patrol."

"I hate leaving you, Hannah," he said with force.

But she'd seen differently at the times he'd ridden out with his troop for a week or more at a time. He felt regret, yes, at leaving her behind; but an excitement had been in his eyes, a deep-running thrill at the chance to soldier, and the little fears only gave a greater buoyancy to his feelings. These were all the things he tried to hide from her searching, memorizing eyes when they said good-bye. She always felt the well of sharpening, tender feelings, the need to clutch and hold on—and to pretend she felt none of those sensations.

"I know you do, my darling." Her fingers smoothed aside the lock of thick brown hair that fell across his forehead.

He kissed her, holding back the roughening needs that ridged his muscles. Her response was a pliant warmth as she combed her fingers into his hair. His hand shifted to cover the mound of her breast, the material an irritating barrier that stilled his caress.

"Hannah?" He made the ancient request against her lips, his breath running hotly over her skin.

"Yes," she agreed to his passion. The precautions to avoid conception were understood between them, not needing reaffirmation.

The kiss spoke of needs and hungers; their hands caressed and urged; their bodies pressed closer beneath the bedcovers. In the enveloping darkness came the love sounds of disturbed breathing, moistly clinging lips, and rustling clothing. Their voices were little more than moans, the words scarcely understandable murmurings.

Their nightclothes were pushed out of the way, bunched high around their bodies, but not removed. It was a deft, exciting touching under the garments, a sensual exploring of breast and nipple peak, shivers of stimulation dancing over skin.

Lovemaking was a world of sensation and near shapes, of things sensed but not fully seen. His hands held her hips, keeping her in position for his penetration. It was a natural fitting, a coupling cloaked in the room's darkness and enhanced by the touch of mystery it kept. It swirled around them, catching them up in the rhythm and its building tempo.

# CHAPTER 4

THE BLOOD BAY GELDING WAS RACY AND SLEEK, LONG-limbed and fine-boned; its glistening neck arched under the stricture of the gloved hands reining on the bit. Hannah Wade sat balanced in her sidesaddle, one leg hooked securely on the rest and the other booted foot in the stirrup. Her long hunter-green riding skirt was draped to completely cover her legs, its matching short jacket darted to show the trimness of her waist. A small green hat with trailing ribbons was perched atop Hannah's head, her darkly red hair coiled into a bun at the nape. Her gloved hands held a leather quirt, which she rarely had to use on her restive mount, more frequently needing its spirit curbed than encouraged.

The soft sand of the dry wash muffled the rhythmic thud of cantering hooves as Hannah moved with the rocking gait of her steed, a pace matched by the two riders accompanying her. Lieutenant Sloane was slightly ahead, while the dark-haired, dark-eyed Lieutenant Delvecchio kept his horse level with the bay gelding.

Here and there along the ever-widening banks, a scrawny, sun-bleached cottonwood leaned toward the sun. The high morning sky was sharply blue and still new enough to retain some of the night's cool, making it pleasant weather for riding. The harsh terrain beyond the wash undulated in seas of bleached tans and clayey reds and yellows, bristling with barrel cacti, chollas, and cat-claw bushes, alive with scorpions and snakes.

When Lieutenant Sloane's horse stumbled in the heavy loose sand, the other two horses automatically slowed, breaking from the slow canter into a jarring trot, at which point their riders checked them to a walk, letting them blow. Hannah leaned forward and gave a rewarding pat to her mount's neck, her gloved hand sliding underneath the jet-black mane to the shiny red coat.

The brisk ride over the two-mile distance from the fort had stirred her blood, giving her face a glow of vitality and freshness. Her dark eyes sparkled with the joy of being alive. She was breathing faster, slightly winded by the exhilarating canter.

"It's wonderful, isn't it?" The remark was made to either of her companions who wished to comment.

"Yes, ma'am." But Lieutenant Mario Delvecchio had trouble keeping his eyes off her, fascinated by every little thing she did.

Dust was stirred up by the striding walk of their horses, the smell of the earth strong and pungent on this spring morning. Recent rains had brought a rare sprinkling of green to the desert, the source of the vigorous odors of fertile ground.

"A mile farther on there's a rock ledge with a view of the entire basin. I'm sure your wife will enjoy seeing it, Lieutenant Sloane." Hannah felt rather like a guide, pointing out all the local sights.

The young lieutenant didn't seem impressed. "Desolate country, isn't it?"

She laughed, not denying it. "Someone told me once that every living thing in this New Mexico Territory either has thorns or bites. It's a hostile land, but you'll see some magnificent sights as well—sunsets that inflame the whole sky or stars that hang so low you swear you can reach out and pluck them like apples from a tree. God had a full palette when he painted this country."

"You sound as though you love it." His look was hesitant, questioning.

"I suppose I do." She had never really thought about it—and didn't now. "As long as my husband is assigned here, nothing good would come of hating it."

"You will be good medicine for my Becky," Lieutenant Sloane declared, letting some of his concern show. "She is homesick, I'm afraid."

A speckled brown bird with a crested head raced past the three riders, its scrawny body leaning forward to lend speed to its black legs. Hannah's horse pricked its ears at the roadrunner streaking down the dry wash ahead of them.

It rounded a bend where a stony bank jutted into the dry streambed and forced the watershed to change its course. Seconds later, the bird came racing back at them. Unconsciously, Hannah checked her horse's walk at the desert bird's erratic behavior, then let it continue forward.

"What do you suppose spooked him?" The almost idle question was spoken as the three of them, riding abreast, halted near the bend.

Action suddenly erupted in front of them. For a stunned instant, Hannah looked at the paint-streaked faces of the Apaches charging at them on galloping ponies and felt a sense of unreality.

With a wrench of the reins, she wheeled her horse

50

about and, keeping her balance in the sidesaddle, sent it leaping forward. She was vaguely conscious of seeing Lieutenant Sloane unfasten the flap on his holster and draw his pistol.

"Ride for the fort!" he ordered, and sawed at his horse's mouth to keep it from racing after its departing companions.

A shot rang out from the army revolver. One fragmented part of Hannah's brain recognized the bravery of his act, staying in the face of the Apaches' charge to cover their retreat. Bending low over her horse's neck, Hannah whipped the gelding into a flat-out run. Off to her right, the ardent young lieutenant was galloping beside her, his gun drawn.

Almost deafened by the thundering sound, the steady drumbeats of noise, Hannah couldn't tell which was the thudding of her heart and which the pounding of hooves, her own horse's, Delvecchio's, or the Apaches'. She felt fear and shock, but little sense of panic.

Chancing a backward look, she saw the pursuing braves and a riderless horse, the stirrups of its McClellan saddle flapping against its sides. A cold finger touched her stomach. After that first shot, she hadn't heard Lieutenant Sloane fire again. And they were two very long miles from the fort.

Three more Apaches appeared, sending their ponies down the embankment slightly ahead of the racing horses. They were being cut off. In a split-second decision, Hannah swung her horse toward the opposite side of the wash. Going cross-country to the fort would be a rougher but more direct route than the smooth-running bottom of this riverbed. The lieutenant guessed her intent and followed, firing from horseback at the new threat.

There was no opportunity for him to take aim at the moving targets, and a hit would be accidental. But the

51

sound of gunshots could carry a great distance in the stillness of the desert air. Hannah mentally clung to the knowledge that the guards at the fort would hear them and send out a patrol to investigate.

The high bank was before her. She urged the big-hearted horse at it and gave the animal its head to choose its own course up the steep, gravelly slope. Its lunging climb nearly unseated her. She had to grab for the saddle horn to keep upright as the gelding scrambled upward, finally making it over the top.

It stumbled, going to its knees, and Hannah was pitched off. She managed to keep her grip on the reins and had nearly made it back into the saddle when Delvecchio came over the top. He swung from his rearing horse to help her, the near edge of panic in his eyes.

Confusion wreaked havoc; the wild-eyed horses whirled away from them, dust flying amidst the blowing snorts and nervous whickers; desperation had them moving too quickly. Hannah tried to haul herself into the saddle before she had a good toehold in the stirrup, the long riding skirt getting in her way. Any second she expected to see or hear the first Apache pony following them up the embankment. Her lungs felt tight, her mouth dry. Fear was a lump in the pit of her stomach.

Delvecchio grabbed the bridle strap of her circling horse so that she could mount, then looked wildly around, hearing the drumming hooves but not yet seeing the horses. His gun was drawn, its black muzzle seeking a target.

Seconds. Everything was happening in seconds.

Twenty yards up the wash, the trio of Apaches rode over the top, the same group that had tried to intercept them. Delvecchio snapped off one shot in their direction. Then Hannah spied the pursuing band thirty yards down the embankment. Again they were being hemmed in.

"Lieutenant!" she warned him.

"We're trapped."

"What should we—" She never finished the question as she looked at the young officer and found herself staring into the muzzle of his revolver.

A terrible look was on his face. "God forgive me, Mrs. Wade." It was almost a sobbing plea.

"Have you gone mad?" She saw his finger tremble against the trigger and slapped at the gun barrel with her quirt, knocking it aside as it went off in a deafening explosion. She flinched from the sound, then watched in shock as he brought the muzzle around to bear on her again.

"I can't let them have you." It was an agonized appeal for understanding.

Hannah suddenly realized that he intended to kill her to save her from the Apaches. No more was it merely talk. As a last resort, the lives of the women and children would be taken before an army officer would let them be tortured by savages.

She drew back, in this last second wanting desperately to live. *Thwack! Thwack! Thwack!* Delvecchio was spun by some sudden force, the pistol spinning from his hand as he clawed at his back. Hannah saw the arrows stuck in him an instant before he fell backward. Her hand choked off the cry in her throat.

Driven by terror, she tried again to climb onto the sidesaddle. The rush of Apache ponies from all sides had her hot-blooded horse in a frenzy. It squatted close to the ground, its legs spread like a cat unsure which way to jump. That was all Hannah needed to gain a seat in the saddle. The reins were loose in her hand, giving her hardly any control of the gelding's mouth.

A gap still existed between the sandwiching bands of Apache raiders, and Hannah used her quirt in an attempt to whip her horse through it. Her gelding sprang for the opening. Amid the terror and confusion, she still carried the conviction that a detail from the fort was on its way. She simply had to reach them.

Her pounding heart felt as if it was in her throat, pumping madly, blood surging through her veins, her body fevered. The gelding slipped through the gap before it closed, but the Apaches were running along on either side. The blood bay gelding was fast, Hannah knew. Stephen had raced it once against the top racehorse in the regiment and been beaten by only a length. With her voice and her rawhide quirt, she urged her mount to an even greater speed. Its stride lengthened as the beast extended itself. But the small, wiry horses of the Apaches weren't left in his dust; they kept pace.

With alarm, Hannah saw that the half-naked riders were drifting in, closing on her from both sides. One leaned over to reach for the reins, his lank black hair flying, and she struck his copper-skinned arm with her riding crop. But while she beat off one, the diversion gave the Apache on the other side a chance. Frantic, Hannah swung wildly at both. One grabbed the rawhide quirt and pulled; she had to let go of it or be jerked from the saddle. A second later, a yank of the reins deprived her of them as well.

The minute she lost control of the bay gelding, there was an immediate slackening of speed, as if the animal knew that the race was lost. The reins were in the hand of an Apache with blue lightning streaks on his high cheekbones, and he led the horse in a wide circle back over the same ground. The feeling of helpless, trapped terror was more difficult for Hannah to suppress now that her hands were empty—nothing to do and nothing to hold.

Until now, there had not been time to think, only to react; no time to wonder, only to run. As they rode up to the dry wash, Hannah saw two breechclouted Apaches on the ground by Lieutenant Delvecchio's body. A sob was somewhere in her chest, but her teeth buried in her lower lip to keep from making a sound as she watched them strip the dead officer of his cartridge belt and revolver and go through his pockets for anything else of value.

In every movement of the Apaches there was a darting swiftness, an efficiency of action and speed. The instant the plundering of the body was finished, they swung onto their horses. Some silent consensus had them ride down the embankment to the dry creekbed, Hannah barely managing to cling to her side perch during the rump-sliding descent of her horse. In a controlled haste, they were fleeing the scene.

Because the fort was too close—the pony soldiers too near—the reason cried out to Hannah. In anguished hope, she looked behind them, straining to hear the clank of bridle chains and the groaning of saddle leather, or to see the raised dust of a cavalry detail.

Then she faced forward and eyed the Apache leading her horse. It was the first good look she'd taken at any of her attackers, their painted faces seeming like glowering masks of evil in some theatrical play, complete with stringy black wigs. A thin layer of dust lay over the brown skin of her captor's broad, powerful shoulders, a sinewy toughness to his naked torso. Something in his profile seemed vaguely familiar.

A horse neighed, distracting her attention. The cavalry mounts of both officers were in the possession of two Apache riders who were waiting at the bend of the sandy wash. Their presence brought the number of the band to seven, now coming together in a single force. A thickset Apache, his fat a solid bulk, sat astride a narrow-chested roan horse. Hannah recognized the horse and rider as the same pair that had been at the desert trading post. Captain Cutter had identified the Apache as a Chiricahua leader named Juh.

Startled by the discovery, she flashed a glance at her

captor, remembering him, too—the Spanish-speaking one with the scar on his cheek. Hannah looked at the others and thought she recognized more from that bunch. It was difficult to tell, especially now that two of them had donned officers' campaign hats and one had on a second lieutenant's jacket.

Her horse was led past the death-twisted body of Lieutenant Sloane, stripped of his jacket, weapons, and valuables, an arrow in his throat. Chilled and sickened, Hannah looked away. For the sake of her own sanity, she tried not to think about what they were going to do with her, but it was there—the fear—gnawing at her.

They rounded the bend of the wash, its red sandstone worn smooth by the desert's flash floods. Hannah considered jumping out of the saddle. There was nowhere to run, nowhere to hide, so she never thought for an instant that she had a chance to escape. But they might shoot her—death might come quickly. Yet if they wanted her alive . . . she shuddered at the unknown horror in the thought.

She mustn't think about it. At this moment, they weren't bothering her. There was still hope . . . there was still a chance that the soldiers from the fort might catch up with them, or that somehow she might get away. The key was to stay alive. Help would come. Stephen would come.

A hundred yards farther on they left the soft, hoofprint-hiding sands of the dry creekbed and headed into rough, broken canyon country. It was difficult riding, the horses always scrambling up some rocky slope or snaking down some twisting trail at a jarring trot, always at the quickened pace, strung out single file.

At the mouth of a barranca, they bunched up behind the leading riders as they stopped. A chubby-cheeked Apache boy of ten or eleven stepped out from the concealing brush of a palo verde. Within minutes, four more horses were driven out of the natural corral, all carrying local brands on their flanks. Apache booty from other raids was tied on two of the stolen animals.

No time was taken to rest. Hannah barely had a chance to relax her leg muscles from the constant strain of maintaining her balance in the side saddle. A pull of the reins lifted her horse's nose, and it stretched out its neck in a brief resistance; then they were moving again.

The commotion outside the post headquarters began with the arrival of the galloper. Hearing the rushed and anxious tone of the relayed message without catching the words themselves, Stephen crossed to the door and stepped out into the shade of the galleried walk. A trooper put spurs to his lathered horse and kicked it toward the stables, obeying an order issued by the officer just turning to report to headquarters.

Stephen observed the small hesitation when Captain Jake Cutter noticed him at the top of the steps. Grim-visaged, Cutter threw him a perfunctory salute as he mounted the steps. Stephen returned the salute, his own restless nature sensitive to the turbulent currents in this windless desert air.

"What's the trouble, Captain?"

"The patrol that went out to investigate the gunfire we heard earlier just sent a galloper back," he said. "They found the bodies of Lieutenants Sloane and Delvecchio. The Apaches ambushed them about two miles from here."

"Hannah?" The hard kick of emotion hit him in the stomach. "What about my wife? She went riding with them this morning."

"I know, sir. They haven't located her yet. I'm having a patrol mounted and I've ordered the Apache scouts to join us."

"Apaches." It was a white-hot thing vibrating in him, an anger and a fear. "We'll find her, Captain," Stephen stated with building force. "We'll find her if we have to chase those red devils all the way to hell!"

"Yes, sir."

A salute dismissed him. It was understood without needing to be said that Stephen would accompany the patrol, and he went to make his preparations.

The army was a fighting machine, but like all machinery, it needed time to get started, to get its men outfitted and mounted. Stephen chafed at the delay. Nearly fifteen minutes elapsed between the time the galloper rode in and the moment when the black troopers wheeled their horses into columns of four to ride out of the fort, a dozen haphazardly dressed agency Apaches in a straggly group leading the way.

By then word of the ambush had spread through the fort, bringing out other soldiers and dependents as well to watch the column leave. Mrs. Bettendorf and another senior officer's wife were hurrying up the row to the rooms belonging to Lieutenant Sloane and his bride—his widow. It was the practice not to notify the next of kin until someone was with them in that moment of grief.

The two miles were covered at a gallop. When they arrived on the scene, the scouts fanned out to inspect the area, then came back to report. Raw with tension, Stephen sat erect in the McClellan saddle, impatiently listening to a recap of information they already knew—where the ambush occurred, bodies found here and here, riding party jumped at this point, flanked by second group of raiders over here. Wade's big, cedar-gold horse stamped at a fly, the saddle leather creaking at the shifting weight.

On his right, Captain Jake Cutter was slouched over in his saddle, shoulders curved in a relaxed hunch. Stephen eyed him, aware again of that irritating ability of Cutter to grab every second of rest, sleep with a blink of the eyes, relax with a looseness of the body. Stephen had the need for motion.

The head of the scouts was a buckskin-clad white man named Amos Hill, with a full-whiskered face and a scar from a knife wound that had blinded his left eye. The Apaches called him "One-Eye." He wore the army's yellow bandanna around his neck, but it was his only concession to uniform. He was hired to translate and to scout, and that's all he did—no camp cooking or water carrying for him. He wasn't no step-and-fetch-it boy, he always said.

Instead of receiving the report from One-Eye Amos Hill, Captain Cutter was questioning one of the Apache scouts using a combination of stilted English and border Spanish. Nah-tay was squat in stature and powerfully built, with deep-set eyes that burned like living coals.

"Ask him if he knows who they were." Stephen abruptly broke into the talk. "Mimbres? Chiricahuas?"

The question did not require translation. Nah-tay understood it. "Chiricahua."

"How many? Where did they take the woman?" he demanded, conscious of Cutter tilting his head down, an act of withdrawal from the conversation.

"Seven. Eight. Maybe some wait out there." A sweep of Nah-tay's brown hand indicated the limitless canyons and rims of the desert. He added something in Spanish, which Stephen was obliged to ask Cutter to translate.

"He says the Apache goes where it will be hard for the army to follow." Cutter studied the end of his cigar.

"What will they do with her?"

"Major—" Cutter straightened in his saddle, his shoulder muscles flexing slightly in protest to this subject, while his gaze made a short sweep skyward.

"Tell him to answer me," Stephen ordered harshly.

59

Cutter nodded to the scout. Nah-tay hesitated, then gave a long, staccato response in Spanish. Cutter did not look at Stephen as he offered an unemotional translation. "Nah-tay doesn't know. He says it depends on many things. They may kill her slowly, or take her to Mexico and sell her to the slave markets. They may keep her for a captive . . . or they may use her for their pleasure. In that case, we will find . . . what's left of her soon."

As Stephen started to rise in his stirrups, anger billowing in him at the ruthless savages, Nah-tay included, a hard hand gripped his forearm. Cutter gave him a narrow-eyed glance.

"You asked for it, Major," he said softly.

With an effort, Stephen controlled his rage, lifting the reins. "As soon as the bodies are loaded in the wagon, send them back to the fort for burial."

As the big, high-bred horse was wheeled away from the circle, its glistening rump swung against Cutter's mount. Indifferently the second horse shifted out of the way. Cutter rolled his cigar to a far corner of his mouth, holding it between his teeth while he let his gaze follow Wade for a short span of seconds. Then he looked back to the flat-nosed scout.

"It is his woman the Apaches have taken," he said in Spanish.

Nah-tay grunted and turned his deep-burning gaze after the officer. "Some 'pache no be with woman on raids. Think they take his power." He seemed to offer the possibility as a remote hope.

"How do these Apaches think?" Cutter asked.

"Quién sabe?" The Apache shrugged.

"Who knows?" Cutter repeated under his breath, and laid the reins alongside of the horse's neck, turning it away from the scouts as he half-saluted them.

He urged the heavy-headed horse into a lope and headed for the wagon that was hauling the dead back to the fort. His quick eyes scanned the ambush site, now a rest stop for his company of colored troopers. The Apaches had been after the officers' horses and guns— and some thumbing of their noses at the fort—but they'd taken the woman as an added prize. Gall burned his throat, the muscles tightening. He remembered her beauty, the shining of her hair, and the dance of her smile . . . and he remembered that hint of pride and strong will in her mouth. That spirit of hers would be hard to break. And it angered him that the Apaches would enjoy the time it would take.

He looked into the vast expanse that tumbled roughly around them, its dry heat waiting, its thorned and spiny plants bristling, and its scorched earth unforgiving. A hostile land.

# CHAPTER 5

HOW FAR OR HOW LONG THEY'D TRAVELED, HANNAH didn't know. She could no longer judge distance and time. Wherever the spotted rump of the pony in front of her went, the blood bay gelding she rode followed. It stumbled frequently, not as surefooted as the desert ponies on this rocky ground, which forced Hannah to be constantly alert.

The muscles in her legs and back were cramped from the sidesaddle position, and there was an aching soreness all through her from the long hours and the grueling miles on horseback. The midday sun, high overhead, added to her discomfort, sending its hot rays into the mountain canyons to bake the rocks.

The ruffed collar of her blouse was damp with perspiration, and the scratchy weight of her riding skirt and jacket seemed to smother her skin. She was so hot; the smell of her own body was strong. Wisps of hair lay wetly along the sides of her face and her hat sat slightly askew, but Hannah was too exhausted to expend the energy to right it. Besides, it seemed of little importance.

With no other means at hand, Hannah raised her arm and used the sleeve of her jacket to blot at the moisture beading on her upper lip. Her mouth and throat were parched, and the salty taste of her own sweat only increased her thirst. Not once had she seen any of her Apache captors take a drink since they had set out. She didn't know how they kept going.

The mental stress, the physical discomfort both pressed on her. Her chin dipped and a wetness gathered in her eyes. Hannah shut them, and made her mind focus on anything that might help her. Someone had once told her that Indians admired courage and bravery; she mustn't let them see she was afraid. Her head came up, her blurred vision slowly clearing, and her lips thinned out, dryly sticking together.

The stillness was broken by the clatter of many hooves on stone, the rattle of a miniature rockslide and the scrape of a hoof, and the gruntings of the horses as they picked their way along the side of a rocky hill. They followed it around to the base of its steep side. The rising bluff threw a wide band of dark shade onto the ground, and the raiders in the lead stopped to give the horses a rest.

After her first rush of gratitude had passed, Hannah experienced a twinge of unease. So far they had ignored her, but for how long? She watched the Chiricahua warrior ahead of her slide from his horse, always with that effortless, catlike grace and quickness. The reins to her horse remained in his grasp, but loosely, it seemed.

All the Apaches had dismounted, save the boy guarding the captured horses, and one moccasined Chiricahua scrambled back along their trail on foot, obviously a sentry. In the seconds it took her to notice these things, Hannah realized she might never have another chance to escape.

She kicked her horse and hit it with her hands to make it pull free of the Apache's hold. It was a slim chance, and a dangerous one. Even if the horse managed to get away, there was always the risk that it would trip on the dragging reins.

The tired and sweat-caked bay gelding made a startled lunge forward, whinnying its frightened confusion as Hannah beat at the animal, urging it to take flight. It tried to respond, but its head was pulled around by the heavy hand on the reins. The pressure never let up, twisting the gelding's head around, doubling it back against its own body until the horse overbalanced. Hannah was thrown from the saddle, falling on the talus slide of the rock face. The shock of the impact stunned her.

Her horse scrambled to its feet and shook itself, like a dog shaking off water, while Hannah cautiously pushed herself up on her hands, dazed but cognizant that she had suffered no injuries beyond a bruising. A sound, a movement, a sense of something above her caused Hannah to turn over, scooting into a half-sitting position. The loose folds of her long riding skirt became tangled around her legs. Her Apache captor stood at her feet, his obsidian eyes staring at her out of the brutish face with one cheek scarred by a knife, his shaggy black hair hanging past his brown-skinned shoulders. The menace in him was silent.

Hannah remembered that he had spoken Spanish and said, in the border tongue, "The soldiers will come. They will catch you."

The smallest flicker of surprise flitted across his wooden expression before it returned to its customary blankness. With a slight turn of his head, he translated her warning to the other members of his party in their own language. A few derisive-sounding responses were offered.

"Yellow legs slow. Soldiers come. Apache no be here," he answered her, harsh and arrogant. "Apache like grains of sand. Sprinkle on desert. No find."

Her stomach knotted into a tight ball. For a second she looked away, trying to find some other straw of hope to grasp. There was a sudden motion and the hat was plucked from her head, her hair painfully pulled until the securing pin was jerked loose. Hannah gasped aloud at the pain and lifted a hand to her hair, its chignon pulled loose. But she thought the better of arguing over Lutero's right to her dark green hat.

To the chortling delight of his comrades, he set it squarely atop his black head. It was barely big enough in circumference to circle it, sitting a good inch higher than the clay-red sweatband around his head. But Lutero seemed satisfied with the fit and made a demanding gesture at Hannah.

"Coat," he said, meaning the green riding jacket that matched the hat.

Once she realized he was serious, Hannah removed her riding gloves to unfasten the looped buttons of the jacket's front. Sitting upright, she shrugged out of the fitted top and handed it to him. She felt immediately cooler without that layer of clothing, and she welcomed the relief on her heated skin.

The jacket was much too small to fit the powerfully built Apache with his broad shoulders and runner's chest. The back seam split and the sleeves ripped as he tugged it on. Angrily he pulled it off and threw it on the ground. Hannah thought it foolish of him to believe it could fit him. She untangled her skirts to stand up and brush away the dirt and debris from her fall.

Lutero caught up a handful of the hunter-green skirt

material. Hannah acted without thinking, pushing at his hand to get it away from her person and to free her skirts. Her show of resistance brought a snarl to his lightning-streaked face. He yanked violently on the material, throwing her off balance. The waistband fastening gave, the cloth ripping as she fell. She was tumbled out of the skirt and its slip, like a pillow turned out of its case.

Clad only in her blouse and pantalettes, Hannah clambered to her feet and backed warily away from the Apache, very much afraid. The rocks at the cliff's base slid beneath the leather soles of her riding boots. Solid sandstone was behind her. Blood pounded in her ears as her breath came in fast, panic-shallow gasps. Her nerves were screaming with the tension, but Hannah fought to still the panic. When he took a step toward her, Hannah bolted for an open space that would give her maneuvering room, but he caught her, his fingers digging into her arms like ensnaring talons. The thin material of her blouse tore like paper under his grip as she struggled to break loose. The ache of her weary muscles was forgotten, renewed strength coming from the surge of adrenaline in her veins. Twisting and fighting, she kicked at him, the toe of her boot squarely hitting his shin and drawing an involuntary grunt of pain.

She was thrown violently to the ground, scraping her flesh on the sharp gravel. Her feet were caught, and after he made one abortive attempt to pull her boots off, a knife blade flashed in the sunlight. Her blood froze at the sight of it, all her limbs momentarily stilled. It sliced through the laces and the hard leather boots nearly slid off of their own accord. Her stockings were stripped off, and when he pulled Hannah upright, the stones cut into her bare and tender feet, the pain hampering her attempts at resistance. She couldn't swallow all the anguished sounds that rose in her throat, while she tried to concentrate on the threat of the knife.

Continuing to struggle, she tried to avoid the blade as it came toward her, but there was no lasting escape. She eluded it here only to have it slice through a piece of cloth there. Her blouse and undergarments were quickly shredded to ribbons. She could feel the exposure, the sensation of air against her bare flesh. Hannah clutched at the scraps of cloth covering her private places, but she didn't have enough hands.

The humiliation and indignity flamed through her body, fear always there but now coupled with a wild desperation. Her mane of red-brown hair tumbled loose, swinging forward to hide her breasts, but the rounded cheeks of her buttocks were unprotected, and the figleaf pose of her hand over the dark pubes was futile. In a fear-driven rage, Hannah struck out against this degradation, this awful helplessness.

The scaly roughness of his hands was abrasive against her soft skin, brutal in its intent to subdue. She was sickened by the strong smell of his body, revolted by the contact with his sweating flesh, grainy with dust and dirt.

By some accident, her pummeling fist got past his defenses, striking his high-bridged nose. A second later, exploding agony spread across her jaw and her lip was smashed against her teeth, splitting it open. The force jerked her head way around, a noise ringing in her ears. She reeled backward, staggering, belatedly realizing he'd hit her. She lost her footing on the loose rock and sprawled onto the ground, grazing her bare skin on the gravel.

Quickly she turned, expecting any second to feel the weight of his body pin her to the ground. But the Apache called Lutero was still standing a foot away, his legs spread in an arrogant stance as he surveyed the white smoothness of her nude body.

Some unintelligible comment was made by one of the others in the Apache tongue, seeming to urge Lutero into action—or so Hannah feared. Her glance darted around the watching band of warriors; she could sense their desire for the sport. A sickening fear curled through her stomach.

Speaking Apache, Lutero said something that held a note of finality, and a response was made by Juh, the malevolent, fat one, which seemed to amuse the others as they made sounds of approval. Hannah was afraid to move, and break whatever spell was holding the Apaches in their places. Then Lutero moved—away from her, rejoining his companions while he kept an eye on her.

When he squatted on his heels in their loosely formed circle, she cautiously sat up, drawing her knees tightly to her chest and hunching over them, hiding behind the curtain of her hair as much as she could. She kept glancing at the pile of torn clothes, wondering if she dared to retrieve them. A moment later he gathered them up and began stuffing them into a pouch on one of the packhorses.

*"Por favor—"* Hannah began her protest with a tactful plea, but she fell silent when Lutero scowled at her, revealing his contempt.

The gelding stood in the shade, its head hanging in exhaustion. After a few halfhearted tugs at the hardy mountain grass, the horse had given up the task as too wearing. The Indian ponies chomped at the scattered clumps, their heads jerking to tear the tough stalks.

Lutero stopped beside the gelding and looked over the strange saddle with its arrangement of leg rest and stirrups all on one side. It did not win his approval. He unhooked the cinch and let the sidesaddle drop to the ground. Hannah wasn't sure what all this meant, but she was still alive. She was still alive. Tears burned at the back of her eyes, but she managed to keep them there.

The lookout came back and spoke in that rhythmic flow of throaty sounds, and the others began moving toward their horses. But none of it carried any sense of urgency. Hannah sat quietly, hoping they might overlook her but Lutero did not do that.

"*Ugashé*. We go," he translated into deep-voiced Spanish.

The mortification she felt at her nudity was an indescribably intense emotion. In her whole life, only her mother—and Stephen, in the dark shadows of the bedroom—had ever seen her unclothed. Now here she was, under a brilliant sun in the company of eight marauding Apaches without a stitch of clothes to her name. It stripped her of all dignity and pride.

Fear impelled her to obey him. Her shoulders hunched, her arms spread across her body in a covering gesture, Hannah rose and gingerly picked her way over the sharp-edged rocks, the mass of thick, darkly auburn hair tumbling about her white shoulders.

Impatient at her slowness, Lutero reached out and shoved her at the horse. The force propelled her into the animal's hot flank, the horsehair coarse against the softness of her breasts and belly. All her life she had ridden sidesaddle, from the time she was seven and her daddy bought her first pony. Few ladies she'd met ever rode astride. It was considered indecent for a woman to spread her legs astraddle a horse. To do so now, when she was naked, seemed the greatest indignity.

Hannah levered herself away from the bay's flank, hotly conscious of her bare bottom. She stiffened at the rough touch of Lutero's hands, one grabbing her waist and the other a handful of round bottom. In one motion, she was heaved onto the horse's back. Automatically she swung a leg over it to straddle the bony, hair-covered hump. The sensations of the horse's coat beneath her made her rigid with embarrassment. Her degradation now seemed complete.

Single file, the Apaches moved out. A tug on the reins pulled the bay horse into a trot. Hannah had to thread her fingers into its black mane to hold on while she learned to grip with the insides of her legs to avoid the awkward and painful slap of her bottom on the horse's back.

As the sun drifted lower in the afternoon sky, the rocky cliff cast a longer shadow onto the canyon floor at its base. The Apache scouts loosely sat their horses in the shade, awaiting the cavalry column riding up. The hooves of the army horses stirred up a dust cloud that could be seen for miles in all directions.

The collective sounds of jangling bridle chains, creaking saddle leather, and shuffling hooves covered the infrequent conversations among the troopers. Horse smell and body sweat combined in a rank odor that swirled around the column when the command to halt came down the line.

"Have the men dismount, Sergeant." Cutter passed the order to his colored top sergeant, John T. Hooker. "We'll rest here for fifteen minutes."

"Yes, sir." Hooker saluted and wheeled his horse around. "Prepare to dismount!" he called.

In between Cutter's order and the shouted command, Stephen Wade muttered his discontent. "I don't see that a rest is necessary, Captain. Those coloreds should be used to the heat anyway."

"Dis-mount!" The bellowed command was followed by the combined creak of twenty saddles as the troopers halted themselves off their horses.

"It's the hot of the day, Major," Cutter said, unemotional in the face of criticism from his superior. "If our horses break down, we will never catch up with those Apaches, sir." No rebuttal of his reasoning appeared to be forthcoming, so he suggested, "Let's see what the scouts have found."

One-Eye Amos Hill was squatting on the ground in the shade of the cliff. When the two officers rode up, he passed the reins of his horse to one of the scouts and motioned for Nah-tay to join them.

"They stopped here." Amos turned his one good eye on the officers as they dismounted and handed their horses over to the scout.

"How long ago?" Energy lay coiled inside Stephen like a spring, capable of carrying him for days without rest if necessary. It was this knowledge of his own stamina that made him impatient with weaker men.

"Better than an hour ago. Closer to two, I'd say," Amos said, reconsidering.

"Dammit, we aren't gaining on them," Stephen protested.

"That's kinda hard to do." Amos scratched at his whiskers. "You see, Major, they got the advantage of knowin' where they're goin', and we got to follow their trail to find that out—and make sure we don't ride into an ambush in the process. It's slow business, especially when an Apache don't want you to follow him."

"You hired on to do a job, Hill. I expect you to do it without a lot of excuses and bellyaching." Stephen had little time for complaints on the job, especially when that job involved finding Hannah. The damned chief of scouts should be out there now, hot on the trail of those murdering Apaches, he thought.

"No excuses, Major," Amos replied, stealing a half-concealed glance at Cutter. "The job comes with some limitations, and I just wanted to be sure you understood them."

"I understand, Hill."

71

"How many were here?" Cutter went back to the original subject as he opened his canteen to wet his bandanna and wipe his face and neck.

"Eight. Nine counting the woman."

"Then she was here?" The idleness of Cutter's tone did not match the sharp-eyed glance he sent the scout.

The hesitation lasted no longer than a pulse beat. "Yeah, she was here."

A heightened tension in the air alerted Stephen to a missed significance of the question. "We've been following their trail, and it led us to this place. Why did you ask if she'd been here, Captain?"

"It's a way of double-checking, Major." He wiped out the sweatband of his campaign hat, his black hair pressed flat against his head where it had sat. "We can be certain we didn't miss any side trips they might have made off the main trail." The hat was set firmly onto his head and pushed back into position before he looked at the scout. "There was something you wanted to tell us."

"No," Hill said in a disgruntled, irritable voice. "But I reckon there's somethin' you've got a right to see."

Cutter lagged half a step behind the major as he followed the whiskered scout across a graveled stretch of talus to a clear area next to some brush. It wasn't the kind of ground that showed much sign, but the scrap of white cloth hooked to a low branch of a bush told part of the tale.

"That's Hannah's." Wade snatched up the piece of cloth, a narrow ribbon woven along the top to make a neckline of sorts. "It's her . . . camisole." His voice faded and his fingers curled the bit of material into his palm, his jaw muscles working convulsively.

Cutter picked up a piece of pink ribbon, torn from the undergarment, and twined it around his forefinger. He stared at the kicked-up gravel and the gouges in it. He felt very flat and very cold inside.

"The ground's purty churned up here," Amos said. "It looks like she put up a struggle."

"Damn them!" The words were an ominous rumble that came from deep within Stephen Wade.

"I seed Mrs. Wade at the fort a time or two. I always thought she was a fine lady," Amos offered as a kind of final comment before he turned to leave Major Wade.

Cutter took a swift step after him and pulled him to the side, muttering under his breath so that Wade wouldn't hear, "What did you mean by that? Is she still alive? Did she leave here with them?"

"Yeah, she's alive." The scout wiped at the sweat trickling down his temples, and his crazy, marble eye directed its gleam at Cutter. "And we both know she'd be better off dead about now. Hell, Captain, between here and Texas, you been fightin' these 'paches for a few years. You seen what they done to white women."

Cutter knew. He had buried some of them. Unconsciously, he wrapped the piece of ribbon more tightly around his fingers. He hoped to God he wouldn't have to bury her, too.

"Get your scouts out. We'll be on the move in another ten minutes." He dismissed Amos. As the buckskin-clad figure moved away, Cutter glanced back at Wade.

The piece of cloth was clenched in his fist and held tight at his side. He was staring at the patch of desert, the gravel all scuffled, and Cutter saw the wetness in the other officer's eyes. A rage of anguish contorted his features, making his long jaw stand out.

A man was entitled to his private feelings, so Cutter walked away, a bitter gall sticking in his own throat at the whole sorry situation.

Fire burned all the way through her, until Hannah felt seared to the bone. The sun had beaten down on her naked skin for hours, the tender white skin that she had always protected with such care from too much exposure to the elements. She had only to look at her thighs and arms to see the redness and understand the searing pain.

Her body ached from riding, every muscle screaming its soreness; the insides of her knees were practically raw from gripping the horse, and her legs felt as if they were being pulled apart.

Her lips were cracked from the dryness and the heat. She'd had nothing to eat or drink since morning. She was on the verge of collapsing, yet some spark of life kept her going, kept her swaying to the horse's stride, kept pushing her to continue.

Everything was a kind of haze, a shimmering agony of fire, thirst, and pain. Her face throbbed where Lutero had struck her, her lip was swollen, and her head ached. Dust and sweat had mixed to crease her skin with muddy rivulets.

They walked their mounts along a gully soft with sand, a single line of horses traveling nose to tail. The thick, fine sand muffled the thud of plodding hooves, a dully rhythmic sound punctuated by the odd snort of a pony clearing its nostrils of dust. The sound enveloped Hannah, coming from beneath her, behind her, and in front of her.

It was several beats before she realized it was also coming from another direction, and she roused herself from the stupor that claimed her to puzzle out the difference. The horses in front were angling out of the gully where a natural ford sloped the sides. Instead of following them, Lutero was riding straight ahead, the blood bay gelding in tow. The riders behind them turned after the others.

Confused and unable to think clearly, Hannah swung her dull gaze to her Apache captor and watched him lift a hand in farewell to his comrades. When he noticed her bewilderment, his mouth curved in a smile that seemed malicious.

"Scatter across desert," he said in Spanish.

It took her a minute to unravel that cryptic message and to recall his earlier likening of the Apache to grains of sand. The band was breaking up, scattering across the desert to disappear one by one. In the half of her mind that was functioning, the part not dulled by physical suffering, Hannah realized that any cavalry patrol following their trail would be unlikely to notice their tracks in this soft sand, splitting away from the main bunch.

She cried out, but it was only a low moan. Her body hurt too much.

# CHAPTER 6

THE SHOCK OF WATER AGAINST HER PARCHED LIPS AND thick tongue lifted Hannah out of her stupor and awakened her pain-drugged senses. The smell of the tepid water, the sound of it trickling from a container made from animal intestines, and the wetness of it reduced her to a primitive drive. The rough hand that had twisted into her hair no longer needed to hold her head back. She clutched at the water bag, tipping it higher to increase the flow. More came than her dry throat could swallow and it slopped over the side of her mouth, its warm wetness cooler than her sunburned, dehydrated skin.

When the flow was cut off and the water bag withdrawn, Hannah greedily reached for it, her thirst not nearly quenched. "No, please." The croaked protest was no louder than a whisper and it lacked strength.

No response came as Lutero walked away from her kneeling form. Her outstretched arms fell limply to her sides, and a sudden gut-wrenching pain convulsed her stomach. The precious liquid she had so greedily consumed was disgorged in a violent upheaval. The desert sand instantly sucked up the watery vomit, leaving only a damp, dark circle to mark where it had been. Hannah wiped at the slimy spittle on her lips while her shoulders lifted with dry, hacking sobs.

She sagged into a sitting position, propped up by one hand, her legs curved to one side. The reviving influence of the water, however briefly enjoyed, had broken the stupor that had kept her from feeling the agony of her blistering flesh and screaming muscles. Salty sweat ran onto her cut lip, making it sting afresh. Prostrated by heat and exhaustion, Hannah felt incapable of further movement. With eyes that blurred and didn't hold focus, she looked around.

They were in the midst of some sort of ruins. Behind her were the crumbling remains of an adobe wall, weathered and old. The area was ringed by trees and encroaching brush. Beyond lay a high range of mountains, the Mogollons. She noticed some broken shards of pottery nearby. But none of this was capable of rousing her interest. She was alive; that was all that counted.

The sun was nearly behind a distant ridge whose spiny top flamed with a yellow glow. Lutero was picketing the horses near a tumbling wall where tufts of desert grass provided forage for them. The bay gelding wasn't interested in the nourishment; it stood with its head hanging and its legs braced apart. They were stopping for the night, and a fragment of relief quivered through her.

Wanting to avoid causing herself more pain, she tried to stretch out carefully on the ground, but the sharpness of the gravelly sand against her raw and tender flesh was excruciating. She collapsed onto it, the single convulsion of pain preferable to a multitude of little ones that clawed at her nerves. She went limp, throbbing all over and much too exhausted to care about the rough bed the desert floor made. She shut her eyes.

The blessed oblivion of sleep was brutally disrupted by a pain stabbing through her ribs. The force of it rolled her over, and sand scraped the raw flesh of her back. When she opened her eyes, Lutero was standing over her, his high-moccasined legs spread slightly.

Dusk lavendered the sky, cerise clouds lying low on the horizon. At first Hannah thought he wanted her to rise so that they could be on the move again. Weakly she moved her head from side to side, a mute, negative answer to his command, while sandy grit entangled itself in the wild mass of her hair.

Her half-closed eyes caught a glimpse of motion. She tried to focus on it. The breechcloth that hung past his knees in front was being unwrapped and drawn away to reveal more of the brown-skinned body. Almost against her will, Hannah's gaze focused on the turgid male erection. All that had been shapes in the shadows with her husband, brief glimpses and sensations of size, was now blatantly there for her to see.

Inwardly she recoiled, trying to shrink from him. With his foot he forced her sore legs apart. More of her raw, sun-seared skin rubbed across the sand and the contact drew sharp gasps of pain from Hannah. When she felt him move between her legs, she raised her hands, trying to ward him off, but her sun-battered and ride-abused body was too weak.

He pressed the weight of his sweat-slick and grimy body brutally onto her, indifferent to the rough scrape of his skin against her sore flesh, and the smell of him saturated the air she breathed. She made puny, ineffective attempts to escape him, her hands pushing futilely at his deep, stoutly muscled chest, and she twisted, trying to arch away from the jabbing prod, writhing at the pain any movement on this gravel bed caused.

"No. No." Hannah repeated the word over and over, crying silently, too weakened and physically beaten by the elements to offer any other resistance.

His callused hands grasped her hips and held them in position while he entered her dryly, ramming into her without a care for her discomfort. Her mouth opened on a cry that never came out, shut off somewhere by a desire to deny the driving animal thrust that rocked her body and ground her seared flesh into the dirt.

In this whirling moment of pain and violation, a sense of unreality took hold. None of this was happening to her. She shrank from it mentally, blocking it out and crawling into a corner of her mind to hide until it was all over.

The pounding increased in tempo, Lutero's bestial gruntings rumbling into her hearing. None of it stopped until he'd spent his seed inside her. Almost immediately he withdrew his still-hardened shaft from her and stood without ceremony. Hannah kept her eyes shut, revulsed by the mere thought of the hanging genitals.

But Lutero was uninterested in her now that he had taken his satisfaction. The tough rawhide soles of his moccasins made a small crunching sound as he stepped over her sprawled legs and walked away, picking up his breechcloth to wind it around his hips again.

Slowly, hurting, Hannah drew her legs up and curled into a tight fetal ball. She ached from the rough usage, the wetness of his sperm making the insides of her legs sticky. She felt dirty and unclean, a defilement that had nothing to do with the honest grime and sweat coating her naked body. She recoiled from the mental image of the broad-faced Apache mounting her like a rutting animal.

"Stephen," she said in a broken sob. "Stephen, where are you?" Her shoulders shook. Then she saw Lutero walking straight toward her. "Oh, God, no." She didn't know what he intended—to rape her again or to kill her—but a spark remained that made her want to live. He crouched down on one knee and caught up both her wrists. "What are you going to do?" Hannah demanded hoarsely in Spanish.

But the Apache wasn't inclined to answer her as his inscrutable black eyes gave her brief glances. Using a piece of rawhide, he tightly bound her wrists together, so tightly that her pulsing blood was just barely able to continue to flow. All the horrifying tales she'd heard about the innovative ways Apaches used to prolong death came rushing back to her with frightening clarity. Half certain that he intended to stake her out atop a mound of vicious biting fire ants, Hannah watched him tie the free end of the strap to the solid trunk of a mesquite not far from her head. He tied her ankles as well and secured their rawhide thong to a thick branch that he pushed deep into the ground. She could roll from side to side, but the rest of her movement was restricted.

With a grunt of satisfaction, Lutero again left her, his footfalls making no sound. Even if she'd had the strength to try, she couldn't have freed herself from the leather bonds. In her condition, it was best simply to breathe and try not to think of past events—or the future.

The campfire was a deep-glowing light in the swallowing blackness. Overhead the stars glistened sharply, and the mountain desert held its mysteries from them. The breeze lifted, carrying the smell of the cavalry horses and their excrement to the soldiers beyond the fringes of the firelight.

The camp was segregated into three parts—four, if the picketed horses and mules were counted. The largest section was occupied by the Negro troopers, the dark blue of their dusty uniforms and the dark shades of their faces blending with the midnight blackness. Off by themselves, away from the campfire, the Apache scouts had bedded down. And the last area belonged to the officers.

After a tasteless meal of beans and hardtack, the officers grouped around Major Stephen Wade. His anger was controlled but palpable as he viewed the circle of men, slicing a pointed look at the one-eyed scout who stood slouching on his right.

"The size of the raiding party has shrunk during the course of the day, gentlemen." Stephen faced them, his shoulders stiffly squared. "Mr. Hill estimates that we may now be trailing as few as five Apaches."

"They been travelin' single file, each pony messin' up the tracks of the one in front of it, which makes it hard for a tracker to gauge how many's in the party." Amos Hill had a cheek full of chewing tobacco, which made a small bulge in his whiskered face. "An' all them extra ponies just makes it tougher. We're purty damned sure we're four horses shy, plus some of the extra stock—and maybe more."

"For how long?" Captain Cutter asked.

"For sure, they was all together at that afternoon stop. My guess is they dropped off one at a time, each pickin' a place where they'd leave few tracks and peelin' off from the rest. Them 'paches are experts at scatterin' and meltin' into the desert."

"Would you care to take a guess whether Mrs. Wade is in front of us—or somewhere behind us, Mr. Hill?" Taut muscles stood out along Stephen's jaw.

"I can't rightly say, Major. If they're still lettin' her ride that big blood bay, then she's behind us." He was careful not to commit himself. "Nah-tay says the hoof marks of that bay gelding are no longer in this trail of ponies."

"If we backtracked along our route, Mr. Hill, what are the chances of finding where Mrs. Wade's horse left the trail?" Stephen unrolled a map of the area with quick twists of his wrists and spread it out for his officers to study.

"We'd find it. Nah-tay and his Apaches could track a fly across this desert, but it would take time," the scruffy scout reminded him. "We'd have to fan out, cut for sign, keep crisscrossing back and forth till we found it. An' for all we know, she might not even be ridin' it."

"I have considered that. Therefore, tomorrow morning, Cutter, I want you to take Lieutenant Sotsworth and half the troopers plus Nah-tay and four of his scouts and continue on the trail of these hostiles. Lieutenant Bones, Hill, and the rest of the men and scouts will accompany me while we retrace our route."

One-Eye Amos Hill sucked in his breath and let it out in a long sound. Stephen gave him a sharp-eyed glance. He didn't ask for anyone's approval of his decision, but if a man had a point to make, Stephen preferred that he speak it aloud to his face. It was much easier to deal with dissension that way.

"It 'pears to me there's two possible reasons why them 'paches have been slippin' off," Amos ventured. "It could be that they're through raidin' and they're headin' back to their wickiups with the loot—splittin' up to go their own ways, so to speak. Or—" He paused deliberately. "Or they're doin' it 'cause they know we want the woman back. Maybe they did this a-purpose, guessin' that you'd separate your force into two groups. It could be they're settin' a trap for us and usin' Miz Wade as bait."

"It could be," Stephen conceded, undeterred. "In which case, we shall see whether your Apache scouts are willing to kill their own kind." His glance swung to Jake Cutter. "First call at 4:45 A.M., gentlemen."

After the dismissal, Wade strode away from his officers, tap-tap-tapping the rolled map along the gold stripe on his pantleg. One-Eye Amos turned his head

THE PRIDE OF HANNAH WADE

so his good eye could watch the major leave, then swung back to look at Cutter.

"I reckon he'd like it if those 'paches turned on us. It's a cold-blooded killin' mood he's in." He made a grimace, his mouth nearly disappearing into his whiskers. "Can't say as I'd feel any different if'n it was my woman them bastards molested." A long sigh of regret came from him. "When you're trackin' Apaches, mistakes are costly. I just plain caught onto their trick too late."

No reply was forthcoming, so he simply lifted his hand in an absent farewell and moved into the night. Cutter noticed that he headed over to join the scouts; he was more comfortable with the Indians than he was with his own kind.

Beside Cutter, Sotsworth inquired, "Coffee?" A tin mug of the black, vile brew was extended to him.

"Thanks." The lieutenant was considerably steadier of hand as he passed Jake the mug than he had been earlier. Sotsworth felt he was doomed to oblivion as a junior officer in a black company—and usually tried to drink himself to that point whenever he could. The smell of whiskey drifting in the rising steam from Sotsworth's coffee didn't escape Cutter's notice. He said nothing. If every soldier who drank on duty was thrown out of the army, only a scant handful would be left to fight the Indians.

"What do you think tomorrow will bring, Captain?" Sotsworth wondered aloud as he stared at the tall shape of Major Wade standing at the fire, one leg cocked, a restless brooding quality about him.

"The sun, Lieutenant," Cutter replied dryly.

"Always ready with the clever answer," Sotsworth remarked into his cup. "Clever and never revealing." He lifted his head to gaze again in the direction of their commanding officer. "I, myself, await the morning and the sun. Nights are lonely, I find. It must be particularly difficult for Major Wade this evening."

"Yes, I expect it is." His curtness was an attempt to end this personal speculation on a topic that was none of their business.

"Knowing your wife is out there, alone with the Apaches. The mind can be a cruel organ, Captain," Sotsworth stated. "He must be visualizing all the things they might be doing to her—"

"That's enough, Lieutenant."

Untroubled by the censure in Cutter's voice, the lieutenant took a long swig of his coffee and gazed into the night with an expression of melancholy. "All this darkness makes a man remember the dreams of his youth, those wonderful nights when there was still plenty of time . . . for everything." A couple of horses began to scuffle along the picket line, disputing territory. "Will we see action tomorrow?" He rephrased the first question he'd put.

"We've been on campaigns many times without seeing a single Apache." One of the most difficult aspects of fighting the Apache was finding him. A cavalry company raised a lot of dust, which made it easy to spot. Even now, the Apaches knew the soldiers were on their trail. Their location was already known, so there was no need for a dry camp.

"But when we did see them, Captain, we were usually under attack," Sotsworth reminded him. "I don't relish the idea."

"If you're lacking courage, maybe you'd better take another swig of that coffee." The suggestion informed his lieutenant that Cutter knew what flavoring was in his brew.

A flush darkened Sotsworth's face. "It isn't that I fear the Apaches, Captain Cutter." A deep, burning resentment flashed across his face as he looked toward the shadowy troopers, dark shapes against an even darker night. "I can't decide which would be worse—the ignominy of dying in the oblivion of this company or the humiliation of having my life saved by one of these coloreds."

Cutter emptied out the dregs of his coffee, a deft flick of the wrist splatting it on the rough ground. "If I were you, I'd worry about the Apaches . . . and staying alive."

A prodding foot started the shooting agonies all over again. Hannah groaned, slowly raising her heavy eyelids partway and letting the soft gray of dawn fill her vision until it was blocked by Lutero's looming figure as he kicked her again. Her second groan was louder and she opened her eyes fully. Further movement was made almost impossible by the rawhide that stretched out her legs and bound her hands above her head. The Apache bent down to free her feet.

No blanket had protected her naked body from the chill of the desert night, and it had seeped into her bones. Tied as she was, Hannah hadn't been able to curl into a ball to conserve her escaping body heat. The minute her feet were loose, she ignored the scream of her sore muscles and tried to bend her body together to find some vestige of warmth.

The sight of her own nudity was not a shock to her anymore; the excruciating experience of having her dignity stripped away was gone. Now she was revolted by the bloody water seeping from the broken blisters and the worst sores. Her body was a mass of scabs.

The rank odor of the Apache came to her as he crouched at her head to loosen the rawhide strip tied to the base of the mesquite trunk. She shrank from him and from the memory of the violation she'd known by him. Some fierce burning inside—fear, hatred, pride, or a mixture of all three—refused to let him see the primitive creature he'd reduced her to.

When he straightened, her wrists remained bound. As he walked away, Hannah realized that she was to stay tied. Dully she hunched over her drawn-up knees, shivering in the dry cold and aching endlessly. Her mouth was so dry there was no saliva in it. Just for a tiny moment she let herself wonder what was to become of her—whether she was to be killed when Lutero was tired of forcing himself on her or if he intended to keep her for his squaw.

Stephen was out there. She must remember that. She must remember that he was looking for her. Hope briefly lifted her flagging spirits.

A shadow fell across her as a shy sun peeped over a ridge and cast its new light on the Apache, throwing his dark outline onto Hannah. She looked up and saw him holding the water bag. This time she was wise and did not drink so much when it was offered to her. Even then it kept trying to come up, and she had to swallow at intervals to keep it down.

The bridled horses were all packed with his stolen goods when Lutero led them from the grassy area. He untied her hands, hoisted her onto the bay horse's sweat-caked back, and tied the reins to the brushy tail of his horse. Hannah had not eaten since breakfast the previous morning. She didn't know if Lutero had eaten anything, but he'd given her no food.

Walking, trotting, always moving, they went up canyons, across ridges, along rocky defiles, and through narrow gullies. To Hannah, it was endless motion, another ache, another hour in the merciless sun. Again it was near sundown when Lutero stopped to make camp for the night. Hannah collapsed onto the ground. He tied her hands to a tree, then staked the horses in a hollow depression close by. He looked at Hannah.

After a second's hesitation, he took the water bag and slipped away into the brush, as soundlessly as a lizard.

Feverish and exhausted, she shut her eyes for a moment. When she opened them, mauve shadows cast an odd tint over everything—and Lutero hadn't returned. The half-light was fading quickly, and she strained to listen for any sound that might signal his approach. The wild thought occurred to her that she'd been tied to this tree and left here to die. She started tugging and gnawing at the rawhide strip with her teeth.

A low voice cursing in Apache burst into her hearing. Hannah ceased her efforts and looked around just as he kicked her in the back, knocking the breath out of her. For a long while, she lay there struggling for air. Vaguely she was conscious of Lutero moving about and of a warm, unusual odor in the air. Finally, she pushed herself up into a sitting position, wary of him as he approached.

"*Eyanh.* Eat." He held something out to her, but in the dark she couldn't see what it was.

"What is it?" she asked, then remembered to use Spanish. His answer was a word she didn't understand. The thought of any food turned her stomach, but she knew she had to eat if she wanted to regain her strength. She held out her bound hands and something warm and wet slid into them. Its softly firm texture and slick feel made her uneasy as she brought the roundish object to her mouth.

The smell of blood hit her, and Hannah nearly gagged at the discovery that it was raw. She started to shove it away, but Lutero stopped her, roughly forcing her hands, with their object, back to her mouth.

"Eat," he ordered again in Spanish.

He pushed it between her teeth, making her tear a chunk from it. Hannah knew at once that this thing wasn't meat, but some part of the viscera. Lutero held her mouth closed and tipped her chin high until she had to swallow. The instant he released her, Hannah vomited. Lutero shoved the regurgitated chunk down her throat again and Hannah threw it back up. The process continued until she kept it down; then he made her eat the rest.

# CHAPTER 7

THE STEEP-WALLED SIDES OF THE ARROYO PROVIDED A respite from the hot, stinging wind, laden with the gritty dust it churned up and blew across the barren and broken land. Hannah sagged on the horse, relieved to be sheltered from the whip of the wind lashing her sore and festering skin.

Her fingers were twisted into the horse's dingy white mane, her wrists still tied. Her head drooped forward, bobbing from side to side in rhythm with the walking horse, matching the swing of its spotted face. She rode Lutero's spotted pony. The bay had quit on her about midmorning, stumbling to its knees and collapsing. Nothing in its soft, grain-fed life had conditioned the once-flashy bay gelding for this ordeal.

But Lutero had pulled Hannah clear of the fallen horse, then mounted it and forced it onto its feet. He rode the sweat- and dirt-caked horse now, always pushing it farther than it believed it could go. Hannah understood that feeling. Many times over the last three days she had reached the limits of her endurance and gone beyond them. It would be so easy to fall off the horse and simply die—and it was so much harder to stay on. The rare times she was capable of stringing thoughts together, Hannah wondered at all she had endured. Last night, he'd come to her again while the nauseating taste of that raw animal organ and her own vomit were fresh in her mouth. She had been as powerless as the first time. Not satisfied, Lutero had assaulted her twice more, but Hannah had retreated into that corner of her mind that disassociated itself from her body.

A rock defile marked the beginning of the arroyo, which was narrow and strewn with boulders. Ahead of Hannah, the bay horse stumbled over the rough ground and the heavy hand on its reins jerked on the bit, keeping the staggering gelding on its feet. If there was a single thought that kept Hannah going, beyond the sheer will to survive, it was the certainty that there must be an end to all this. It couldn't last forever.

The narrow trail led up to a high mesa, steep bluffs rising on three sides. Its long top rolled in smooth dips and swells, covered with grass and sage and a scattering of scrub trees. Hannah's pony broke into an eager trot, its ears pricked toward some distant point, but its desire for haste was hampered by the flagging bay to whose black tail it was tied. At an angle, it trotted forward, pulling the bay's tail around its haunches and hurrying its pace. The bay horse labored under its load, carrying not only Lutero but also the carcass of a deer, which had provided Hannah's meal the previous evening.

*"Hoh-shuh, hoh-shuh,"* Lutero murmured to the spotted horse, the low, firm tone quieting it.

It slowed to match the bay's gait but didn't drop behind, its head bobbing alongside the dust-streaked haunches. The wind cut into them again and threw a haze over everything atop the plateau. Hannah made herself as small as possible astride the horse to lessen the sting of the wind-blown dust. With her mind and senses dulled by abuse, she rode on, indifferent to her surroundings or their route through them.

A dog barked—not the shrill yip of a prairie dog, but the fierce, throaty sound of a dog. It roused Hannah sufficiently for her to make a frowning attempt to focus her gaze in its direction. A rounded hump in a clearing amidst the scrub brush took on the dome shape of the Apache *jacal*, thatched with the grass that grew in abundance atop this mesa so that it blended into its surroundings.

More *jacals* were scattered in the general area, in no discernible pattern. Children came running to meet them, while mangy dogs darted out to trot alongside the horses, barking between grinning pants. Several women appeared and one old, bent-over, and white-haired man shuffled toward them. A handful of men sat beneath a *ramada*. Hannah vaguely recalled Stephen mentioning Apache villages, *rancherias* he had called them.

As Lutero rode past rounded brush huts to one situated near the center of the cluster, the *ranchería*'s residents came trailing behind him, crowding around on either side of Hannah. She looked at the women, small and shapeless in buckskin tops that hung past the hips and buckskin skirts that came to mid-calf, high moccasins modestly covering the rest of their legs. Most wore their black hair in twisted coils at the nape of the neck, but the older ones let it fall in a silvered black curtain down the middle of their backs. Their expressions held loathing and disgust for Hannah, no sympathy or pity. She wanted to cry, but she didn't, simply looking straight ahead instead.

An Apache woman stood in front of a *jacal*, waiting for them to ride up. She was small-built, not more than five feet tall, with a maiden's slimness. Her hair was shining black, her eyes dark and luminous. She had the same strong-boned features as the other women, but there was a softer curve to the proud cheekbones and a straighter bridge to her nose, resulting in an uncommon beauty. A smile parted her lips as Lutero stopped the bay horse next to the *ramada* outside the wickiup.

He vaulted from the horse with a pantherish litheness and approached the woman with a proud, lordly bearing. Some emotion gentled his fierce looks, and Hannah stared, amazed, at the warmth in his face. In low, murmured voices they exchanged private greetings; then Lutero turned to gently guide the woman to the horses so that he could show off his plunder. A chance movement briefly pulled the woman's loose-fitting buckskin top tight and outlined her swollen stomach. She was with child, Hannah realized. This woman was Lutero's wife, obviously several months pregnant.

A babble of voices broke out, all speaking in that unintelligible—to her—Apache language, questions obviously being put to Lutero and answers given back that generated excitement. Although they seemed pleased, almost jubilant, about what he told them, Hannah was subjected to a variety of cruel pokes and jabs. After Lutero yanked her off the horse, she was kicked and hit, new bruises being added to those on her already battered body. Hannah shrank from the blows, but she could not elude them.

After the initial excitement of Lutero's arrival in the *rancheria* cooled, the gathering slowly dispersed. Lutero led Hannah to the *ramada* and tied her to an upright post.

He stood before Hannah with his wife at his side, and glowered at his captive. "This my woman, Gatita." He gave her the Spanish name that meant "Little Cat." "You belong to her. You do what she say."

Gatita's luminous dark eyes were turned to her

husband in respectful adoration and pride. She hardly took any notice of Hannah. When the couple moved away, Hannah leaned against the post, gratefully using its support and ignoring the painful scrape of its rough bark against the scabbing blisters on her dull red skin. The children scampered around her conducting a mock war, throwing stones and striking at her with sticks, but they quickly lost interest in the game and rushed away to something else.

Much later in the afternoon, Gatita approached Hannah, holding a gourd hollowed into a saucer. An impassive expression claimed her features as she knelt on the ground beside Hannah. A clear, gel-like substance was in the gourd dish. Without ceremony, she dipped her fingers in it and began smearing it on Hannah's back. The first contact drew a sharp gasp of pain from her, followed almost instantly by a moan of relief at the subsequently soothing sensation.

"Medicine?" Hannah ventured to question.

"*Anh,* yes." Once she had Hannah's back thoroughly covered, Gatita untied her hands and pushed the saucer at her indicating for her to finish the task alone. Some effort was required for Gatita to push herself to her feet with the baby's added weight changing her center of balance, but the Apache woman succeeded in doing so with a measure of grace.

As she disappeared behind the skin flap that served as a low door to the *jacal,* Hannah used her fingers to scoop up some of the wet, cool gel and gently rubbed it onto her sun-blistered and festering skin, massaging it over her breasts and stomach and between her chafed legs. Sandy grit clung to the gel coating, adding to the grime she'd accumulated over three days of travel, but Hannah used every bit of the natural salve.

Shortly after she finished, Gatita came out of the wickiup and crossed the *ramada,* a folded buckskin bundle in her small hands. She dropped it at Hannah's feet and walked away. When Hannah unfolded the buckskin, she discovered that it was a skirt and top. They were worn thin in places, the tanned leather rank and stiff from many wearings, but she had clothes again.

She stared after the primitively beautiful woman, whose glistening black hair was fashioned in two loops and decorated with beads. The lotion, the clothes, were the first kindnesses Hannah had received since her capture. Yet there was no reason for the Apache woman to want to be friends with her, so why? The answer was very likely a practical one; of what use is a captive if she is hurt and fevered? Hannah was of no value to them sick. She couldn't be sold or traded; she couldn't work.

With her weary mind whirling, Hannah put on the buckskin clothes, finding the confinement strange after days with nothing but the air of the canyonland touching her skin. She sank into the shade of the brush arbor. With a balm on her raw skin and the protection of garments covering her body, Hannah was able to shut her eyes so that her exhausted being could steal some much-needed rest.

Before the afternoon was over, three more Apache warriors rode into the *rancheria*; two of them Hannah remembered seeing in the raiding party that had captured her. With the arrival of the last, a celebration started, complete with singing and dancing. From the *ramada* where she was tied, Hannah watched the festivities, remembering all the tales she'd heard on the frontier about the savage and barbaric customs of the Apache.

The chants with their odd pitch and repetitious sounds were unnerving and the thumping drums seemed to vibrate through her body. One dance flowed into another with no perceptible break, and she watched the Apache women move around the ring, choosing partners from among the men on the side-lines.

The beat changed, becoming more insistent, heavier. The air became charged with some undercurrent Hannah couldn't identify, but she could feel the building tension.

First one woman, then a second, and a third began slowly stripping off their clothes until they were almost naked. All were lean-shaped, with muscled legs and blunt shoulders. The woman partnered with Lutero was heavy-breasted and taller than the others. She danced close to Lutero, twisting and writhing in a lewd manner and rubbing her hands over her body.

Repulsed yet fascinated by the erotic exhibition, Hannah stared at the changing shimmer of light on the woman's bucking hips as they thrust forward and back in sinuous motion. It was obvious that Lutero couldn't take his eyes from the action of her hips nor from the beckoning pump of her hands, drawing him nearer still. The dancers' bodies were sweating and the smell of lust filled the air when the dance ended.

Lutero did not leave the Apache woman with the full, firm bosom. Curious, Hannah scanned the circle, finally locating the small and proud Gatita. She seemed untroubled by Lutero's public behavior with the woman as she talked and laughed with other women. When Hannah looked back, Lutero and the lewd Apache dancer were leaving the circle, walking to one of the *jacals*. Immoral heathens, she thought, bitterly recalling her own treatment at their hands—the cruelty, the savagery. The rhythmic beat of the drums and the chanting voices filled the night as Hannah slowly drifted into an exhausted sleep.

The next morning, Gatita put Hannah to work scraping the remaining flesh off the inside of the hide of the deer Lutero had brought back. Too weak to work at long stretches, she had to pause frequently to rest. Flies buzzed around her, attracted by the smell of the fetid meat bits and interested in nibbling at the sores on Hannah's body. She slapped at one nasty biter and caught a glimpse of green out of the corner of her eye—the hunter green of her riding skirt. Hannah stared at the Apache woman wearing her riding skirt. She was the one who had danced so obscenely with Lutero the evening before.

Gatita came out and berated Hannah for slacking. Firm and in command, but plainly hostile to Hannah, she ordered her back to work and derided her ineptness before curtly showing Hannah again how to use the tool.

The cavalry column rode into the fort with trail-weary horses and riders. The slope of the men's shoulders and their long faces foretold the negative results of their expedition. While the troop continued toward the stable, Stephen swung his horse out of the column to ride to the post headquarters, accompanied by Captain Cutter. Colonel Bettendorf was waiting under the *ramada* to meet them when they dismounted and passed the reins to their horses to a waiting trooper.

"No luck, Wade?" Bettendorf guessed after both went through the motions of saluting, observing the dictates of military protocol.

"None, sir." Stephen removed his gloves and slapped them into the palm of his left hand. Frustration dogged him—frustration and the aches and tortures of the mind. "The wind started blowing and wiped out all trace of their tracks. We lost them."

"I was afraid of that," the colonel said, and breathed in deeply, the sympathy he had trouble expressing contained within the subsequent troubled sigh.

"Sir, I request permission to lead a detachment of

men from the fort to make a search of the canyon country to the north," Wade demanded.

"Denied," the colonel refused flatly and impatiently. "We're trying to make peace with the Apaches. You don't do that by riding into their *rancherias* with armed soldiers. Sure as hell, they'd resist such action—and rightfully so! Some fool would start shooting, on their side or ours, it doesn't make any difference. The Apaches that are on the agency now would head for the hills. Then we'd have all of them to round up."

"Very well." Stephen understood the military's position, even though his concerns were more personal in nature. "Then have Amos Hill and his Apache scouts spread the word that I will pay a ransom for my wife's safe return."

"Are you certain she's alive, Stephen?" the colonel inquired very gently.

The cords stood out in Stephen's neck and his jaw was ridged by severely controlled emotion. "I don't know that she's dead—sir." His tone bordered on insubordination.

It was hot. It was always hot in this desert basin. The colonel looked across the military complex toward where the small cemetery was not quite visible beyond. It was neatly sectioned into graves for the dead of the white ranks, the Negro troops, and the odd civilian.

"We buried Lieutenant Delvecchio and Lieutenant Sloane yesterday. You may wish to call on Mrs. Sloane to pay your respects before she leaves tomorrow to return east." Bettendorf again faced Wade and folded his hands behind his back. "I am extremely saddened that your wife was captured by those Apache renegades, Major Wade. All of us are. We plan to hold a prayer service for your wife at the chapel this evening. It will be a great deal easier for you, Major, if you accept the fact that she's dead. It's unlikely her body will ever be found."

Stephen's fingers tightened around his leather gauntlets, crushing them together. What Bettendorf suggested was unthinkable. Rage railed through him, but that imbedded discipline allowed Stephen to keep his composure. "Will you instruct Hill to have the word spread among the Apaches about the ransom?"

"Yes." The agreement was uttered resignedly, as if Bettendorf knew that this resistance should have been anticipated.

"Very good, sir." Wade was stiff. "Cutter can fill you in on any other details you may wish to know. If there's nothing else you need me for, sir—"

"Dismissed, Major." Bettendorf inclined his head in a releasing nod and perfunctorily returned the Major's precise salute. Wade walked briskly away in the direction of Officers' Row. "I didn't say that to offend him, dammit." His brows bristled thickly above his eyes, increasing the disgruntled and irritable look about him when he turned to Cutter. "Tragic. Very tragic."

"Yes, sir." The response betrayed no emotion.

Bettendorf seemed irritated by the noncommital reply. "I can imagine the agony Wade is going through, not knowing if she's alive or dead—the thought of her in the hands of those . . . barely civilized savages. It's hell, I'm sure."

"I'm sure it is, sir."

"We all know that her chances of being alive are slim," Bettendorf insisted. "How many white women taken captive by Indians have ever been seen again? Damn few, I'll wager—and then they're usually not right in the head afterward. It's a damned shame that Delvecchio or Sloane didn't shoot her before they died. Now we can only pray to God that she knows a merciful death." He paused, glowering at Cutter for his continued silence. "You're a seasoned officer, Captain. Apaches don't burden themselves with women captives unless they intend to rape them or sell them into slavery. Children they will take into their tribe, but it's an exception for a grown woman to be accepted."

"You're right, sir. If they keep her alive, she'll be a slave." And, like camp dogs, at the first hint of enemies in the vicinity of the *rancheria,* slaves were killed so that the location of the Apache wickiups would not be revealed by a dog's bark or a slave's betrayal of his master. In severe circumstances, Cutter knew, the Apache was known to kill fussing infants or toddlers, sacrificing one for the safety of many. Supposing she lived long enough to accompany them into their Mexico range, she'd be sold or bartered to some slaver for a rifle or a horse.

"She's going to haunt him." Bettendorf looked after the retreating figure of Stephen Wade. "That's why it is better if he believes she's dead. Then he can grieve over her passing and the pain will be clean. Eventually, the memory will dim."

The colonel had it worked out too neatly for Cutter's taste. That was the easy solution—to turn your back on what was unpleasant. To some, it was simpler than dealing with it.

"That may be, sir," was the most he would admit. "Is there anything else you wished to ask me about?"

"No. I'll expect your written report." Bettendorf dismissed him, apparently realizing how long he'd kept Cutter standing there listening to his defensive explanations of why he wanted to shut the book on Hannah Wade.

Before he reached his quarters, Wade was intercepted by the owner/editor of the *Gazette* in nearby Silver City. A derby hat was perched atop Boler's head and his checkered jacket was unbuttoned around his large middle, his chest spanned by the gold watch chain hooked to his vest. His sideburns were long, flowing into his heavily jowled cheeks, a style popularly called

Dundrearies. Shrewd and intelligent, Hy Boler had the look of a man who knew a good story was before him and intended to have it.

"Major Wade, I can't tell you how badly I felt when I heard about your wife's abduction by the Apaches." He'd already run one story when the word had first spread to Silver City. Below the *Gazette's* banner, the headlines had read, "Army Wife Carried Off by Savages" with the subheading, "Gallant Cavalry Officer Pursues Apaches to Rescue His Wife." It was a sensational story, and the eastern trades had already picked it up. "What happened? Were you able to catch up with those murdering savages?"

"No. We lost the trail. The wind came up and wiped out their tracks," Wade admitted tersely, in no mood for this questioning, yet aware that it was never wise for an ambitious officer to ignore the press.

"You didn't find your wife, then?"

Grimly, Wade recognized this as a tactful way of asking whether she was dead. "No. The Apaches still have her."

"You believe she's alive?"

"Yes," he said forcefully. "And I will not quit looking until I find her. Our scouts will be spreading the word to all the friendly Apaches that I'll pay a ransom for her safe return. You can put in your newspaper, Mr. Boler, that I'm offering a reward for any information about her."

"Will you be going out again to search for her?"

"Every time I leave this fort, sir, I will be looking for my wife. I will not be content until I have her back," Stephen asserted. "Now, if you will excuse me?"

Upon entering the rooms he had shared with Hannah, Stephen immediately felt the force of her absence, the sense of something vital missing. An emptiness seemed to ring through the place. His steps slowed, then stopped altogether as he looked around. He removed his dusty campaign hat absently and laid his gloves inside the crown, then set both on a side table.

Some invisible weight dragged at him, increasing the slant of his broad shoulders. Inside he was emptied, a hollow ache occupying the void. He looked at a framed sampler hanging on the wall, its finely stitched design all Hannah's work, and thought of her soft, smooth hands, the gentle strength of their touch on his arm. So many memories came to him—the evenings they spent together when he read aloud the latest novel to come their way; the picnics she arranged, complete with wine and crystal, at some surprisingly idyllic site she'd found; the times they had raced their horses across the flats and she'd let him win.

How he adored her! She was more than an officer's lady, more than his wife and companion; she was his island in a sea of sand, the one who made his life bearable. He needed her—her intelligence, her wit, and her love. She had believed in him, which had allowed him to believe in himself.

Stephen followed the narrow hall to the bedroom door and walked through it into the room where they'd spent so many nights together. The shock of seeing a woman standing in front of the wardrobe stopped him short. At first his glance couldn't get past the gown she held, the brown one shot with gold threads that Hannah had worn to the party for Lieutenant Sloane and his bride. When he could drag his gaze from it, Stephen noticed the coffee-brown color of the woman's skin and recognized the laundress, Cimmy Lou.

"I didn't mean t' startle you, Majuh." Her voice was a throaty drawl, a match for those knowing eyes that watched him.

"What are you doing here?" he demanded, finding her presence disruptive.

"Miz Goodson asked me to come by an' tidy up some." She smoothed a hand over the shimmering gown. "What d'you want me to do with Miz Wade's things? Miz Goodson said maybe you want 'em packed away."

Turning, Stephen unfastened the front of his army jacket and crossed to the vanity table and mirror. The table was nothing more than packing crates disguised by material from an old blue satin gown of Hannah's, pleated and flounced to skirt the wooden boxes. Stephen picked up the gilded hairbrush, part of a vanity set of comb, brush, and hand mirror. A strand of dark auburn hair was caught in its bristles. Memory played a cruel trick, flashing him the mental image of a scalp he'd seen once—freshly taken and bloody.

"She shore did have some pretty things," Cimmy Lou declared.

"No!" Mindless of her comment, Stephen shouted at the image in his head, a roar of pain and anger. It vanished.

"Majuh?" A long-fingered brown hand touched his arm.

He jerked away from the contact. "I don't want anything done. Leave everything as it is," he ordered, and finally looked at the colored woman. "Put the gown back where you found it. I don't want you touching anything of hers."

"Yes, suh."

"Hello? Hello-oo?" A female voice trilled the questioning call, the sound seeming to originate in the vicinity of the front parlor.

Frowning, Stephen left the bedroom to find out who else had gained entry into his living quarters. In the parlor doorway he paused and refastened his uniform jacket when he saw Captain Goodson's wife standing by the side table, his hat and gloves in her hands. Her amber hair was arranged atop her head in rolled curls, a single ringlet dangling from the back, and a small navy blue hat that matched the trim on her serge suit in a lighter shade of blue crowned it all.

"Mrs. Goodson, forgive me." He apologized for his disheveled appearance, belatedly noticing that he still held Hannah's hairbrush in his hand. "I didn't know who was here."

"I knocked, but you must not have heard me." Her hand made a small, graceful gesture toward the front door.

"I was . . . in the rear." He glanced at the hairbrush, his hold tightening on it slightly.

Maude Goodson looked at it, too. A shimmer of tears glittered in her china-blue eyes when she lifted her glance to his face. "I knew you had returned and I—I wanted you to know how sorry I am about your wife."

Her sincerity was unmistakable, but Stephen was conscious of her delicate phrasing, not actually stating whether Hannah was dead, missing, or captured. He knew that she and Hannah had been close, as close as any army wives could be, considering their peripatetic lifestyle.

"You are most thoughtful, Mrs. Goodson."

"While you were gone, I had Cimmy Lou come by to clean." She appeared hesitant. "I wasn't certain what you wanted done with your wife's things."

"Nothing." He was quietly emphatic about it. "Everything stays exactly as it is."

Her expression grew tender. "Of course, Major." She smiled in warm understanding and sympathy. "Would you care to accompany Captain Goodson and myself to chapel this evening?"

His hesitation was slight. "Thank you, yes."

"We must remember, Major, that the Lord knows of our sufferings, and we must believe that Hannah is in his care."

"Yes." Stephen deferred to her faith, since she was

the daughter of an army chaplain. Hard facts were more his line. As far as he was concerned, his wife was in the hands of the Apaches. And if that thought didn't tear a man's guts out, he wasn't much of a man.

Mrs. Goodson laid his campaign hat and leather gauntlets aside. "We will come by to pick you up later this evening, Major."

"I shall be waiting." He walked her to the door.

Bathed, freshly shaven, and dressed in a clean uniform, Cutter angled his body against a post supporting the *ramada* roof outside the bachelor quarters. Water-filled ollas hung nearby, an occasional cool stir of air reaching him. Mess call had sounded some time ago, bringing the soldiers to the hall. Retreat was over and stretching shadows covered more and more ground as the sun settled in the western sky. He smoked his cigar, the first one in four days that didn't taste of desert alkali or salty sweat, and watched the flow of officers, especially those with wives, into the chapel. Wade was among them, in the company of the Goodsons and the Bettendorfs. Cutter made no move to follow them.

Not long afterward, he heard the muffled resonance of their voices lifted in praiseful singing. His cigar was smoked down to the butt, so he shoved away from the post and went down the steps to the walk. Strolling, Cutter made a slow circle of the fort's grounds, the children playing and laughing along Suds Row drawing a rare smile from him.

When he reached the small cemetery that lay on the fort's perimeter, he paused to search out the two freshly dug graves among the little mounds. They stood out sharply from the older ones. The elements here were quick to reclaim what belonged to them, the older mounds of disturbed sandy soil being slowly leveled by the desert wind until they blended with the rest of the ground, leaving only faint outlines of the graves' dimensions. Soon, even those would be gone.

As Cutter stood by the new graves, he remembered how distraught Mrs. Sloane had been when he'd stopped by her quarters before supper to pay his respects. She had not wanted comfort. Sloane would live in his wife's memory forever. But a time would come when no one remembered the way he laughed or recalled the firm way he shook hands. Just as the desert absorbed his grave, time would absorb him, too. Nothing would be left.

"Death makes it easier to forget." Cutter recalled the essence of Bettendorf's words during their discussion of Hannah Wade.

With an obstinate set to his features, he dug a heel into the sandy ground and drew a small trench around the oblong shape of Sloane's grave, more sharply defining its outline. The desert would require that much more time to weather it away. The inevitable was merely postponed. He left the cemetery, taking the long way to his rooms. The evening wind lifted around him, scented with the night's coolness.

Dark was settling and he felt the loneliness of his evening walk. On the edges of his mind were memories, still sweet, and wounds, still aching. He'd heard it said that when a man finds a woman, he finds his ambition, too. In his case, it worked the opposite, he supposed.

All by choice. And the decision was still one he wouldn't change even if he could go back and do it over. There was too much hate—the hate of a high-born southern aristocrat's daughter for a blue-bellied Yankee officer of the occupying army. Eventually she had been able to forgive him that sin, but the idea that his command would be a company of colored soldiers had been more than her plantation-bred heart could tolerate. She had issued an ultimatum—her or the army. In the end, it hadn't been much of a contest.

The army hadn't wholly satisfied him, but it fed his prime hungers: for the hard discipline and the thrill of action, of men riding, fighting, and sweating, and the wicked satisfaction that burns in a man when he's in the middle of a good fight. But the army had disappointed him, too, with its politics and prejudice, its seniority system that put inferior men in superior ranks, and its bureaucratic corruption that put an ill-equipped, ill-supplied, and undermanned force in the field. Lately, he'd been giving a lot of thought to quitting the service. After twelve years in the cavalry, following the guidon had lost its glamour.

But if he left the army, where would he go? What would he do? The only knowledge that the army had given him that was worthwhile on the outside dealt with horses and the kind of remounts the army needed in large quantity. Cutter supposed that if he ever got his bellyful of the army, he might go into the horse business.

# CHAPTER 8

GATITA APPROACHED THE MORNING FIRE WHERE HANNAH sat, absorbing some of its meager warmth. The Apache woman moved at the stately pace of a woman growing heavy with child. She stopped beside Hannah and dropped a worn pair of the distinctive curl-toed Apache boots on the sand next to her.

"*N'deh b'keh,* boots. Wear feet," Gatita told her.

"*Gracias,*" Hannah responded in Spanish, and quickly gathered up the high moccasins with the red strip painted on the seams of the turned-up toes.

After a week of doing chores around the *rancheria* from dawn to dusk, she had almost reached the point where the bottoms of her feet were so callused she didn't need shoes. Perhaps Gatita had noticed that and no longer regarded her bare feet as a guarantee that Hannah wouldn't try to run away.

Her body had healed. Almost all the scabs were gone and her skin had turned a shade of toasted brown from the sunburn. The meager helpings of food she received were not sufficient to enable her to put back on the weight she'd lost, but she was acquiring a wiry toughness, a resilient strength that came back after shorter rests. The diet of the Apache left a lot to be desired. She kept remembering what a delicious turkey galantine Mrs. Bettendorf made, and Maude Goodson's salmon croquettes.

"Is time of Many Leaves," Gatita said.

*"No comprendo."* Hannah shook her head, grateful for this second language they had in common. She could not imagine the terror of everything they said being so much gibberish to her.

"When things grow, Many Leaves." Her explanations, if Gatita deigned to make any, were invariably curt. *"Ugashé,* we go—all women—gather mescal before flower come."

This explained why she had been provided with the moccasins. But the expedition was not the simple foraging walk along the mesa top that Hannah surmised it would be. Supplies were packed to last for several days and loaded onto horses along with large baskets. Seven Apache women plus Hannah set out from the *rancheria* and took the rocky, boulder-strewn trail down the barranca. Three of the older women rode on horses.

Many exchanges were made in Apache as they traversed the rough trail, the voices pitched low but lilting with a gossipy flavor. Hannah listened to them, catching a feeling of sisterhood and a sense that maybe all women were the same when they got off by themselves away from the menfolk.

When they were out of the narrow, steep canyon, they headed in the direction of some dry hills. Gatita appeared to be tiring. When she stumbled, Hannah happened to be closest and steadied her with a supporting hand.

"Do you wish to ride the horse?" Hannah was leading the spotted horse. Always she seemed to be caught in a state of ambivalence toward Gatita, at one moment hating anyone who deprived her of her freedom and the next seeking a scrap of human companionship. Hannah didn't understand it. This female Apache treated her like dirt, kicking and striking her; yet she also gave her salve for her burned skin, buckskin clothes and moccasins, food and water. Gatita was everything evil and everything good; she was the madonna with child and the mother carrying Satan's seed.

"No horse," Gatita said, and patted the rounded arc of her stomach. "Because of baby, no can ride horse, no can carry basket, no can eat piñon nuts, no can watch *Ganhs*—" The list of restrictions placed on her was enumerated in fun.

"—and no can have Lutero's *pico*," one of the other women giggled.

"No can do that till baby stops sucking. Be crazy by then," another declared, and laughed with a tittering sound.

The conversation lapsed from Spanish into Apache and Hannah couldn't follow it anymore. But she'd gleaned enough from the previous exchange to realize that an Apache couple were not intimate during the term of the woman's pregnancy or while the infant nursed. So all the lust Lutero couldn't expend on his wife he had unleashed on Hannah those nights on the trail. The wrenching physical and mental agony of all she'd been through nearly swamped her. Her mood veered toward rage. She didn't deserve any of this!

But it was all so much wasted energy. The sun and the heat and the walking soon drained her of her anger.

The plant the Apache called the mescal was the same that Stephen had once identified as the century plant or agave. The heart of it, which the Apache women had come to gather, was contained within the basal cluster of leaves. And the stretch of hills where they stopped abounded with the desert plant.

Once the base of the stem containing the head was cut off, the sharp-pointed leaves had to be trimmed. Hannah soon learned to keep her eyes half-closed against the squirting juice from the leaves as the women were slicing them off. The end result was a mescal heart about the size of a cabbage head with the appearance of a giant artichoke.

Not trusted at this early stage of her captivity with a knife, Hannah had the task of carting all the mescal heads, as well as the edible stalks, to a central location. A huge pit was dug, roughly three feet deep and twelve feet long. She lugged firewood to the spot until the pit was filled, then helped to bring flat stones to lay on top.

After two days of gathering mescal, the Apache women made a ceremony of lighting the pit fire while praying to their gods. When it burned down, all of them hurried to throw a thick layer of wet grass onto it, followed by a layer of mescal, more wet grass, and a foot of dirt. Then another fire was built on top of that mound. And the mescal baked.

All one day and part of the next, they waited for the mescal to finish cooking. The time wasn't idly spent, since Many Leaves was also the season when the first wild onions appeared and other edibles were ready, certain flowers and berries. Hannah's inexperience made her useless at foraging, so her tasks were mainly camp chores, the hard menial work she had always hired someone to do.

Not far from where the baking pit and their camp were located, some rock tanks provided their water source, reservoirs carved out of solid stone by the elements eons ago, natural containers to catch and hold the rare downpours of rain in the desert. Steep walls leaned protectively over the series of three basins and shaded them from the sun, thus preventing rapid evaporation. They were completely hidden, no trees or green things growing within the barren tumble of stone and boulders to betray their presence.

Sent to fetch water, Hannah snaked in and around the maze of fallen rock worn smooth by time and the elements, following an unseen path whose twists she knew because she had traveled it so often these last few days. The natural tanks themselves were small, bathtub-size and almost that deep. The rock lip around them was smooth, a solid slab of stone. The stone retained a cool temperature, rarely getting much direct sunlight.

When the containers were filled, she surrendered to an urge that was too strong to resist and scooped up a gourd-full of water and doused her dirty, smelly hair with it. She had some of the soapweed Gatita used when she washed her hair, and quickly lathered her own with it. The sensation was as close to heaven as she'd come in a long time. When she rinsed, Hannah was careful not to foul the water in the tanks, and used as little as possible.

Then she sat in a wedge of sunlight, her long, burnished hair spread across her arms to dry, brushed straight with grass bristles as Gatita did with hers. As yet she hadn't acquired the knack of fashioning her hair in the double loops and securing it with the *nahleen,* a strip of leather shaped like a bow. Among her many other duties, Hannah was also being trained to do Gatita's hair.

The thought made her laugh aloud. The sudden sound in the stillness instantly silenced Hannah. She drew her knees up to her chest, the rawhide soles of her moccasins making little scraping sounds on the bald rock.

She looked to the south, an inner compass telling her that in that direction home lay. Tears trickled slowly down her cheeks. The injuries of the flesh were almost all healed; there was no more pain. Yet she ached inside. She was aware of the distance, not merely in miles but in the vast change from that life to this one. That one had a dreamlike quality of unreality. It was another place, another time. And it was over.

The loneliness, desolation, and despair washed over her, and she cried. The tears she hadn't shed during this whole ordeal flowed freely, while she wept for all the times she'd been afraid or in agony or humiliated or abused, for the rage that had no release.

When the emotional storm abated, she pressed at her eyes with a thumb and forefinger, pushing at the last few tears squeezing through her lashes. She breathed in deeply, sniffling at her runny nose, and lifted her head.

Slowly an idea took shape in her mind. Instead of feeling sorry for her present state, she needed to change it. With the water bags filled, she'd have more than enough water. All she had to do was slip back to camp and take one of the horses. If she was lucky, she'd be miles away before anyone noticed she was gone.

When Hannah returned to camp, one of the older Apache women was tending the fire atop the baking pit. She didn't even glance Hannah's way when she walked past the camp to the tethered horses. Lutero's spotted horse knew her and didn't raise any fuss as she scrambled onto its back. She walked the horse quietly away from the others, her heart in her throat in anticipation of the cry of alarm that would give her escape away. But the silence held.

The minute they were out of sight, Hannah kicked the patch-colored horse into a gallop. The speed lulled her in the beginning, the miles falling away to accumulate and separate her from her Apache captors. When the pony slowed, she felt the first nudgings of panic. She was in unfamiliar country. The fort was somewhere to the south, but that covered a lot of territory—and she didn't even know if this was the right direction.

This mountain-wrinkled, boulder-tumbled stretch of country was an obstacle course. Rare were the places where she could ride straight ahead for a prolonged time. Usually she could only angle in a given direction, following a zigzag course. In some places a lot of zigging had to be done before the zag was available.

Hannah reined in her horse, feeling the weight of hopelessness. It was foolish to think she could make the fort. If there were settlements, ranches, or mines in the vicinity, it would be purely chance for her to find one. Behind her was the misery, drudgery, and abuse of Apache enslavement, and ahead of her was a maze of canyons. She had no food, but plenty of water and a horse to carry her.

The narrow-chested pinto looked to the side, its ears pricking and a low whicker vibrating from its chest. Following its glance, Hannah saw the four mounted Apaches, motionless as statues, watching her from the spiny ridge of a low bluff not fifty yards away. She recognized Lutero almost at once.

Her first impulse was to dig her heels into the ribs of the spotted horse and make good her escape. It lunged forward under the first prod. Two strides later, she knew she hadn't a chance of getting away from the Apaches. This was their country, Apacheria. There was no place she could hide from them, even if she were able to outrun them.

She hauled back on the rawhide strip of rein hooked around the pony's lower jaw and roughly checked its flight. Turning it, she rode toward Lutero and the other Apache riders. The look in his eyes when she stopped the horse in front of him made her blood run cold. Since he'd brought her to the *rancheria* and given her to Gatita as a personal slave, Lutero had not forced himself on her. Now, his anger made her afraid of what he might do.

"I got lost." She tried to bluff her way through it, speaking as always in border Spanish.

He snarled something in Apache and dropped a rope loop around her, snugging it tight, then wrapped more lengths around her, trussing her arms to her sides. Another Apache with a bad knife scar disfiguring his face rode close to take the braided rawhide rein and lead her pony. Lutero used the loose end of the rope to whip her several times across the arms and shoulders, the hard, sharp lashes numbing bands of her skin. Hannah could not hold in the low cries of pain that escaped each time he struck her.

The punishment was brief, almost a release of savage temper, but she could feel the welts raising on her skin. They moved out. Within minutes she saw the thin smoke from the baking pit, and the camp itself was in sight shortly afterward.

"I be here all time," Lutero said, very much the predator playing with his captured prey.

"*Como?* What?" Hannah frowned.

"We"—a circling slice of his hands included the other riders—"guard. Watch and see if maybe you try run away."

It had all been a trap, a test to see how much they could trust her. Hannah kept her gaze directed to the front and her chin level. It had all been so easy because they let it be. There never had been a single chance of escape, she could see that now. And it would be a long, long time before her every movement would not be watched by one of them.

The women were grouped near the pit fire, awaiting their arrival. Their high-cheeked and wide-nosed faces were expressionless, yet the black wells of their eyes held a glare that was directed at Hannah. Nowhere was the enmity more obvious than in Gatita's look.

A shove of Lutero's moccasined foot pushed Hannah off the horse. With her arms bound to her sides, she couldn't break her fall and landed heavily on the hard ground near Gatita's feet, momentarily stunned by the impact. Lutero tossed the free end of the rope to the pregnant woman, a returning of property.

The first bite of the rope across the fresh welts lifted Hannah from the half-daze of her fall, the new pain screaming through her senses. As more blows from the rope rained on her body, she hunched into the ground, the harsh desert soil swallowing her moans while its smells and tastes filled her nostrils and coated her lips. The other women joined in the beating, poking and kicking until it seemed that all her ribs were broken and every breath was torture.

She was almost senseless when the blows stopped and hands grabbed her and roughly turned her onto her back. The rope was dragged from around her. There was a moment when she thought it was all over; then her arms were twisted to spread them away from her sides and the front of her buckskin blouse was ripped from its shoulder seam.

Hannah saw a red eye coming toward her, oddly stuck on the end of a stick held by one of Gatita's older sisters. As it came closer, she caught a whiff of smoke and the smell of burning wood. The red eye was the red-orange center of a stick from the fire, surrounded by white-hot coals. Her shock turned to horror as Hannah realized they intended to use it on her. She pulled in her breath and tried to flatten herself into the ground, but the imprisoning hands held her fast.

She screamed as the fiery end seared through the layers of skin above her right breast. The acrid smell of burning flesh, her own, implanted its sickening odor in her mind. Again, and once again, it was pressed onto her shoulder before she mercifully fainted.

Later Hannah learned that she had missed several

opportunities to escape while the mescal was being gathered. Because she had waited until this important crop had been harvested and buried in the baking pit, her life had been spared. It was still possible that she would be a good slave because she had finished her work before she tried to run away.

Three deep burns made an irregular pattern above her breast. The pain of the charred flesh was excruciating; it throbbed through her body as she labored under the weight of the basket filled with baked mescal hearts. The basket was carried behind her, Apache-style, a cloth strap stretched around the basket and up across her forehead. The muscles in her neck ached with the strain of leaning against the heavy pull dragging her back, but this method distributed the weight over her entire body and made it easier to walk over the rough terrain.

As the season wore on, Hannah became conditioned to the harsh Apache way of life. More mescal gathers were made before the agave flowered, and the baked hearts were spread on the ground around the *rancheria* to dry in the sun. Hours were spent pounding them into thin sheets, keeping the juices to make a preserving glaze. The dried mescal would keep almost indefinitely, making it a vital food source for the Apache. With hunger ever present, Hannah eventually grew to like its squashlike flavor.

Always there was work: food to be gathered and prepared, firewood to be hauled, water to be carried, and meals to be fixed. In addition to all the regular chores, there were animal hides and skins to be tanned and meat to be cooked and dried whenever the men returned from a hunt.

She was a slave, constantly at the beck and call of her mistress, physically punished if she was slow to obey and treated as an inferior. She hungered for the sound of a friendly word spoken to her, but she never heard it.

She'd been given the name Coloradas for the red in her hair, but if she was addressed at all, it was usually in some abusive term.

As the days wore on, her previous life seemed more and more distant. On cold nights while she lay on the bare ground, huddling close to the fire because she had no blanket, she would recall the warmth of Stephen's body when she used to curl against him in bed, and wonder if he was lying there now thinking of her. Sometimes she woke in the night, shivering, with his name on her lips.

Many Leaves passed and the season of Large Leaves came. The Apaches abandoned their camp on the mesa top and packed all their belongings on their horses, carrying what couldn't be loaded on the animals, and set out. They moved frequently, Hannah learned, going where there was more game or where a wild food was ripe for gathering, like the juniper berries and the wild grains during the time of Large Leaves. Sometimes the spring or water tanks went dry. Sometimes Hannah didn't even know the reason they were on the march again. Often they came in contact with other Apaches, sometimes camping together in an area where the food, game, and water were plentiful.

When a hunting party went out, Lutero was seldom among them, Hannah had observed; yet when Apaches from two or three groups gathered to form a raiding party, he was the one they addressed as *jefe*, leader. It was confusing, but she supposed it could be likened to a quartermaster and a field commander; one was good at tracking down supplies and the other excelled at fighting.

Several times Lutero left the group to raid, sometimes being gone for weeks on end. When he and his band returned, sometimes together, sometimes singly, it was always a cause for celebration—for the safe return of the men and the goods and horses they had stolen. Each time, the heavy-breasted woman created her vulgar display with some man at the dancing. Cactus Pear Woman was a *bi-zhahn*, a young divorcée, and cousin to Gatita. Her behavior seemed to be acceptable because of that, although Hannah noticed that it was only exhibited on the occasion of a successful raid.

Fatigue was ever with her. Sometimes she worked by rote, too tired to think. At other times Hannah made herself recall things from that far-off past to keep them fresh, or made odd connections like the one with the quartermaster and field commander simply to keep that link with the past. She'd hum the melodies of songs that were favorites of hers or Stephen's while she scraped the flesh from the hide of a freshly skinned deer, or recite the names of the officers of the Ninth and the companies to which they were attached while she picked up firewood. Hannah was determined not to let her memories of that other existence fade during this struggle to survive. Somehow she'd return to Stephen, and she wouldn't allow that hope to die.

All hell had broken loose in the Apache country of Arizona and New Mexico. It began in April when factions of the Chiricahua tribe, which the late Cochise had once united, were again divided. A band under an Apache called Skinya was making raids into Old Mexico. With gold from one of their raids, a warrior bought whiskey from a station keeper along the Overland Stage route. He came back drunk and tried to buy more. A fight erupted; the station keeper and his cook were killed.

The wild country around Fort Bayard was ceaselessly patrolled, from the mining district in the mountains around Silver City to the stage and supply routes in the desert to the south. Two detachments were constantly in the field to discourage raiding in the area. The patrols were staggered so that a third of the cavalry's force always remained at Bayard.

It was hot, the ground throwing off the day's accumulation of heat to add to the baking glare of the late afternoon sun. Cutter paused in the shade of the trader's store, bending his head to light a black Mexican cigar and scanning the road beyond the main guardpost over his flickering match flame. Wade was due back with his detail any time now. His return would signal Cutter's departure on his patrol.

The Apache scout Nah-tay appeared beside him, his approach soundless. "One comes to this person's *jacal* with white captive for *pindah* with leaves on shoulder. He no here. You come. Talk to him."

Cutter shook out the match and used the delay to ask, "Why doesn't he come to the fort?" They conversed in border Spanish.

"One who comes afraid *pindah* become angry, not let him leave after they buy his white woman. You come," Nah-tay repeated insistently.

"Lead the way." He indicated his agreement with a nod of his head, then followed a step behind the silent-walking Apache. At the main guardpost, Cutter stopped and informed the soldier on duty of his whereabouts. "I'll be at the scouts' encampment if anyone wants me. If Major Wade returns, have him meet me there."

"Yes, suh." The order was acknowledged with a stiff salute, which Cutter idly returned before continuing on with the scout.

Since Wade had issued his promise of a ransom for his wife's safe return, several attempts had been made to collect it. Cutter knew the chances were remote this time as well, so he allowed himself no expectations.

At Nah-tay's *jacal*, Cutter ducked inside the traditionally east-facing doorway and stepped into the sour-smelling interior. The unmoving air was hot and stale in the shadowed gloom. Two figures squatted on the beds made from blankets and robes. Cutter sank to his haunches opposite the pair while Nah-tay sat almost in the middle, serving as the link between them. Abiding by Apache etiquette, Cutter preserved the silence, meeting the stares with the natural gravity of his features.

When a satisfactory interval had passed, one of the Apaches spoke in his quick, loose-sounding native tongue, which Nah-tay translated into Spanish. "He says you are not *pindah* who asks for captive."

"Tell him that I am not. Tell him also that I bargain for the *pindah* who seeks the white woman with fire in her hair."

The reply was relayed, and its subsequent answer. "He asks how much you pay."

"It was promised that fifty dollars in gold would be paid." Cutter repeated the reward that had been offered by Major Wade.

One Apache, an older, round-faced man, did all the talking and haggling, while the other sat silently and looked disagreeable. The fifty dollars was finally accepted as the price as long as the smooth-faced *pindah* gave his assurance that they would be allowed to leave.

"Agreed," Cutter said. "But tell them I will pay them nothing until I see the woman."

After Nah-tay had told them that, the older Apache replied. "He says they left her tied in the brush. You are welcome to go see the woman."

"Ask if he thinks I look like a *tonto,* a fool? Tell him to bring the woman here," Cutter replied.

It was agreed that the Apaches would bring the woman captive into the camp. They slipped out of the *jacal.* A few seconds later, Cutter and Nah-tay vacated the hot, rancid hut to wait for them under the *ramada* outside. From the main road came the scuff of a horse column, the creak of leather, and rolling snorts. The patrol had returned.

A movement on the edge of the encampment directed Cutter's attention back to the matter at hand. The two Apaches pushed a cowering, blanket-wrapped figure into the clearing. The hooding blanket and the woman's downcast head made it impossible for Cutter to see anything of her face. She had the cowed look of a broken-spirited animal. Cutter eyed her with a growing resistance.

When she stopped in front of him and the old Apache pulled the blanket from her head, he was relieved to see that it wasn't Hannah. The sallow complexion identified her as a Mexican even though her black hair had been dyed with red juice, probably made from boiling the bark of the mountain mahogany. She whimpered like a beaten puppy, too frightened and too ashamed to look at him.

From behind him came the stumbling clatter of tired horses being hurried over the desert rock. Cutter turned to observe Major Wade's approach, seeing his uniform caked with sweat and alkali dust and the weariness of two weeks in the saddle about him. A black armband encircled his left sleeve. He wore it constantly as a reminder of his wife's abduction, refusing to regard it as a symbol of mourning. The dramatic affectation had been picked up by the local newspaper, and fresh stories were circulated about the noble cavalry officer.

Driven by some kinetic energy, Wade appeared, as always, on edge, his nerves rasped thin. The chief of the scouts, One-Eye Amos Hill, rode with him, bringing up the rear.

"What is this about?" Wade demanded.

"The Apaches have brought you the woman with fire in her hair," Cutter answered dryly.

"The bastards dyed it." He cursed the ruse they'd used to collect the ransom. "Tell them that is a Mexican with red hair. I want the white woman."

"What do you want to do about the *señorita?*" Cutter watched the officer sitting his horse so stiffly. Beside him, a buckskin-jacketed Amos Hill sat slouch-shouldered on his dun horse, whiskered and weary.

Irritation ruled Wade's expression, then gave way to a hard impetuosity. "I'll buy her, of course. She can't be worth much. Offer them ten dollars." He looked at the white scout. "Afterward I want them interrogated. Find out everything they know."

Amos Hill gave a slow nod and dismounted with poky deliberation. After he walked forward to stand beside Cutter, the haggling began. Eventually the Apaches settled for the ten-dollar price, but Wade didn't pay them until the questioning was through. They seemed anxious to leave, disappearing into the brush the moment Amos Hill told them they could go.

The huddled figure of the Mexican captive continued to cower underneath the blanket. She had again pulled it up around her head and held it tightly closed near her mouth. When Cutter approached her, speaking quietly in Spanish, she made odd protesting sounds in her throat and shrank away from him.

"What do ya want us t'do with her, Major?" Amos shifted his plug of tobacco to the other cheek.

"Find out where she's from, and we'll try to get her back to her family." Stephen's horse kicked at a biting fly, the saddle leather creaking at the action.

"That'll be a problem." With difficulty, Cutter pushed the bitter rage from his voice at the discovery he'd just made. "They cut out her tongue."

Everything went still, a heavy silence suddenly weighting the air. It lasted for three long heartbeats; then Wade wheeled his horse toward the fort and kicked it into a lope. Cutter eyed the pitiful creature for a moment more, then bowed his head in an attitude of near-defeat and frustration. He doubted the Mexican girl's sanity.

"Poor dumb thing." Amos shook his head.

"I'll have one of the women at the fort clean her up and fix her something to eat."

"She won't thank you for takin' her in there for everyone to gawk at," Amos interposed. "Best if she goes to my wickiup where Mary Rose can look after her." He didn't wait for Cutter's agreement. Instead he turned and called to the plump squaw dressed in bright calico sitting under the *ramada* of the next *jacal*. She came hurrying over, her white-powdered face creating an odd contrast to her naturally bronze skin. Amos said something more to her in the mushy-sounding language of the Apache and indicated the Mexican. As the squaw led the mute girl away, Amos spat a yellow stream of tobacco juice onto the ground. "Wish she wouldn't wear that damned powder. She's got it in her head I want a white woman. Women. Don't matter what color they are; they're all alike." He started after them. "See ya, Cutter. Ridin' out tomorrow?"

"First light," he confirmed.

"Have a good scout."

The arrival of the patrol roused the fort from its hot afternoon somnolence. The inhabitants came to the edges of the shade to watch the column ride in. Cimmy Lou Hooker was among them, carrying a bundle of freshly laundered clothes to be delivered to Major Wade's quarters. She scanned the troopers slumped in their saddles, even though she knew John T. was with the second detail that was still out on patrol and not due back for another week.

Four of the cavalry horses were carrying double.

Most of the mounts in the regiment were poor excuses for horses. Invariably a patrol came back minus a couple who had broken down in the long, hot rides through rough terrain. But no blanket-wrapped bodies were tied over any saddles this time. From the shade of the dispensary across the way, the post's surgeon, Doc Griswald, scanned the ranks to see if he had any new patients among them, but there seemed to be nothing beyond the usual cuts, bruises, and occasional snake-bites of a normal patrol.

Cimmy Lou looked into the sun-sore eyes of the fatigued troopers as they rode past her. She spied Leroy Bitterman, the near rider in the columns of two. His long, narrow shape was loose in the saddle. When he saw her, a smile parted his lips, showing the uneven row of his white teeth, his mustache a long and thin black line against his dark chocolate skin. He nodded to her as he went by. Cimmy Lou watched him for a minute or two, her body absently moving with a rocking sway.

The detail halted at the front of the parade ground. The hot and weary troopers in their wool uniforms and thirty-pound packs sat motionless on their horses, waiting for Major Wade to give the order dismissing them. Seconds after it was given, the major left the parade ground at a canter, heading off the post.

The trumpeter blew mess call as Cimmy Lou sauntered in the direction of Officers' Row, in no hurry. Dismissed by their sergeant, the black troopers headed for the stables in loose files. Cimmy Lou saw Bitterman swing out of line and dismount. He lifted his horse's left foreleg to check its shoe. He was still tinkering with it when she came by, the corners of her full lips pulled up in a knowing smile. He straightened, letting the horse's foot drop to the ground and absently patting its side.

"Saw yore sergeant." In a faint swagger, he lazily

pushed back his shoulders and arched his spine in a catlike stretch. "I asked him if he wanted me t'give you any message from him, but he didn't seem to think much of the idea."

"You like to make trouble, don't you?" She stopped with the laundry bundle held in front of her, idly rocking it from side to side while she eyed the long, lean shape of him.

"Not half as much as you do with them hips of yores always in motion." He watched their faint movement with obvious interest, letting her see the turn of his thoughts. The swaying motion stopped, and he laughed.

His humor and bluntness offended her pride. She held her head unnaturally high, a bandanna bound around her black curly hair. On the verge of getting angry with him, Cimmy Lou suddenly changed her mind, her curiosity getting the better of her—curiosity and the heavy appetite a man's attention always stirred in her. "What makes you think it's fo' you?"

He didn't like her answer and it showed in the sudden hardening of his expression. "Whatcha doin' over here?" He looked behind her at the row of adobe housing reserved for the white officers.

"I'm bringin' Major Wade his laundry."

"That who you got yore eye set on now?" Bitterman challenged. "Yore done playin' yore games with Cap'n Cutter, now yore figurin' on messin' about with the major. You don't want yoreself no white man, Cimmy girl."

"What makes you think that thought's in my head?" she retorted.

"That thought's always in yore head." The slant of his mouth held amusement and irony.

"You don't know. You don't know me," Cimmy Lou asserted.

"I know you better than you think I do. You want purty things—an' a man who's got what it takes to satisfy them churnin' hips of yores."

"An' that's you, I s'pose." His boldness revived her interest.

"You an' me don't belong here, Cimmy Lou. This kind a life ain't fo' people like you an' me." From the other side of the quadrangle came the tramp of weary soldiers answering the call to mess and the low chatter of tired voices.

"What would you do instead?"

"I been a faro dealer befo'. Might get me a job dealin' in one of them gamblin' halls in a minin' town." Then he asked, "Do you know how much them miners pay to have a shirt washed in Silver City? Five dollahs."

"For *one* shirt?"

Bitterman held up his hand, spreading his fingers and thumb to show all five digits. "Five dollahs for one shirt. An' two dollahs is all you get fo' a soldier's laundry the whole month."

She shifted the bundle of clothes to a more comfortable position and looked across the parade ground toward the company mess. "If you want anythin' t'eat, Private Bitterman, you best be gettin' on yore way, an' I'll be gettin' on mine."

"I ain't keepin' ya."

Cimmy laughed, throwing her head back and letting her eyes dance, once more in control the way she liked it. "Then it's me what's keepin' you here." She walked away from him, letting her hips swing leisurely with her steps, and the length of time that passed before she heard the clop of his horse's hooves going toward the stables made her smile. She knew it meant that Bitterman had been watching her all that time in between.

The door to the Wades' quarters stood open to allow the entrance of any vagrant wind in the lingering heat of late afternoon. Cimmy Lou knocked on the door frame and peered into the shadowed rooms. "Hello? Delancy? You here?" she called.

A movement in the rear of the hallway where the kitchen was located drew her glance to the glimmer of something white. Good smells, new smells of something cooking, came from the same direction. She could barely make out the tall, keg-round shape of the striker, Delancy.

"Is that you, Miz Hooker?" He waved her inside. "Come on in."

He disappeared into the kitchen without waiting to see if she did as he said. Cimmy Lou went down the narrow hallway and paused in the kitchen doorway, appreciatively sniffing the air. "Somethin' sure smells good." All that waited for her back at the tent was chili with a slab of raw onion between two pieces of bread.

"The boys shot me some doves, an' I stuffed 'em with rice an' sage. The major is fond of it." Always proud of his culinary skills, Delancy artfully arranged the golden birds on a small platter mounded with brown rice.

"I brung the laundry," she said sulkily when he ignored her, not even offering her a taste as he sometimes did.

"Go ahead and put it away." Without turning around, hc motioned her toward the bedroom, then straightened when she started to leave to add a word of caution. "An' be quick about it. The major won't like it if'n he finds you pokin' 'round Miz Wade's things."

"I'll be quick." But she laughed at him as she danced out of the kitchen to the bedroom off the narrow hall.

When the major was away, Delancy sometimes let her try on the missus' hats and gowns. Cimmy Lou had her favorites, like that silver shawl crocheted in a rose design she'd found in the bottom of a trunk. Since discovering it, she kept it on a shelf in the wardrobe. Now she set the laundry bundle on the bed and went straight to it, taking it out and sweeping the shawl around her shoulders to admire herself in the vanity mirror. In its reflection of the room, she spied the copper bathtub with its curved backrest, but Cimmy Lou was more interested in her own image than that of a half-full tub of water.

Not five minutes later, she heard a horse come galloping up and grunt to a stop close to the adobe. The sound was followed by the hard crunch of boots approaching the front door. Moving swiftly, Cimmy Lou returned the shawl to the wardrobe shelf and began putting away the laundry, slowing down to take her time.

"Delancy?!" A hard impatience underlaid the bellowed summons that rang through the quarters, and she recognized Major Wade's voice.

The anger in it was all the more reason to linger until the fury had been spent elsewhere. Cimmy heard the striker hurry from the kitchen at the same time that the bell-like sound of glass against glass came from the parlor.

"Where's all the damned whiskey?"

"I'll get it fo' you, suh." There was more rattling from the parlor. "Dinner's ready to suhve whenevah you say, suh. We're havin' dove tonight—succulent with golden-crisp skins an' stuffed with rice jest the way you like 'em, suh."

"I don't want any damned dinner. Throw it out and just give me the whiskey bottle. I don't need it decanted." A short pause held the sound of liquid being poured. "My horse is outside. See that he's groomed and fed."

"But, suh—"

"That's all, private. You're dismissed."

"Yes, suh."

After Delancy left, Cimmy Lou waited in the bedroom, listening to the restless movements in the parlor. She kept thinking about those roasted doves in the kitchen. No one would know if she took two of them and slipped out the back door. On the parade ground, the bugler blew first call before retreat while the sun sat on the western horizon. At last the sounds from the parlor died into silence, and Cimmy Lou slipped into the hallway.

"Delancy!" She stopped short at the impatient call and looked toward the front rooms. Major Wade stood in the doorway facing the parade ground, only now swinging around when his summons was answered by silence. "Delancy?! Where the damned hell are you?"

Cimmy Lou caught the faint slur in his voice and wavered indecisively. An instant later, impulse pushed her away from the kitchen and toward the front rooms.

"Delancy ain't here, Major." She spoke as she emerged from the deepening shadows of the narrow hall. "You dismissed him."

"I did?" He frowned, then trod heavily to a parlor chair and collapsed loosely in it, holding a whiskey bottle and a glass in his hands. "I did," he remembered, and sighed heavily. "Dammit, I wanted a bath." Then, "What are you doing here?"

"I brung yore laundry," Cimmy Lou answered as she eyed him with a considering look. "Want me t'heat some water fo' you, Major? The tub's already in yore bedroom waitin' fo' you."

"Yes." He lifted the whiskey glass to his mouth and tossed the liquor down.

In the lingering early summer heat, it wasn't desirable for the bathwater to be hot, just somewhat warmer than tepid to relax weary muscles. Cimmy Lou carried the last kettle of water into the bedroom, where the major sat in the copper tub, his knees bent and his hand holding the whiskey glass. The half-empty bottle stood on the floor beside the tub. He took no more than passing notice of her as she poured the heated water into the tub. For all his brooding stillness, she could sense the restiveness that stirred beneath it. He downed another swallow of whiskey and wiped at the wet ends of his mustache, his hand scraping the light brown stubble on his cheeks.

"I need a shave," he mumbled irritatedly to himself.

"Want me to do it?" Cimmy Lou set the kettle down, seeing a lot of possibilities in the situation, which seemed not so different from the stories she'd heard about the Devereaux plantation. "I shave my John T. all the time." Her dark eyes watched him, so knowing as she calculated each step.

Water sloshed around his bare white skin as he settled deeper into the tub and tilted his head back to rest it on the long curving end. "Go ahead." He closed his eyes, but he didn't relax. Whatever the thoughts that railed through his head, they continued to work on him while she lathered his face and stropped the razor.

When she began shaving him, the long, sure scrape of the blade was the only sound in the room. Beyond the adobe walls, the muffled tramp of a guard detail could be heard, posting sentries around the fort's perimeter. When she finished, Cimmy Lou laid the razor aside and picked up a towel to wipe away the residue of lather.

His tormented thoughts finally twisted his features as he hoarsely wondered aloud, "What do you think they'll do to her?"

Cimmy Lou knew who he was talking about—and she also knew that he didn't really want an answer. The major was conjuring up his own horrors in his mind, but he wanted to block them out. That's why he was drinking, and Cimmy guessed it was what he was seeking from her. One thing was sure: she knew all about making a man forget, and she didn't figure black or white mattered much.

"Po' Major." She picked up the cake of soap and began lathering his shoulders and neck with it, rubbing the taut tendons. "You've shore had a bad time of it lately, haven't you? So lonely, an' not a soul to comfort an' ease the hurtin' in you."

"No, no one," he murmured.

"Well, Cimmy Lou will take care of you," she crooned softly, fascinated by the whiteness of his skin and the mat of golden-brown hairs on his chest that curled so tightly when they were wet. Her soapy hands traveled down his flat stomach and under the surface of the murky water, exploring with an age-old curiosity, while she knelt beside the tub, on eye level with him.

He looked at her with flat eyes that gradually began to show an absent interest. Water had splashed on her, dampening the front of her green blouse. He noticed it, his attention lingering on her full bosom. "You're getting wet."

"The water feels cool." She continued to scrub him gently, working on his legs and the insides of his thighs.

"My family once owned slaves. Did you know that?" His speech was lazy, the words being drawn slowly out. He wasn't drunk, but he was feeling the liquor. That, the warm water, and her stroking hands all combined to loosen him.

"You from the South?" Cimmy Lou looked at him in idle surprise, but he shook his head.

"St. Louis. But we had house slaves when I was a boy. My wet nurse was a colored woman," he recalled, his gaze never leaving the front of her blouse and the faint jiggle of her breasts as she washed him. "I was nearly two years old before she stopped suckling me. But even after that, if I was upset or hurt and needed comforting, she'd let me crawl up on her lap and unbutton her blouse." As if he was reliving the past, his fingers moved to the front closure of her top and unfastened it. Cimmy Lou felt that first run of excitement, the stimulation of success and its accompanying sense of power. It was a powerful aphrodisiac.

"I can still remember gazing at them, putting my hands around those chocolate-colored mounds." Stephen held the weight of Cimmy Lou's breasts in the cups of his hands and methodically rubbed his thumbs across the sensitive nipples, keeping it up until the ache he created nearly drove her wild.

"Is that all you did?" Cimmy Lou urged huskily, a groan rising in her throat.

"No. No, that wasn't all." His mouth was opening to encircle a tautly erect nipple even before he dragged the upper half of her body over the tub's rim so he could reach it.

Her long fingers dug into the ridges of his shoulders to both brace and balance her as he greedily consumed her breast, his full mustache bristling against the skin as he butted and pulled at it, his hand roughly kneading its hanging firmness. The occasional nipping tug of his teeth created a sensual pain that took her breath away. When he transferred that same suckling attention to her other breast, a curling sensation traveled all the way to her toes and she clamped her legs tightly together to ease the throbbing between them.

But their positions were awkward and the water made their skins slippery. Cimmy Lou was unable to maintain her precarious balance across the copper tub with her feet on the floor, and splashed into the tub, her feet in the air, soaking all but the hem of her skirt and the very top of her blouse. Their combined volume sent the water sloshing over the copper sides onto the floor.

Laughing, Cimmy Lou scrambled out of the tub, dripping water everywhere. "You got me soppin' wet. I'm gonna hafta take these clothes off an' wring 'em dry," she declared in her most provocative manner, and deliberately looked him in the eyes while she stripped off her clothes. Last of all she removed the bandanna restraining the mane of curly black hair and stood before him in Nubian splendor, proudly naked.

"I guess I should see if'n I can't find somethin' to wear while my clothes is dryin'."

As she crossed to the wardrobe, she heard the major climbing out of the tub. She made a bold play, taking the silver shawl from the shelf and draping it around her shoulders. When she turned to face him, the crocheted material was drawn together under her breasts and the fringed corners dangled to a point at the V of her pelvis.

"How do I look?" The thrusting angle of her hips invited him.

"Beautiful." His erection confirmed the power she had over him. He walked to her like a man in a dream and pulled apart the shawl to feast his eyes on all of her. His hands wandered over her in slow discovery, traveling from the lamb's-wool softness of her hair to the sleek curve of her dark buttocks, gradually drawing her into the circle of his arms.

"No." Cimmy Lou grew impatient with his gentle handling. "Be wild with me." She curled talon-fingers into his hair and showed him the wanton ways of loving with the straining press of her rounded body and the tonguing excitement of her kiss.

Later, after she had drained him of all the pent-up energies and taken the sting from him, Stephen watched her pick up her wet clothes, still enthralled by the dark sheen of her body. Not a single whore he'd paid to bed had ever encouraged him to give full rein to his passions the way she had tonight—to be as wild and as wicked as he pleased.

"Cimmy Lou." He could see by her expression that she knew how well she had satisfied him. "I . . . want to see you again," he admitted after a brief hesitation.

"Maybe." She shrugged, and he knew that she refused to commit herself just to torment him.

It rankled him that she could do so, when he was a major and she was just a colored laundress. Stephen reached for his money pouch to settle up for the "special services." "How much do I owe you?"

A hot flash of temper crossed her expression. "I ain't no whore, Major," she snapped. "You cain't buy me. I gives 'cause it's my pleasure."

Surprised to find that he had misjudged her, he was taken aback. "I—I'm sorry," he offered stiffly and awkwardly.

Cimmy Lou immediately softened. "Now, if'n you be wantin' t'give me a present 'cause I pleased ya, I'd like it fine if'n you gives me this shawl."

His hesitation over giving away this article of Hannah's was brief. She had never been fond of it that he recalled. "By all means, take it."

"Maybe I can wear it fo' you again," she half-promised, quickly gathering it up.

"Tomorrow," Stephen said.

She laughed, but he knew she'd be at his quarters the following night.

## CHAPTER 9

THE LARGE BUNDLE OF DEAD STICKS AND BRANCHES rattled together like a bunch of dry bones as Hannah dragged them to the *jacal*. A length of rawhide was hitched around the stick bundle and the slack center of the rawhide rope served as a tumpline across her forehead. She stopped and slipped the rawhide band off her forehead with a duck of her head, then paused for a minute, pressing one hand against the stitch in her side while she caught her breath.

Underneath the crude *ramada,* which offered the only shelter from the broiling sun of late summer, Gatita knelt to mix *penole,* a kind of cornmeal mush, for their night meal. Her protruding stomach was huge. Hannah didn't think it could be much longer before her time came.

A two-year-old toddler trotted close to the fire in his unsteady stagger. Like all children, he had free run of the *rancheria.* All the adults looked out for the children and kept them out of harm's way. If the Apaches had any redeeming quality, Hannah thought, it was their deep affection for the children. She crossed to the fire and steered the little tyke away from the hot coals.

A gasp that seemed to mix surprise with pain came from the *ramada*. When Hannah turned, Gatita was pressing a hand against the side of her baby-swollen stomach.

"Do you have pain?" Hannah questioned.

*"Anh,* yes. Is nothing." The smallest of smiles edged her mouth, a glimmer of pride showing through. "Baby kick. Strong. I think *ish-ke-ne,* boy-child."

Hannah's mouth quirked briefly, but she was too tired to hold the smile. It seemed to be a common belief among both white people and Apaches that if a baby was active, it was a sign that the unborn child was a boy, while a quiet one was a girl.

"He-who-is-father comes." Gatita put aside the *penole* and used the aid of the cedar post supporting the brush roof to pull her ungainly bulk to her feet.

A half dozen horses skittishly approached the *rancheria,* driven by the riders in the rear. Dust boiled around their legs as the Apache men who had not gone on the raid came out to herd them into a brush corral. The return of the raiding party meant a partial respite from work, at least until the excitement diminished. Hannah sought the shade of the brush arbor where Gatita stood, searching among the indistinct riders in the billowing alkali cloud for her husband.

Those closer and better able to see yelled something to the rest of the *rancheria* inhabitants. Something changed; the pitch of the voices became different, the tension almost tangible. Everyone gravitated toward the incoming riders, and Hannah was drawn into the flow, caught by the animal instinct that something was wrong. The voices became low, troubled murmurs.

A piercing wail suddenly broke from Gray Dove,

Gatita's sister, and she threw herself in the path of the brown-and-white-spotted war pony that Lutero rode. Her hands were lifted in pleading beseechment, while her wailing voice sobbed with questions. He was sullen and grim as he spoke to her. As fresh screams of anguish quavered from Gray Dove, Hannah noticed that the Apache who was her husband was not among the returning warriors. But another man was!

Something leaped in her chest when she saw straw-brown hair poking from under a floppy-brimmed cowboy hat. Another rider was in the way and it was a moment before she saw the panicked face, a sickly white color. The man's glance darted wildly about as he started and trembled in his terror at every sight and sound.

For a moment, Hannah went a little crazy herself. She shouldered her way through the Apaches to get close to the riders, and hurried alongside the horses in a kind of running walk. "Mister. Hey, mister!" she called to make herself heard above the tramp of the horses and the collective wails of several mourners. "Hello!"

His startled look finally located her. "Are you a . . . white woman?" His voice sounded so young and frightened. Hannah doubted if he was more than twenty-five, her own age. He was wearing full, sweeping *chaparejos,* and on the blaze-faced roan he rode was a high-horned western saddle.

"Yes." She rushed the answer and spoke quickly as Lutero used his horse to block her from his captive. "My husband is Stephen Wade! Major Stephen Wade! Tell him . . ." She knew he couldn't hear her anymore with all the commotion in the camp, but the cowboy kept turning in the saddle to look back at her. "Tell him you saw me," she finished lamely.

*"Ugashé,* go." Lutero ordered her back to the wickiup.

Hannah went slowly, watching to see where they

took the cowboy. It was difficult to see with the dust rolling from under the horses' hooves and all the Apaches on foot crowding around them. The women relatives of the slain warrior were wild with grief as they raged at the enemy, the white cowboy. They bound his feet and tied his hands behind his back, then sat him in a large patch of bare ground with two braves guarding him with rifles. The unrelenting sun blasted him. Hannah could see the sweat dripping off his forehead and the end of his nose, plastering the front of his shirt to his skin. She took a water bag and tried to approach him, but Chavez, Gatita's father, blocked her path.

"Lady?!" the cowboy called anxiously to her as she started to turn away. "Lady, you gotta help me. What are they gonna do to me?"

"I . . . I don't know," Hannah admitted. It was a question she kept asking herself, now that she'd gotten over the shock of seeing a white person after all this time. The rest of the band was meeting in a large communal area they used for ceremonies and council talks.

Chavez gave her a push and made a threatening gesture. She took a couple of steps, then stopped on the pretense that a stone was lodged in the seam of her moccasins.

"Ya gotta help me get away, ma'am." It was almost a whine.

She knew that. "How?"

"Cut these ropes and I'll figure out the rest." His voice caught on a sob. "Sweet Jesus, don't let them bastards torture me."

"Where are you from? How'd they get you?" She shied from his explicitly expressed fear and sought information, something that might give her an idea of the nearest towns or ranches.

"Me an' this *hombre* from Chihuahua were driftin' some cows out of the Mogollons an' they hit us. We tried to stand and make a fight of it, but . . . My name's Jack Bledsoe, from over Uvalde way." It suddenly seemed important to him that she know his name and hometown.

The meeting ended with a loud ki-yipping that reminded Hannah of a dog pack with the prey in sight and closing in for the kill. She turned as they came streaming toward the open ground, the women all in a pack with a wild-eyed Gray Dove in front. They surged on him and pulled the struggling, protesting cowboy to his feet.

"What do they want with me?!" His voice lifted hoarsely to Hannah while he kept his frightened gaze on the women who were tearing and yanking at his shirt. "Help me!!"

She couldn't stand there and do nothing. "No!!" Hannah rushed toward them and tried to get between the women and the cowboy. "Leave him alone!" she cried in Spanish. They pushed and kicked to get her out of their way. "Don't hurt him!"

Lutero dragged her back, his hands clamped around the solid flesh of her upper arms. "*Coche!*" he said gruffly, the deep snarl of his voice warning her not to interfere.

"What are they going to do to him?"

"He kill Knife-Open-Cheek. Gray Dove asks for him. It is her right." Lutero maintained an iron hold on her arms while Hannah unconsciously strained against it.

Helpless, she watched the women strip the man stark naked, even taking his hat. Young Jack Bledsoe kept screaming over and over again, "What are they gonna do to me?"

She couldn't tell him. She didn't know whether Lutero meant that he'd been given to Gray Dove as a slave and his treatment would be the suffering she'd known, or whether Gray Dove had been given the right to punish him for the death of her husband. A bundle of firewood was dragged over, and Hannah recalled the branding fire that had burned into her chest. It still ached when the skin pulled just right.

"My God!! They're gonna burn me!! No! Please!" he sobbed. His body was thin and very white except for the weathered tan of his face, neck, and the vee of his throat where his shirt collar had flopped open.

Hannah felt his terror and wept for him, large tears spilling over her lashes and running slowly down her cheeks. But rather than being used to build a fire, the wood was broken into long splinters that were sharp and thick. One by one the women began to stick them into his flesh, while he kept yelping and crying in his terror, "What are they gonna do? What are they gonna do?"

They took a long time, covering every inch of his body with the splinters, turning him into a walking porcupine. He writhed in agony. Then Hannah saw Gray Dove carry a flaming stick of wood from one of the campfires and touch it to the splinters. She screamed and tried violently to wrench herself from Lutero's hold.

The boy's full-throated shriek of horror spiraled above hers as the flames enveloped him within seconds, racing through the dried bits of wood like tinder. Before Hannah shut her eyes, a living ball of fire rolling on the ground was the last thing she saw. Lutero let go of her and she stumbled away, the stench of burning flesh filling her nostrils, the smell lingering long after his screams ceased to echo through the night. She vomited, emptying her stomach until only bile was left, and most of that came up, too.

She moved blindly with no thought of a destination and eventually sank to the ground with no idea of the place. For a long time, she sat with her knees bent and her forehead resting on them, while the tears dried on her face. She felt completely blank; everything was a void.

Once she had been so proud of her milk-white skin; now it was the color and texture of the buckskin of her clothes. And her hands had been so soft and smooth; now calluses gave them the roughness of sandpaper. No more afternoon teas with watercress and cucumber sandwiches; she was grateful for a drink of water and a chunk of *zigosti,* bread.

Why did she still want to live? Why, when maybe she would die like that later on?

*"Vámonos,* come," Gatita ordered.

"No." Hannah stated her rebellion quite simply. She saw no reason to live in subjugation any longer. When she lifted her head, she met Gatita's glare with equanimity. "How can you kill a man like that? How can a woman kill a man like that?" she demanded.

Gatita stretched to attain every imperious inch of her five-foot height and looked down on her seated slave. During a long pause she studied Hannah's upturned face, then rested a protective hand on the top curve of her stomach. Maneuvering her bulk with care, she lowered herself to the ground, kneeling and then sitting back on her heels.

"It is way of Apache."

"To set people on fire? To burn them alive? No one deserves to die like that. It is the way of animals!" Hannah retorted.

"Look there." Gatita motioned toward the barren, inhospitable reaches of the desert spilling out before them. "Desert kills like that. Takes man's power piece at a time. Slow die. Power leave—slow."

"That's crazy." Irritated, Hannah grabbed up a handful of sand and shook it inside her closed fist.

"No crazy. This Apache land. Take lot of power to live here. When white-eyes kill Knife-Open-Cheek, take power from Gray Dove. She must avenge and take power back. Man lets go of it piece at a time. Longer he take to die, more pieces Gray Dove have. It is way of Apache."

"Could you kill like that, Gatita?" Hannah looked at the proud woman with a long sideways glance.

"*Anh,* yes."

"Women and children?"

"Women and children have no power. Man has power."

A throaty sound that was almost a laugh bubbled from Hannah. "That's some consolation, I guess," she said in English. "We may not have any power, but at least we don't have to die like that." Gatita gave her a puzzled and wary look, not following any of it. Hannah's bitter amusement faded to a dry smile. "Maybe the desert is cruel. Maybe man is cruel. We are the earth. I just don't know any more."

"*Mañana, ugashé,* tomorrow we go," Gatita stated. "This place smell of *dah-eh-sah,* death."

"*Anh,*" Hannah replied in Apache, agreeing with the Indian woman.

It was the time called Thick with Fruit. The *rancheria's* wickiups were erected amid towering saguaro cacti to harvest its fruit and preserve it. But none of Gatita's female relatives were out among the giant cacti. They were gathered at her wickiup, including her mother, Salt Lips, and a *di-yin,* a medicine woman skilled in midwifery. Observing the tribal taboo—where his mother-in-law was, he wasn't—Lutero absented himself from the event.

Lifting aside the blanket flap over the low, traditionally east-facing door of the wickiup, Hannah carried in the water warmed over the campfire. Gatita knelt on an old blanket and held onto an upright post to brace herself during the contractions. Apache women did not give birth lying down, Hannah had been informed. The *di-yin,* a tall, stately, gray-haired woman, had given Gatita four salted pieces of the inner leaves of the yucca, a medicine that would make the birthing fast and easy. While the *di-yin* rubbed the extended abdomen, a solution made from a root powder was used to bathe Gatita's genitals.

Hannah passed the water to Gatita's mother, then hugged close to the rounded side of the wickiup, wanting to be present when the baby was born. Minutes later, a flurry of excited murmurs announced its advent as the head emerged to be cradled in the palm of the *di-yin*'s hand. An exhausted and sweating Gatita was smiling, her head thrown back, arching her throat for that last effort.

*"Ish-ke-ne."*

*"Ish-ke-ne."*

It was a boy-child; the happy words were repeated and spread as the newborn infant was gently drawn away from his mother. Hannah saw that the baby hadn't begun breathing on its own and waited for the customary slap. Instead, the *di-yin* splashed cold water on the infant. After one tiny startled gasp, he breathed on his own but didn't cry. There were approving nods all around the wickiup.

The *di-yin* called for the warm water Hannah had brought and began the ritual washing of the baby, followed by the sprinkling of the *ha-dintin* pollen to the four directions and on the baby and then the offering of the proper prayers. Gatita's mother and sisters administered to her, bathing her and making sure all was normal.

Finally the blanket-wrapped baby was handed to his mother for his first meal. His mouth was open and blindly searching, and a small red-brown fist waved in the air. Then, as if it all became too much for him, he yawned widely.

Gatita laughed tiredly. *"Go-yath-khla."* Everyone

seemed to agree; only Hannah was confused. Gatita noticed that as she guided the milk-wet teat to her son's mouth. "I call him Sleepy," she explained in Spanish.

An appropriate name. For the first week, that seemed to be all he did.

A rosy yellow was tinting the sky on the eastern horizon, a fingering light softly stealing into the desert chaparral to show the breaks in the mesquite, palo verde, and creosote bushes. Soon the night shadows would lift and they would be able to see clearly with dawn's blush on the land.

Stephen stood in the stirrups, feeling the stretch of his leg muscles, and looked over his shoulder at the column of men. Their faces were haggard from the night's forced march; they had traveled better than twenty-five miles under the cover of dark. But he was satisfied to see a tension in their expressions, the nerves tightening the way they always do just before the enemy is engaged. Combined with the solid, sure feeling that steadied him, it became a smooth exhilaration, a readiness that made the blood flow and the heart pump strongly.

But he bridled his impatience for the time being. Stephen could feel the tiredness of his horse after the all-night trek. The light wasn't quite right and the horses could use the extra few minutes' rest. He curbed his own energies and waited.

The buckskin horse Amos Hill was riding soft-footed over to the tall chestnut that was Stephen's personal mount. Amos came up on the side of his good eye and eased himself into a better position on the horned saddle.

"Do they know we're out here yet?" Stephen asked, sotto voce.

"Ain't got a whiff," Amos assured him in a mumbled

whisper, and looked at the spreading color in the sky. "Be light enough soon."

"Yes." Too much energy was contained in him for Stephen to remain still. He swiveled partially in the McClellan to take another look at the men behind him and make certain they were ready to move out at his signal. On his right, he noticed Cutter rubbing a hand across his jaw and cheek, the beard stubble making a scraping sound.

"Need a shave," Cutter murmured. He lowered his hand to a uniform-covered thigh with its yellow stripe. "How many should we expect, Amos?"

"Nah-tay thinks most of the men are away—hunting or raiding. Not many horses. Figure maybe ten, fifteen men. The rest are women and children, maybe thirty or so."

Stephen measured the sky's light with another look. "Let's move up."

The signal was given to move forward at a walk. All sound was subdued—the sand-muffled plod of hooves, the small moans of leather, the muted chomping of bridle bits, and the hush of silent men, faces somber and eyes alert. The last quarter mile to the *rancheria*'s eastern extremity was a long one. Nah-tay and a dozen of his *nan-tans*, best scouts, waited for them.

There was a stir of movement around the *jacals*, of women adding fresh fuel to the smoldering fires, dogs stretching and wagging their tails at the children wandering out of the brush-covered huts, and men hunching over the rekindled fires. Then the early-morning quiet was shattered by the thundering charge of the blue-suited cavalry.

The ensuing chaos was a harsh blend of shouts and screams and sporadic bursts of gunfire. The Apache men along with two war women leaped for their weapons, while the rest of the adult females tried to get the children to safety. It was a stampede of animals and people, in a dozen directions, women and children fleeing, soldiers chasing, and warriors trying to cover the retreat of their families. The smells of sweat, blood, and panic mixed with the sharp-scented dust and woodsmoke in the air.

The fury of the clash was expended within minutes as the troop overran the *rancheria* and captured all who didn't make it away in the first dash. Five Apaches were killed in the battle, including one woman, and seventeen were taken prisoner, while the company suffered only two casualties, both relatively minor. A detail was dispatched to comb the area for fleeing stragglers, the search patrol composed mainly of Apache scouts and a handful of troopers.

The rest of the troopers remained at the *rancheria*, where they rounded up their prisoners and herded them into one of the stick corrals, constructed out of ocotillos. Stephen's long-striding chestnut swept back toward the center area of the *rancheria*, the war-horse's neck arched in excitement from the smell of blood, its reaching trot giving the horse and rider the appearance of gliding across the ground. Stephen reined the prancing horse to a jiggling stop by one of the smoking fires. Cutter rode over. "Get that fire going," Stephen said. "I want these wickiups burned to the ground. Their weapons, food, supplies—everything destroyed."

The intent was simple: deprive the Apache of food, shelter, and weapons, and thus force him to seek the reservation. It was brutal, but effective.

"Ser-geant!" Cutter summoned Sergeant John T. Hooker as he rode by, and passed along a briefer version of the directive. "Torch them."

"Yes, suh." Hooker threw a salute as he hauled his horse into a turn and yelled to a private, the order finally getting to the bottom rank.

Jake Cutter kicked his horse into motion after the

high-striding chestnut, following Wade to the corral where the captives were being held. One-Eye Amos Hill swung out of his saddle and waited by the thorny-sticked fence at their approach. The chestnut slowed to a reluctant stop, tossing its head and chewing noisily on the bit between snorts. Wade sat the constantly shifting horse and surveyed the sullen and silent Apache prisoners. A couple of toddlers made the only sounds with their muffled sobs of bewilderment. From the side, Cutter watched him. It was a scene he'd seen played out many times before.

"Open the gate." The command was given calmly as Wade twitched his horse to one side.

Amos Hill motioned to the Apache scout inside, and the crossbar was let down. Knowing its role, the high-bred chestnut settled down immediately and entered the enclosure with parade poise. While Wade slowly walked his horse around the prisoners, stopping to visually inspect each one, Cutter reached inside his pocket for a cigar and lit it. After a long abstinence, the cigar smoke made a pleasing sting on his tongue.

Amos scuffed the toe of his boot into the ground, glancing up briefly in the general direction of their commanding officer. "Kinda makes me wonder what he'd do if he ever found one of 'em wearin' somethin' of his wife's."

"The odds are against it." Cutter continued to watch with a noncommittal expression.

"He was over checkin' the dead ones almost before the flies landed on 'em." Behind them, the first torch was set to a brush-thatched wickiup. After an exploratory crackle, the flames whooshed over the hut. "He's persistent as hell, I'll give him that." Amos squinted his good eye against the sun's low angle of light. "Ya know, some authorities claim there's twenty-five thousand Apache out here. I bet there's less than ten thousand, an' probably only a third of 'em is males of fightin' age."

"You could be right." Cutter absently flexed the tired muscles in his shoulders, catching the smell of gunsmoke on his clothes. "Hey, John T.," he called to the colored sergeant. "As long as we've got all these fires going, tell somebody to throw some coffee on one of them."

"Yes, sir."

Wade rode behind the huddled group of Apache captives one last time, and headed for the corral's opening. The big chestnut swung outside it and responded to the curb by prancing sideways, snorting at the blazing native huts aflame all around.

Wade looked directly at the scout. "You know what to ask." He didn't wait for a response, easing the restraining pressure to send his mount forward.

"Yeah, I guess I do," Amos said to the major's back as he rode away, then gave a small shake of his head. "D'ya really think he expects to find her after all this time? What was the last tally—d'ya remember, Cutter? Wasn't it two Mexican señoritas and one yellow-haired boy he's bought off the 'pache?"

"Something like that." Cutter conceded that it was roughly the number for whom Wade had paid ransom to the Apache.

"One of them women had a papoose on her back an' the other had one in the oven. An' the boy—he was wild an' savage as any Apache tot ever thought of bein'." Amos moved the cud of chewing tobacco to his other cheek and spat out the extra juice. "'Pears to me, he's better off not askin'."

"Mrs. Wade is a rare woman, Amos." Cutter gathered up the reins to his horse and leaned idly back in the saddle, the steady pressure on the bit backing his mount from the corral.

"Now, there ya go. Yore doin' it, too—talkin' like she's still alive," Amos declared in exasperation.

"I guess I've been around the major too long. It must

have rubbed off." Cutter's grin was dry as he reined his horse from the corral and urged the tired animal into a canter.

The commissary building was pressed into service as a ballroom, its stores stacked away and its bare adobe walls and its rafters festooned with bunting, shields of colored paper, and crossed sabers. At one end of the room, a platform was erected for the regimental band to play at the ball honoring the visit of the territorial commander, Colonel Edward Hatch, a visit that was covered by Hy Boler from the Silver City newspaper, arriving in his best bib and tucker and his derby hat.

While the band played its best rendition of a quadrille, the officers, resplendent in their full-dress uniforms, danced the sets with the ladies, elegant in their best satins and taffetas. The floor was a whirl of color, the gold epaulets and regimental cord and sash glittering on the military uniforms while the vibrantly hued gowns gleamed. An exuberance filled the night as the men were filled with a sense of importance at this visit from their regimental commander.

After leading off the ball, partnering Mrs. Bettendorf in the grand march, Colonel Hatch stood near the punch bowl, flanked by a semicircle of officers. Prominent among them was Major Stephen Wade, the dramatic touch of the black armband around his sleeve giving him an even more striking appearance.

"It seems to me you had some very good hunting, Major," the colonel declared in response to Wade's report of the number of captives they'd taken in their recent action.

"Luck was on our side, Colonel. Our scouts were out combing the area for the hostiles who had fled the *rancheria* we had attacked. They heard a dog barking, and discovered another *rancheria* not four miles distant. I regrouped my forces and hit the second camp immediately." Stephen paused and idly took a sip of fresh lemonade. Hannah had often fixed lemonade for them on the hot, hot days when their thirsts seemed unquenchable. He had found nothing of hers at the second *rancheria* either, nor had any of the Apache captives admitted knowing anything about a white woman taken from the pony soldiers. He resumed his narrative. "Obviously the Apaches didn't realize we were in the vicinity. If they think the Army is close by, they usually kill the dogs so their barking won't lead us to their camps."

"It was very commendable work." The colonel brushed aside Stephen's modesty. "You were out with your company for two weeks, destroyed seven *rancherias,* killed twenty hostiles, and captured fifty-two—and all without losing a man, and suffering only minor casualties. Very commendable."

"That's kind of you, sir."

"Nonsense," the colonel said gruffly. "To be honest, Major Wade, one of the reasons I decided to visit the fort was to meet you. I've been seeing your name on so many reports lately." His glance drifted to the black armband around Wade's sleeve. "Naturally, the tragedy regarding your wife came to my attention. Most regrettable, sir. Most regrettable."

It was still a knife in him, a raw and painful wound that festered. Stephen tasted the bitter irony that it should be Hannah's fate that had brought him to the attention of his commanding officer.

"I appreciate your kindness, Colonel." Stephen stiffly accepted the expression of sympathy.

"Well, I'm sure you know you're not alone in all this. You have the prayers of a lot of people, both friends and strangers."

"Yes, sir. Since the newspapers picked up the story from the *Gazette* about my search for her, I have received a good many letters of encouragement from people I don't even know."Some of the eastern trades had carried it, and Stephen was well aware that the military hierarchy was particularly sensitive to the press. General Crook was even known to include two reporters in his entourage to ensure that his activities got proper coverage. Hy Boler was serving the same purpose for Stephen.

"That's to be expected. I like you," Hatch said abruptly. "General Pope thinks you are the kind of officer we need at command. What would you say to that, Major Wade?"

"I would be deeply flattered." Stephen inclined his head in acknowledgement of the honor while expressing regret. "But you understand that I would not be happy to leave the area until my wife is found. If nothing else, I owe her a Christian burial." He was aware that the newspaper publisher was listening closely to the conversation.

"Of course, of course. However, the army may feel that you are needed elsewhere," the colonel suggested diplomatically.

"Naturally I will obey any orders the army gives me."

"I never doubted it, Major." The mustached colonel smiled, and finally shared his attention with the rest of the officers gathered around. "This strategy against the Apache is beginning to show results. As we destroy his *rancherias,* burn his winter supplies, and take his horses, we are driving him to seek the reservation. It does us absolutely no good to chase a band of raiders for a hundred miles. It wears out our men and our horses. We have already proven in the plains that if we take away the Indians' food supplies, deprive him of the mobility of his horses, he must seek the refuge of the reservations to survive . . . he must accept peace."

"Have you heard the old adage about the Apaches and horses, sir?" Jake Cutter had been standing well back from the half-circle of officers, listening to the run of talk as he drank lemonade and wished it was diluted with whiskey. He strolled into their midst after voicing his question.

Even in his dress uniform, he exuded a kind of loose indifference to military dictates. The black, unkempt thickness of his hair curled into his collar, and the uneven lines of his face gave him a roughness that was out of place amidst all this polish.

"I don't believe I know the one to which you refer," the colonel admitted with a summing look that found Cutter of skeptical worth.

"It's claimed that a white man can ride a horse until it drops; then a Mexican can come along and ride that same horse another twenty miles before it quits; finally an Apache will come by and ride the same horse thirty more miles, and then he'll kill it and eat it—and walk two hundred miles."

"The point, sir?" the colonel inquired.

"These Indians aren't the Comanches and Mescaleros we fought in Texas. You take away an Apache's horse and he's twice as dangerous on the ground. I'd rather fight two hundred mounted warriors than a dozen Apaches on foot."

"They are masters at camouflage and skilled, silent stalkers," the Yankee-born colonel conceded. "But what are you suggesting? That we are not achieving our objective of forcing the Apaches into a peace treaty by our destruction of their supplies?"

"I think we are all aware that the Apache bands we have struck so far have not been the ones that have been committing most of the depredations in this area." Cutter was careful how he answered the question, not openly opposing the present plan. "The Apaches we want are followers of Juh and Geronimo, and they spend half their time on the other side of the border in Mexico laughing at us. And I wouldn't be a damned bit surprised if it was one of that bunch who took Mrs. Wade." No argument came from the rest of the officers. "And the only way you'll get those boys to honor a treaty is to beat them in a fight—a military victory they'll respect."

Colonel Bettendorf cleared his throat. "I believe we have forgotten that this is a ball. That's a waltz the band is playing. Where is Mrs. Bettendorf? Do any of you see her?"

Balls had never been much in Cutter's line, any more than polishing brass and playing politics were. He walked back to the punch bowl and left his cup with the trader's ringlet-haired daughter, then left the commissary and ultimately the post.

An hour later he was riding his horse up to the hitching post in front of Lomas Cherry's house, strategically situated on a back alley between two Silver City saloons. The inside lights gave off a rosy glow behind the curtained windows as Cutter climbed the steps to the porch. Someone plunked on an untuned piano, the sour notes distorting the melody. A laugh came from an upper story of the frame house, whose gingerbread seemed oddly out of place in this rugged clime.

Cutter opened the door and walked in, slapping the trail dust off his blue uniform with his gloves. Two slick-haired, spit-polished miners sat in the gawdy parlor with its red-rose-patterned rug and red-rose brocade sofas and gilded mirrors that endlessly reflected the vibrant pink shade. Cutter ducked his head to avoid the huge crystal chandelier, gilded as well, which was too large for the room.

"'Ello, Cutter." The heavily painted woman at the piano smiled when she saw him, but lost interest quickly. "If you want Cherry, she's upstairs. A guy gave Nita a little trouble. The kid's gotta toughen up. The game's in back . . . as always."

His glance went to the stairwell, but Cutter continued through the parlor to a door half hidden by a fringed and tasseled drape. "I think I'll play a little poker."

When he opened the door, the room reeked of smoke. He walked into the haze, found an empty chair at the game table, and sat down. He knew most of the players already.

Roughly an hour later, Cherry came through. The heavy powder on her face was beginning to cake from the heat, showing the hardness in the features that had once been pretty. Cherry was of the belief that a man liked to do his sinning in splendor, so she gave it to him—the Victorian house, the chandeliers, the brocades and silks. She gave Cutter a look that said the night had been a wild one—one old friend to another—and went on to the little office she had in back.

The poker game broke up about midnight and Cutter wandered into the parlor, finding some whiskey and a quiet corner, while the rest of Lomas Cherry's clientele finished their business and went home. The last one to leave had drunk a few too many, and Cherry hooked his arm around her shoulders, half-carrying him to the door. Cutter made a move to help her, but she waved him back to his chair.

With the door shut and locked, she leaned against it. All the vitality seemed to ebb from her. Even the vivid scarlet of her hair looked artificial.

"Hell of a way to make a living, isn't it?" she murmured, and walked through the parlor, picking up glasses and depositing them on a tray. Then she flopped into a chair near Cutter, her arms hanging loosely over the sides and her head tilted back.

"Drink?" He offered the whiskey bottle.

She looked at it and made a face. "I can't even stand the smell of it anymore. Nita!!" she hollered. "Bring me a cup of coffee!!" An affirmative reply came from the back of the house. Cherry shifted, bracing an elbow on the chair's curved armrest and supporting her forehead on her hand. "Why do you suppose all men are worms? Present company excluded, of course."

"Of course." He smiled wryly. "If you feel that way, maybe you oughta get out of the business."

"And do what?"

His shoulder lifted. "Get married." Cutter raised the shot glass of whiskey to his mouth.

Her interest aroused, she looked at him. "Are you proposing?" But she already knew the answer. "I thought not." Her red mouth twisted, but Cherry did straighten a little in the chair and push at the cherry-red hair from which she got her nickname. "I must look a sight."

"Scrape off some of that rice powder and rouge and that kohl around your eyes, and a man might find a pretty woman." The idle observation came as the girl Nita entered the parlor with Cherry's coffee, her face all swollen and bruised around one eye.

"The later it gets, the hornier a man gets and the more desperate he gets, until finally the ugliest hag looks beautiful to him." Cherry took the coffee cup, but ignored the girl. No acknowledgment appeared to be expected as the young Mexican crossed to the staircase and climbed the steps without a backward glance. "It isn't kind to say such things to a woman like me, Cutter." A trace of sadness was in her hardened expression, and a bit of resentful anger. "It gets her to wishing for things she can't have."

"Why?"

"Maybe there was a time when I could have walked outta that door—and outta this way of living," the woman mused; then her expression turned cynical and amused. "And if you're asking how I came to take up this profession . . . naturally there's a man involved. He came along at the time when I was ripe for picking. Well, he picked me—and a few hundred miles later, he dropped me. What was I to do then? How does a woman make a living out here if she hasn't got a man? Some do," Cherry conceded. "But a gal makes a mistake, and she gets marked. So what fair town would want a soiled woman like me teaching school or sewing clothes or cooking in a restaurant? I didn't have any money, nowhere to sleep . . . Hell, I did it!" Her tired laugh derided the justifications she was making. Almost immediately it faded away. "And, no doubt, I'd do it again."

"An honest woman." Cutter lifted his glass to her, sincere even as he smiled at the irony.

She sipped at her coffee, her red lips pursing around the cup's rim, then lowered it to release a long sigh and eye Cutter with a speculative glance. "You almost make me believe that you mean the things you say to me."

"I do." He frowned slightly, studying her closer.

"Maybe so," Cherry conceded, then laughed a husky laugh that had been roughened by years of whiskey and smoke and raw living. "But, honey, you still ain't gonna get it for nothing." She reached over to grab his hand, and led him up the stairs.

# CHAPTER 10

DURING THE TIME OF EARTH REDDISH BROWN, LUTERO'S band packed up and moved again. Hannah looked at the low-running river they waited to ford, presently being checked for quicksand by Lutero and Angry Dog. Lutero rode Hannah's bloodbay gelding, but the desert-toughened animal bore little resemblance to the sleek, flashy steed she'd once ridden for pleasure.

The dun horse Gatita was riding shifted sideways, its hindquarters jostling against Hannah, who as a slave was relegated to walking. Hannah stepped closer to the head of the silver-gray packhorse she led and gazed at the mud-colored water moving slowly between the wide banks.

"What river is this?" She had picked up some Apache, but, as now, she still mainly used Spanish.

"The one you call the Rio Grande. Mexico." Gatita pointed to the other side.

Hannah had never seen the Rio Grande before. They

had ranged farther east than she'd thought. The signal was given to cross, and the first of the band urged their mounts into the clay-colored water, the horses splashing as they waded in. The forward flow began around her, but Hannah hung back, her feet rooted on the American side. The dark, scrubby tail of the dun horse swished at her as it passed, Gatita astride and *Go-yath-khla*, Sleepy, on the cradleboard strapped to her back.

The river was the border. The U.S. Army could not cross it. If she crossed it, Stephen could not follow her. It was irrelevant that he didn't know where she was; crossing that river was the abandonment of another chance, however remote, of being rescued.

*"Ugashé*, go!" The rawhide-curled toe of an Apache boot struck her between the shoulder blades, roughly shoving her forward. Herded from behind, she was driven down the embankment into the water and swept into the train of horses and riders, unable to turn back. On the opposite bank, Hannah paused for one last look at the American side, her throat tight and her eyes hot.

Most of the dead wood around the *rancheria* had already been picked up. Each time, Hannah had to go farther afield to gather firewood. She stacked an armload onto the accumulating pile and started out for more. A sound, almost like the wail of a small baby, drifted into her hearing. Sleepy had been acting colicky lately, fussing and cranky, not at all his usual benignly contented self, so Hannah supposed it was him.

The distant crying continued. It was unusual for Sleepy to cry at all, and never that long and that hard. As Hannah stooped to pick up a dead branch, she listened to the baby's cries and realized that they weren't coming from the direction of the *jacal*; instead, the source was somewhere in the chaparral. She dropped the branch and the other firewood in her arms and went to investigate.

Deep in the brush twenty yards from the wickiup, Hannah found the squalling baby tied in its cradleboard and strung from a bush. The angry, heartbroken cries were wrenching sounds, impossible to ignore. Not a soul was in sight as Hannah hurried to comfort the red-faced infant, crying so hard that he was shaking. The crosses and parallel tracks decorating the stretched rawhide hood of the cradleboard and the amulets of hummingbird claws, splinters from lightning-struck wood, and bags of *ha-dintin,* ferrous dust, that hung about the frame were protective charms.

"Sleepy," she crooned in some surprise, and gathered up the cradleboard to untie it from the bush, looking around in some confusion for Gatita. "Sssh, we didn't forget you, Sleepy." Instinctively she spoke in Spanish. She rarely lapsed into English anymore even when she was alone.

When she had the cradleboard with its crying baby freed from the bush, Hannah started toward the *jacal,* all the time comforting him with her voice and the soothing touch of her hands. His crying became less strident and more tearful, self-pitying.

"What you do?" An angry Gatita suddenly confronted Hannah and grabbed the cradleboard and her son away from her.

"I found him out there. Someone tied his cradleboard to a—" She broke off as Gatita swept past her to walk back into the brush, not interested in the answer.

Confused, Hannah followed. The baby began crying afresh, but Gatita appeared unmoved by his wails and made no attempt to comfort or silence him. When they were well away from the clearing of the *rancheria,* Gatita stopped and began to tie the cradleboard to the limb of another scrub tree.

"You aren't going to leave him there?" Hannah protested when Gatita left the cradleboard suspended from the limb and turned her back on the angry, frightened wail of the boy-child.

"Sleepy must learn is bad to cry. We leave alone until he stops." Gatita stated her position quite emphatically.

"But—" The baby was so small, and the action seemed so heartless.

"He must learn he not get what he wants if he cries. If he silent, then will get," Gatita explained. "Noisy baby is bad. Enemy might hear. Learn early to stay quiet. That is way of Apache."

And Hannah noted that the lessons always seemed to be cruel ones. Compassion, tenderness, sympathy—they had no place in these environs. She tried to shut her ears to the baby's bawling, but it didn't come easily to her.

When she had the firewood gathered into a bundle, she dragged it into camp. A bright-eyed Sleepy was cooing happily in his cradleboard, this time hanging from an upright post of the *ramada,* and batting at the shiny baubles dangling from the hood.

Cactus Pear, the *bi-zhahn,* young divorcée, was at the fire with Gatita. Since she was without a husband, Cactus Pear supported herself by making clay pots, which she gave to the others in the *rancheria* in the expectation of receiving gifts of game or other goods and supplies. Small red circles were tattooed in a line across her forehead, a form of adornment affected by some Chiricahua women.

The scrawny camp dogs set up a barking, advising the *rancheria* of approaching riders. Hannah looked to the southwest and saw a faint haze of dust. Minutes later she heard the lowing of cattle and the first shout that indicated the return of the Apache raiders. This was the harvesting of another crop. The desert home of the *Nde-nda-i* Apache did not provide enough food and game for them to subsist on it alone. To survive, they had to raid the farmers and ranchers on both sides of the border, sometimes using stolen goods to trade for other things they needed. In truth, the Apache didn't want to drive the white man or the Mexican from his lands since he would thus be depriving himself of a source of food, supplies, and goods for trade, such as these scrawny Mexican cattle. Whenever there was trading to be done, Hannah wasn't allowed to remain in camp, where she could be seen by illicit traders, white or Mexican. She·was always taken into the brush and tied there, guarded by Apaches.

The dust haze thinned and Hannah's gaze picked out Lutero astride the blood bay gelding on the herd's right flank. Always at the sight of those flat, high-boned features, Hannah stiffened with dislike. She could never completely block out the memory of his violations of her. At times she still felt unclean from the past rape, but he had never again approached her, although sometimes she caught him watching her. Apache custom insisted that a man abstain from sex with his wife while she nursed their child. Hannah wasn't sure whether he didn't want to risk the tribe's censure or whether he stayed away because she was his wife's property. Either way, he didn't come near her.

And the only time he broke his celibacy was after a successful raid when there was celebration and dancing. As a skilled raider, Lutero was invariably chosen by one of the *bi-zhahns* or young widows as a partner in the Property Dance. Payment was expected for the privilege out of his share of the raid's plunder. Only the unattached women were allowed to dance in such a lewd and lascivious manner, or to slip away with the warrior to her *jacal*. A *bi-zhahn* had no husband to satisfy her needs—her every need. At this special time, custom allowed her to seek out a man and obtain a share of the plunder while relieving the inner pressure of long abstinence, both hers and the warrior's, who'd spent weeks away from his wickiup. So tonight, Hannah could be fairly certain that Cactus Pear or one of the other *bi-zhahns* would seek Lutero's attentions . . . with the tribe's blessing.

She turned away from the sight of the returning raiders and rubbed a hand down her sinewy thigh. The hard work was endless and little time was available for her to reflect on her plight beyond a moment now and then for the flashes of bitter resentment, the odd flickers of hope, and the poignant flares of memory. Even in her moments of greatest despair, Hannah could not imagine living this way forever, always on the edge of hunger, fatigue, thirst, and pain. Yet the Apaches' bright moments had become hers—the laugh of a child, a full stomach, and the fresh scent of aloe-washed hair.

By now she looked Apache. The unrelenting sun had deepened the red hues in her mahogany-dark hair, but its fire was contained in the traditional double loops, held at the nape of her neck by a *nah-leen*, a bow-shaped piece of leather. The sun had also darkened her fair skin to a deep shade of bronze. The loose-fitting buckskin top and calf-length skirt were duplicates of the first Apache clothes she'd been given, only these Hannah had made herself, as well as the *n'deh b'keh*, the tall, curl-toed Apache boots that came up to her knees. Her vocabulary included more Apache words all the time. She knew many of the rituals and taboos. Slowly she was being absorbed into the Apache way of life.

But not completely.

Following the celebration of the highly successful raid, the Mexican traders came to the *rancheria* to barter for the horses and cattle with whiskey, ammunition, and guns. As always, at any time strangers, especially non-Apache, came to the camp, Hannah was taken a mile or more away, where she was left tied. She never came in contact with anyone outside Lutero's band.

All day and all night, Hannah remained bound to a tree with a rawhide rope. Accustomed to privation, she thought little of water for her dry mouth or food for her empty stomach or the stiffness caused by restricted movement. She only hoped no one came for her until well after all the whiskey had been drunk, so that she could be spared the bursts of hot temper, fueled by the "fire water," and the randy advances of drunken, pawing Apache braves.

By now, she knew they would eventually come for her and not leave her tied out there to die. As long as she was healthy and strong and did what she was told, she was useful to them. She was a good slave, if there was such a thing. But on the day that she became a burden, she would be sold or killed. That was the way.

The morning sun had been burning in the sky for more than an hour when Gatita walked silently out of the brush. She offered no greeting as she approached Hannah. And Hannah said nothing either, not even when she noticed the large, purpling bruise below Gatita's eye. The ropes were untied, freeing Hannah, and she rubbed at her limbs to speed the slow return of circulation while she eyed the small-built Apache woman, sensing something was wrong.

Gatita passed her a water *tus,* a small wicker jug woven out of sumac. Hannah lifted it to her lips and tipped it to let some liquid flow into her mouth, enough to wet its dryness. The warm water had the faint flavor of piñon from the pine gum used to caulk it. After a second swallow, she gave the *tus* back to Gatita, and they started in the direction of the *rancheria.*

"We get *thlees,* horses," Gatita said. "Take back so we can pack."

"Why?" Hannah looked around at their mountain stronghold in the Candelaria Mountains of Mexico. They had plenty of food, water, and graze.

"He-with-whom-I-go-about say *ugashé*, we must go." She referred to her husband, Lutero; his order would normally have ended discussion, except that Gatita too seemed to resent the necessity of leaving this camp where they had plenty. "Last night, the pepper-eating one who came to trade for cattle, he drink whiskey and tell of raid by Apache on the *kinh*, house of Mexican *jefe*, leader. Many slow-die. Much power taken. Mexican *beshes*, long-knives, very angry. Many, many search mountains." Her hand made an arc to indicate the mountainous country all around them. "Pepper-eating one may tell of this place. He-with-whom-I-go-about saw crow this morning. Bad sign. *Ugashé.*"

"Who took the power?" Hannah wondered if Lutero had tortured the Mexican family at the hacienda that had been attacked by Apaches.

"It was Juh. He is *hesh-ke.*"

"*No comprendo.*" Hannah frowned, the Apache word completely unfamiliar to her.

"One of the crazies, the unreasonable haters," Gatita replied. "Juh is *hesh-ke.*"

Unreasonable hater. The phrase triggered a vague memory of a conversation with Captain Jake Cutter. In her mind, Hannah saw him again: the hard, grave features, the keen blue eyes, and the shaggy black hair curling into his uniform collar. The clarity of his image was brief, and the thought was forgotten as they approached the horse herd.

After catching two of their packhorses, they led them to the *jacal*. Sleepy jabbered away at them from his cradleboard hanging on a *ramada* post. The packing of belongings and supplies began. The hut, which had taken half a day to construct, was quickly dismantled, the canvas kept and folded to be loaded on the horses, the rest discarded. Each time a *rancheria* site was abandoned, the procedure was the same. Nothing would be left as it was; even the fire pit would be smoothed over so that anything that happened in this place while they were gone would not affect the Apaches when they returned.

An impatient, glowering Lutero watched them begin the long task of loading the horses. Restive and irritable, he growled at their slowness, but made no move to help them. It was women's work. Hannah could see the dullness and lethargy of a hangover about him, the flatness that dragged at him and soured his mood. She stayed well clear of him, so it was Gatita he sent to fetch his horse.

At the first gunshot, Hannah paused to look around, wondering which liquor-laden Apache had awakened with sufficient rowdiness to do some hoorahing. When drunk, the Apaches were a noisy, brawling bunch, quick to laughter and quick to anger.

The single shot was followed by a flurry of gunfire and yells of warning. A second later, riders charged the *rancheria,* uniformed Mexican soldiers in their high-crowned, small-billed hats, flashing their sabers. Hannah spared one glance over her shoulder at Lutero as he grabbed his weapons and bolted for cover.

But joy leaped through her, the blood rushing through her body. Laughing and crying with relief, she turned and ran to meet the charging soldiers, these riders in the uniform of the Mexican army.

She waved her arms at them, shouting, *"Americano!! Americano!!"*

A soldier angled his mount at her, lifting his saber. At the last instant, Hannah realized that he intended to ride her down and threw herself out of the path of his slashing saber and his horse's hooves. Her hands absorbed much of the impact of her fall, but it was their darkly tanned color Hannah suddenly noticed, and the Apache dress she wore. She claimed to be white, but with her dark hair, dark eyes, and tanned skin, she looked like one of them. Her cries of *"Americano"* had probably made no more impression on the soldier than the rest of the screaming going on around them.

Hannah scrambled to her feet, finally becoming aware of all that was happening in the chaos of the moment. Apaches were running in every direction— men, women, and children, pursued by soldiers who hacked at them with their sabers. It was a bloody scene; bodies were split open like ripe melons, arms severed from shoulders.

Suddenly she heard the scared whimpering of a baby who knew it shouldn't cry. Sleepy was still in his cradleboard, dangling from the *ramada*, his big dark eyes looking about in frightened confusion. As she ran toward the brush arbor, a soldier also caught the distressed sounds and hauled back on his horse's reins to locate it. When he saw the Apache infant in the cradleboard, he swerved his mount toward it, saber raised.

There were no weapons within reach, nothing of size that Hannah could throw at the soldier. All she could find was a water-filled *tus*, which she grabbed and hurled at the horse and rider. The spray of water in the horse's face startled the animal and it shied violently, unseating the soldier on its back. As he fell, he lost his grip on the saber. Hannah snatched it up and, in one swift motion, cut the rawhide strings suspending the cradleboard from the *ramada* post.

Grabbing the bulky cradleboard with the baby, Hannah ran toward the *jacal* and past it, taking a direction opposite to the marauding soldiers while avoiding the open ground. They were everywhere, shooting and slashing. The whine of bullets was all around her; some were fired by Apaches to cover the retreat of their women and children. There was no safe direction to run, no clear way to break through the encircling ring of soldiers and escape into the mountain wilds.

So Hannah hid in the only place she could find, crawling into the small space between a boulder and some brush and hugging close to the ground. Through the sharp-edged leaves and the thorny twigs, she could see the rampaging soldiers, killing those who didn't get away in time and mutilating their bodies, horrible scenes of children pulled apart, women eviscerated. She saw a Mexican soldier impale Cactus Pear's young daughter on his lance and hoist her body into the air, then hurl it off, a rag-doll figure. The smell of blood and gore scented the dusty air.

When the killing ended, the burning started, and the Mexican soldiers scoured the *rancheria* and the surrounding terrain to flush out wounded victims. The smoke from the burning, half-dismantled *jacals* was thick and choking. As the soldiers passed close to her hiding place in the crevice under the brush-shielded boulder, Hannah struggled not to cough and reveal her location. Sleepy made protesting little movements, but issued not a sound. Her fingers rested lightly against his mouth, ready to smother any cry he might make, but there was none.

For a long time—it seemed hours—she heard the soldiers moving about; there came the stamp of a horse's hoof, the distant utterance of some command in Spanish, or the clip-clop of a passing horse. Then there was nothing but the crackle of flames burning low or the crash of a collapsing wickiup's charred frame. Still Hannah didn't leave her hiding place with Sleepy.

Buzzards began a slow circling overhead, surveying the scene before coming in to land near the bloody corpses scattered about. The flap of their long wings was an ominous sound, nearly as unnerving as the sight of their cadaverous heads. Other wildlife, frightened away by the gunfire, screams, and smoke, began to return. Their presence reassured Hannah that the soldiers were no longer in the vicinity.

She had started to crawl out from beneath the shielding branches when the buzzards took off with a lumbering flap of wings. Immediately she pressed her body flat to the ground, breathing in the sharp-scented dust while her senses strained to locate whatever had disturbed the scavengers. Her heart pounded loudly in the stillness of the smoke-trailed scene, only a scattering of burnt ruins within her range of vision.

A second later, Hannah saw Lutero's deep-chested figure walking among the smoking fires and heard the first mourning wail of an Apache for his dead. The Mexican soldiers must be some distance away and under observation, or none of the Apaches would have risked returning to this place. Hannah scrambled from her hiding place, carrying the cradleboard with Sleepy in her arms, and hurried to join the gathering survivors of the small Apache band.

All that remained of Lutero's *jacal* were the fire-blackened ribs of the bent saplings. There were charred and smoldering shapes in the ash-strewn center, none of them recognizable. A distraught Gatita stumbled around it, blindly looking around.

*"Hola!"* Hannah called to her, relieved to see that she had survived the attack.

Gatita cried out with joy at the sight of her son alive and well, and rushed to take the cradleboard from Hannah. Hugging and touching the baby, crooning to it while she assured herself it was unharmed, Gatita hurried to her husband so both could share in this miracle. Then together they faced Hannah, a deep gratitude welling even in Lutero's look. *"Asoog'd,* thank you," Gatita said simply. Something Hannah had never heard expressed before by any of the Apache.

*"De nada,* it was nothing," she assured them, but she smiled faintly, for the first time feeling a warmth of emotion—and a reciprocation of it.

Then the destruction around them reasserted itself. Death's stench permeated the air with its reek of blood and roasted flesh. In shock, Hannah gazed about her. Some of the dead had been thrown onto the pyres of flaming *jacals*; others had been eviscerated or horribly mutilated, breasts removed from the women and genitals from the males. She recoiled from the sight of all the bloodied heads from which scalps had been hacked away and ears cut off. Such butchery was sickening. That soldiers had done it—soldiers, regardless of whose army—was beyond Hannah's ken.

Altogether fifteen of their small band had been brutally murdered; all but three of them were women and children. With the threat of the soldiers' return ever present, the dead were quickly removed from the scene and carried deeper into the mountains to be walled into crevices that would become their burial chambers.

Virtually nothing could be salvaged from the *ranchería.* Everything had been destroyed except what they carried on their persons and the clothes they wore. All else was gone—their foodstuffs, their household goods, their weapons, everything. Hannah kept thinking of all the food they had gathered and spent hours preserving; their entire store of winter supplies—gone. Homeless, they had nothing—no food, no blankets—and the time of Ghost Face was approaching. Only two ponies from their herd were recovered and one of those horses was lame, but they brought the limping beast along. If nothing else, it would provide the night's meal for the surviving members of the band.

A cache of extra food and supplies had been stashed in the Florida Mountains of New Mexico earlier in the year. With it, they would have a chance of making it through the winter. They started out, on foot, for the Rio Grande.

All along the way they encountered Mexican patrols. There was constant skirmishing, with the braves and war women engaging the soldiers to cover the escape of the women and children. Hunger, thirst, and exhaustion were their constant companions on the dangerous journey.

On a cold, moonlit winter's night, they waded across the wide river. All Hannah could think of when they reached the American side was that the Mexican army could not pursue them past this river. They were safe at last.

They recovered their cache of supplies from its walled-in hiding place in a cliff face, then headed for the site of the *rancheria* in the Mogollons where Hannah had been taken as a new captive, the one located atop the mesa and reached by a narrow, tortuous defile. The stronghold was virtually impregnable, the mesa rising sheerly from the desert floor. The narrow, snaking trail was the only access to the top. With his band thus safe, Lutero took three of his men and went to raid and replenish their storehouses with the essentials.

They were lean times, cold times. Many times Hannah went to sleep with little food in her stomach, huddled close to the small fire by the *ramada,* staring at the icy stars visible through the brush-thatched roof. Often she heard Sleepy whimper with hunger inside the *jacal* and guessed that Gatita did not have enough milk to satisfy the fast-growing infant.

When Lutero returned, his booty was considerable— ten horses plus twenty head of *wohaw,* agency steers, which he'd herded into a grassy canyon. The grazing would keep them there and allow the Apache to hunt and kill them as meat was needed. The blankets Hannah recognized as the kind issued at the reservation. She could guess where Lutero had done his raiding. The bags of flour and some of the other staples bore the stamp of the Indian Agency. Strangely, she did not particularly care how or where Lutero had obtained the goods. The needs of the *rancheria* were desperate; even the children were gaunt and hollow-eyed.

Now they could feast on *wohaw,* and the cowhide would make them new clothes, new moccasins; the blankets would keep them warm on the cold nights. She did not wonder at this new attitude of hers but accepted the bare comforts.

With a blanket draped over her head and around her shoulders as a shawl, Hannah left the fire and walked into the chill of a desert winter morning. She carried the empty wicker jugs that held their water and walked toward the spring that supplied the *rancheria.*

The water at the spring was icy cold, numbing her hands as she filled the *tus.* She rubbed warmth back into them, then started back to camp. Halfway to the *rancheria,* Hannah met Lutero on the trail. This was the third time in as many days that she had encountered him away from camp. She was wary of this sudden interest he was showing in her and these meetings when she was alone.

Against the cool temperature, he wore a long-sleeved buckskin shirt with fringe on the shoulders and the forearms of the sleeves. The long tails of his breechcloth helped protect his legs in their high mocca-sin boots. Lutero watched her approach with an impassive expression. Hannah avoided his eyes as she drew near him, catching the fragrance of wild mint on his body.

His hand moved toward her; she thought he intended

to grab her, and jerked back. Belatedly, she saw the carcass of a cottontail rabbit in his outstretched hand. She ventured a glance at his broad, flat features, plucked smooth of all facial hair. He watched her impassively. The preparation of small game was women's work, so Hannah took the dead rabbit from him and started again for the *rancheria*. Lutero didn't follow her.

In her months of captivity, Hannah had learned the Apache way of cooking, specifically the Chiricahua method. Small animals were partially roasted whole, then skinned and gutted and cooked the rest of the way. That was the method she used to cook the rabbit back at camp. While it was roasting over the fire, Lutero returned and set to work making arrows.

When the rabbit was done, she took it to him. He regarded her gravely before he accepted it, a satisfied expression finally showing on his face. *"Enju,* it is well," he said.

*"Anh,* yes." She nodded and returned to her work.

Late that day, Hannah knelt beside the large, flat stone called a *metate,* grinding cornmeal. The accumulated meal flour she gathered and placed in the *tsah,* a shallow basket; then she put more kernels in the stone's natural depression and picked up the oblong *mano* to pulverize it. Gatita came and sat cross-legged on the ground at an angle to Hannah.

"My husband spoke and told me his wishes," Gatita announced with formal dignity. It was a curious statement, but Hannah said nothing. If she was to know what it meant, she would be told. That much, too, she had learned. "He seeks to marry with you. I have no unmarried sisters who would have this right first. You are my property, so he comes to me." Shock deprived Hannah of her voice. "He brought food and you cooked it. That is a sign you willing to be his woman.

You work hard and you learn good the way of the Apache. You gave back the life of my son. I agree with the man who is my husband that you become his second wife and stepmother to the sleepy one."

Hannah didn't bother to explain that she hadn't understood the significance of the rabbit. "But I have a husband."

"He is a *pindah,* white-eye." Which dismissed him completely in Apache logic.

"If it is not my wish to marry with him?" She wondered how much choice she had in this.

"Then you are a *tonto,* a fool." Even the suggestion of it had reduced Hannah in Gatita's estimation. "Why should you wish to be treated like a dog, eating scraps and sleeping outside in the cold and the rain?"

"What you say is true," Hannah admitted cautiously. "I will think on this."

After Gatita had left her, Hannah made slow work of grinding the corn into meal for tortillas. The proposal of marriage was an honor, she realized, and signaled her acceptance into the tribe. A refusal by her was likely to be regarded as an insult. They were a proud people.

She paused in her work, aware of the heavy pressures grinding on her. The reality of her situation had to be faced. She had survived this long by adapting. She didn't know exactly how many days or months she'd been with the Apaches, nor how many more days and months would go by before she would be free . . . if she ever would be. The doubt finally crept in.

Yet how could she quit now? It would mean that she had gone through all this in vain. She couldn't do that. While she was still alive, there was always a chance. Marriage to Lutero would drastically improve her living conditions, and refusal could deny her the few comforts she presently had. On one hand, it seemed unthinkable to marry the man who had so brutally raped her eight or nine months ago; but on the other hand, it was imminently practical.

Perhaps it was strange, but Hannah could separate in her mind the woman she had been from the woman she had become. And the same with Lutero. At the time of the rape, they had been two enemies separated by their hates and fears. In these last weeks since the Mexican tragedy, they had worked together for the band's common good. While she could never forgive nor forget what he'd done to her, she couldn't hate him with the same ferocity she once had.

When she was finished with her task, Hannah collected the basket of ground meal and the parfleche in which the dried kernels were stored and carried them to the *jacal*. Gatita was working outside, weaving a basket, a *tuts-ah*, of willow and devil's claw. At Hannah's approach, she looked up. Their glances locked for a long minute; then Hannah slowly nodded.

*"Enju,* it is well," Gatita said, and went back to her weaving.

As was custom, the marriage ceremony was arranged to take place within two days after Hannah had agreed to the proposal. A feast followed the Apache rites of marriage. Hannah sat composedly through the celebration, stiffly aware of the man at her side and the fragrance of her skin, rubbed with the crushed leaves of the wild mint.

At the appropriate time, two horses were brought to them. While Lutero held the nose of the tan-and-white-spotted horse, Hannah sprang onto its back and waited for him to mount the dappled buckskin. A heightened tension tightened her stomach. She had spoken little to Lutero during the festivities, and now they were going off alone, away from the *rancheria* and the watching eyes, to become accustomed to each other. Hannah was not sure if she was grateful for that.

However, certain things were done to survive. She had to regard them in that light to preserve her sanity, had to put them in appropriate compartments in her mind and then close them off. When she rode out of the camp with Lutero, she had no sense of infidelity; she was trying to stay alive in order to get back to Stephen. It wasn't Hannah Wade who had married Lutero, but Coloradas, the name she'd been given for the red in her hair. These things were separate. They had to be.

# CHAPTER 11

UPON LEAVING THE *RANCHERIA* ATOP THE MESA STRONG-
hold, they traveled roughly three miles to a small box
canyon. Lutero led her to a *jacal,* half-concealed by the
scrub juniper and pine crowding the north side of the
canyon floor. While Lutero staked the horses out to
graze on the winter-brown grass, Hannah explored the
newly built honeymoon retreat, stocked with several
days' supply of food, utensils for cooking, and a bed
frame covered with blankets.

Lutero ducked through the low opening to loom
before her. "It is as you wish?"

She managed to stand her ground and not back away
from him in an instinctive recoil, sensing his attempt to
please. *"Enju."* She indicated her approval.

"I will start a fire." He moved past her to the center
of the bower, where firewood and kindling were laid in
preparation.

The winter sun left the sky early. Outside, shadows

176

were already lengthening in the late afternoon. They had brought food with them, so Hannah didn't have to fix a meal that night. She began unpacking it while Lutero used a fire drill, twirling it in his hands to ignite the grass and bark shreds around the small hole in the foot-long sotol stick. It was a slow, tedious process. On occasion, Hannah had seen the Apaches use flint boxes to start fires, but she had learned that they seldom relied on the white man's devices.

When the flame was burning strongly, Hannah passed him the food she'd set out and they ate, a weighty silence between them. Several times she felt his eyes on her as she chewed on the tough agency beef, but she never caught him looking at her. She guessed that he watched her covertly, as she did him.

The sky above the smoke hole in the thatched roof had a purple hue and the flickering pool of light cast by the small fire played across the bronze planes of Lutero's face. His hair hung black and straight from the blue calico band around his head, the blunt ends brushing the fringed shoulder seams of his buckskin shirt. Hannah felt tautness running through her nerves and rejection growing in her stomach for the food she was putting there. She put aside the rest of her portion.

"You do not eat," Lutero observed.

"My stomach is filled. I can eat no more." She wiped her greasy hands on the sides of her tanned leather skirt.

"*Enju.* I cannot eat anymore." The suggestion of a smile gentled his bluntly carved features, but Hannah didn't acknowledge it. She was too stiff with a dread that had to be controlled. He waited, motionless by the fire, while she stored away the uneaten food; then he rolled to his feet in one lithe motion, swinging a blanket around his shoulders. "I will check the horses before we sleep. You will come."

Her hesitation was slight; then she followed him

through the opening as he held the skin flap aside for her. The deep purple of night had settled over the canyon, masking their surroundings in black shadows. Her footsteps were almost as noiseless as his as they walked to the small clearing to check the horses.

"The moon rises." The tilt of his head directed Hannah's gaze to the gleaming white crescent above the black horizon.

"It looks cold."

"It is cold." Lutero raised a blanket-draped arm and started to put it around her shoulders to bring her inside its warm protection. Hannah instinctively flinched at his touch, and he drew back. "Do you have fear of me?"

"No." She could honestly say that she wasn't afraid of him.

"Then come where it is warm." The end of the blanket was again raised, while he waited with calm patience for her to join him inside its cloak. Steeling herself to impassivity, she moved within the open curve of the blanket and felt the outline of his hard, muscled body all down her side. She remained detached from the contact as she listened to the munch of the horses, barely discernible pale shapes against the darker shadows of the trees.

Absently, Hannah realized she was probably no different from many women who married to have a roof over their heads and food on their tables—and endured the touch of their husbands because there was nothing else they could do. For the first time, she saw the injustice of it. But it was ingrained from childhood that they needed men, that without them they were less than women. She found herself objecting to the subjugated role she had always played. It was a new thought and one to ponder.

"It grows late," Lutero stated, his head turned toward her.

Hannah stirred, roused from her wonderings; yet she maintained her stoic indifference. She held her end of the blanket, ignoring the feel of his hand on her waist and the rub of his hip against hers as they walked back to the secluded *jacal*.

Inside the structure, the low-burning fire threw little light to ward off the encroaching shadows. Under the cover of the darkness, Lutero pulled the buckskin shirt over his head, and she caught the glistening sheen of his muscled chest. She turned her back to him and began undressing.

For one instant, just before she slipped beneath the blankets where Lutero lay, she let herself remember that other time when her body had been blistered and raw. She tried to school herself to feel nothing when his hands moved onto her. She sank her teeth into her lip to silence her automatic protest, relieved that Apaches regarded the practice of mouths touching as revolting. Hannah stared up at the twinkling of stars through the wispy trail of smoke rising through the roof's hole, and disassociated herself from the things that were happening to her.

In a wholly abstract way, she was conscious that his hands were not rough with her but caressing. She was not rigid under his touch, but neither was she responsive. When he levered himself on top of her and moved between her legs, a hot rage seethed through her and she shifted under his pinning weight, resisting the jabbing probe of his male-head. He stopped, his hand gliding down to rub her mound and stimulate the flow of female juices until she was moist and ready for his entry. And Hannah discovered that the body was capable of accepting what the mind rejected. Even though she received no satisfaction and little pleasure, the coupling was not the objectionable act she had expected. There had obviously been a healing of the mind as well as of the body. Here was one more thing she could endure.

During the next five days, they spent nearly every minute together. Sometimes they worked at separate tasks doing camp chores, and other times they walked, but never venturing outside the confines of the box canyon. Lutero talked, mostly recounting details of successful raids when he'd outwitted the stupid *pindahs* or telling amusing stories about this or that person. Sometimes Hannah listened, but mostly she feigned attention, smiling and nodding at the appropriate times.

*"Mañana, ugashé."* As always, their conversation was a mixture of Spanish and Apache as Lutero informed her that they would be leaving this place the following day. Hannah wasn't sorry. While it would be crude and totally unfeeling to say she only tolerated him—there were moments when his company was actually pleasant—she longed for time to be by herself.

"It is time, I think." She nodded, and glimpsed the flash of blue as a jay took flight from the tree just ahead.

"Do you wish for your own house?"

*"No comprendo."* Hannah didn't understand why he asked the question.

"Do you wish to live in house with first wife or do you wish to be separate?"

"Separate," she was quick to answer.

*"Anh,* yes." He smiled knowingly. "Two wives seldom happy under same roof—even sisters. Fight."

*"Anh."* After putting up and taking down so many wickiups as the band constantly moved to new sites to hunt and forage, it would be a novelty to erect her own when they returned to the *rancheria.*

"Look." Excitement was in his voice as he pointed to something high on the canyon face.

Hannah scanned the sheer rock, but her eyes were not as keen as Lutero's. "What is it that you see?"

"Bees make hive where think we cannot reach to steal their honey." His confident expression indicated differently, but when Hannah spotted the dark comb, she wasn't convinced. "You wait. I get."

In disbelief, she watched him move to the base of the canyon wall where it rose almost perpendicular to the ground and begin his climb, finding hand- and toe-holds in the smooth ledges of the layered rock where none appeared to exist. It was an exhibition of agility and strength, partly to impress her with his skill and daring, and partly to satisfy his boyish sweet tooth with honey.

Higher and higher he went. Hannah's head was tipped back as far as it would go to keep him in sight. When he was almost within reach of it, Lutero stopped and snapped a dead branch off the twisted trunk of a tree. At any other time of year, the bees would have swarmed from the hive and attacked, but now, heavy with winter, they slept. Still, Hannah held her breath as he pried at the encrusted nest. Two large chunks of it broke off and careened off the canyon face, falling to the ground not far from her. Sluggish, disoriented bees crawled from the broken honeycombs, keeping Hannah at a distance while Lutero descended.

When he reached the ground, he scooped up the two chunks and shook out more bees, then urged Hannah to run before the bees woke up. Lutero followed, yipping cries of success. They were halfway back to the *jacal* before they stopped running.

Lutero gave her the larger piece, all sticky with oozing dark honey. She bit into the waxy comb, the thick, sweet honey running down the sides of her mouth and dripping from the comb, and she cupped her hand, trying to catch it. It was like nectar on her tongue, richly flavored and sweet.

She licked at her fingers to get every drop, making appreciative sounds in her throat. *"Bueno. Muy bueno."*

"Is good for you. Good for women," Lutero informed her. "Honey make woman fertile, so her stomach will grow large with baby."

Hannah knew that the Apaches had many superstitions centering on pregnancy, but she had not heard this one before. The honey lost some of its flavor. Not because she believed what Lutero said, but simply because she hadn't considered that she might have his child. For so long, she had wanted Stephen to give her a baby. She felt a sharply bitter pang at the thought that eventually it might be Lutero's she carried. She put a hand on her stomach, wondering if she had already conceived.

"We begin to make baby," Lutero stated with certainty. "It takes many times to make all the parts. *Eyanh.*" He urged the honeycomb to her mouth, encouraging her to have more.

She bit into it and slowly chewed on the honey-coated wax, almost letting his superstitions sway her into believing. That was nonsense. But the chance of her becoming pregnant was very real.

The hour call traveled the circuit of the sentry posts around the fort's perimeter. Stephen Wade listened to the lonely call running through the darkness from inside the Goodsons' parlor. His stance by the wood heating stove resembled a parade rest, one arm cocked behind his back and his feet slightly braced apart. The glass of port in his hand took away some of the stiffness of his pose. His glance strayed to the window, as it had repeatedly during the last twenty minutes . . . ever since he saw the gleam of light shining from a window in his own quarters across the way.

This morning, Captain Jake Cutter had taken a detail

from A Company on patrol. The colored sergeant who accompanied him had been John T. Hooker. From that, it was easy to deduce that Cimmy Lou had come to see him, as she often did when her husband was away from Fort Bayard.

Damn, but that black wench excited him. He shied away from the erotic images that flashed through his mind. His damned cock would get hard if he didn't stop thinking about her. Stephen tossed down the rest of his port. When he'd first glimpsed the light, it had been too soon after the fine dinner the Goodsons had prepared for him to take his leave without breaching social etiquette. But now . . .

"After such a delicious meal and such excellent port"—Stephen lifted his glass to salute Captain Goodson's taste—"I don't know how to thank you for inviting me tonight."

"It was our pleasure," pretty blond Maude Goodson assured him.

"Have some more port, Major." The captain reached for the wine bottle to refill his glass.

"No more for me, thank you." Stephen set the glass on a doily-covered side table. "I am behind in my correspondence, so I hope you won't think me rude if I tell you that I must retire to my own quarters."

Protests were made, mostly by Maude, since Captain Goodson deemed it inadvisable to argue with his superior officer. Finally Stephen's hat, coat, and gloves were fetched and he bid them good night.

When the door had shut behind him, Stephen stepped from beneath the *ramada* and paused to turn his collar up against the night's winter chill. The sleepy eye of a quarter moon shone on the darkened parade ground. On the other side of the quadrangle, gleams of light came from the black silhouettes of the barracks, the source of the occasional sound of men's voices drifting on the desert air.

It was a mean post, brutal duty. He'd served his time in these harsh, unsavory conditions. Now there was a chance that it would all change. God, how he wished Hannah was here. After all this time he'd finally been recommended for promotion, and he wanted to share the news with her. There was even a slim possibility he'd be transferred out of the regiment. Custer's massacre last summer had decimated the ranks of the Seventh Cavalry, and the army was waging a full-scale war against the Sioux, whom Crook called the best light cavalry in the world. Stephen wanted to be part of that campaign against an enemy who could be engaged in battle, instead of fighting these hit-and-run guerrilla tactics of the Apache. It was all happening—slowly— but still it was happening. If only he could find Hannah.

Restlessness pushed at him, all the coiled, driving energies sending him striding across to his quarters where Cimmy Lou waited to ease them. He wondered how he could manage to take her along with him if he was transferred. Now, that would be ideal.

He didn't regard it as unseemly to think of Hannah and Cimmy Lou at the same time. Gentlemen had always kept mistresses for their personal enjoyment. In Stephen's mind, Cimmy Lou had no effect on his feelings for Hannah, not lessening his devotion in the slightest.

The minute Stephen entered his quarters he pulled off his hat and gloves, hardly breaking stride as he tossed them on a table and headed down the hall to where the faint light shone, shedding his coat as he went. He opened the door and walked in, then stopped cold.

"Why, Majuh Wade, it's so good to see you at last," Cimmy Lou declared in her best imitation of a lady, and sank in a low curtsy.

The metallic gold threads in the gown's bodice glittered in the lamplight, the brown satin shimmering and rustling softly as she straightened. Outrage built within him at the sight of that gown—the one Hannah had worn to that last dinner party before the Apaches captured her—on that coffee-colored body.

"What the hell do you think you're doing in that dress, you damned little slut?! Take it off!" He threw aside the army coat draped over his arm and advanced on the startled girl, too enraged to wait for her to obey. "Dammit, I said take it off!!"

Cimmy Lou took a step backward in alarm, but before she could stop him he grabbed the high bodice and ripped it down the front. Roughly manhandling her, he tore the dress off her, his force sending Cimmy Lou stumbling, wary and half-naked, to one side. Stephen picked up the shredded gown, belatedly noticing its destruction, and clutched it in his hands, desperately holding onto that piece of his wife.

He was slow to hear the scurrying sounds of Cimmy Lou pulling on her plain blue skirt and drab green blouse. The swift tread of her footsteps finally aroused him, and he turned to see her walking to the door, the usual provocative sway of her body stiffened by an angry pride.

"Where are you going?" He frowned in vague confusion.

"I'm leavin'." She yanked open the door.

"Come back here," he ordered, his frown deepening.

She stopped to glare at him. "You don't own me, Majuh. I comes here of my own free will an' I ain't comin' no more."

"Cimmy Lou, wait!" Stephen urged, crossing the room to the door. "I don't want you to leave yet. Look, if it's a new dress you want I'll buy you one."

"I don't want nothin' from you—not anymore." She slammed out of the bedroom.

Instead of slipping out the back the way she always

did, Cimmy Lou went out the front door. She hugged the blanket shawl tightly around her as she hurried across the parade ground at a trot and headed between the long barracks, taking the shortcut home. The deep shadow between the buildings enveloped her in its blackness, forcing her to slow down.

The sudden appearance of a figure directly in her path momentarily frightened her. Then she recognized the man and her heart started beating again, faster and heavier than before. "Leroy Bitterman, you shouldn't pop out of the dark like that. I thought you was an Apache," she muttered angrily, in no mood for him or any man.

"You left the majuh's kinda early t'night, didn't ya?"

"Early or late, it ain't none of yore business." When she tried to walk by him, he sidestepped to block her path again. "Let me by."

"You been goin' there purty regular when yore man's away. I been watchin' . . . and wonderin' what it is you 'do' fo' the majuh in the dark."

"I thought you was watchin'," Cimmy Lou retorted sarcastically, and tried to shoulder past him, but he caught her arms and pulled her against his long, lean frame.

"Why don't you do fo' me what you been doin' fo' him?" His narrow face with its thin mustache moved close to hers.

"You let me go, Leroy Bitterman, else'n I'll scream," she warned through bared teeth.

"No, you won't." He ground his mouth onto her full lips, the pin-sharp whiskers on his upper lip stinging her skin.

Cimmy Lou twisted her head away from his grating kiss. He grabbed a handful of her hair and tugged harshly on the roots to force her back, but the smarting pain only made Cimmy Lou fight him all the harder, kicking at his legs and curling her fingers to claw at his face, incensed that he, too, thought she would stand for such rough treatment. He struck her, cuffing her on the jaw, then hitting her a second time with force.

She stopped fighting suddenly and shut her eyes, offering no resistance when he clamped her face between his hands. "Yore always playin' with men, first one, then another, an' ain't a one of 'em full-blooded enough fo' you or you'd be with him yet. I can show you what it is yore missin'—an' it'll be more than you ever dreamed it could be." She remained silent and passive, motionless and indifferent to his claims, her eyes closed. "Look at me." His hands tightened their viselike grip on her face, but she didn't respond.

Again he kissed her roughly, driving his mouth against her lips, but they stayed slack under his pressure, neither taking nor giving. A groan came from his throat. "Kiss me," he murmured hoarsely, and tried again, rocking his lips across hers.

The anger and frustration that riddled him pleased Cimmy Lou. She'd show him that she wasn't to be mastered—not by him or anyone. A run of quiet satisfaction moved through her when the pressure on her lips ended and he leaned his forehead on hers, dropping his hands to her shoulders.

"There ain't nothin' there." His breathing came in hard, laboring gusts, the sound of it heavy like the beat of his pulse. She opened her knowing eyes to study his face, and the lack of peace in it. "Not fo' me. Not fo' any man. Yore hollow inside. All there is, is them hips of yores."

"If you say so," she mocked him softly, and saw the hot anger come back.

"Yore a she-bitch. That's what you are—a she-bitch dog. I oughta bend you over that rain barrel and mount you the way the dogs do it." He released her with a shove that pushed her backward a step. She waited, her lips parted in unconscious anticipation of what he would do, but he merely looked at her, finally motioning for her to leave. "Git! I don't want you."

"Yore a liar, Leroy Bitterman." Cimmy Lou moved close to him and tilted her head until her face was only inches from his, while she reached down to trail a forefinger up his crotch, unerringly finding his hardened shaft. "You want me." She slid away from him with a silent laugh and disappeared quickly into the black shadows behind him.

On the day they returned to the *rancheria,* Hannah selected a site a discreet distance from Gatita's wickiup and constructed her own dwelling. She constructed the frame of saplings, in a circle, roughly fifteen feet in diameter, then bent them and tied them together in the center, thatching the space in between the poles with yucca leaves. A tanned hide served as a door flap, and Gatita brought her a fire-scorched canvas that had once covered a settler's wagon to stretch around the exterior and keep out the winter drafts.

At first Hannah was reserved in the presence of her former mistress, but she soon realized that Gatita felt secure in her role as Lutero's first wife and confident of his affections. Hannah had witnessed the tenderness of their meeting after the newlyweds returned, Lutero and Gatita standing close together and letting their eyes speak, and knew that she had been a practical choice for a second wife, a means to satisfy his physical needs and provide him with more children.

When an Apache married, he became responsible for his wife's family. If he acquired a second wife, it was usually a sister of the first so that he wouldn't have to support two families. Since Hannah was a captive, Lutero had no such obligation to fulfill on her behalf. She was a highly practical choice, and Gatita appeared willing to accept her as a sister and occasional workmate.

In the mornings after Lutero had spent the night in her *jacal,* Hannah sometimes felt awkward and a trifle guilty when she first saw Gatita, but there was too much work to be done for that self-consciousness to last. In addition to her daily chores, she had to make or obtain many of her household items, although a few were given to her as gifts.

When Hannah approached Cactus Pear's fire to trade some beef she had jerked for the pottery jugs and cups the young divorcée made, the woman was boiling the juice from some root. Hannah couldn't identify the plant source and frowned curiously, aware that Cactus Pear was a *di-yin,* a medicine woman possessing power over pregnancies and births.

"What is this you are making?" she asked, after she had given the tattooed woman the beef and sat crosslegged on the ground beside her.

"It is liquid for washing the mother before baby is born."

"You can help a woman be fertile so that she can have a baby, can't you?" She remembered hearing that power attributed to Cactus Pear in the past.

*"Anh,* yes."

Hannah watched the liquid bubbling in the clay pot. "What if a woman doesn't want to have a baby? Can you help her?"

*"Anh,* it can be done."

"How?"

"There is a potion that can be made from certain rock powders." She couldn't reveal all of her knowledge or she would lose her power.

"Would you make this potion for me?" Hannah was conscious of the inspection by the *bi-zhahn,* so close that it was nearly an exhibition of curiosity.

*"Anh,"* she agreed at last. "I will find the special rocks to make the potion for you."

*"Enju,* it is well." Hannah straightened fluidly and left the woman's fire, preferring to trade the jerked beef for the potion instead of the pottery. She'd seen some of the shamans' medicines work on the wounded when they had all fled Mexico. She was willing to try it.

## CHAPTER 12

"WELL, JOHN T., WHAT DO YOU THINK?" WITHOUT THE aid of the field glasses, Cutter studied the narrow, twisting trail up the steep side of the canyon to the mesa top. Boulders bigger than horses elbowed into the rocky path, squeezing any approach into single file.

The black hands holding the binoculars directed the magnifying lenses from the bottom of the trail on the canyon floor all the way up to the jagged opening on the top. When the long, slow study was completed, Sergeant John T. Hooker lowered the glasses to look at the area again.

"If those Apaches catch us goin' up that trail, it'll be like shootin' tin cans off a fence rail," was his sober judgment as he passed the binoculars back to Cutter.

"That's kinda the way I saw it, too." Cutter absently thrust the glasses at his lieutenant to be returned to their case as he swung away and angled down the graveled slope to the shallow gully where the cavalry patrol rested.

His boots started a tiny avalanche of stones, its clatter echoed by the following footsteps of Lieutenant Sotsworth and Sergeant Hooker. Cutter's blue eyes made a swift study of his dismounted troop, slumped and worn after more than a week away from the fort. Five horses had given out and they had no remounts, which put five of his buffalo soldiers on foot or riding double.

"Do you believe these are the Apaches who stole the agency cattle?" Sotsworth caught up with Cutter and matched his easy, rolling stride as they headed toward the trio of scouts surrounding their recently captured prisoner.

"It would seem likely, Lieutenant." It was a dry response, accompanied by a look that noted the rivulets of perspiration running down the junior officer's temple despite the fact that the afternoon temperature was on the cool side. Cutter guessed that his lieutenant's liquor supply had given out. "John T., picket the horses." He gave the order to his sergeant. "It's a dry camp. No smoke—not even a cigarette. Tell the men to get all the rest they can, 'cause they're going to need it."

A black hand was waved in a careless salute as the sergeant turned away to direct the setting up of camp. Beside Cutter, Sotsworth frowned at the directive.

"Excuse me, sir, our orders were quite clear regarding the pursuit of—"

"I am well aware of the orders," Cutter interrupted in a flat voice. "And, Lieutenant, I don't think even Major Wade would order a charge up that trail in broad daylight."

"Sir, I wasn't suggesting—" Indignant, Sotsworth halted.

Cutter paused, the effects of the long days on the trail

fraying his temper, and settled his glance on the man. "Yes, you were, and I don't give a damn, Sotsworth. You want to grab onto Wade's glory and ride out of this regiment with him. That's fine with me, but just stay out of my way in the meantime."

A dark flush ruddied Sotsworth's skin as he lagged a full step behind Cutter. Nah-tay was one of the three Apache scouts guarding the squaw they'd caught. Cutter joined them, his gaze straying from the scout to the Chiricahua woman of indeterminate age. She watched them all with a mixture of sullen distrust and fear. Cutter had no idea what threats Nah-tay had made to force her to disclose the location of the *rancheria*, and figured it was just as well he didn't.

"Ask her if there's another way to the top. A trail on the other side." One that might be easier, less exposed.

The clipped exchange in Apache was accompanied by a persistent shaking of the woman's head in a negative response. Her high-boned face showed the gauntness of hunger, something her blanket-wrapped, lumpy body concealed. A set of small red lines was tattooed across her forehead, a facial adornment that some bands practiced.

After a lengthy parley, Nah-tay had a simple response. "She say 'no.'"

"Have two of your *nan-tans*—your best scouts—see if they can find another path to the top of that mesa," Cutter ordered in Spanish, then scraped a smooth place in the sandy soil with the edge of his boot. "And get the woman to show us how everything is laid out up there."

The cooperation was grudgingly given, each piece of information dragged from the Apache woman, at the threat of what Cutter neither knew nor cared. He didn't have Nah-tay let up on the interrogation until he was satisfied that there was nothing more of strategic importance to be learned. Hooker joined him in time to hear most of it, crouching beside Cutter and sitting on his heels to study the rough map drawn with a stick in the gravel.

"I guess this means we're goin' up there," Hooker concluded, and tried to keep any opinion from his voice.

"That's right." Cutter used the drawing stick for a pointer. "So far, they don't know we're down here. The squaw swears there aren't any lookouts posted. I'm sure they regard their stronghold as impregnable."

"Ya mean it isn't?" Hooker smiled tiredly.

"Nothing is. As soon as it's dark, we're going up that trail. Presuming we make it to the top without being discovered, we'll deploy the men in skirmish lines." With x's, he marked the approximate positions in relation to the *rancheria*. "At first light, we'll attack. According to the woman, there's only one way up or down that mesa. We'll have them trapped."

"Yes, suh—or they'll have us," Sergeant Hooker pointed out.

"We've been in tough spots before, John T.," Cutter chided, and caught the slash of an answering grin. They understood one another, and shared a mutual respect. They were about as close as a Negro and a white man could get in these times and this military society. And it never quite occurred to either one of them to want more.

No fires meant no coffee and no hot food. The men drank stale water from their canteens and chewed on dry hardtack. No fires meant no warmth to take the place of the sun buttering the horizon, and the chill crept in to numb the body.

The first stars glittered as a handful of troopers was assigned to stay with the horses and the captured squaw, while the rest formed up to climb the trail under the cover of darkness. A quarter moon came out to watch and shed some of its faint light on the expedition, making shadows in the blackness of the boulder-strewn path.

The buffalo soldiers practiced the Apache art of stealth and silence, wrapping their boots in burlap sacking to muffle the sound of their footsteps. Nah-tay and his Apache scouts led the way up the trail, mere shadows flitting from rock to rock. Cutter followed them, with John T. about midway back with the men and Sotsworth bringing up the rear.

Tension magnified each sound—the roll of a stone became a resounding clatter—or it altered the pitch, to transform the hoot of a night-hunting owl into the hollow call of an Apache warrior. Winter nights on the desert were chilly, but sweat beaded on black and white skins alike. Fear had a way of playing tricks on a man when he didn't know what was waiting for him in the darkness, when he felt eyes watching him that he couldn't see. It dried his mouth and tightened his stomach and roughened his breathing. It strained his senses until the pounding of his own heart, the smell of his own body, and the taste of his own sweat drowned out practically everything else.

They reached the top undetected and lay in wait for first light, silent huddles of men, listening, looking, and thinking of the morrow. As soon as there was enough light to see, Cutter gave the signal to attack, beginning with a rush at the first loose cluster of wickiups.

At the first sound of gunfire, disbelief paralyzed Hannah. She stared in the direction of the reverberating explosion, the carnage of the Mexican attack too fresh in her mind. It couldn't be happening again, when the wounds of the last raid had barely healed and their bellies were only now growing full again!

Lutero ducked into the wickiup and came out with his new Spencer rifle and the repeating Winchester.

Hannah was galvanized into action when Gatita pushed the cradleboard, with Sleepy strapped securely in it, into her arms and shoved her in the opposite direction of the gunfire. A war woman before her pregnancy, Gatita took up the fighting again and went with her husband to cover the flight of their small band.

All around, women and children were scurrying to escape. The trail was the only way Hannah knew off the mesa, and it was blocked by the enemy. Some of the fugitives went that way, obviously hoping to slip behind their attackers. Hannah looked for a place where she and Sleepy could hide until the fighting and killing were over, as they had done the last time.

With the sound of sporadic gunfire in her ears, she ran across the undulating plateau dotted with juniper and scrub oak. A half mile from the *rancheria,* she found a fall of dead timber and crawled into it, trying to drag the leaf-brittle branches around them.

Long after the shooting stopped, she lay there in a repeat of the nightmare, listening to the rustle of men moving about and completing the mopping-up operations. Distantly she heard voices, but she listened only to judge how close they were, how still she and the infant had to be to escape detection.

The Ghost Face season had colored everything tan and brown. The dead branches and limbs were a many-hued collection of browns and grays. The natural tones of her buckskin clothes let Hannah blend into the earth, and she covered her head and the cradleboard with the charcoal wool of the blanket, breathing in the same air her breath warmed and inhaling the strong earth smells.

The swishing of someone walking through the tall, dead grass around the fall of timber tensed her nerves. Her body hugged tighter to the ground, half-curled in a protective arc around the cradleboard. Hannah cautiously lifted an edge of the blanket hooding her head and face and managed to peer out with one eye. All she could see was the blue pantlegs of a soldier's uniform as he moved cautiously through the grass.

Sleepy made a sucking sound as he chewed on his fist. It was a very small sound, but Hannah saw the legs stop and remain motionless. Carefully she let the edge of the blanket down and held her breath, willing the baby into silence. Seconds later, she felt the ground vibrate under the thud of feet approaching the fall of timber, then a brief stillness came.

A branch was lifted aside and something jabbed at her leg. "Awright, we sees ya. *Vámanos,* come on outta there," a voice ordered.

Turning onto her side with an arm resting protectively on the cradleboard, Hannah looked warily into the dark faces of the two Negro soldiers, their rifles aimed directly at her. "Do not shoot. We cannot harm you," she responded automatically in Spanish, pleading with them not to hurt her or the baby. There was a blankness in her comprehension: she saw the uniforms, but not the U.S. Army insignia; she understood their words, but didn't realize what language they were spoken in.

When one of them reached out a hand to touch her, Hannah lifted her arm in a defensive gesture. The blanket slipped, showing more of her face beneath its draping hood.

"Hey, Kirby, she don't look like no 'pache to me. Does she to you?" the heavy-lipped soldier queried his buddy, a taller, blacker man.

"She sho' don't," the second man agreed as he bent closer to study a cringing and wary Hannah. Something kept telling her to be afraid of them, not to let them touch her, even as her fear was receding.

"I think we got ourselves one of them *señoritas.*

Better go tell the sergeant we found ourselves a Mexican captive," the first one said, then began crooning to her as his partner hurried back toward the *rancheria.* "We ain't gonna hurt ya, *señorita.* You jest come along outta there." His long black fingers with their inner pinkness beckoned to her, urging her to come out.

But it was his voice, the thick southern accent, that began to sink into her consciousness. Frowning, Hannah picked up the cradleboard and scooted slowly free of the timber fall, her eyes watching him. She began noticing details, the Union blue of the uniform, the insignia.

"Sir?" The English word coming from her lips sounded strange, but she went on, a daring hope building inside. "What is your regiment? Is it the Ninth?"

His brows pulled together in a frown of incredulity. "Be you a white woman?"

"Your commanding officer?" She looked toward the *rancheria.* "Where is he? Take me to him. Now." Her voice grew firmer, an old authority coming through.

"Yes, ma'am." Stiffly, the proud soldier swung around to escort her to the temporary field headquarters at the overrun Apache camp.

The cigar Cutter had been waiting to smoke all night and morning was between his lips, and he savored the taste and feel of it. The wounded were being patched and bandaged by Private Grover. Hooker left him to approach his commanding officer.

"How many casualties, John T.?" Cutter jerked his head in the direction of the wounded men.

"Four. All flesh wounds, Grover says." The sergeant confirmed that their losses were light, but didn't pause. "These Apaches had a Mexican captive. House is bringin' her in. You speak their lingo, Cap'n. Might be good if you come along."

"Sure." Cutter swung into step beside him.

Through the spiraling smoke of his cigar, he saw the trooper escorting a female captive. She carried an infant strapped in an Apache cradleboard in her arms. Something about her—the way she moved, the way she carried herself—bothered him. It wasn't until they were a few feet apart that he felt the kick of discovery go through him. Stopping short, he stared into her clear brown eyes, and slowly removed the cigar from his mouth.

"Hannah—" It was the way he'd come to think of her. After the initial check of his impulsive familiarity, Cutter let it carry him. "Hannah Wade."

"Captain . . . Jake Cutter, isn't it?" Her dark eyes seemed extraordinarily bright. Then she touched a hand to the rough shawl, self-consciously aware of her blanket and buckskin attire. She straightened with a dignity that Cutter was sure few women could match. "They . . . they took all my clothes."

A smile gentled his hard-etched features. "Don't apologize for your appearance, Mrs. Wade. We weren't even sure you were alive anymore." His voice was made husky by the emotions tightening in him.

"My husband . . . Stephen . . . is he well?" An awkwardness seemed to claim her as she struggled with the question.

"Yes, he's in good health." Cutter could have added that Wade was mourning her and missing her, but for some reason he didn't. His attention shifted to the black-haired infant in the cradleboard, and a muscle flexed in his jaw. "Is the child yours?" The question sounded remarkably detached.

"No." Her answer came automatically; then she looked at him, realizing what his thoughts had been. Cutter didn't meet her glance as he kept all expression from his face and indifferently studied the Apache boy-child. "He is Lutero's son. Lutero and his wife, Gatita."

"I suggest we give him to one of the captured Apache women," Cutter said, and turned to Hooker. "Sergeant, have one of your men take the child over with the rest of the Apache captives."

The sergeant stepped forward to take the baby from her, briefly meeting her glance before centering his attention on the child. She gave the baby into Hooker's care, displaying only a faint reluctance to surrender her small charge to him. Her gaze followed them as the sergeant carried the infant away.

"The Apaches will look after the baby," Cutter said to assure her. "His parents may be among the prisoners." Although he didn't recall seeing Lutero in the bunch.

"Of course." She rubbed her hands over her arms, and Cutter sensed the nervousness that was just below the surface.

The blanket that had hooded her head slipped to her shoulders, and the sunlight fired the hidden red tones in her dark hair. It was smoothed back from her face, a headband circling it, and coiled into two vertical loops at the base of her neck. The style suited her, at once sleek and contained, yet primitive in its simplicity.

"We've boiled some coffee. Would you like a cup?" He gestured in the general direction of the camp's center, where the casualties were being treated and a hot meal was being cooked, the first in two days.

"Yes, I would. It's been a long time since I've had any *tu-dishishn*, black water." There was a brief softening of the tension around her mouth, something akin to humor tugging at it.

"It's camp coffee, so it's likely to be strong," Cutter warned as he swung around to walk on her right. She didn't stroll across the enclave as she once would have, but strode like an Apache, taking long, fluid steps instead of the sedate, measured walk of a lady.

Cutter's glance briefly touched on the two troopers with firebrands heading toward the *jacals*. It was standard procedure to torch the brush-thatched dwellings of the Apache, to burn their homes and supplies, thus driving them onto the reservations. Cutter took note of their actions merely as a detached observance that orders were being followed.

"What are they doing?" Hannah demanded when she saw the first of the colored soldiers approach a wickiup, a torch in his hand.

"Setting fire to the huts." His tone dismissed the activity as being of minor significance.

"No!" Her protest was strident and angry as she glared at him. "You have to stop them. You can't let them do it!"

A frown darkened his face, and deepened as she broke into a run to go stop the soldiers herself. Her long, muscled legs flashed with a sheen of golden bronze, the side-slash of the buckskin skirt showing her bare thighs above the tall moccasins. Within a half dozen strides, he'd caught her, but she was stronger than he'd expected and Cutter found that he had his hands full trying to keep her from breaking free.

"Mrs. Wade. Hannah!" He was harsh with her as she twisted and strained to break loose, fighting him with a wildness that was difficult to contain. "We have orders to burn them!"

Beyond them, flames crackled, catching hungrily at the dry brush thatching the dome-shaped native huts. Within seconds, the smell of smoke stung their nostrils. She suddenly abandoned her resistance to clutch at him.

"You've got to stop them!" She appealed again for his help, raw desperation in her expression. "All our food, everything is in there! You can't burn us out again!"

"Hannah, stop it. Stop it!" Understanding was a cold weight in his stomach. "You aren't one of them! You aren't an Apache!" Cutter shook her with jarring roughness and watched the comprehension finally dawn in her eyes.

All the fight left her as Hannah bent her head down and away from him. She felt lost and confused, caught somewhere in the limbo between what she was and what she had been. She had forgotten how to act, how to walk, what to think, what to say. It was a long way from being an Apache woman to being an officer's lady. The things that had happened to her suddenly made Hannah doubt that she could be the same person again.

Quietly he asked, "How about some of that coffee now, Mrs. Wade?"

She felt the light pressure of his hands through the buckskin sleeves covering her upper arms; a faint throbbing remained where they had gripped her moments ago. Her glance lifted from the brass buttons of his uniform to his rough-hewn features, the look of his blue eyes keenly measuring.

"I'd like that fine," she agreed quietly to his second invitation for coffee. Her composure regained, she turned from him to walk toward the campfire.

A self-consciousness stayed with her, not allowing her to be completely at ease with her escorting officer. At the fire, Hannah sank gracefully to her knees, rocking back to sit on her heels in a position that had become natural to her over the past months. It was only when Cutter brought her a tin mug of coffee and squatted low, balancing on the balls of his feet, that she realized it was unladylike to sit on the ground. But it seemed pointless to move now.

She peered at him across the lip of her cup, wondering what he must be thinking of her. Nothing showed in his face, deep sun-creases splaying from the outer corners of his eyes. Beyond him, smoke billowed as fire engulfed the nearest wickiup. The sight caught her glance and held it for long seconds until she became aware of Cutter watching her.

"Almost two months ago, the Mexican army attacked the *rancheria*." She stared into the bitter black brew that was camp coffee, old grounds boiled and boiled until only acid and oil remained to flavor the water. "They burned everything . . . our winter food, our blankets and clothing, weapons, baskets, pottery—everything. Even the mutilated bodies of some of our dead." She spoke in the personal pronoun again. At the time, she had been one of them; the incident had happened to her. "They—the soldiers slaughtered everything in sight, butchering like animals. The stench of the place after they'd gone . . . the death smell—" Hannah shuddered in remembrance.

"I see." It was a taut but noncommital response.

And the vagueness of it flashed through Hannah like a white-hot spark through kindling. "Do you?" she challenged suddenly. "When I saw those uniforms, I went running to them, certain that at last I would be saved. But all they wanted to do was kill—women, children, white, Apache; they didn't care." The burst of anger was quickly spent, and she lowered her gaze again to the battered tin mug and her work-roughened hands.

"And they tried to kill you," Cutter guessed.

"Yes." She sighed and passed a hand in front of her eyes, trying to free herself from that remembered terror. "I got away and hid. They chased us for days. We had nothing to eat and nothing to keep us warm."

"It's over now," he said.

"Yes." Hannah pressed a hand to her forehead. "I've waited so long." A sob was in her throat and her eyes

203

were full of tears, but she kept both choked down, along with her fear that maybe it was too long.

"Something kept telling me you'd make it, Mrs. Wade." The directness of Cutter's gaze when she straightened was oddly soothing. "It's hard to break a strong spirit." After taking a last swallow from his coffee cup, he emptied the dregs in the sand and pushed himself to his feet. "We'll be pulling out in an hour or so to head back to the fort with our prisoners. We're short of mounts and equipment, so we'll be using the Apache ponies. If you don't object, I'll assign one to you."

"Not at all, Captain. By now, I'm used to riding them."

All the surrounding wickiups were ablaze, and the troopers were returning to the *rancheria* in pairs. Hannah watched Cutter walk back to the cookfire, where a colored soldier was scraping green mold off a slab of bacon. He left the tin mug with the cook as he went on to confer with his subordinates and see to the last details of the operation. Hannah was glad of these minutes alone to adjust to this sudden change of circumstances and the subsequent conflict of identity. It had all happened so fast.

An hour later, Hannah was sitting astride a sand-brown-and-white pinto and holding the reins. No side-saddle, no voluminous riding skirt for her now. She had vaulted agilely onto the horse's back, unaided. It had not occurred to her to wait for assistance in mounting.

The split sides of the buckskin skirt showed the sun-browned skin of her knees and thighs, lean-muscled and firm. During the long months she'd lived with the Apache, Hannah had lost much of the con-sciousness of her body. It didn't come back until she saw the way the young lieutenant was staring at her legs. With a heated remembrance, she recalled that in civilized society, only loose women showed their limbs. In her situation, though, there was little she could do about it. Hannah sat straighter on the paint horse and held her head a little higher.

Cutter came riding up from the rear of the split column and checked his horse when he neared Hannah, bringing it to a side-dancing halt. "Would you care to ride with me, Mrs. Wade?"

"Yes, thank you." She kicked her horse forward with a moccasined heel, usurping the lieutenant's place and leaving him to ride with the sergeant.

The Apache scouts formed a scattered advance wedge ahead of the column. Cutter raised his hand and signaled the troops to move out. "Column, ho!" came the sergeant's shout, the words drawn out in the familiar rhythm of army commands. All around them were the burnt-out shells of the *rancheria* buildings, their timbers still smoldering and smoking.

With their Apache captives on foot, the very young and the very old alike, their pace was necessarily slow. The severely wounded among them were transported on travois. Hannah tried not to think about the men, women, and children being herded like animals in the middle of the column. Her own treatment at their hands had not always been humane. But she wanted to forget that, and she wanted to forget them. She wanted to blot the past months out of her memory. She wanted to stop this warring ambivalence.

"At this pace, I'm afraid we won't make it to the fort until midday tomorrow." The campaign hat was pulled low on Cutter's forehead, the wide brim shading his rough, angular profile. "I'm sorry I can't spare a detachment of men to escort you back ahead of the column."

"I understand, Captain." She almost welcomed the delay, and wasn't sure why.

That night they bivouacked near the mouth of Hell's

Canyon on the Gila River. All remaining supplies were used to fill the empty bellies of soldier and prisoner alike. When it came time to distribute the food among the Apache captives, Hannah accompanied the Negro cook and his helper. The black sergeant named Hooker stayed nearby with half a dozen soldiers standing guard. As the food was dished out, she looked to see which members of the band had been caught and who had escaped. Gatita was there, *Go-yath-khla* strapped to the cradleboard on her back. She gave Hannah a stony-faced look and went on.

"He isn't here."

Hannah stiffened when Cutter spoke mere inches behind her. His words caused a break in her rhythm as she spooned beans onto a corn tortilla. She didn't pretend ignorance of his meaning, nor protest when he motioned for one of the troopers to take her place in the chow line, dispensing the meager servings.

His hand cupped her elbow as he guided her out of the prisoner encampment toward the glowing heat of a fire beneath the stark cottonwood skeletons. "Lutero escaped." Cutter was more specific in his statement. "He wasn't one of the Apaches we killed in this morning's attack either."

"You know, don't you? How?" Her voice was low, but her face was smooth.

"The scouts interrogated some of the prisoners. They told that Lutero had taken you as his woman," he stated. "I don't think you could have kept it a secret, Mrs. Wade. That wouldn't be like you."

"But what am I, Captain?" she mused wryly.

"A woman who survived what few could."

"Thank you." Darkness enfolded them as they walked. Her steps slowed as her gaze turned to the night's shadows that surrounded them, and Hannah realized that this experience, this ordeal would never allow her to feel completely secure again. She stopped underneath the cottonwoods; overhead, their branches made a web against the night sky.

"It's hard to believe I'm going home." A tremor of relief rippled through her, suddenly washing out all the rigid supports that held her emotions in check. Tears of relief and muted happiness welled in her eyes. "I'm sorry . . . it's just that after all this time, it's so good." The apology and the explanation became all tangled.

"Considering all you've been through, Mrs. Wade, I would have been worried if you hadn't cried," Cutter said.

His easy acceptance of her need for the release tears would bring allowed Hannah to give way to them. His arms went around her and he gathered her loosely to him, while she cried softly at the rare pleasure of something good happening to her.

He breathed in the sweet fragrance of her hair while the heat of her body and the vague pressure of it against him made their impressions on him. The night had a sharp edge to it, and every whisper of sound was a song. Cutter stood stock-still.

"Your husband is a very lucky man, Mrs. Wade." The thickened words were low and faintly gruff.

The close-paired figures under the trees made a dark silhouette, which John T. let his glance linger on. A lot could be read into Cutter's rigid tension, the hands that wouldn't stroke or comfort. With a small, wry shake of his head, John T. turned away from the sight and reached down to pick up a burning stick from the campfire to light his pipe. Sotsworth sat sprawled atop his bedroll, a wicker jug of Apache *tizwin* beer grasped loosely by the neck, obviously a spoil of this morning's foray and obviously partially consumed. He stared at the couple in the tree shadows.

"How many Apache bucks do you suppose she's had,

Hooker?" Sotsworth took another swig of the native beer. "I'll bet she's developed a craving for it by now."

"If I were you, I wouldn't speculate about such things in front of the captain." Hooker clamped his teeth on the pipe stem and sucked to draw the flame into the tobacco-packed bowl. "But I never did think you was any too bright, Lieutenant."

# CHAPTER 13

THE PAINT HORSE STEPPED HIGH AND TOSSED ITS HEAD, catching the eagerness of its rider as they approached the collection of adobe buildings. Cutter's easy-striding cavalry mount kept pace with the Apache pony Hannah rode. Tension stiffened her spine and squared her shoulders and put a shining light in her eyes. Her calico headband still encircled her head, its faded dark blue pointing up the luster of hcr thick hair the color of burnt sienna. She still wore it Apache-style, smoothed back into the twin loops secured by an oddly shaped piece of leather. The way she sat her horse, the way she held her head, everything about her reminded Cutter of her deep pride and strong will.

Earlier, Cutter had sent a galloper ahead to alert the fort to the patrol's return and specifically to inform Major Wade of his wife's rescue. Cutter noticed the way her lips lay softly together, tremulous and ready to smile at the first glimpse of her husband. He knew that

209

Hannah wanted to break this slow pace, but he also understood why she didn't leave the column and ride ahead of them; she disliked arriving dressed the way she was—like an Indian. So her pace remained sedate, and the distance to the fort slowly narrowed.

As they rode into the quadrangle, Cutter spotted Stephen Wade standing at the edge of a long adobe's shade. He swore under his breath at the damned black armband Wade continued to wear around his sleeve. All around them, work details paused to gawk at the Apache-dressed white woman, an officer's wife straddling an Indian pony's back, her bare legs showing. An apron-clad black soldier stood in the doorway of the bakery, watching them pass.

After turning over command of the column and the captured Apaches to his lieutenant, Cutter veered his horse toward the adobe where the major waited, and Hannah kept her pony abreast of the bay. Other officers stood well back in the adobe's shade, keeping a discreet distance.

As they rode up to the *ramada*, Wade stepped out to meet them and grasped the rawhide rein close to the jaw of Hannah's pinto. Disbelief and doubt seemed to lurk in his expression while he scanned the bronze-skinned woman on the horse.

"Stephen!" The smile she'd held back for so long finally broke across her lips as she swung one leg over and slipped off the brown-spotted horse.

Cutter dismounted and took the pinto's rein from Hannah, unwillingly watching their meeting. Wade placed his hands very tentatively on her shoulders, while his running gaze seemed to pick her apart, from the sweatband around her forehead and the double coil of burnished hair at the nape of her neck to the buckskin clothes and the sun-browned skin.

"Hannah, it is you." The words were breathed out,

and Cutter wanted to yell at him to take her into his arms. Couldn't Wade see the way she was straining toward him? Couldn't he see the ache in her eyes?

The moment seemed trapped forever; then Stephen's arms were hauling her into his embrace and Hannah was crushed against him, breathlessly laughing and crying with joy. Her own hands found their way around his wide shoulders so that she could hold onto him with the same clutching fervency.

Finally Stephen pulled back and cupped her head in his hands, framing her face while his restless gaze inspected it again. "We'll go to our quarters. They've been so empty without you. I know you want to get rid of those squaw clothes . . . and you'll want to bathe, wash the smell of those savages off you." His attention swung from her to Cutter as his hands came down to clasp both of hers. Hannah felt the swirl of his energy all around her. "Cutter, have someone fetch Cimmy Lou to our quarters."

"Yes, sir." Cutter lifted a booted foot into the stirrup and remounted his horse, then paused to touch the brim of his hat and nod to Hannah.

"Thank you, Captain." She smiled up at him, seeing little details: the thick black line of his brows, the crookedness of his nose, and the hidden things in his keen blue eyes. His lips widened briefly in response, and Hannah remembered how his steady calm and easy silence had comforted and reassured her.

"Fetch Doc Griswald, too," Stephen ordered, his gaze coming back to Hannah. Before she could protest that nothing was the matter with her, he said, "We'd better have him check you over and make sure you aren't suffering from something."

"I'm not. I'm fine—now." Now that she was here with him.

His fingers tightened around her hands before Stephen was distracted by the crunch of gravel under the hooves of Cutter's horse as the captain turned to leave with the pinto horse in tow. "I want to speak to you later, Captain. I'll be at my quarters."

"Yes, sir." Cutter saluted and reined his mount away from the couple.

In his side vision, Cutter saw them start toward Officers' Row, but they were soon out of his view as he rode to the infirmary. Like everyone else, curiosity had brought Dr. Benjamin Rutledge Griswald outside. Cutter saluted him, but remained in the saddle.

"Major Wade would like you to come over to his quarters and examine his wife," he said, relaying the request.

"I figured as much when I saw her ride in with you." Griswald nodded and picked up the black satchel sitting on the ground by his feet. "I expect after her being with the Apaches, she isn't right in the head. Sad thing. A refined woman like her."

"I think you'll find she's sound of mind—and body," Cutter asserted tersely and saluted again, then swung his horse away from the adobe building, tugging on the pinto's rein for the animal to follow.

Along Suds Row, ragtag pickaninnies played behind the tent houses. The boys were wielding sticks as if they were sabers and charging at imaginary Apaches crawling along the encroaching desert. They came running up when they saw Cutter leading a real Indian pony. A tolerant smile edged Cutter's hard mouth. Until the captured Apaches were taken to the reservation, he knew they'd have trouble with the young 'uns slipping around to get an up-close look at some of the "savages" their daddies had fought, and to get a good scare, too.

In front of the third tent, Cutter halted his horse and swung down. He picked out the oldest child in the encircling group, a girl of about ten with rag ribbons tying the ends of her much-braided hair, and handed the horses' reins to her. "Don't let them loose," he said in a mock warning, amused by her ear-to-ear smile; she was so proud to be chosen over the boys.

The door flap was tied open and Cutter ducked through, automatically removing his wide-brimmed campaign hat and combing his fingers through the unruly thickness of his black hair where the crown had flattened it. His glance skipped by the crudely made pieces of furniture to the iron stove where a flatiron heated and Cimmy Lou stood, so dark against the light walls. An iron was in her hand, poised above the half-ironed shirt lying atop a cloth-cushioned board.

"Well, if it ain't Cap'n Cutter come to call." Her drawl mocked the way he came to a stop just inside the opening. The iron was returned to the stove to stay hot while she moved away from the ironing board to cross the room.

Cutter straightened, his body rearing slightly away from Cimmy Lou's potent beauty with her fine, high-boned features, luminous jet-black eyes, and softly full lips. The dark kerchief around her hair made a cameo of her face.

"I saw the patrol come in, but I shore never expected you to beat John 'T'. here." When she cocked her head to the side to taunt him, Cutter saw a faint bruise purpling the flesh along her jaw, nearly invisible against her coffee-brown skin.

"Who hit you?" At his demand, she immediately turned her head to conceal the discoloration, but Cutter laid his fingers against her chin and turned it back.

"Nobody. I ran into a post," she answered sulkily.

"And what was the post's name?" he queried derisively.

"Always so clever, ain't you, Cap'n?" She laughed

and drew away from him, uncaring of what she'd admitted.

A hard anger made him tight-lipped. "Someday John T. is going to kill a man over you and wind up on the gallows before he realizes you aren't worth it."

"How do you know? Maybe I am." Wickedness danced in her eyes. "It ain't my fault he's gone for weeks—months at a time. A girl gets lonely." Always she flirted with him, baiting Cutter with her body and watching to see if he'd rise to the lure. "And don't try to convince me John T. wouldn't find hisself some 'company' if'n he had the chance. 'Course, it's okay for him."

"Mrs. Hooker—"

"Why don't you never call me Cimmy Lou like everybody else does, Cap'n Cutter?"

"Mrs. Hooker, Major Wade requested that you be sent to his quarters. As you already know, we brought Mrs. Wade back with us, and the major would like you to be of assistance to her," he stated.

"Fo' a white woman, she didn't look no worse fo' wear. Maybe she found out it wasn't so bad after all. Did she talk about what-all they did to her?"

Cutter swung away in disgust. "The major is expecting you."

She laid a long-fingered hand on his arm, halting him. "Ain't you gonna pick up yore laundry while yore here, Cap'n?" she asked in a silkily innocent voice.

After a split second's hesitation, Cutter pivoted back, a closed expression on his hard and trail-weary features. "Yes, I will."

With a swing of her hips, she sashayed across the earthen floor to the piles of neatly folded clothes. "That'll be five dollahs fo' the month." She came back, cradling the stack of his clothes in her arms. The gold coin was between his fingers, his hand extended toward her offering the payment. "My hands are full," she reminded him, her look and gesture provocative. She turned at right angles to him, standing close to give him a clear view of the deep cleavage between her upthrust breasts. "Why don't you do like all the rest of the officers an' put the money in my private bank?"

It was a challenge, a husky taunt that said she knew he wouldn't do it. Cutter made a two-fingered drop straight down the middle, barely brushing the firmly rounded skin. Then he took the bundle of clothing from her arms. She looked disappointed, while trying to hide it.

"I don't know if'n I'll ever figure you out, Cap'n," she declared. "Most of yore white officers gots to feel around a little before they find the bank. What makes you so high an' mighty? White men have been messin' 'round with colored gals ever since they found out the color don't rub off."

"Good day, Mrs. Hooker." He pushed his hat onto his head, nodding curtly.

"I guess it bothers you that I ain't lettin' you do the chasin'. Let me tell you somethin' about women, Cap'n, colored or white. You men think you do the chasin' an' the winnin'. But there wouldn't be no chasin' if we didn't surrender. You'd never catch a woman less'n she made up her mind to let ya. So ya see, she always gets what she wants."

"What is it you want me to see?"

"John T. thinks yore somethin' special, but I say yore jest a man."

"Maybe, or maybe it's something as simple as having more respect for your husband than you do, Mrs. Hooker." This time Cutter stepped out of the tent and crossed to the young girl holding the horses.

With the freshly laundered clothes tucked under his arm, he swung into the McClellan and searched with his toe for the other stirrup. Cimmy Lou sauntered over to his horse, looking at him as she started stroking a hand slowly along his thigh.

"How long you been out on patrol, Cap'n?" she teased, noticing the taut flexing of his leg muscles. His horse sensed the hot agitation that fired his blood, and danced nervously. "Why do you suppose yore horse is gettin' all excited?" She laughed.

Her throaty laughter followed him as Cutter caught up the braided rawhide rein of the pinto and rode away with it in tow. Halfway down Suds Row, he met John T. on his way home. The black sergeant saw the laundry under his arm, and a closed-up look came over his face. Cutter gave a cursory response to Hooker's salute, and continued toward the stables. Out of the corner of his eye, he saw John T. start walking a little faster toward his makeshift dwelling. And Cutter damned that woman; he damned her to hell for twisting a man up like that.

It was all so sweetly familiar. Hannah moved slowly through the rooms, her fingers trailing over precious objects—so many little discoveries to make, so many little things she'd forgotten, but she had only to see an item again to recall it afresh. When her circle of the parlor was complete, she stopped in front of Stephen. A wondrous feeling of moving through time claimed her.

"It's all exactly the way you left it," Stephen told her with an encompassing gesture. "Not a thing has been moved."

This demonstration of devotion and loyalty touched her. She gazed at him, seeing in his face the changes that the room did not show. With the tips of her fingers, she traced the gauntness of his cheeks.

"You've lost some weight," she murmured as he

caught at her hand and lowered it. She studied his face, the glitter of gold in the tobacco-brown of his mustache. The thick sweep of his lashes hid his eyes from her, but she sensed that he was looking at her hand. Its calloused roughness was a far cry from the velvety-soft texture it had once had. Then Stephen lifted his head and she felt the hard thrust of his gaze, so intense and probing.

"Did they hurt you?" he demanded in a voice made harsh by raw feelings.

She shut out the horror of her own memories to reassure him. "I'm all right now." Her body swayed toward him, wanting his kiss, needing it.

She pressed her fingers to his lips as he tightly shut his eyes, as if in fervent prayer. He spoke against her desert-chapped hands. "Sometimes I thought I would never see you again."

"I know," Hannah said gently, surprising him with her answer.

"How?"

"The armband. Or has someone died in your family?"

"No one died." Stephen released her and drew away to remove the black cloth from around his sleeve, all his attention becoming rapt in it. "This was my reminder of you. You were always with me. Wherever I went, whatever I did, I carried the thought of you. Whatever pain and grief I endured, I knew that it was small compared to what you must be suffering." He paused to look at her. "Does that make sense?" Then he seemed to see her, and all that restless, intense energy was channeled into another subject. "We've got to get you out of those clothes. Where is that Cimmy Lou to help you with your bath? I had my striker put water on to heat. You wait here."

Alone, Hannah turned back into the center of the

room and caught a glimpse of her reflection in the wall mirror. She stared at it. The image of the woman the Apaches knew as Coloradas gazed back at her, clad in hand-sewn buckskins, curl-toed moccasins, and a colored headband around her forehead. Her skin was so brown, and her eyes were so dark. Yet Hannah recognized herself.

She remembered the last time she'd looked in this mirror; it had been the night of the Sloanes' party, but the face of that other woman seemed to belong to a stranger, even though the features were the same. All the things in the parlor were familiar to her—except the remembered image of that other Hannah. During her captivity, she had forced herself to remember objects, acquaintances, places, details about Stephen; but she had forgotten what she used to think and feel, what she had wanted, what she once believed. She wasn't sure anymore who that well-bred, well-schooled, and blissfully ignorant woman was.

Hannah turned away from the mirror and faced the parlor, a room meant to hold lavender scents and silks and the rustle of long skirts—not crushed mint and buckskins and the cat-footed silence of moccasins. In so many ways she hadn't changed—not in her loyalties nor in her love for Stephen—yet an uneasy feeling plagued her. She couldn't be that other woman anymore. She didn't know her.

When Cimmy Lou Hooker came to the back entrance of their quarters, Stephen's striker, Delancy, showed her through. Hannah had forgotten how much water was needed to fill the copper tub; the amount seemed prodigious after her desert existence with the Apaches. Luxuriating in the bath, she forgot her nudity in the pleasurable sensation of immersing her body in so much water. She didn't display any of the modesty she would have shown before with servants present.

"Miz Wade, where'd you get them scars? Did them

Apaches do that to you?" Cimmy Lou stared at the burn marks gouged into the skin below her collarbone.

"Yes." She covered the marks with the large bath sponge. Time had dulled the memory of that sharp-searing pain, but not the sight of the red-hot stick coming at her. "I tried to run away once," Hannah admitted in an emotionless voice. "They punished me."

"I bet you didn't try to escape from them again."

"Only once." Hannah dipped the sponge in the soapy water, then raised it and squeezed the liquid over her outstretched arm. "When the Mexican army attacked the *rancheria,* I tried to give myself up to the soldiers so they could bring me back. But they thought I was an Apache and tried to kill me."

It was good to talk, to release some of the words. It let some of the horror out. And Hannah knew that the colored woman's questions were only the first of many that would soon be asked by others. This was merely practice, she thought wryly.

"Well, yore as brown as one, that's fo' shore." Cimmy Lou shook out a toweling blanket and held it up for Hannah to step into as she climbed out of the copper tub. "How'd you get like that, all over?"

"They took away my clothes." The towel was wrapped around to swaddle the full length of her.

Cimmy Lou stopped rubbing her down. "Every stitch?"

"Every stitch," Hannah answered flatly. The knock that came at the bedroom door was a welcome intrusion. "Yes?"

"Doctor Griswald is here." Stephen's voice came from the other side.

"I'll only be a moment." She turned to Cimmy Lou, concerned now with the task of making herself presentable. "My robe, Cimmy Lou."

After donning a minimum of underclothes, Hannah

slipped on the long robe and tied the sash snugly around her waist. Freed of its ribbon, her auburn hair tumbled loosely about her shoulders as she crossed the room to the hall door and opened it.

"Please come in, Doctor Griswald." The army surgeon and her husband were conversing in low tones in the narrow hallway. They stopped abruptly when she spoke, and Hannah felt the doctor's close scrutiny. She was becoming uneasy with the way everyone was watching her, as if expecting to see something, some mark of her captivity perhaps.

"Your face is thinner," Doc Griswald announced, and tilted his head back to look at her up close through his bifocals. "It appears you've lost weight. Your color looks good though, even with that tanning from the sun."

"I am feeling well," Hannah insisted as he walked past her into the bedroom, his medical bag banging against his leg. Actually she'd had more rest in the last two days than she was accustomed to having in a week, and more food and water, too.

Stephen smiled at her, but remained out in the hallway. "You're beginning to resemble the Hannah I married." The look in his eyes was as warm as the low comment. "I'll leave you in Doctor Griswald's capable hands."

"Miz Wade, what you want me t'do with these buckskins?" Cimmy Lou inserted.

"Burn them." The order came from Stephen, quick and firm, before Hannah had a chance to speak. "Burn the moccasins, everything."

Hannah didn't like the hard set of his jaw, the sudden blaze of light in his eyes; she remembered the temper that boiled behind them. But she held her peace, turning instead to the colored laundress to confirm, "Yes, burn them, Cimmy Lou."

"Whatever you wants, Miz Wade." She shrugged to indicate that it made no difference to her and picked up the naturally tanned leather garments, folding them loosely over her arm. "You be needin' me fo' anythin' else, Miz Wade?"

"No, you may go." Hannah dismissed the woman and walked to the dresser, where the doctor had spread open his black satchel. Again, she felt herself the target of his close attention.

The minute the door closed behind Cimmy Lou and they were alone, the doctor inquired, "What's the date today, Mrs. Wade?"

The question startled her, especially the tone in which it was asked; he seemed determined to trip her up in some way. "I don't know," she replied. "I haven't asked anyone. It's late winter, the season the Apaches call Ghost Face, and it's almost the time of Little Eagles, which I think is early spring—so it might be February . . . of 1877." The answer was the most complete one she could give him.

"Well, it doesn't appear that you're addle-witted," he concluded, and took out his stethoscope.

In the hallway outside, Cimmy Lou turned away from the bedroom door and started for the kitchen. Stephen followed her, his stride quick and determined. "Is she all right?"

She answered him over her shoulder, half angry and half mocking. "If'n yore askin' me if I could tell how many of them 'paches she bedded, once a field's been plowed it's purty hard to know who done the plowin'." Cimmy Lou chucked the buckskin clothing in a box that was kept in the kitchen for garbage. "I do know they took her clothes from her an' made her go 'round naked as the day she was born fo' awhile. It's fo' shore she ain't pure an' white no more." She swung around to give him a knowing look, smug and self-satisfied that she was getting back at him through his precious wife. "You been wantin' her back an' she's here. Now we'll see how you like it."

Stephen took a step toward her, then stopped, his body rigid. "You don't know what you're talking about. You're only saying it because you're jealous."

"She's welcome to you." Her short laugh mocked the arrogance of his assumption. "'Course, there's the other thing. With her bein' without clothes for so long, her body's almost as brown as mine. Maybe you won't miss me so much. At night in the dark, you jest might mistake her fo' me. An' who knows, Majuh? Maybe them Apaches taught her a few things."

"My God, I'll—" His hands were clenched into fists at his sides.

"You'll what, Majuh?" she flared in challenge. "You know I'm sayin' the truth. Last week you called me a slut. Well, jest what does that make her?"

He raised a hand to strike her, hesitated, then stalked from the kitchen. Outside the bedroom door, Stephen paused, all the raw turbulence of his temper stirring beneath the veneer of severe discipline.

An imperious knock rattled the front door in its frame, the sound traveling down the narrow hall to break through his harsh musings. Several seconds passed before he responded to its summons and went to answer it. His first rush of pleasure at Hannah's return, apparently unharmed, was gone.

When Stephen opened the door, the colonel's wife, Ophelia Bettendorf, and Maude Goodson confronted him. He stiffened at the avid curiosity not quite hidden by their expressions of concern and remained standing in the doorway, blocking their entrance.

"How is she?" demanded silver-haired Ophelia Bettendorf, reigning queen of the officers' wives.

"We came as soon as we could," Maude Goodson

interposed. Her delicate white skin and blond hair reminded Stephen of how different from them Hannah had become.

"She's fine," he said tersely. "The doctor's with her now."

"One of us should be with her," the colonel's wife stated. "At a time like this, she needs the company of another woman. I'm sure there are certain things she simply can't tell a man, things that would be too painfully embarrassing."

"All those months of captivity—it must have been a horrible ordeal." Maude Goodson clutched her Bible. "I know she'll want to relieve her mind of the dreadful experience."

"You ladies are kind." A stiff politeness marked the faint smile that curved his mouth. "But I'm sure you'll understand that, with all the excitement of coming home, rest is of the first importance. Perhaps she'll be up to seeing you in a day or two."

"Really, Major—" Ophelia Bettendorf began haughtily.

"I'm afraid I must insist."

Their disappointment at not being able to see Hannah was not fully concealed. "You will tell her we called?" the captain's wife requested anxiously.

"Of course. And thank you for your concern, ladies." Stephen remained in the doorway until they turned away, then stepped inside and shut the door. He crossed to the parlor window and stood to one side to watch them.

It was an empty sky, as washed out as Cutter felt. Sunlight glinted on the ground, catching the brittle flashes of mica particles in the sand. He left the stables and headed up Officers' Row, his long body weighted by fatigue. His uniform was travel-stained and he needed a shave. But more than that, he wanted to kick back and relax, let all the jumble of thoughts and events spill from him.

His bachelor quarters were closer than the Wades'. He kept thinking of a wash, a shave, a change of uniform, and maybe a shot of whiskey and one of those black Mexican cigars he'd been saving. Cutter went to his quarters, but only to leave his laundry; then he went out again and down the walk to the adobe building where Major Wade resided.

Before Cutter reached the *ramada,* Wade stepped outside to meet him and moved into the deep shade below the raftered roof. Cutter followed him partway, then stopped and came to attention to salute him. A driving tension charged the air despite the forced calm Wade showed him as he returned Cutter's weary salute.

"At ease, Captain."

"Thank you, sir." He shifted to a loose and relaxed stance, his mind tired but alert to the unsettling currents in the still air. "You wanted to speak to me, Major."

"Yes." Wade paused as his striker, Private Delancy, came onto the porch to bring him a drink. "Whiskey, Captain?"

"Thank you, no, sir." The whiskey he had in mind Cutter planned to drink with his feet up and a cigar in his mouth, while his striker lathered his face and shaved off the crust.

Wade took the glass half-filled with the amber liquor and dismissed the striker. "That will be all for now, Delancy." As the enlisted man went back inside the adobe structure, Wade turned and looked across the parade ground at the limp flag hanging from the pole. "Griswald is inside examining my wife." He gave the impression of being in agitated motion even though he didn't change position or even lift a hand.

Cutter waited, making no response to the reference to Hannah, and watched Wade take a drink of the whiskey. Then Wade put the glass down and swung around, confronting Cutter with a narrow-eyed look.

"I want a full account of yesterday's action, Cutter, everything you can tell me."

Cutter frowned and made a small, vague shrug, troubled by the question. "We learned the location of the *rancheria* from an Apache woman after some interrogation. During the night we climbed into position, and then attacked at dawn, completely surprising them. It was a small band, led by a subchief named Lutero."

"Where did you find my wife?"

"When the fighting broke out, she had taken cover. We found her when we were securing the perimeter."

"What had they done to her?"

Cutter noticed the way the major's fingers clenched around the whiskey glass, his knuckles whitening, and was careful in the wording of his answer. "From what I could ascertain, she appeared unharmed."

"That isn't what I asked."

"Maybe you should question your wife about that." Cutter felt angry, disliking the answers Wade was seeking to obtain.

"Dammit, I'm asking you, Captain," Wade snapped. "She rode in here looking like an Apache squaw. I want to know whose and where he is now."

"If you mean Lutero, he got away." Cutter's own temper was fraying, the hardness settling into his expression.

"You know damned well who I meant!" Liquor sloshed over the sides of the glass as Wade took an abrupt step toward him, his voice getting louder. "You had Nah-tay question the Apaches you captured. I want to know what they told you. I want to know what happened to my wife while those savages had her!"

"You've got her back, for crissakes! Be happy about that and put the rest behind you!" Cutter flared. "Don't you know how damned lucky you are?!"

"One more remark out of you, and I'll have you hauled up on charges of insubordination!" Wade thundered, his hand doubled into a ready fist.

"Stephen." Concern and confusion were mixed in Hannah's voice as she stepped out of their quarters and stared at the two men confronting each other in bristling silence. She wore a day dress of cinnamon brown trimmed with white lace, the material smoothed over her corseted waist and drawn into a small bustle at the back. "What is it? We heard you shouting all the way inside." Her mahogany hair was drawn into fullness at the back, completing the symmetry of the bustle's silhouette.

Cutter backed down first, dropping his glance although all his resistance continued to simmer. "Did you wish to receive a full account in writing, Major?" he questioned with deadly quiet.

"Yes." Wade was not so quick to control his agitation, finally bolting down the rest of the whiskey to wash it away.

"Very good, sir." Cutter came to attention and held his salute until Wade returned it to dismiss him. He left the *ramada,* barely touching his hat to Hannah as he passed, and briskly walked away from the adobe.

"Why were you shouting at each other?" Hannah eyed Stephen, troubled by something she couldn't name.

"Shouting? You exaggerate." He dismissed her description. "Cutter sometimes forgets his place in this company. I was merely reminding him." He came and took her arm to escort her back inside. "What did the doctor have to say?"

The question was overheard by Griswald, who was in the act of taking the whiskey glass offered by Wade's striker. "A little on the thin side, but in damned better shape than you or I, Major."

# CHAPTER 14

STANDING IN THE DOORWAY, HANNAH LEANED AGAINST
the frame, the rough board supporting her spine and
her head as she listened to the first clear note of tattoo
trumpeted into the night. It was followed by the ritual
passing of the sentries' hourly call from their perimeter
posts, the assurance that "All's well." The smells were
familiar too, the rank odor of the stables and the
aromas of freshly baked bread, leather, and water-
cooled air from the hanging ollas. Few lights showed
along the quadrangle.

"I've missed all this." She turned her head against
the door frame so she could look into the parlor at
Stephen. His mouth curved in a smile, but he said
nothing. She pushed away from the door and let the
lace shawl slide to her elbows as she came into the
room. "It was kind of Mrs. Bettendorf and Maude to
bring those covered dishes for our dinner this evening."

Hannah wanted to confide in him the strangeness of

eating again with a full set of silverware and china plates. And she wanted to tell him how natural, yet how odd, it felt to wear so many layers of clothes. This dress, one of her favorites, felt cumbersome and bulky with its voluminous skirts and bustle. Her clothes were suddenly so constricting when she'd grown used to complete freedom of movement. But Stephen's growing silences were making her reticent, creating an awkwardness Hannah was determined to smooth away.

"You haven't told me how I look, Stephen," she prodded, and walked toward him, her head high and her smile set to conceal her unease. His brooding gaze swung to study her.

So many times during her absence, Stephen had summoned her image to his mind, that face with its lively eyes and warm, full lips. He tried to match that remembered image with the face of the woman before him, to lay one atop the other; but there were differences, a blurring of lines that didn't match, small shadings of change. They'd been apart for only eleven months, yet she was not the same woman.

He had known that such an ordeal would alter her, but it hadn't done so in the ways he had expected. There was an inordinate amount of pride in the way she carried herself now, a boldness of manner and look. Gone were the soft persuasion of her smile and her gentle, well-bred demeanor, replaced by a frankness of eye and a strength of will. She had not come back to him cowed and ashamed, frightened and needing him. He could see no gratitude in her reaction to him. He didn't like this new independence—these changes that went deeper than her sun-sullied skin. Instantly he was angry with himself for the thought and sought to make amends.

His hands caught her shoulders, the pressure of their grip drawing her toward him. "God, how I've missed you, Hannah," he vowed with deep intensity. "Losing you was like losing a leg. I was always off balance, teetering, without you at my side. I was half out of my mind." He scanned her upturned face, seeing the trembling of her lips and the ache in her eyes. "Sometimes at night I could feel you lying next to me in bed, but when I'd go to touch you, you wouldn't be there."

The depth of his torment made her cry for him as she slid her arms around him and arched her body against his length. His mouth covered her lips in a crushing attempt to blot out all the past misery and sufferings, the memories of anguish and rage. Hannah didn't care about the physical pain of his fiercely possessive embrace: it was contact. No longer did some unseen thing keep them apart. Stephen was holding her, loving her; everything would be all right.

At last he dragged his mouth from hers, his mustache brushing across her skin. His hand cradled her head against his chest, stroking one smooth cheek. Hannah closed her eyes to listen to the hard drumming of his heart, aware of the quicksilver run of her own pulse.

"I'm so glad to be home, Stephen," she said in a low and fervid whisper.

"Hannah." By his tone, the probing edge to it, he attempted to prepare her for his next, hesitant question. "Were you . . . violated?"

"No." The false denial was startled from her; then she instantly corrected, "Yes." She was angry with herself for wanting to hide the truth from him; only there was a kind of truth in the denial. She swung out of his arms, turning her back to him, but his hands rested on her shoulders to keep her close. She dreaded this subject, the sense of shame she could never quite shake. "My body was taken, but I never let him touch my mind."

"Him? Only one?"

"Yes."

His fingers dug into her shoulders. "Who was he, Hannah? What was his name?"

"He's an Apache. What difference does his name make?" She didn't want to tell him, but the very compulsion that insisted that she conceal his identity prompted her to tell Stephen, lest he think she had a reason to keep it from him. "Lutero." She pulled free of his hands and walked a few steps away, drawing the shawl up higher around her shoulders, fighting a chill that came from inside.

"The leader." The very flatness of his voice was telling. "He wasn't caught with the others." Both comments were statements of fact.

"Yes." Hannah realized that Stephen knew of him, which probably meant that Cutter had reported this information. Their argument—had it been about her?

"How . . ."

Hannah guessed at the rest of his unfinished sentence, a sense of painful irony twisting through her. "How could I let him do it? Oh, Stephen." She laughed without humor. "In the beginning, all I could think was that the shots Lieutenant Sloane fired would be heard here at the fort; a detail would be sent to investigate. I was sure you were coming. I kept telling myself that if I could just hold on a little longer, you'd come charging in with the rest of the cavalry to save me."

"We followed your trail for three days," he said, insisting that the blame wasn't his, then added lamely, "A windstorm came up and wiped out all the traces. The patrol had to turn back. We had nowhere to look."

"Three days," she recalled with bitter regret. "You wouldn't have recognized me, Stephen. By then I'd been three days under that sun without any clothes. My whole body was blistered and burned, scabby and bleeding. I'd had no food and hardly any water. That's how he took me . . . when I was too sore and too weak to move." A tightness clutched at her throat, and she arched her neck back, trying to ease the constriction as hot tears scalded her eyes. "Oh, God," she murmured in prayer at the ugliness of that memory.

"I'm sorry." Stephen gathered her into his arms and rocked her against his length, his head bent and his mouth moving against her hair. "I'm sorry, darling. It was horrible, I know." The solid wall of his body radiated solace and comfort. "So many times I was told that the Apaches would kill you when they were finished with you."

"But he wasn't finished with me," Hannah murmured, and pressed closer to him. "He needed a slave. His wife was heavy with child, so I had to do all the lifting and carting and carrying—all the hard labor. During that time, he never came near me. But—" She hesitated, but recognized that Stephen would only wonder if she didn't tell him. "The Apaches have a belief that it's forbidden for a man and woman to have any further contact once it is discovered that she's going to have a baby. She must abstain and cannot be bedded by her husband until the infant is old enough to stop nursing. Lutero didn't have another wife, so he married me. Captives make good wives."

She could feel his resistance to her implication, his body stiffening at the thought. "My God, Hannah." There was condemnation in his confused mutter.

"You don't understand, do you? I had no choice, not really." She pulled back to search his expression, frightened. "I wanted to come back to you, Stephen. As long as there was a chance, I wanted to come back."

He didn't answer, he couldn't answer, because he didn't know what was right. It was emotion warring with reason, morality with immorality, love with hatred. The conflict seemed irreconcilable.

"You don't understand," Hannah realized, and felt the shock of it. Stephen made no attempt to stop her when she moved out of his arms.

"Hannah, I'm trying." It was the best he could offer, but even that admission brought a rise of bitter gall into his throat. "All I want to do is get my hands on that bloody Apache bastard." His hands were curled into talons while his lip curled away from his teeth. "I want to kill him for taking what was mine."

"But I am still yours—in my heart, in my mind." That was what she was trying so desperately to make him understand.

"Don't you think I'm trying to convince myself of that!" He raked his fingers through his sun-streaked brown hair and paced in agitation, then suddenly spun around and moved to trap her with his body against an adobe wall. "I love you, Hannah." His warm breath fanned her skin while his mouth hovered an inch away. "These months have been hell. A man's mind can be cruel. Not knowing, one starts imagining all sorts of things."

"We . . . we both probably need time." Her head was tipped slightly to avoid his eyes.

This was not the way she'd envisioned her homecoming. Now she could see how foolish she had been to think she could return with no questions asked, no recriminations. Her ordeal with the Apaches had been harsh and abhorrent, and the repercussions of it were only beginning.

"Hannah." His fingers stroked her cheek in a delicate caress, his face so very near hers. She could hear the desire in his voice, and the reluctance that was ground into it.

Once his touch might have thrilled her, but tonight she was oddly unresponsive. The bloom of the evening had faded; the moment when she could have gone freely into his arms had passed. He wanted her, but it was still in his mind that she'd lain with Lutero. Her own memories were too strong. When Stephen touched her, she wanted no thought of Lutero in her mind.

"It's been a long day, Stephen," Hannah said quietly, and felt his slow withdrawal before he straightened away from her. "I think I shall retire."

That hard-driving energy, so tightly leashed, turned him away and carried him to the whiskey decanter on the side table. "I'll be along . . . directly."

A quilt covered the straw-tick mattress, creating a cushiony soft bed. It formed to her body as she lay on it, surrounded by inky darkness. Occasionally she could hear the chink of a glass from the parlor or footsteps impatiently pacing. Everything was so familiar, yet the sensations had been forgotten and had to be discovered all over again. She wished Stephen was beside her so she could tell him all these things, share the wonder of returning to all the things she'd taken for granted in the past, but that was denied, and the pleasure of these discoveries was lessened.

The agitated tempo of Stephen's footsteps changed to a decisive sound as he entered the narrow hallway and approached the bedroom. Hannah tensed, without being sure why. He came into the room and stopped, a dark shape blending into the black shadows, indistinct.

"Hannah, are you asleep?"

She hesitated a moment, debating whether to feign sleep, then replied, "No."

"I've decided. You will tell no one the details of your capture."

"Stephen." She raised herself up on an elbow, protesting his words.

"Did you tell Griswald?"

She was confused by this compulsion to defend her

actions, to justify her behavior. "He asked. He's a doctor. I wanted to be sure—"

"I'll speak to him," Stephen cut in, almost as if he was thinking aloud. "He'll keep his mouth shut."

All her feelings flattened out and she lay back on the mattress to stare blankly at the ceiling. "What do you want me to tell them, Stephen?"

"The truth. That you were a slave, a handmaid to that Apache squaw."

"If I say it often enough, will they believe it? Will you believe it?" Hannah asked in a sad voice.

"It isn't that, Hannah." He came to the bed and sat on the edge, leaning over her and stroking her auburn hair. "I don't want them to be looking at you and wondering things that are none of their business. You've been through enough. If I can, I want to protect you from any more unpleasantness. Do you understand?"

"Yes. Yes, I see," she murmured.

Out on the parade ground, the trumpeter blew taps. The long, sad notes made a lonely call across the night, the song rising, reaching, and fading into a final sigh. Its silent echo lingered, holding them motionless for several seconds. Then Stephen leaned down and pressed a kiss to her forehead, the thick broom of his mustache again sweeping her skin.

"Good night, my love." It was a husky whisper of longing and regret.

Hannah shut her eyes against the churn of emotions, the hurt and the want, the warmth and the cold, the bitterness and the sweet. He straightened, then moved away from the bed.

The strangeness of her surroundings, the half-forgotten sounds and smells and sensations, made it impossible for Hannah to sleep soundly. Much later she heard Stephen come to bed. For a long time, he lay beside her, not touching her, an arm flung above his head. She wondered if he knew she was awake, but said nothing.

The adobe house in which the commanding officer and his wife resided was considerably larger and better appointed than the rest of the quarters along Officers' Row. A large four-poster bed with an elaborately carved headboard dominated the bedroom, crowding a tall armoire into a corner. Mrs. Bettendorf sat on a cloth-draped steamer trunk disguised as a bench, which was positioned near the window where the morning light was good.

She held a mirror in order to watch and approve every curl and wave Cimmy Lou's long, deft fingers made in her hair. Such a contrast they made—the staid, large-bosomed matron with her silver hair and powdered face, and the earthy, high-breasted woman with her coffee-colored skin and black, shining eyes holding all of night's mysteries in their depths.

"You do have fine healthy hair, Miz Bettendorf." Cimmy Lou combed the blue-gray strands, already curled by the hot iron, around her finger and fashioned them into position in a nest of long rolls.

"I believe this side is too full. Smooth more of it away from my face." Mrs. Bettendorf critically examined her reflection, not responding to the compliment from one who was of the servant class, yet preening slightly.

Cimmy Lou skinned back more of the gray hair, accomplishing the feat that made her hairdressing skill in such demand, that of firming the age-slackened facial skin. "Yep, you have good hair, Miz Bettendorf. This hot, dry sun ain't damaged it a bit. You should see what it's done to Miz Wade's hair."

"Oh?"

"I went an' did her hair yestiday. I looked close, but she didn't have no nits in her hair. It worried me some, her livin' all that time with the Apaches an' all." Deftly she pushed at the rolled curls on top, giving height to the crown. "My husband was there when they found her hidin' under that pile of wood. You know my husband, Sergeant Hooker?"

"Why was she hiding?" The mirror shifted, its angle changing to include the reflection of Cimmy's face.

"Scared, I guess." She lifted a shoulder in a careless shrug. "I s'pose there was a lot of shootin' goin' on."

"There is always the risk of a stray bullet," Mrs. Bettendorf reasoned aloud.

"I 'spect yore right. It's jest natural that she wouldn't want anythin' to happen to that baby."

"What baby?" The mirror was tilted sharply back to reflect Cimmy's image.

"My husband said it was a shore 'nuff Apache baby. 'Scuse me while I get some mo' pins for yore hair." She crossed the room to the vanity table and picked up a squat glass dish with an enameled lid.

"Whose baby?" came the impatient demand.

A shell-adorned box sat open on the table, filled with fine lawn kerchiefs edged with lace. "I don't rightly know whose baby it was." Cimmy Lou touched the tip of her finger to the delicate lace edging. "You have such purty things, Miz Bettendorf. I always did admire these fancy hankies of yores."

"Yes, yes. What about this baby?" Ophelia Bettendorf insisted.

"I don't know nothin' 'cept what my husband tole me. Didn't you think Miz Wade looked like an Indian when she came ridin' in?" With calculated avoidance of a more informative answer, Cimmy Lou remained preoccupied with the exquisitely fashioned linen squares. "Ain't you so lucky to have so many of these purty things?"

Mrs. Bettendorf released a long breath. "Why don't you take one for yourself, Cimmy Lou."

"Why, thank you, Miz Bettendorf. Yore so generous." She quickly picked out the one she'd had her eye on and tucked it deep inside her blouse. Gathering up the wire pins for the woman's hair, she turned back to the window. "Ya know that baby must not of belonged to Miz Wade 'cause she shore didn't keep it. Cap'n Cutter tole her to give that baby to my husband and she did. 'Course he gave it to them Apaches to take care of theirselves." She went back to work on the gray hair.

"How old was that baby?" Ophelia Bettendorf frowned thoughtfully, mentally doing some calculating of her own.

"John T. never said exackly. It was a little tyke, though, tied on one of them boards like they do with the small ones."

"What else did your husband tell you about Mrs. Wade?"

Half an hour later, Cimmy Lou came to the rear door of Captain Goodson's quarters. Maude Goodson was in the kitchen, supervising the meal preparations. A bundle of soiled table linens and other laundry sat just inside the doorway.

"Sorry I'm so late, Miz Goodson. Miz Bettendorf kept me a-fixin' her hair." Cimmy Lou sniffed the air, a sleek, feline gesture. "My, my, somethin' shore smells good."

"I will need these washed and ironed by the weekend," Mrs. Goodson reminded her. "You will have them done for me, won't you, Cimmy Lou?" She pressed her hands onto the laundry bundle, as if to keep the dirty linens should the laundress reply in the negative.

"Never you fear, I'll have 'em done by Friday. You have lovely hands, Miz Goodson, so smooth and white. Miz Wade's skin used to be like that, but it ain't no more. The majuh fetched me when she came back yestiday, so's I could help her bathe an' all." Her wide-eyed look said there was more she could tell, but she turned away. "Mmm, that's peaches I smell." She walked toward the open jar sitting on a kitchen worktable, and breathed in the fruity scent. "It's been a month of Sundays since I had any peaches."

"How is Mrs. Wade?" Maude Goodson followed after her.

"As well as can be expected, considerin'." Cimmy Lou lowered her voice. "You know how brown her skin looked? Well, it's that way all over." Only a few peaches remained in the bottom of the jar. "Whatcha makin' with these peaches?"

"A torte." It was an offhand, uninterested response as Maude pushed the nearly empty jar of peaches toward the colored girl. "Have the rest. We don't need them." She strove to sound very casual. "You didn't really say that Mrs. Wade was dark *all* over, did you?"

"Oh, yes, ma'am." Cimmy Lou used a knife to stab the peach halves from the jar. "She tole me the Apaches took all her clothes. She had to go 'round without a stitch."

Maude Goodson drew back. "I don't believe that."

"S'truth," Cimmy Lou swore, her mouth full of peaches and the juice oozing out the sides.

"Why do you suppose they did that?" Maude wondered with an avid kind of horror and fearful curiosity.

When Cimmy Lou left Officers' Row, she made a side trip by the parade ground, where dust boiled under the cantering hooves of cavalry horses, which were more familiar with the shouted commands than their riders. She was aware of the heads turning in her direction.

The air was pungent with the smell of horses and manure as she approached the stables. The rasp of a blacksmith's file came from a shed nearby, and Cimmy Lou altered her course to walk toward the sound. She slowed at the sight of her husband, John T., stripped to

239

the waist, the hind foot of a bay horse between his legs. A sheen of perspiration made his muscled torso glisten a chocolate black, the hard flesh rippling as he rhythmically buffed the file across the hoof of the newly shod horse. His slouch hat was pushed to the back of his head, showing the mat of thick black curls.

Finished with his task, he set the horse's foot on the ground and straightened, giving the horse's rump a slap. His suspenders drooped in two loops from the waistband of his trousers, falling loosely against his small, tight flanks. He walked to the horse's head, untied its lead rope from the snubbing post, and turned to lead the horse away before he noticed Cimmy Lou. The leap of pleasure that lit up his expression was greatly satisfying. He reached for his blouse, a small bundle on the ground, and led the horse over to her, waiting until he had reached her to put on the gray uniform blouse.

"What are you doin' here?" He stood close, looking down at her with warm, half-closed eyes.

"Haven't seen you since reveille." Her upward glance reminded him of how difficult she had made it for him to leave the bed that morning.

Hooker chirruped to the horse and headed toward the stable, a half-smile showing on his face when she walked with him. It was at times like these that John T. felt he had everything the world could offer him. He was top sergeant, the best damned soldier in the regiment, and married to a beauty, the envy of every man in the regiment . . . and she was here with him by choice, and he didn't have to wonder whether she was making time with someone else.

"Whatcha got there?" He looked at the large laundry bundle she carried.

"Miz Goodson's table linens. She's havin' a big party this weekend, a fancy welcome for Miz Wade. She's havin' oysters, John T. Can you remember what they taste like?" A ring of longing was in her voice, wistful and seeking. "Must be five years back that the regiment was in Brownsville. They was good, I remember that."

From the brightness of the day they went into the shadowed interior of the stable, the cloppity-clop of the horse directly behind them. A myriad of smells assailed them, horse and saddle leather mingling with grain and excrement. Cimmy Lou left her laundry bundle atop a wooden barrel just inside the stable doors and followed John T. to the empty stalls.

"Maybe we should get us some oysters." John T. led the horse into the stall and tied its lead rope to the manger ring. As he walked back to Cimmy Lou, he ran a hand along the animal's curving neck and withers. "Oysters make a man strong in bed, you know."

"Is that right?" She slid her fingers over his chest, running them under his shirt to feel the muscled flesh.

"Being married to you, I could use that," he declared in mock seriousness as his hands settled on the curve of her bottom. He fitted himself into the cradle of her hips and pushed against her in the intimate way husbands and wives have of expressing their desire.

"Maybe you could," Cimmy Lou agreed in order to provoke him as she moved suggestively against him, feeling the beginnings of his arousal.

Bending his head, he blazed a kiss across her full, coral-tinted lips, and his hands moved around to the front and cupped the undersides of her breasts, holding the weight of them. He felt something else, too.

"What's this?" His fingers probed inside and came up with the lacy kerchief.

"Miz Bettendorf gave that to me," she said, taking it and tucking it back inside her bodice.

"And what piece of information did she obtain in return?" John T. knew her game.

"She wanted to know 'bout Miz Wade."

241

"Poor woman. She's been through plenty."

"Poor woman," Cimmy Lou scoffed, and snuggled against him. "What about me? I ain't had plenty."

"I swear to God ain't nobody can use you up. It's like tryin' to drink a river dry." But his mouth came down on hers just the same. She was soft and silken, and he felt himself sinking. Her parting lips dragged him inside to all the sweetness of her mouth and mating tongue. When John T. came up, needing air, he murmured thickly. "You taste like peaches."

"I had some at Miz Goodson's." She didn't stop, her warm, moist mouth traveling along his neck and under the rolled collar of his shirt, while her hands slid down to tug at the cinched belt of his trousers. "That's all right, 'cause you taste of salt," she said, the tip of her tongue licking his skin on a downward journey.

"Will you stop it, Cimmy Lou?" he protested vaguely and looked around the shadowed barn, belatedly seeking any observer.

Her hands were inside his pants, cupping him. "I always did like my meat salty." Her lips continued inexorably downward.

"Jeezus, woman, what d'ya think yore doin'? Stand up!" Then a moan convulsed him as the stroke of her lips surrounded him.

## CHAPTER 15

IDLENESS MADE THE MORNING PASS SLOWLY FOR HANNAH. Things that she recalled as having taken up so much of her time actually took very little. She had approved the day's menu that Delancy had submitted, unable to remember why it used to take her so long to decide whether cornbread stuffing would go better with the smoked turkey than sage dressing. It had been the same with selecting her dress for the day. Few of the routine housekeeping chores required her assistance, let alone her supervision.

By later morning, she could stand the idleness and confinement no longer. She left their quarters to re-explore the fort, reincorporate the military rhythm of living, and walk off some of this restless energy.

It was a mild February day as she turned up Officers' Row. To the north, the jagged edges of the Pinos Altos mountain range cut into the sky, with Hermosa Mountain nearby and tall Signal Peak beyond. Everything in between the fort and the mountains was a jumble of desert canyons and stony parapets, like the land beyond them—the Mogollons and the Gila River country where she had lived with the Apaches. Hannah brought her attention back to the row of adobe housing that faced the parade ground.

A large, heavyset man in a derby hat, checked jacket, and a solid vest was walking her way. It was not uncommon for civilians to visit the fort, but it was sufficiently unusual to attract her notice, as were the eastern-style clothes he was wearing. The man studied her with close interest as they approached each other. He lifted his hat to her, revealing the bald crown of his head, which had been hidden under the derby. The lack of hair on the top of his head was compensated for by the long, flowing sideburns on his cheeks.

"Mrs. Wade?" he inquired as he stopped before her. Politeness obliged her to pause as well.

"Yes?"

"We haven't had the pleasure of meeting before. The name is Boler, Hy Boler from Silver City." The careless charm he exuded did not reach his eyes, so very piercing in their study of her. "I'd like to be one of the first to welcome you back."

"That's very kind of you, Mr. Boler." Hannah was polite but reserved. Between the Apache's suspicion of strangers, which she had not yet lost, and Stephen's attitude concerning her captivity, she was very much on guard.

"Not at all. It must have been quite an ordeal you went through, Mrs. Wade."

"I survived. It was a pleasure meeting you, Mr. Boler." She nodded to him and resumed her walk, but he fell into step beside her.

"Your husband and I became well acquainted while you were living with the Apaches. I've taken a very deep interest in your story right from the beginning.

You see, I publish the newspaper in Silver City. I ran a lot of stories about your husband's gallant search for you and printed all the posters with the reward offers."

"I didn't know."

"It isn't often that a story like this has a happy ending. I'd like to write about it," he said.

"I'm sure my husband will give you all the information you need to know, Mr. Boler. Why don't you speak to him?" From the stables came the angry squeal of a horse being broken to saddle and the muffled shouts of men encouraging its rider to stay on.

"I will, but I was hoping for some comments from your viewpoint." A glint of appreciation for the way she was eluding his questions shone in his eyes, but he persisted. "People would like to know what it was like, living with the Apaches all that time. Were you treated harshly?"

"Naturally it's something I'd rather not talk about." She continued walking, her strides lengthening. The high leather shoes were beginning to pinch her feet and the heels made walking over the rough ground slightly hazardous. Her moccasins had been much better suited to this, Hannah realized.

"I understand you became the wife of an Apache chief."

"Who told you that?" She froze inside, but her pace never altered. She didn't want to believe that Jake Cutter would tell.

"I've spoken to some of the Apache prisoners who were brought in. Spanish is a useful language in this part of the country. They said you were given the name Coloradas." The newspaperman waited for a comment, but Hannah remained silent. For several seconds, there was only the crunch of their shoes on the gravel. "Perhaps you could describe an Apache marriage ceremony."

"I didn't live with the Apaches long enough to

understand their rituals." Hannah stopped and faced him. "And I don't wish to discuss the subject any further. I bid you good day, Mr. Boler."

When she continued on her way again, he didn't follow. At the end of Officers' Row, she turned to walk past the headquarters building, the commissary, and the trader's store, nodding to those she met. Gradually, Hannah became aware of the heads turning, the stares, the murmured comments too low for her to catch.

She left the quadrangle and walked along the less-traveled route in back of the buildings. Behind the barracks, the tent housing for the families of the enlisted men stood—Suds Row. Hannah lingered along it, watching the colored children at play, some of them minding little brothers and sisters and carrying babes almost as big as they were.

A horse whickered and Hannah lifted an idle glance toward the stables. She turned toward the corrals where the brown and bay cavalry mounts lazed in the warm sun. Cimmy Lou Hooker came out of the barn, her arms making a wide circle around a large laundry bundle. Her husband, the black sergeant, was only a step or two behind her, smiling and looking loose and relaxed.

"Mornin', Miz Wade," Cimmy Lou drawled, a secretive gleam in her eyes as she passed Hannah.

"Good morning, Cimmy Lou," Hannah responded, and observed the slight sobering of Sergeant Hooker's expression. "Hello, Sergeant."

"Good day, Miz Wade." His glance followed his wife for an instant, then came back to her with sharp attention. "Were you lookin' for the major, ma'am?"

"Is he around?" She hadn't anticipated that she might encounter him on her walk, but she welcomed the chance occurrence.

"I haven't seen him, ma'am, but I'll see if I can find him for you."

"No. Thank you anyway, Sergeant." Her long skirt swished mere inches off the ground as she walked toward the corral, where a curious sorrel horse stood with its neck arched over the fence.

The sergeant moved toward the corral as well. "It ain't accordin' to regulation, I know, but it is nice to see your wife durin' the day."

"Especially when she is as lovely as your wife." The corners of her mouth deepened with a hint of a smile.

"Yes, ma'am." His wide, pleasant smile agreed with her. Turning, he hooked a boot heel on the lower rail of the corral. "If you're thinkin' of gettin' yourself a good ridin' horse, we've got a nice-travelin' blaze-faced roan with four white stockin's. Too nice a horse for these troopers of mine to be poundin' through the desert on."

"I hadn't thought about getting another horse yet." She studied the blue roan he'd pointed out, but only with vague interest.

"No riders are permitted off the post without an escort. Too many Apaches around. If you get another horse, I'm afraid you wouldn't be able to do much ridin' 'cept around the parade ground," Sergeant Hooker informed her.

"I suppose not." She moved away from the corral. "Thank you, Sergeant. And I'll remember your recommendation of the roan if I do get another horse."

For a moment, he watched her wander away from the stables in the general direction of the parade ground, then slipped his suspenders onto his shoulders and went back to his work.

Hannah was diverted from her path by a trace of movement, the low mutter of the loose-sounding Apache language. Impelled by an inner force, Hannah turned toward it. She traveled several yards before she saw the brush-covered *jacals* and the dozen or fewer Apaches around them, a temporary encampment for the prisoners erected on the fort's perimeter. She was oddly drawn toward her former captors.

"Halt!" A guard moved to block her path, a stout soldier with muttonchop whiskers. His fierceness quickly dissolved into uncertain apology as the black private recognized her. "I'm sorry, ma'am, but nobody's s'posed to go near the prisoners."

"I understand, Private," Hannah assured him, and moved away at right angles to the camp.

A small Apache woman came out of one of the dome-shaped huts, a cradleboard holding an infant tied to her back. Hannah stopped when she saw Gatita. If the Apache woman noticed her, she gave no sign of recognition. Hannah wasn't certain whether she had expected any. They hadn't been friends. Yet she had gone through more in the company of that Indian woman—hunger, pain, thirst, danger, birthings, deaths —than she had with any other female, including so many of the officers' wives she called friends. She and Gatita weren't quite friends and they weren't quite enemies. In many respects, theirs was an oddly close relationship between two strangers.

Hannah had started to turn away when she heard the hard gallop of a horse, which quickly turned into a clattering slide to a halt. Stephen dismounted before his horse came to a full stop. Everything about him suggested a contained riptide of feeling as his long, stiff-legged strides carried him toward Hannah.

"So this is where you are," he said in accusation. "I've been turning the whole damned fort upside down looking for you." His glance flashed to the Apache encampment. "Couldn't you stay away from them for one day?"

"I was out walking. I had no idea they were here." His whole attitude stung her. She lifted her skirts, turned from the camp, and started back toward the quadrangle, a faintly stubborn set to her chin.

Stephen caught the crook of her arm. "Don't lie to me, Hannah." He managed to keep his voice down so that the onlooking guard couldn't overhear, but it shook with anger. "I know they found you with a baby. Did you come to see it? Is it yours?"

"No." She was hurt and angry. "No, he isn't." She removed her elbow from his grip with a trace of disdain and set off once again toward the parade ground, walking as fast as the high-topped leather boots would permit on the rough, uneven ground. Stephen came after her, leading his horse.

"Hannah, I'm sorry." But the clipped edges of his words indicated that anger, not regret, was still the foremost of his emotions. "I don't think you appreciate my concern when I returned to our quarters and discovered you weren't there. You didn't even tell Delancy where you were going."

"I wasn't aware that I was confined to quarters." She steadfastly refused to look at him, concentrating all her attention directly ahead, looking to neither the right nor the left.

"You aren't, but you could have told someone where you were going," he snapped in return. "Mrs. Bettendorf wanted to come by, but I told her you weren't receiving yet. Why couldn't you have been content to stay in our rooms?"

"I was restless. I wanted to walk and re-explore the fort. I'm not used to sitting around doing nothing." A horse whinnied to Stephen's mount as they approached the stables.

"Of all the places to walk, why did you have to go to that damned Apache camp?" Stephen muttered in exasperated anger. "If they treated you as horribly as you claim, I would have thought you'd never want to set eyes on any of them again—that you'd keep as far away from them as possible."

"I didn't know they were there," Hannah reminded

him tersely. "I presumed that they were being transported to the reservation. I came upon the camp by accident." Hannah walked close to the stable wall, her skirts up, in order to avoid the horse apples in the main path. She spared one glance over her shoulder at Stephen, the snap of anger striking deeply through the brown wells of her eyes. "And I dislike your insinuations to the contrary."

Immediately she returned her attention to the possible obstacles in her path as she rounded a corner of the stable. Too late she saw the boots in front of her and bumped into the officer coming from the opposite direction. His hands were quick to reach out and steady her, and she looked up to find Jake Cutter's weathered countenance before her, a startled expression on it.

Those keen and quick blue eyes darted a glance at Stephen coming up short beside her. Relief gentled the set of Cutter's features. "I see you've found her."

Irked by the comment, Hannah corrected it, enunciating very clearly. "I wasn't found because I wasn't lost." Before she swept by him, she caught the flash of amusement in his face.

"Have someone see to my horse." Stephen thrust the reins at Cutter and walked after Hannah.

The mounted company returning to the stables after morning drill broke their column to let Hannah cross in front of them. Quickly, Stephen was at her elbow to escort her. The air was sharp-scented with stirred-up dust, damp horsehide, and sweated leather, all of it warmed by the high yellow sun. Hannah walked quickly toward the row of adobe buildings that lined the parade ground.

"Tell me, Stephen," she began on a challenging note, still angry with him for his intolerant attitude, "what would you have done if that baby was mine?"

"Since the matter doesn't arise, I don't see how I can answer that question." He was very stiff and contained.

"Obviously it would be very difficult for me to accept an infant conceived . . . under such circumstances."

It was an extremely honest answer, Hannah felt. She herself hadn't wanted a child fathered by Lutero. The subject triggered a memory of her earlier encounter with the newspaper publisher. "When I left our quarters, I was stopped by a man named Hy Boler."

"What did you tell him?" Stephen demanded.

"Nothing. But it doesn't matter. He knows." She had hated the idea of secrecy. Secrecy had guilt and shame attached to it, and she felt neither. "He spoke to some of the Apache prisoners. They told him that Lutero had married me."

"Stop using that word. You are *married* to me!" Stephen reacted with taut anger, using the trivial issue as a release for his frustration.

"I told you it wouldn't do any good to try to keep it a secret," she reminded him.

"I know." He sighed heavily, then swore. "Damn, the Goodsons are having a dinner party on Saturday for us—actually a welcome-home party for you." As they reached the walk in front of Officers' Row, Stephen reached out and put an arm around her cinched-in waist and rested his hand on its narrow curve. The faint pressure of his fingers urged her to a slower, more refined pace, one befitting an officer and his lady out for a morning stroll. "That's what I came home to tell you."

"I see. And did you tender our acceptance?" She guessed that he had, and she was irritated that he hadn't bothered to consult her first.

"Naturally I did." He was curt. "They are honoring you—celebrating your return. These are your friends. Surely you want to go to the party."

"Of course." A sigh of self-impatience accompanied the response. She went through the motions of smiling and waving to Mrs. Bettendorf, who was out tending her rosebushes in front of the commanding officer's quarters. A wide-brimmed straw sunbonnet was perched on her gray head.

"And the next time you go for a walk, wear a bonnet or carry a parasol," Stephen advised as they turned up the path to their quarters. "The sun has done enough damage to your skin."

"Oh, goodness me, that's what I was missing—a parasol," Hannah mocked. Everything was rubbing her the wrong way—his insinuations, his presumptions, his short temper, and his doubt of her. It was all so unsettling and she couldn't seem to handle it gracefully, her tongue becoming sharp and quick.

She swept into their rooms, her skirts whirling about her legs as she stopped in the parlor, feeling heated and stiff. Stephen followed her into the shadowed interior where the sunlight couldn't reach.

"Will you be here when I come back, or will I have to tear the fort apart looking for you again?" He stood rigidly before her.

"Why don't you simply put me under house arrest?" she retorted. "Then you won't have to worry about me wandering off."

"Dammit, Hannah, can't you see that I was worried about you? I was afraid something had happened to you—" Stephen began in half-angry, half-irritated explanation.

Her temper flared, ignited by something in his answer. "Don't be afraid! If there's one thing I learned from the Apaches, it's don't ever be afraid. No matter how badly something hurts, you'll forget the pain in time. You can be driven half mad with hunger and thirst, but you can live longer than you think without food or water. You would be surprised how much you can stand."

The strident declaration rang loudly in the still room. In the ensuing silence, Hannah saw the stunned and frowning look on Stephen's face; he gazed at her as if he was staring at a stranger. She turned away, her head tipping downward in contrition.

"I'm sorry. I shouldn't have shouted at you." It troubled her that she had done it. "I had no call to raise my voice like that."

Abruptly, Stephen said, "I have to get back to headquarters," and walked to the door.

Hannah made no attempt to stop him and smooth over these harsh feelings. Instead, she wheeled from the room and walked swiftly down the narrow hallway to their bedroom. This disagreement with Stephen merely amplified all her other irritations. The hard leather boots hurt her feet, and the layers of skirts and petticoats got in the way when she bent to remove the shoes. In a temper, she stripped off her day dress and the slips, down to her ruffled pantaloons, corset, and chemise. As she went to fetch her robe from the wardrobe, the bedroom door opened.

Stephen paused in mid-stride, arrested by the sight of her disrobed state. Slowly he reached up and took his hat off, then stepped the rest of the way through the opening and shut the door. Hannah stood still beneath the slow rake of his dark amber gaze, a small thumping in her chest.

"I don't want to fight with you, Hannah." His low-pitched voice vibrated with the force of his repressed feelings. "We have to stop pushing each other away."

"Yes." She agreed completely that this wedge had to be removed before it drove them farther apart.

He hesitated for a heartbeat, then came toward her, absently tossing his hat onto the dresser. Her pulse accelerated slightly as he stopped before her, whether in tension or excitement, Hannah didn't know. His hands touched her bare arms, lightly rubbing them as if to discover how that golden-brown skin felt. He warmed to its satiny texture as his gaze traveled over the cotton bodice of her chemise, paying special attention to the beginning swell of her high breasts.

She didn't know. She wasn't sure. She felt an uneasiness in the pit of her stomach, but she didn't back away from him. Her hands moved to his flat, muscled torso, lightly bracing herself as Stephen bent his head and devoured her lips.

"It's been so long since I've held you." His mouth grazed the side of her face and nuzzled into her neck with aching force. "So damned long, Hannah."

"I know." Her fingers slid into the thickness of his hair as his hands slipped the chemise off her shoulders and reached for the hooks of her corset.

The bed stood in the deep shadows of the room. Stephen carried her to it, her pantaloons and chemise discarded but the gartered stockings and corset intact, only the top hooks loosened to free her breasts to his intimate attentions. He was quick to shed his uniform and climb onto the bed with her, while her gaze clung to his. She ignored the whiteness of his body, intent on keeping the face of her husband before her.

She was enveloped in a fevered heat of kisses, his hands touching and urging, their bodies thrusting and recoiling to thrust again. Maybe it was the relentless grinding of hips, the straining of their bodies that made it all too intense. When the release came, it wasn't enough.

Afterward, Hannah made slow work of tying the sash of her robe in a precise bow while Stephen put on his uniform. Going over it in her mind, she knew that it had not been good between them. They had tried too hard, because both had images they were trying to blot out of their memory.

"Why, Hannah?" With his second boot pulled on, Stephen stood up and reached for his uniform blouse.

"Why what?" She turned to look at him, golden sunlight shafting through the window to make a silhouette of her.

"Why did you make love during the daytime? You never have before," he stated.

"I don't understand." She gave a confused shake of her head, her faint contentment still alive but fading. "What do you mean?"

"Are you used to making love during the daytime? Is that when you did it with the Apaches?" The questions were made blunt by the grudging anger he felt.

Her mouth opened in shock. For a moment she was unable to get any words to come out; then they rushed from her. "Why on earth would you ask a question like that now? Why ruin—"

"Tell me which is worse, Hannah," Stephen demanded, "to ask the question or to wonder?"

The ache inside her was very painful. "Mostly at night, since I had work to do during the day." Her voice was flat and emotionless. "Why are you doing this to yourself, Stephen? Why do you keep asking?"

He looked down at her, troubled and aloof. "Maybe because I don't understand how you could let him touch you . . . why you didn't kill yourself before you let that savage get his hands on you."

Her smile was gentle, almost pitying. "That's easy to say, but it isn't easy to choose not to live."

"I've faced death before." Stephen rejected her insinuation.

"Have you? A soldier's death, maybe—the quick kind, never knowing where it will come from or when. But I'm talking about another kind—when you can reach out and touch death and invite it. When you're faced with it, you'll slap it away and hang onto that last scrap of life for as long as you can. Because while you're alive, you have hope. When you're dead, you have nothing. I know, Stephen," She laid her fingers along his jaw. "You are a soldier. You'd fight with the last breath in your body."

"But you were a refined woman. You should never have been subjected to such handling." He could not shake that thought.

Hannah moved away from him, laughing under her breath without humor. "I agree. It is not at all lady-like."

"Do you have any idea how helpless I feel? How impotent?" Stephen faced her, taut and angry. "A savage brutalized my wife, held her captive, made her his squaw, and I could do nothing. I was powerless. A man's wife is his most precious possession. You belong to me. You're mine. The thought that anyone else has touched you—" The rage swelled within him, choking him with its bitter fury. "I want to kill him. I want to kill him for damaging my property, for violating it in the meanest sense. I never should have let you go riding that morning." Stephen began a bitter recrimination. "We knew Juh and his band were in the area. Sloane was so damned green, so new to this country—and Delvecchio was so lovesick over you that he never saw anything else. I shouldn't have let you go with them."

"Stephen, I did. We can't change the past." She rubbed her hands up her arms to her shoulders, hugging herself to ease some of the ache.

"Damn them for ever letting the Apaches take you alive," he muttered.

"Delvecchio tried to kill me," Hannah informed him. "It was the very last thing he did. But I knocked the gun away. I wanted to live." For all the complexities of the moment, the decision was always remarkably simple. "Stephen, do you really wish I were dead? Are you sorry that I'm standing here right now?"

"No. No," he insisted more forcefully, but even as he

gathered her into his arms and held her close, Hannah could sense the conflict. Every time he looked at her, the thought was in his mind that another man had known her. She suddenly wasn't sure whether Stephen would ever be able to forget.

When he finally released her, her robe slipped off one shoulder. The fiery red burn scars were clearly visible. Hannah started to pull the robe back in place and cover them, but he stayed her hand and stared at the ugly scars, against his will.

"He even left his mark on you," Stephen said stiffly.

She didn't attempt to contradict him nor to explain that the scars were the result of punishment by Gatita. They were part of the result of her months of captivity at the hands of Lutero.

"They'll fade . . . in time," she replied.

"Yes." But it was an empty response as Stephen turned and scooped up his hat from the dresser; his attitude clearly said that they would never fade enough. He jammed the hat onto his head and strode to the door, then stopped, his back to her and his head down. "Hannah, was he larger—" He stopped, biting off the rest of the question. "I mean, all men aren't the same size . . . the—" He slammed the flat of his hand against the wooden door frame, the force of the blow disturbing the dust in the rafters so that a fine powder came sifting down. "Damn!" Stephen jerked open the door and charged through it.

Hannah listened to the stride of his steps carrying him out of their quarters, then walked slowly to the bed. She sank onto the mattress, a sick feeling in her stomach, beginning to realize what an enormous amount of pride Stephen had and how sorely it had been damaged.

A sob rose in her throat at the complete injustice of it. She had lived. She had survived, and she wasn't sure whether Stephen would ever forgive her for that.

What was right and what was wrong? Hannah didn't think she knew anymore. She stared out the rectangular window and watched the sunlight's pattern through the thatched *ramada* roof. Some code of conduct had been broken. Somehow in Stephen's eyes she had lost her respectability.

# CHAPTER 16

THE PEACH COLOR OF HANNAH'S GOWN FLATTERED THE bronze tan of her skin and the red tones in her hair as she sat in the soft glow of the lamplight, the center of everyone's attention, including Cutter's. He stood well back, supporting an adobe wall as he had for much of the evening and nursing a glass of champagne, while he watched the party's guest of honor. He'd seen the article in the newspaper the day before. Cutter hadn't read past the headline, "White Woman Becomes Squaw in Heathen Ceremony," before he'd thrown the paper away.

Hannah's head was held high all evening, rarely bowing to any look or comment, and her dark eyes were direct and faintly challenging. Her lips were softly composed, a slightly willful, slightly fatalistic set to them. Cutter had the distinct feeling that Hannah Wade was stronger than anything that had happened to her. She had learned to bend, and not break.

"Tell me, Mrs. Wade, did you meet any of the Apache chiefs? Geronimo, Vittorio . . ." The questions put to her were as endless as the expressions of sympathy. This time, it was Colonel Bettendorf who was getting into the discussion.

"Juh came to the *rancheria* several times. Twice to visit, I guess, and the other times when the warriors were going out on raids. They—the Apache woman called Little Cat who was my mistress —referred to Juh as a *hesh-ke,* which means a 'crazy,' an unreasonable hater."

"What of the others?" the colonel persisted.

"Geronimo came to the camp once, but I didn't know it was him," Hannah admitted. "I only learned he had been there after he'd gone. They regard him as a *di-yin,* a kind of medicine chief. He has the power, they say, to see the outcome of a battle before it occurs."

"You surely don't believe that," Captain Goodson scoffed.

"So far, the Apaches say, he hasn't been wrong." She shrugged, unconcerned about whether they believed her or not. "Many people claim that the Irish have second sight."

"That's true enough," Lieutenant Hennessy agreed. "My mother had a dream that Lincoln would be shot just a week before he was assassinated."

"Do you know, this is fascinating," the colonel declared, sitting back on the horsehair sofa. "She is actually giving us an intelligence report on the enemy. We need to get her up to headquarters and have her go over the maps, give us an idea of their travel routes, where they go, when. Valuable information, important and valuable information."

"Not tonight, Colonel," his wife interjected. "This party is celebrating Mrs. Wade's return. She is to relax and enjoy herself. Isn't that right, my dear?" She reached over to pat Hannah's arm affectionately.

"Yes." Hannah's lips formed a smile, but Cutter observed the tension that was behind it.

"I understand that Apaches are abusive to their wives. Is that true, Mrs. Wade?" Lieutenant Digby's young wife leaned forward with avid curiosity.

"I don't know how they treat their wives. I was a slave." Smoothly she turned to look elsewhere.

"Well, I certainly wouldn't be surprised." Maude Goodson responded to the inquiry with her own opinion. "The Apaches are a brutal race. I shall never forget how on our journey here to Fort Bayard we came across a burnt-out wagon train. The Apaches had attacked only hours before, and there wasn't a single survivor, which was horrible enough. But worse, they had mutilated the bodies almost beyond recognition. It was barbaric."

"It's fortunate that you didn't see what the Mexican army did when they attacked the *rancheria* below the border," Hannah remarked calmly, a sparking of temper in her eyes. "I saw them split babies open with their sabers and tie ropes to children's legs, then ride in separate directions—"

"Hannah." Stephen Wade stood behind her chair, pressing a hand upon her shoulder.

"Forgive me, ladies," Hannah apologized to her horrified counterparts. "I was trying to make the point that cruelty and barbarism are not limited to the Apaches."

"Gracious me, I don't understand how you could go through any of this." Mrs. Digby pressed a delicate lace kerchief to her nose as if needing its heavy gardenia scent to revive her. "Why, I would have killed myself before I let them lay a hand on me."

A small stirring in the room seemed to indicate that this opinion was shared by the majority of those present. Hannah's reaction was a tightening of the lips;

a strong light shone in her eyes as she faced this silent condemnation.

"You'll find that the will to survive is very strong, Mrs. Digby," she informed her with a forced pleasantness. "No pain is so great that you can't endure it. Many times you may *think* you want to die, but when the choice is offered, you'll want to live." Her quick upward glance in Wade's direction gave the distinct impression that the subject had been previously discussed.

"Still, Mrs. Digby does raise a good point," Colonel Bettendorf remarked, nodding thoughtfully. "Women of refinement and breeding should not be subjected to certain horrors at the hands of the hostiles. It is our duty to protect them. It is ultimately our responsibility to see that they aren't taken alive. The last bullets in the chamber must always be saved for the women and children in our midst. Why, at Fort Phil Kearney, they have a standing order that if the post is overrun, the women and children are to be put in the powder magazine and an explosive charge set off."

It was a favorite and much-used illustration of the colonel's on the topic of protecting the "innocents," the category into which women and children fell in the army's classifications. Once Hannah would have laughed and teased the colonel that perhaps wives had more to fear from their husbands than from the Indians. She no longer found any humor in the topic.

"I have often wondered who gave that order," Hannah ventured with idle curiosity. "It's so dramatic —it sounds like something the reckless and dashing General Custer would do. Did the furor he caused in Washington with his charges of corruption in the Indian Bureau ever die down?"

A telling silence spread through the room before the colonel responded, "No one has told you about Custer?"

"No." Hannah looked around the room at the sober, knowing expressions.

"A third of the Seventh Regiment was wiped out." Lieutenant Digby volunteered the information. "There was a battle up in Montana along a river they call the Little Big Horn. Custer is dead, along with nearly two hundred of his men. It happened last June. No one survived."

"Except for Major Reno and the three companies Custer put under his command." It was Stephen who spoke, the hardness of condemnation in his voice. "Custer would be alive if Reno had attacked the Indian encampment as he was ordered to and created a diversion. Instead, he tried to make a stand and it turned into a rout. Custer was battling the Indians not three miles distant. Reno should have charged through and come to Custer's aid."

"Reno's companies were under attack," the colonel reminded him. "They were defending themselves. It would have been extremely difficult to mount an offensive under those circumstances. And even if Reno had joined up with Custer, the Indians still had a superior force in the field. The whole regiment could have been wiped out."

"Captain Weir took a company without authority and went to Custer's aid, because Reno wouldn't do it. By then, it was too late. But Weir did try—he did move."

The entire battle obviously had been hashed over many times, the strategy, terrain, and conditions discussed again and again. Hannah could hear the bitterness in Stephen's voice, and knew precisely what he was thinking: if he'd been there in Reno's stead, he would have reached Custer—he would have saved Custer. The glory would have been his.

Murmuring an excuse, Hannah rose from her chair, leaving the men to refight the battle without her. As she crossed to the side table where a moderately cooled bottle of champagne rested in a bucket of snow water, she reflected on how different things might have been if Stephen had accepted that captaincy in the Seventh after the Civil War. All the battles and the focus of national attention were in the Plains. He might have had his glory, might have realized his ambitions and achieved military acclaim with the Seventh Cavalry Regiment, instead of being forgotten here in this sun-baked, canyon-scarred land, frustrated and restless. And she—she would never have been taken by the Apaches. Of course, it was also entirely possible that if Stephen had joined the Seventh, she might have been a widow by now.

"May I?" A large-knuckled hand lifted the champagne bottle from its bucket, a linen towel ready to hold under the dripping sides.

Hannah looked up, a sense of ease touching her when she met the glance of Jake Cutter's steady blue eyes. "Thank you, Captain." She held out her glass and idly studied his deeply tanned features. There was a deliberateness about him that indicated that he was slow to judge, and an indolence that masked the swiftness of his mind and the sharp attention of his gaze. Hannah remembered that when his eyes lifted to her again. Behind them, the talk rose as a detail of Custer's last battle was disputed. "The wall is standing without your support, Captain," she remarked idly. Ever since the dinner party had retired to the parlor, she had noticed, Jake Cutter had leaned against one wall as if he were a permanent brace. "Or were you assigned to that post by Mrs. Goodson?" She sipped at the champagne, which had gone as flat as the evening, as flat as her attempts to engage in the social patter at which she had once been so adept.

"A bachelor learns to stay close to the refreshment

table." Cutter countered with an equally empty and meaningless remark.

Four days she had been back. Four days she'd tried to live as she had previously lived, and discovered that very little filled her days. They were empty, the time taken by afternoon teas or literary meetings or preparing for afternoon teas and literary meetings, and supervising the household help. Somehow she had lost the sense that these things were important.

She sipped at the champagne, her back to the room as she faced the side table, and listened to the arguments, the second-guessing. Bettendorf's voice lifted. "Never forget, the Sioux and the Cheyenne are among the best light cavalry the world has ever known."

"Cavalry," Hannah said, and felt Cutter's attention come fully to her. "The war with the Sioux and the Cheyenne and the other northern tribes is a cavalry officers' war. That isn't the way of the Apache. I'm afraid my husband is in the wrong region. He wants the action and the swiftness of a cavalry war."

Cutter lifted a shoulder in an idle shrug. "People want too much."

Hannah looked at him with some surprise. "I've often thought that."

"It's true. Sometimes it's enough that life is good—that the air is fresh and the sun rides high." He stood at right angles to her, his look steady. She listened to his words and felt the stirring of interest.

For an instant, she blocked out the others in the room, forgot their existence, until a whispered exchange caught her attention. People didn't speak in whispers unless they didn't want their remarks overheard. In the last four days, there had been far too many whispers and behind-the-hand murmurs in her presence.

Without turning, she asked, "Are they all watching me, Captain?"

His pause was slight. "Yes."

"Pity," she said shortly. "I would have liked to see the back of someone's head this evening. Their eyes are on me all the time." A faint bitterness came into her voice. "I know what they're wondering—it's the only question they haven't had the nerve to ask. How many has she had?"

In the following silence, Cutter set his nearly empty champagne glass on the side table, then turned away. It startled Hannah that he should leave so abruptly—but he didn't leave. Her glance rose from his wide shoulders to the long, shaggy hair curling into the collar of his dress uniform. *"The back of someone's head"*—the phrase came back to her as Cutter swung around to face her again, the corners of his eyes crinkling in a smile. She tried to suppress her laugh, but some of it bubbled through, and the awful tension that had been stretching her nerves suddenly eased.

"You should smile more often," he said, and picked up his glass. "It makes everything easier."

She sobered, growing thoughtful, but her expression remained warm. "I don't know that I ever properly thanked you, for—everything." His presence had been so steadying during those days of going from being an Apache captive to a free woman.

"Thanks aren't necessary, Mrs. Wade," Cutter insisted with a withdrawn air. "I did no more than anyone else in my position would have done."

"You were doing your duty." Hannah recalled the phrase she so identified with the military.

Cutter studied the pale liquid in the bottom of his glass. "Yes, my duty." He raised his glass, downing the last of his flat champagne.

The sound of a footstep behind her broke into the accord between them. Then Stephen was at her elbow, his head inclining solicitously toward her. "How are you feeling, Hannah?"

At last she turned, bringing more of the room and its occupants into her range of vision as she faced Stephen. She felt everyone's attention on them, surreptitiously watching and speculating.

"I'm fine." The smoothness of her answer belied the returning tension she felt, but it was there, traveling along her nerves.

His critical glance took note of the full glass of wine in her hand. "More champagne?" He arched an eyebrow in a gesture of disapproval.

"It's only my second glass." Hannah heard the defensive note in her voice, and resented it. "Don't worry, Stephen. It's not likely to loosen my tongue." Her stiff, low answer referred to his previous admonitions that she not discuss her fate in the Apaches' hands. She knew how worried he was that she would reveal certain details to his friends and fellow officers, confirm all the things they so strongly, and often accurately, suspected.

His mouth tightened in displeasure as he glanced briefly at Cutter, whom he'd previously ignored. To Hannah, Stephen said, "I thought perhaps you were getting tired. It might be best if we have an early evening."

Five minutes before she would have welcomed the opportunity to escape. The strain of coping with the probing questions, the implied censure in the comments, the speculating looks, had been an ordeal. Yet Stephen's attitude irritated her. She suspected that his concern was not so much for her welfare, but for the risk of a too revealing word.

"Not yet," Hannah demurred. "I haven't finished the champagne Captain Cutter so kindly poured for me." She lifted the crystal goblet to her lips, sending a brief glance at Cutter over the rim of it.

"Would you care for more, Major?" Cutter reached for the bottle.

"No!" The sharp refusal was belatedly tempered by a stiff, "Thank you."

With a small shrug indicating that it was Wade's choice, Cutter picked up the bottle and filled his own glass. Hannah's respite from the questions ended as Mrs. Bettendorf approached the refreshment table.

"Champagne, Mrs. Bettendorf?" Cutter still held the bottle in expectation of filling the empty glass she carried.

"No, no. Another glass and I'd be tittering." She set the crystal goblet at the back of the table and turned her attention on Hannah. "I'm sure it must be so wonderful to be among civilized society once more. I truly don't know how you managed to endure such a heinous life. As I told the colonel, it must be a miracle."

"Yes." Hannah's glance lowered to an absent contemplation of the lead crystal in her hand. The bitter irony of trading one ordeal for another was the foremost thing in her thoughts.

"I mentioned to the colonel that it would be a fine thing to have the minister from Silver City come to see you. I'm sure that after all you've been through you feel the need to talk to a man of God." Mrs. Bettendorf smiled, but her look was curiously intent.

Affronted, Hannah stiffened. "I would welcome the opportunity to pray with a man of the cloth on any occasion, but I have committed no sin for which I feel the need to confess."

The clear ring of her voice echoed in the room's silence, her declaration heard by everyone present, reminding her that they were always listening and always watching. Bitterness welled in her, and hurt and anger.

Before the talk could pick up again, a call came from out of the night, muffled by the building's walls.

"Corp'ral of the guard! Post number one!" And the call ran back along the sentry line.

Immediately a shift of attention stirred through the room. The fort's rhythm had been disturbed, and everyone was keyed to the change, sensing trouble. Lieutenant Digby excused himself and quietly left the quarters as the running tramp of booted feet crossed the quadrangle.

The wives made a concerted effort to start up the conversation again, but the talk was desultory. They went through the motions, each with one eye and one ear tuned to what was happening outside, awaiting news of the cause of the alarm. Hannah welcomed the distraction that relieved her of their attention. An agitation gripped her, which she tried to quell with a gulp of the flat champagne.

Within minutes, Digby slipped back inside, breathing hard and barely containing his excitement. "Colonel Bettendorf." He crossed quickly to his commander. "A wagon carrying supplies to the mine's been hit by Apaches. One of the outriders got away to come for help."

Outside a bugler sounded the call to horse. Everyone moved toward the door, the party abruptly ending. Stephen left Hannah's side to go to his commander, his shoulders squared in military attention. She saw in him the eagerness for action, a need to engage the enemy in a blood-battle, and knew that this thirst to fight did not come solely from the soldier in him. Some part of it was a desire for vengeance for what they'd done to him through her.

"I'll go, sir," he volunteered.

"Take twelve men," Bettendorf said, nodding his agreement, and started for the door, inquiring of Digby, "The rider, did he say where the wagon was? Any estimate of the Apaches' strength?"

Many times in the long-ago past, Hannah had lived through these moments when her husband prepared to head a patrol responding to some call of trouble. As she followed him outside into the cool of a high desert night, the familiarity of it all contained a strangeness as well. Hastily moving men spilled out of the barracks, their voices raised, and the air was charged with tension. Stephen headed for the parade ground at a trot.

"Hooker!" His hard command rang out clearly as he called to the top sergeant. "I want the first twelve men you find ready! Either company!"

Dark shadows moved through the night, shapes outlined by the starlight above and the lantern light spilling from the barracks windows. Hannah saw a rider being helped from his horse and Doc Griswald's pudgy shape hurrying in that direction.

A light flared near her. Cutter lit one of his long, thin cigars, his hand cupping the flame, and released a puff of aromatic smoke that scented the night. His watchful gaze was on the activity boiling around the parade ground. As if sensing Hannah's eyes on him, he glanced her way and seemed to absorb her with a look. Hannah was slow to turn from it.

Troopers lined up in the middle of the parade ground, hustling under the urging of their sergeant. Stephen conferred with Colonel Bettendorf and the corporal of the guard. From her position on the walk, Hannah could hear snatches of their words, information about the number of supply wagons, drivers, and guards, and the approximate location along the canyon road.

"Prepare to mount!" Hooker's deep voice lifted across the parade ground. "Mo-ount!"

The resounding noise of legs slapping leather as a dozen soldiers mounted in unison, the horses grunting and snorting, filled the night. The column was ready to move out. Almost belatedly, Stephen remembered Hannah and rode over to say a quick farewell. His fresh, eager horse curvetted in place, its hooves beating a tattoo on the hard-packed ground.

For a few seconds, he looked down at her, controlling his restless mount with little effort. When his glance fell away from her, his expression was riddled with tension, the straight lines of his mouth partially hidden under the dark bristle of his mustache. Hannah folded the wool shawl more tightly across her breast.

"You'll be all right?"

"Of course," she said.

"I'll see Mrs. Wade safely back to her quarters." Cutter held the cigar between his fingers, white smoke trailing upward. "Good hunting, Major."

A salute acknowledged both comments; then Stephen wheeled his horse away and sent it toward the mounted column. The signal was given. "Right by twos, march!" The line began moving, dark and indistinct, a mass of serpentine shadows. "Gallop!" The ground rumbled with the pounding hooves as the column swept out of the parade ground and headed toward the road to Silver City. They melted quickly from sight, but the clatter of horses' hooves and equipment echoed through the night for several minutes.

The party guests had begun dispersing when Hannah turned to take her leave of her hosts. She felt the weight of the group against her, the veiled disapproval and censure that lurked behind their unsmiling glances.

"Thank you so much for this evening's party, Mrs. Goodson." Her good manners prevailed to keep everything proper and polite. "From both my husband and myself."

"Not at all, Mrs. Wade. Although I must say, I was surprised that your husband volunteered to take the patrol out," Maude Goodson remarked with open

271

speculation. "I would have expected him to be less eager to leave you alone so soon."

"Duty has always come first with him," Hannah replied stiffly, and turned in the direction of the cigar smoke. "If you're ready, Captain? Good evening, Mrs. Goodson."

It was difficult to walk at a sedate pace with this desperate, driving anger pushing at her feet, but Hannah tried to control the length of her stride. Cutter walked beside her, the Mexican cigar clamped between his teeth.

Hannah was glad of his silence, preoccupied as she was with the sense that she had been on trial tonight, her actions judged and found improper. It was all so unfair! She had been an unwilling victim of all that had happened to her, yet she was being condemned for it. She carried the stigma of having been an Apache squaw, and in their eyes that made her tainted and unclean. If she had died at the hands of her assaulters, she would have been widely mourned. But she had lived, and they blamed her for it. She was rigid with anger, her nerves strained, her emotions in conflict as a raging temper brought her close to tears.

At the door to her quarters, Hannah paused. "Thank you for seeing me home, Captain." She reached for the door latch.

"It's difficult, isn't it?" The quiet, low-voiced words checked her movement. She stopped, facing the door, her head bowed but turned in his direction.

"I'm afraid I don't know what you mean, Captain." She was stiff with pride, yet drawn by that hint of understanding she so badly needed.

"I think you do, Mrs. Wade." He removed the cigar from his mouth, its tip a glowing red ember in the night. "I heard what they said, what they asked. Nobody gave you an easy time of it tonight."

"Why?" The slope of her shoulders increased,

bowed under the weight of the blame she didn't understand. "What have I done?"

"It isn't what you've done so much as it is what they've been taught." Cutter studied the thread of blue-gray smoke from his cigar as Hannah half-turned toward him to listen. "Some mothers teach their children that if their candy gets dropped in the dirt, it isn't good anymore because no amount of washing will ever make that piece of candy clean again."

A humorless sound came from her throat. "Maybe you should never have picked me up, Captain. Maybe you should have left me where you found me."

"You don't really mean that, Hannah—I'm sorry: Mrs. Wade," he corrected his uninvited familiarity.

"Please call me Hannah." She gave her permission, then became conscious of the pleasure she'd felt at the sound of her name from his lips. "Do people ever outgrow their aversion to washed candy?"

"They just have to get hungry enough." Cutter took a last drag on the cigar and tossed it to one side, its red tip tracing an arcing path in the black night.

"And if they don't?" The question was almost a challenge.

"Then they're fools," he concluded evenly.

"You are good for my morale, Cutter."

"I'm not sure that was in my mind." He straightened. In the shadows, she could see the wide cut of his shoulders against the night's darkness. Somehow she knew he wasn't smiling when he touched his hat to her. "Evening, Hannah."

She watched him move off the porch and stride into the night, her thoughts on Cutter rather than her own situation. She wondered at this taciturn man who seemed to shrug away so many things that troubled others. They just didn't bother him. He had the desert's hard vitality and strength—and its impartial acceptance of all that lived. Yet Hannah suspected that he had once been hot-tempered and reckless, until the Civil War had cooled his fiery ardor and the Apache frontier had taught him caution and forced an indolence on him. And he had a sense of fairness. She lost sight of him in the shadows and finally turned to enter her quarters, regretting that Stephen did not share some of Cutter's views.

On the other side of the parade ground, the call to horse had summoned families from their Suds Row housing. Wives emerged with sleepy, sobbing youngsters on their hips and older children scattered about them. They watched the patrol depart, most with their husbands at their sides and a few whose men were among the troop galloping into the night.

When the blackness had swallowed them and distance muffled the drumming hoofbeats, Cimmy Lou lingered with the others, mentally following the patrol. With vague reluctance, she turned to join the growing numbers of onlookers who were wandering back to their canvas shacks. She dawdled, walking with a slow swing of her hips, hugging the heavy shawl around her while she gazed at the star-dusted sky.

Frustration and irritation increased the longing in her. She didn't want to go back to that empty cot, still warm from John T.'s body, and the bedcovers all musky with the smell of him. He was top sergeant; he had to be the first to respond to the call—he kept telling her that. Sometimes Cimmy Lou hated the chevrons he wore with such pride, even though she had married him because of them—because he was the best, because he had top rank, and because John T. could satisfy her—when he was around.

Something stirred in the deep shadows between the close-standing tents. Cimmy Lou sent a quick glance that way to probe the darkness, the ever present danger from the Apaches too real for suspicious movement to be ignored. A shadowy form motioned to her, a tall, narrow figure. A heady sureness went through her as Cimmy Lou looked around to see if anyone else had noticed him, a secret smile on her lips.

"Why, Private Bitterman. Ain't it late fo' you to be comin' by fo' yore laundry?" she chided, knowing full well what had brought him around. She looked into his avidly shining eyes, so catlike and black.

"I been waitin' fo' you," he said with some reluctance, a hard tension making him curt. "You know that."

"How could I?" Cimmy Lou half-turned away, punishing him for his bluntness.

"I knew Hooker'd go with that patrol an' leave you all alone t'night." His glance traveled down her profile to the shawl-covered mounds of her pushed-up breasts, her arms crossed under them. Reaching out, he stroked a finger along the line of her jaw and, applying pressure under her chin, turned her face toward him. He wanted her and didn't like the idea. That pleased her, and made her wonder how much command she had over him. "I never shoulda kissed you."

"I know what yore thinkin'—what yore wantin', Leroy Bitterman," she taunted him. "You ain't no different than any other man."

"I came to tell ya to leave me alone, woman. Don't you be a-waggin' that tail o' yores at me, an' givin' me yore looks," he warned. "I ain't like the others. That top sergeant of yores ain't gonna stop me."

For a moment Cimmy Lou stiffened against his accusations; then a rising curiosity eased her. "I never asked you to wait here fo' me t'night. You did that on yore own."

"An' I'm tellin' you, woman, leave me alone if'n you don't want me," he repeated.

"Who'd want you?" A toss of her head dismissed his appeal as she took a step away.

His hand grasped her arm and roughly jerked her back, and he caught hold of her other arm. "Don't be walkin' away from me. I ain't through."

She struggled against his hold, resisting him and the sudden shift of power. She no longer had control, something she'd always exercised over men. He shook her hard, but still she fought him, kicking and pushing. He hauled her against him, pinning her arms to her sides and holding her face in the grip of his hand. His mouth seared across her lips, driving against them and demanding. But she went still, totally unresponsive to this fierce attempt at sexual dominance. The absence of any response, passion or resistance, angered him.

"Have it yore way this time." He drew back, breathing roughly, but she looked at him blankly, giving him nothing, no reaction. "But yore wrong about me, Cimmy Lou. I'm different. I could wear you out."

When he released her, she felt as if she'd lost something instead of winning the battle. While she resented his manhandling tactics, her interest was highly piqued by him, and by the appetite so strong within her.

"Yore like all the rest," Cimmy Lou taunted him as she adjusted the shawl around her shoulders, and studied him with a considering glance. "Nothin' but brag."

But Bitterman merely smiled, the thin mustache a dark line on his upper lip. "Every man what looks at you wants you, Cimmy Lou. That sergeant of yores keeps 'em from doin' anything but lookin' and wishin'. You love a-teasin' 'em. But you ain't gonna tease me. I'm gonna have you—Wait an' see."

Her low, soft laugh mocked him, but her expression was thoughtful and reflective as she moved away again in the direction of the one-room canvas shanty.

# CHAPTER 17

SLEEPY GURGLED WITH LAUGHTER, WAVING HIS SMALL fists excitedly in the air when he saw Hannah. A smile tugged at the corners of her mouth, but the sight of the Apache prisoners crowded together in the bed of the army wagon quickly froze it. The men among them were shackled with ankle-irons, the rattle of a chain making itself heard now and then. She stood about six feet from the wagon. A black trooper from the guard escort eyed her with misgiving, but he didn't order her back.

It was difficult to summon any hatred for these people. Hannah knew of the stealings and depradations they'd committed—and she had not forgotten the brutal way she had initially been treated by them. Yet when she looked at them, she remembered also Angry Dog's skill as a hunter and how he'd always managed to provide them with some game during that long flight from Mexico, or Loco, the group's clown, who always made his wife laugh.

Few on the post would understand her reasoning if she tried to explain it, least of all Stephen. Five days ago he'd brought his detail back before daylight; there had been no survivors from the supply wagons that had been ambushed by another band of Apaches. The bodies had been mutilated. There was no forgiveness in his heart.

The Apaches in the wagon, the remnants of Lutero's band, were being transported to the agency at Ojo Caliente in northern New Mexico. They were a silent and sullen group, except for Sleepy, and Gatita turned his cradleboard away so that her son couldn't see Hannah. She wasn't one of them anymore, and they no longer trusted her.

Still, Hannah said to them in Spanish, "Ojo Caliente is a good place." The area of the hot springs was a favorite stopping place for the tribe.

Gatita looked at her. "If place is good, then let the yellow legs take *pindahs* there and leave this land to us."

Saddened by the words, Hannah stepped back. She knew that the fate of the Apaches was already sealed. Their nomadic life of raiding, foraging, and warring might continue for a time, but it couldn't last. They would either be confined to reservations or vanish from the earth, as so many of the eastern tribes had. The two cultures, white and Apache, were too different to coexist. The Apaches would have to be assimilated or die.

There was a stir of activity along the forming escort detail. Stephen cantered up and dismounted beside her, suspicion and displeasure darkening his expression at finding her by the prisoners. He caught her arm and drew her away from the wagon.

"Were you talking to them?"

"Yes." Hannah bridled at the censure in his tone.

"What did you say?"

A deep bitterness welled in her heart at his question, and she hated Stephen for asking it. More than anything it revealed his loss of faith in her. "What does it matter? You wouldn't believe me anyway." She stopped when he did, unable to look at him.

His hand fell away from her arm in a telling gesture. The escort detail was mounted and ready; the driver and the armed guard sat on the wagon seat while the mules dozed in their harness.

"Hannah." Many things were in his voice, above all a longing for the woman she had been, but the year she'd been away stretched widely between them. There seemed to be no way to bridge it. Stephen could not bring himself to forget the past and build on the present. When Hannah looked at him, she saw the conflict, the wanting and the rejecting of the dirty piece of candy. Finally he spoke. "When we get these Apaches out of here and on the reservation where they belong, things will be better. They won't be around to remind you of that time. You'll be able to put it behind you."

Hannah smiled faintly, finding irony in the assurance that was given to her but needed by him. And she knew that he was still trying to whitewash her. "Of course."

"I'll be back in a week." After a visible hesitation, Stephen bent and brushed a kiss across her cheek, the first physical affection he'd shown her in a week. A moment later, he mounted his horse and rode toward the head of the column.

A slap of the reins awakened the mules and they leaned into their collars, the trace chains jingling. With wheels squeaking, the wagon rumbled out of the yard, surrounded by its cordon of mounted soldiers. Hannah caught one last glimpse of Gatita before the wagon rolled out of sight. When she turned to go back to her quarters, she saw Cutter watching her from the *ramada* of the post headquarters. She smiled and nodded to him, feeling a fine run of warmth at the interest he showed in her, an interest that held no hint of judgment. He touched his hat to her.

Since her return, Hannah hadn't taken an active role in post life, mostly because Stephen wanted her to stay in the background, but partly because she hoped that with the passage of time she wouldn't be treated as such an oddity and looked at askance. With Stephen away, however, her days would drag with nothing to do, so she resolved to begin participating again. She invited the officers' wives to come to afternoon tea two days later.

As she was going through her wardrobe to find her blue dimity day dress, Hannah noticed that her brown satin gown wasn't there. She checked the trunk and discovered that her silver shawl was missing. A further search of the rest of her things revealed that more items were gone—a dreadful glass brooch an aunt had given her, a chipped tortoiseshell comb, two old skirts she'd kept for the material, and a few other items. Except for the brown satin, all of them were things she had seldom or never worn or which she disliked.

"Delancy," Hannah called, and went to the kitchen to question the striker.

Cimmy Lou was with him, hurriedly licking away the crumbs from a ladyfinger. "I brung yore linens, Miz Wade." She nodded to the stack of serviettes on the table.

"Thank you." It was an absent acknowledgment as her attention focused on the striker. "Delancy, I can't find my brown satin gown with the gold threading. There are some other things missing, too. Do you know anything about them?" She caught the look so quickly exchanged between the soldier-servant and the laundress. Her suspicions were immediately roused.

It took him a moment to phrase his answer. "I found it in the garbage one mornin', all ripped. I mentioned it t'the majuh an' . . . he said he knew 'bout it."

"I see." Hannah frowned. "Thank you, Delancy." As she turned to leave, she noticed a yellow glitter from beneath one edge of Cimmy Lou Hooker's shawl. She stopped. "Isn't that my brooch you're wearing?"

Cimmy Lou's hand covered it protectively. "The majuh gave it to me," she insisted.

"And my shawl, the hair comb, my skirts, and all the rest—did he give you those, too?" Hannah questioned, stunned that Stephen would do that.

"Yes, ma'am."

"But why?" She hadn't meant to ask; the question just popped out.

A secretive look stole over the laundress's face, turning her expression very smug and knowing. "I guess he jest wanted t'give me a little somethin' on the side. Mebbe you should ask him."

"Yes."

When Hannah walked out of the kitchen, her cheeks were flaming at the implication behind the answer. Every army wife knew that if she didn't accompany her husband to his posted assignment, he would seek out some fallen woman to satisfy his carnal needs. Such straying was never mentioned. Even if Hannah never had real evidence of it, in her heart she knew. Men were lusting creatures; they couldn't be expected to remain faithful. Hannah knew all that, but to be confronted with it was quite another thing.

By the time the ladies arrived for tea, she had regained her composure. They gathered in the parlor and Hannah poured the tea. The order of service followed the rank of their husbands. Hannah passed the first cup of tea to the colonel's wife, Ophelia Bettendorf, and the second went to the captain's wife, Maude Goodson. Since Lieutenant Digby had seniority over Lieutenant Mitchell, Grace Digby was served before Sadie Mitchell, and, as hostess, the last cup was for herself.

The chatter began with regimental gossip concerning other companies of the Ninth stationed in various New Mexico forts. Some of the names were new to Hannah, so a lot of what was said was meaningless to her.

"I thought he was such a personable man, didn't you, Mrs. Wade?" At the blank look she received from Hannah, Ophelia Bettendorf prompted, "Surely you remember meeting Lieutenant Austin from Boston?"

"No, I don't." Hannah sipped at her tea, holding the fragile cup in one hand and its china saucer in the other.

"That's true, she wasn't here. That was after the Apaches had carried her off," Maude Goodson recalled, and turned to Hannah. "You were with them such a dreadfully long time, my dear."

"Yes, I was," she agreed quietly, and set her cup aside to pick up the china teapot. The contrast between her sun-browned hand and the pastel-flowered pot was marked. "More tea, anyone?"

"Please." Little, doll-like Maude Goodson offered her cup. "I've been meaning to suggest that you should bathe your skin in lemon juice. That's what I do whenever I get too much sun. It whitens your skin really wonderfully."

"I'll try it." But Hannah wondered if the woman realized how many lemons it would take.

"Is it true that they took all your clothes?" Grace Digby stared at her with wide, wondering eyes.

Little shocked sounds came from the others at the temerity of her question, but Hannah noticed that not a single one of them objected as they waited with bated breaths for her answer. She suddenly had a very real sense of why they'd come today—to garner juicy tidbits to gossip about later, and to voyeuristically experience what had happened to her and thank God it wasn't them. Of them all, Maude Goodson was likely the only one who felt even a modicum of pity and a desire to help.

"A lot of things that happened are too unpleasant to recall." A stiff politeness masked her bitter anger. "I'd rather put all that behind me."

Ophelia Bettendorf looked down her long nose and gave Hannah a false smile. "I must say, my dear, I was surprised that Major Wade would leave you so soon after your ordeal. Considering how long you've been apart, I should think he would want to spend every minute he can with you."

Hannah was not surprised that others had noticed how little time Stephen spent with her. He always managed to stay busy at something until after retreat had sounded, thus avoiding her and the problems they were having.

"Duty always comes first with Stephen. That's what makes him a good officer." She remembered when she would have said that with pride—the good, understanding wife praising her husband. Now, she was making excuses for his conduct. "After all, Captain Goodson is on patrol and Captain Cutter just came in, so it was Stephen's turn."

"But the colonel informed him that, under the circumstances, the major should have the time with you, and Lieutenant Digby would have charge of the detail. But your husband insisted that he go."

Hannah hadn't known, and Ophelia Bettendorf had guessed that. More separation was not the answer to their difficulty, yet Stephen had chosen it. Hurt twisted through her, raw and angry. "My husband would never allow his personal life to take precedence over his obligations to the army." None of them were fooled by her response, and they covertly exchanged snide glances. Hannah saw the looks and raged silently.

Plump Grace Digby reached for another of the

dainty sponge cakes. "These are delicious, Mrs. Wade. I must have your recipe."

"I'm afraid you'll have to ask Delancy for that. I didn't make them."

"You never have done much cooking, have you, my dear?" The colonel's wife took a delicate sip of her tea.

"Not in the past, although I do make a very good tortilla now. And I learned to cook a very tasty thick stew by filling a deer's stomach with blood, chili peppers, and wild onions." Hannah saw the shock and revulsion on their faces and didn't care. It was what they had come to hear.

"You didn't eat it?" Grace Digby's ladyfinger was laid aside, only one bite taken.

"Of course. And the next time you have rabbit, you should try partially roasting it before skinning and gutting it." She deliberately gave them all the worst examples, not leaving out a single lurid detail.

Later, Hannah watched them leave. They were barely out the door before their heads were together and their tongues were wagging, but she found no satisfaction in the sight. Sighing, Hannah turned away, fighting depression and loneliness.

Stephen's return did not bring any improvement to their troubled marriage. He went through the motions, pretending that everything was fine, but he never touched her or mentioned the past year. Not that they were together very much; but when they were he rarely looked at her, and when he did, Hannah saw what he was thinking and remembering.

His return coincided with a step-up of Apache activity in the area. Their favorite targets were the ore trains, the twelve- and fourteen-horse teams hauling wagons loaded with silver ore from the mining camps in the Mogollons. Fort Bayard was in a constant state of flux, responding to reports of ambush or near-ambush.

One evening just before retreat, a wounded outrider from an ore train reached the fort. A mounted detachment was dispatched to the scene. Hannah wasn't surprised to see Stephen at the head of it. It was becoming clear to her that Stephen was obsessed with settling what he considered his private score with the Apache.

It was pitch black, shadows pressing in from all sides as the column of riders walked their blowing and winded horses along the gravel track up a high canyon. Other than the striking of metal horseshoes on rough stone, the only sound was the far-off yip of a coyote crying to the lonely sliver of moon. All else was quiet, a mountain chill breathing down on them.

Hooker leaned forward in his McClellan, calling in a low voice to advise Major Wade, "The rider said the Apaches hit 'em along that spot in the road where the fallen chimney rock is. That'd be less than a quarter of a mile."

"It's quiet." Lieutenant Digby rode beside Wade, his anxious gaze darting into the lurking shadows. "What do you think, Major?"

"The Apaches might have broken contact. They seldom fight at night." Stephen turned in his saddle and looked back down the double line of riders. "Stay alert."

Word passed among the troopers that they were approaching the ambush site. Stephen wished that they had more than a ghosting of light from the moon to alleviate this utter blackness before them. He strained to hear any misplaced sound, to catch the smell of smoke or gunpowder.

About four hundred yards farther down the path, his chestnut pricked its ears at an object ahead of them. Stephen could make out little in the trail. His horse snorted, disliking something, and he reined in, stopping the column with an upraised hand. A large and long black shape loomed before them, its dark outline vaguely showing against the lighter-colored ground. He lifted the flap on his holster and loosened his gun.

"Hello, the wagon!" Stephen called in a low, strong voice across the intervening distance. For a long span of seconds, there was only silence. Stephen kicked his horse forward while pulling out his service revolver.

The wagon had been overturned, lying on its side and blocking the trail. From the well of darkness behind it came a low moan. Stephen directed his horse toward the sound as he continued to scan the dark tumble of rocks and brush. The rest of the column advanced behind him.

The closer to the wagon he came, the more he could make out. A horse lay dead in the harness, its teammate obviously having been cut free, and the wagon had half a dozen arrows projecting from it. Stephen dismounted, catching the acrid odor of powder smoke lingering in the air, and passed the reins of his horse to Digby. Another moan, louder than the first, came from the other side of the wagon, near the front wheels. Stephen found the man propped against the undercarriage, half-conscious.

"I've found one of them—alive," he called in that same low but clear voice. "Check around, Sergeant."

While the troopers fanned out under Hooker's direction to comb the surrounding area, Stephen crouched beside the wounded man. The faint moonlight glistened on the barrel of a carbine, lying across the man's legs.

"Where are you hurt, mister?" Stephen picked up the carbine, and felt the man's weak attempt to resist slacken at his words.

The man's head lolled, his mouth slack, his eyes opening, white-ringed. "Curly . . . made it." His breathy laugh became a cough. "Arrow in my . . . shoulder." From the frothy sound of his breath, Stephen suspected that it had pierced a lung. "Bullet in . . . leg. My ribs, maybe. Don't . . . know."

The arrow was still lodged in his left shoulder, the feathered end of the shaft broken off. Stephen left it alone and searched for the leg wound, hampered by the darkness and the deep shadows. "What happened? Where are the others?" Warm, sticky blood oozed from a hole in the man's right thigh. Stephen used his kerchief to make a tourniquet.

"Hit us. Came out of . . . the rocks. Five, maybe six of 'em." Pain and weakness took the man's breath, turning his voice hoarse and making it waver. "Gillis in first wagon . . . got it right away. The 'paches jumped on horses . . . stole wagon. Irish and Shaughnessy took cover in . . . rocks when wagon turned . . . on me. Held 'em off."

"Take it easy." Stephen came to his feet and moved away, his own weapon and the man's carbine in his hands. Lieutenant Digby still sat his horse nearby. "Have someone see to this man."

"Two mo' men over here, suh," a trooper called from the vicinity of the boulder tumble. "Both is dead, suh."

Chunks of ore from the overturned wagon littered the ground, ready to trip the unwary. Stephen picked his way through the jumble, past the dead and bloating horse to the top of the mine road, where Hooker joined him. Stephen looked into the night with a brooding restlessness. They were always too late on the scene, arriving long after the battle; they were never able to catch the bastards.

The impatient edge was in his voice when he spoke. "Get that wagon righted. We'll use it to transport the wounded driver to the fort. And send half a dozen of your men ahead to see if they can locate the second wagon and the body of its driver. In this rough country, the Apaches couldn't have driven it far. They were after the horses. Somewhere up ahead they must have cut them loose and left the wagon."

"Yes, suh. Suh, do you want me to pick up the trail of the 'paches an' send a detail in pursuit?"

"It's a waste of time, Sergeant." Stephen was curt. "You can't follow their trail until daylight. By then they'll have a six-hour lead. No, sergeant, we won't pursue."

"Yes, suh." Hooker saluted and swung away.

Sound carried a long way on the night air of the dry mountain desert. From some distance away in the canyon reaches came the whinny of a horse. The sound caused both the white officer and the colored sergeant to pause.

"From the north, suh, maybe two, three miles as the crow flies," Hooker guessed. "It could be one of the team of horses runnin' loose."

"It could," Stephen agreed. His head was cocked at a listening angle for a second longer; then he stirred. "Leave five men here and mount the rest, Sergeant."

An hour later, the patrol still wound its way through the rough canyon country, always riding as much as possible in the direction of the horse's neigh, though their way was often blocked by dead-end canyons or unscalable cliffs. Like a signal beacon, the horse had given out its frightened call at irregular intervals. Its shrill whinny again shattered the stillness. This time it was very close, only yards ahead. No spoken command, only an upraised hand, brought the double-file column to a halt. Leather creaked under the shifting weights of the troopers in their saddles as Stephen stared into the darkness, listening and trying to gauge the situation.

Digby gave him an anxious glance. "That horse has

been in the same place the whole time." His subdued tone was just louder than a whisper.

From behind them, Sergeant Hooker advised, "It could be the bait in an Apache trap."

"Send two men ahead," Stephen ordered.

Hooker turned in his saddle to look down the line of black troopers. "Henry. Beaufort." His hand motioned them forward.

A shuffling of hooves, munching of bridle bits, and groaning of leather filtered through the night as the column shifted, giving up two of its number. With weapons drawn and at the ready, the advance detail rode forward and the shadows soon swallowed them; only the muffled plod of their horses' hooves marking their presence.

The seconds of waiting seemed interminable, the silence and the stillness magnifying them. Then a single horse trotted back toward the column, its rider halting it within view of the patrol. "All clear, suh."

They moved forward, Stephen holding his horse and the column to a walk, wisely wary for all his restless urgings. The reporting trooper waited for them.

"The horse is still hitched to the supply wagon—what's left of it," he explained, sotto voce. "Wheel broke an' the box got wedged in some rocks."

They came upon the missing second wagon, its contents scattered by the Apaches. The ground was strewn with silver ore rock and ransacked bedrolls. This time Stephen sat on his horse while he surveyed the shadowed scene. His instincts had been right, but it was like chasing the wind. They were always ahead of him.

The gravel of impatience and frustration was in his voice, along with fatigue. "Look for the body of the driver."

In the darkness, a trooper stumbled over something on the ground and the object rolled with a glassy rattle.

over the stony soil. The soldier's shadowy form bent to the ground as he picked it up. When he straightened, he had a bottle in his hand.

"Whiskey. Ya might know de Apaches got it fuhst," he complained as he turned it upside down.

"Unhitch the horse from the wagon," Stephen ordered.

"It's strange that the Apaches didn't take the horse with them—or kill it," Lieutenant Digby remarked.

"I know." It bothered Stephen, too; but the Apaches were seldom predictable in their actions.

"Major." Hooker walked his horse over to them, a troubled frown on his face. "I smell smoke."

The chill mountain air was sweet and fresh with the scent of pine and aromatic shrubs when Stephen tested it. Yet faintly there was the smell of burning, the smokeless kind of fire that the Apaches made.

"They built a fire around here somewhere, Sergeant. Find it." And Stephen suspected that they'd find the wagon driver, too. It seemed likely now that he hadn't been killed in the first assault, only wounded, enough of him alive for the Apaches to torture.

The search had barely started when scouts found the Apache camp not fifty yards away in an arroyo pocket. The fire was a dull red eye on the ground; long, dark shapes lay around it, motionless. Stephen ordered his men to fan out, distrusting the situation but playing it as he found it. The longer he stared at the seemingly sleeping figures on the ground, the steadier his nerves grew. The hard metal butt of his revolver comfortably fitted his hand, the joint of his thumb heavy on the hammer and his forefinger curving hard against the trigger. An icy run of calm sliced wickedly through him.

He gave the order to attack and they hit the sleeping camp, everyone doubting that they were actually taking the Apaches by surprise. But in the first barrage of shouts and gunfire, it was all explained as the Apaches staggered to their feet, reeling drunkenly and quickly abandoning any attempt at defense in order to flee, the smashing of bullets around them having a sobering effect.

The soldiers charged through the camp, giving chase to two warriors who were attempting to escape on foot. Stephen stopped at the fire circle and reloaded the empty chambers of his revolver, gunpowder an acrid scent in the air and on his hands. Crumpled along the edge of the fire circle were the bodies of two dead Apaches who had tried to make a stand, and that of a third Apache, badly wounded, his fingers digging into the dirt.

"Sweet Jesus," someone cursed in a voice sickened with revulsion; then it steadied, and Stephen recognized Hooker's voice. "Major. Yore wagon driver is here."

Stephen backed away from the dead Apaches and crossed to the high shape of a tree and the black form Hooker made against it. The smell was bad, cooked hair and flesh making a malodorous combination. Hooker struck a sulfur match and Stephen saw the flame's orange light flare over the wagoner's body, which was hanging upside down over the hidden coals of a second fire. Stephen's stomach heaved violently as he swung away from the revolting sight, a sick sweat breaking out across his face.

The match was shaken out. "They roasted his brains." Hooker's voice was sick and flat, hard with the effort to keep emotion out of it.

"Cut him down." The low order was almost inaudible. Then anger vibrated through his voice, giving it vehemence. "Dammit, I said cut him down!"

"Yes, suh," John T. Hooker responded. It wasn't something he had to be told. "Cooper. Johnson. Over here." He summoned two of his men as he watched Wade stalk to the Apaches' fire.

Someone had tossed wood on it, and a bright blaze burned. John T. left the two soldiers to see to the driver's body and followed the major. The sounds of pursuit, of running boots and rattling brush, could still be heard in the broken terrain around the camp. Empty whiskey bottles from the supply wagon rolled around the fire, evidence of the reason they had been able to slip up on the Apaches. They'd passed out.

"Hey, Sarge." Trooper Moseby was bent over the wounded Apache, cautiously peering at the bloodied bullet holes torn in his copper flesh. "We'd better do somethin' for this one. He's bleedin' bad."

"Don't touch him," Wade snarled.

"But, suh, he's hurt."

"I said leave the bastard alone!" He took a threatening step toward the trooper; then he seemed to catch himself, and turned away. John T. released a slow breath and came forward.

"He needs mo' than a patch job, Moseby," was John T.'s only comment at the sight of the gut-shot Indian, neither confirming Wade's order nor countering it.

The hounds had caught their quarry, and John T. turned toward the sounds of their approach as they shoved their Apache prisoners in front of them with the muzzles of their rifles. When the first one stepped within the upreaching glow of the firelight, something clicked in John T.'s memory. He stared at the deep-chested Apache with the wide, heavy-boned features, lank black hair hanging to his shoulders, and the small scar on his cheek. With recognition came a cold feeling of dread as John T. looked at Major Wade. Very slowly he remembered that Wade had never seen Lutero before. And Amos Hill wasn't with them, so there would be no questioning of the prisoners. John T.

stared at the Apache Major Wade had hunted these past weeks with so much zeal and hatred—and kept silent.

Reveille, stable call, mess, fatigue, and drill call—the cavalry routine was a timeworn system. Hannah stood beneath the *ramada* and watched the close-order maneuvers of the company upon the parade ground, columns splitting, fours left, fours right, at a walk, a trot, a gallop.

"Right by twos!" The shouted commands had a deep-voiced cadence to them.

Mrs. Mitchell passed by, a parasol raised to shade her face from the morning sun, and nodded to Hannah. She bobbed her head in acknowledgment of the greeting, but neither spoke. Here, too, was a routine Hannah recognized—the morning ritual of tea at the commander's quarters. She was not surprised that her previous standing invitation had not been renewed. If she was there, they couldn't very well talk about her. What better food for gossip than delicious scandal?

It was so bitterly and tragically ironic that she had been the victim of a violent act, perpetuated over many months, yet it was her morals they questioned, her virtue they doubted. Perhaps if she acted more humble, showed some shame, instead of defending her actions and holding her head high, they . . . That ubiquitous "they" included her husband. About the only person who didn't expect her to feel guilty was that man drilling the company on the parade ground, Captain Jake Cutter.

"Detail's comin' in." Someone shouted to alert the post.

Word of the night patrol's return spread quickly to all corners of the post. There was a stirring and a gradual drawing of people to the quadrangle to observe the arrival. Hannah left the porch and wandered toward the top of the parade ground, watching as they filed through the gate.

Stephen sat tall and erect in his saddle, leading the detachment that entered the fort, his beard-darkened face the only evidence he showed of the all-night ride. The troopers were round-shouldered with fatigue, but their heads were up. In the first glance, searching for signs of casualties, Hannah took little note of the two Apache prisoners, astride a pair of horses that were harnessed together, their hands tied behind their backs.

When he saw her coming to welcome him back, Stephen brought his fingers to the brim of his hat, saluting her with a faint nod of his head. She saw the tired hollows under his eyes. A bitter hurt claimed her. Stephen had preferred the bone-weary fatigue of a night's ride after Apaches to the sleeplessness of lying beside her with all his thoughts, questions, and insecurities.

Her glance strayed from him and was caught by the Apache prisoner riding the near horse. The easy sway of his slouched body to the horse's rhythm struck a familiar chord. Hannah stared, her steps slowing as she recognized Lutero. She felt flattened, too stunned to think for several heartbeats.

Then all the silent loathing and virulent emotion that she had kept bottled inside came pushing to the surface. The mental and physical tortures she'd suffered, the long months of slavery, the forced marriage were his doing. Hannah gazed at him and saw the source of all her problems. Everything that had gone wrong could be traced directly to him. Stephen's rejection of her, however reluctant and bitterly fought, and the failure by her peer group to accept her into their fold once more had been caused by Lutero's capture of her. The whispers, the pointed fingers, the looks that followed her wherever she went, all related directly back to him. Why did he have to show up now?

She walked faster, her hate growing along with the heated emotions feeding it—the wounded pride, the offended dignity, the damaged self-respect, and the remembered fear, the impotence and revulsion. At that moment she hated him with a violent passion.

Her attention was centered on him to the exclusion of all else. She did not smell the hot odor of lathered horses and sweating men or taste the dust in the air, stirred by the scuffling hooves. Her face was taut and her eyes burned blackly; she had doubled her hands into fists. She failed to see Stephen turn in his saddle and look back to discover the object that pulled her so strongly.

And Hannah didn't see the horse and rider approach nearly at a gallop, didn't see Cutter sliding off its back as he pulled the horse up so abruptly that it almost sat on its haunches. She saw nothing but Lutero until Cutter put himself in her path. When she tried to go around him, he caught her by the arms.

"Hannah, no." The low, insistent words cautioned her against any action.

"Let me by." Her stiff arms pushed against him, straining in angry resistance as she continued to stare over Cutter's shoulder at Lutero. "Don't you see who it is? I want him! It's my right!" She demanded the Apache privilege of being given the life of the one who had wronged her.

He shook her to bring her attention to him, and his hard, blue gaze bored into her. "What is it you want with him, Hannah?" Jake demanded roughly, keeping his voice low. "Do you want to kill him, is that it? What will it solve? What will it change?"

She stopped struggling and bowed her head to elude his eyes, but the rage inside her was not something that responded to reason or logic. "I don't know."

Stephen hauled up his tired horse alongside them. "What's going on here?" he demanded, then looked suspiciously at the Apache. "Who is he? Do you know him?"

"Lutero." Cutter might as well have said Lucifer.

Wade stiffened, sitting erect in the saddle and reacting to the name as Hannah had known he would. Regret raged through him at the chance he had lost to kill the Apache last night; the time and place were wrong now. He couldn't do it here in front of the colonel and the other officers, not in cold blood. He had his reputation to consider.

Stephen urged his horse toward the animal Lutero rode. Violence was coiled in him like a vibrating spring of tension. He stared into the dour, brutal face and trembled with the urge to kill the man who stood between him and his wife, the one who had taken her.

The silence stretched, and he became aware of the post's attention on him and recognized how odd his behavior must seem. He gathered his composure and looked at the surrounding soldiers, who were eyeing him with tired interest.

"I'm bringing charges against this Indian. Take him to the stockade," Stephen ordered. He didn't look at Hannah as he rode to the front of the column, where Colonel Bettendorf awaited his report. "Dismiss the detail, Sergeant."

A pair of troopers swung Lutero out of line. For a moment he faced Hannah. He looked at her. He looked *through* her. Hannah watched him ride past her, conscious that Cutter had shifted to stand beside her, one hand gripping her arm above the elbow. A rigid tension held her still, while hot, angry tears scalded her eyes.

"I'll escort you home." His statement was underlaid with a heavy tone of disapproval.

"No." She resisted the guiding pressure of his hand, her gaze still following Lutero. "I want to see him locked up."

Cutter said nothing, merely looking at her for a long moment; then he released a heavy breath and escorted her in the direction of the guardhouse. He didn't like it, but he'd seen the determined set of her jaw. She would go—with or without him. They angled across the parade ground as the detail of tired men and horses passed them, heading for the stables.

Standing at attention in front of the colonel, Stephen was conscious of the colonel's wife and Mrs. Mitchell standing close by. Curtly he gave a brief outline of the night's mission.

"The wounded driver, where is he?" The colonel looked toward the recovered supply wagon, with four blanket-wrapped bodies lying in the back.

"He was lung-shot, sir. He didn't make it."

"And the Apache?"

"He led the raid. He's responsible for the murder and torture of those miners." Stephen maintained a stiffly correct posture, raw energy relentlessly driving him beyond the bounds of fatigue.

"Your wife appeared to know him." The colonel's look probed for more information. "Is he—"

"Yes, sir." Stephen interrupted so that he wouldn't have to hear the rest of the question.

"I see."

The absently expressed remark stirred Stephen's anger and bitter resentment. He knew precisely what Colonel Bettendorf was "seeing" in his mind—Hannah and that Apache—and there was nothing Stephen could do about it, no way he could stop people from thinking about his wife and speculating about what the Apache had done to her.

His temper wasn't helped when he overheard Mrs.

Bettendorf murmur, "Did you hear that? The Apache they just brought in is the one who took Mrs. Wade as his squaw."

Bettendorf said in dismissal, "Good job, Major."

Stephen responded with a stiff salute, then grasped the pommel and swung into the saddle. His tired horse turned toward the stables, but Stephen reined it in and headed for the guardhouse, spurring the animal into a canter across the quadrangle.

The sun glinted on the deep red fires in Hannah's dark hair as she stood outside the iron-barred door and looked through the thick grate. Standing to one side of her, Cutter bent his head, lighting a cigar. He shook out the match as Stephen rode up and dismounted from his horse.

"Why did you bring her here, Cutter?" Stephen demanded in reproof, short-tempered and impatient.

"She insisted," Cutter replied through his cigar, watchful beneath his indolence.

Stephen crossed to Hannah's side. "You shouldn't be here." His gauntleted hand curved around the back of her arm, and he felt her rigid resistance. His glance stabbed at the dark form sitting on the cot in the deep shadows of the cell's interior, silent and unmoving.

"What will they do with him?" Hannah didn't take her gaze from the jailed Lutero.

"We'll hold him here until the U.S. marshal comes; then he'll be tried." The roughness in his voice bespoke his rancor toward such civilized procedures in this Apache's case. "I'll take you home."

She let herself be led away from the guardhouse. Hannah and Stephen walked together, but they were very much separate. Cutter watched them through the wisps of cigar smoke and sensed the friction that split them.

He noted Hooker's approach and the way he looked after the departing couple. The sergeant came to stand beside Cutter. For a minute, silence held between them; then John T. cast a glance at the prisoner behind the iron-barred door.

"If I'd told him last night that was Lutero, he'd have killed him sure," John T. stated with a shake of his head that questioned the rightness of his choice to keep silent.

"He would have." Cutter nodded slowly.

# CHAPTER 18

AFTER SHE PLACED HER ORDER, OPHELIA BETTENDORF wandered to the front of the trader's store and browsed over the limited assortment of threads and sewing items. Her glance strayed out the narrow window and paused on the figure walking by. She immediately motioned for her companion.

"Mrs. Mitchell," she hissed in urgent command, and waited until the woman had joined her to point discreetly. "There she is. I'll bet she's going to the guardhouse where they have that Apache locked up. The colonel said it'll be another week before the marshal comes."

Mrs. Mitchell's tongue clicked in a reproving manner. "It's shocking, isn't it? I should think she would not budge from her quarters until that murderer was taken from here."

"*I* certainly wouldn't," Ophelia Bettendorf remarked. "This thing has ruined her—simply ruined her. It's so sad. Everyone knows about those months she spent with the Apaches. Her reputation is permanently stained. A decent, respectable woman can't risk being seen with her."

There was complete agreement in Sadie Mitchell's expression. "I've said it before: she should have killed herself before she let them touch her. Why, there's just no knowing what all they did to her. And what kind of women let strange men touch them?"

As they watched Hannah Wade walk past the post trader's store, their lips were pursed in unforgiving lines. To have one of their own fall from grace was a reflection on them. As officers' wives, a certain standard of conduct had to be kept, a certain propriety observed. They simply couldn't let their husbands think that they might be like her and welcome the attentions of an Indian over death. It seemed to them that she must have wanted it or she would have fought or tried to escape; and failing that, she should have killed herself. But everyone could see that Hannah Wade was in remarkably good health, so it couldn't have been that much of an ordeal—which meant that she must have been willing. It would have been best if she'd stayed with the Apaches instead of coming back and shaming her husband this way.

Out on the parade ground, the sprinkling cart was dampening the dust, raising the sharp-scented smell of wet earth. The sun was warm on Hannah's shoulders; heat was beginning to dominate the days again. The long skirt of her pearl-gray Irish poplin dress swished briskly with the stride of her legs. When she reached the guardhouse, her steps slowed and stopped.

The colored soldiers on guard knew her and didn't challenge her when she approached the door's iron bars. Beyond the grate, Lutero sat cross-legged on the hard-packed floor, a still figure in the shadowy cell. Hannah stopped just outside the bars and stared inside.

His bronze face was in shadows, but she could feel Lutero's eyes on her. The atmosphere simmered with a wild tension, induced by the prolonged confinement. For all his outward stoicism and his seeming acceptance of the imprisonment, she knew he was haunted by the view of the desert mountains.

Having lived with the Apaches, Hannah knew that pain and physical suffering and even death were things the Apache understood. But they were a nomadic tribe, accustomed to coming and going. To be held within four walls was the cruelest punishment to a creature that had run wild all its life. He came to his feet and placed his hands around the bars, revealing himself for an instant. A second later, he swung away, his muscles flexed and taut. He kept his back to the bars, denying her presence.

She felt no pleasure at seeing him locked in the guardhouse. She had thought she wanted to see him punished; yet it didn't accomplish anything. Lutero was like any other Apache. He hadn't committed a crime against her so much as he'd done what any other Apache would do.

Maybe that was true; maybe it was just the way of the Apache. Hannah knew only that it was becoming more difficult to blame Lutero for everything—for Stephen's inability to accept her, the judgment of her peers, and the prejudices of society. Her feverish need for revenge had diminished to a less consuming level. She still hated, but now that hate was directed toward the injustice being done her. She had gone through hell, and now she was judged a sinner for surviving it.

"What a surprise to find you here, Mrs. Wade." The footsteps behind her had made little impression a moment ago.

Hannah stiffened, becoming defensive in the presence of the newspaper publisher, and turned from the cell door to face him. "Somehow, I'm not surprised to see you here, Mr. Boler."

His mouth quirked at her slightly caustic remark, showing a wry respect for the sharpness of her tongue, but he directed his attention at the cell. "That's him, is it?" It was a flat statement that required no confirmation from her.

"That's Lutero," she said coolly, as if the name made a difference.

"I understand that your husband brought him in two days ago." Boler rocked back on his heels, his hands folded behind the checked jacket. His profile reminded her of a bulldog, with its jutting lower jaw and jowly cheeks.

"That's correct."

"What do you suppose he was doing around here?" Speculation already showed in his small, shrewd eyes.

Lutero's back remained to the bars, showing his indifference to the presence of another *pindah*. The impassive black face of the guard revealed no interest in their conversation as he kept his eyes averted from the officer's lady and the heavyset white man.

"I'm sure you already know that he was a member of a war party that attacked an ore train bound for Silver City, but maybe you should ask him, Mr. Boler." Lifting her skirts, Hannah turned and walked away from the guardhouse. She had guessed that the dogged editor would follow, and he did.

"There's been talk that he was coming for you."

"Why should he do that?" The sprinkler cart finished its rattling circuit of the parade ground and headed for the stables. Its bump and clatter gradually receded.

"You were his squaw." For a big man, he moved with ease, keeping pace with her reaching stride. She suspected that his protruding stomach was not flab but solid muscle, as hard as he was.

303

"His wife and son are at the agency in Ojo Caliente. I am quite certain that if he was seeking anyone, it would be them."

"How do you feel about seeing him behind bars? Does it bother you to see him caged up like that?"

"He was a party to the killing of two drivers and two men riding guard for those wagons," Hannah reminded him with stiff-necked anger. "Surely you don't think I condone that."

"I've found that women tend to be notional creatures, especially the ones who love bad men. According to them, the men aren't bad, just misunderstood. They get caught up in a lot of romantic foolishness. Some are like a dog that loves the master who beats it."

"And do you think I'm one of those 'notional' women?"

"I don't know, Mrs. Wade. Are you?"

She stopped walking. "I am certain that it would make a sensational story to write about forbidden lovers and claim that Lutero was coming to carry me off into the hills where we could live the wild and free life of the Apache. But there wouldn't be a scrap of truth in it," she declared in a heated voice. "I am beginning to wonder, Mr. Boler, whether it's a newspaper you publish or dime novels."

Her outburst drew a smile from him. Out of the corner of one eye, Hannah saw the blue uniform of an officer. She half-turned as Stephen approached them and took a moment to bring her temper under control.

"Is there a problem?" He looked accusingly at the man in the bowler hat.

"None," was the publisher's calm reply, and then he doffed his hat to Hannah. "It's my job to ask questions, Mrs. Wade. I apologize if any of them offended you. Good day to you, ma'am. Major." Belatedly he bowed to Stephen, and walked away in the direction of the trader's store.

"What did he want?" Stephen demanded.

"He was asking a lot of questions about Lutero, putting his own conjecture into all of them."

Stephen reached for her arm. "I'll walk you to our quarters."

She was tempted to protest that she wasn't ready to go back yet, but it would only antagonize him, so Hannah submitted to his pressure and let him escort her in the direction of Officers' Row. Lately she'd caught herself giving in more and more often to his wishes rather than arguing and placing more stress on their already strained marriage.

"Why did you do it, Hannah? Why did you speak to him? There's no telling what kind of story he'll print this time. He'll rake all of that mess up again about you being his squaw. It'll start people wondering all over again."

"I can't help what people think about me." It was a frustration she had learned too well, creating a situation impossible to combat.

They took several more steps before Stephen spoke again, this time with all that hard, explosive energy tamped down. "Colonel Bettendorf has suggested that it might be a good idea if you went east for a while. It would give you a chance to rest."

"I don't need a rest, Stephen." The last thing she needed was more idle time. She treated his suggestion with the tolerant patience she would show a child.

"You do need a change of surroundings. Here you have too many reminders, you are under too much strain. You've gone through enough without having to endure more."

Hannah listened to his voice and read between the lines, a hardness growing inside her. "You want me to leave, don't you, Stephen? I'm an embarrassment to you."

"I never intimated that at all."

"You didn't have to."

"I merely think a change of scenery would be good for you, and your absence would give all this talk a chance to die down," he reasoned with cool logic.

"I'm not leaving, Stephen," she stated. "I have done nothing to be ashamed of, and I won't run."

"Hannah, you don't understand," His patience was thin. The inner force that always drove him was pushing at him now. "You are making things awkward."

"For you?" she challenged.

Stephen ignored her comment. "I've requested a transfer—"

"Oh, Stephen." It was Hannah's turn to be exasperated with him. "Don't you think the rest of the regiment knows about me? I'm sure they've all heard about it at Fort McRae, Fort Wingate, and Fort Stanton, as well as all the others."

"I've asked to be transferred out of the regiment," he finished the statement she had interrupted. "It will very likely mean a demotion in rank."

Her anger faded into a kind of pitying sadness. "What happens if the story follows us to another regiment?"

"It won't—especially if you spend some time in the East, until my transfer comes through. Then, when you join me, you'll be fresh from the East, as far as they're concerned." He had it all planned.

Hannah turned her head away, troubled by his inference that her ordeal was damaging his career. It wasn't fair that she should suffer when she'd done no wrong—and it was doubly unfair that Stephen should feel any backlash.

"I'll think about it, Stephen," Hannah promised in a subdued voice.

A patrol approached the front gate, returning from a five-day scouting expedition. The increasing volume of grunting horses, scuffing hooves, and jangling metal bits claimed the attention of the fort. Stephen stopped short of their quarters to glance at the column riding in, and Hannah paused as well.

"Cutter's back. That means I'll be going out in the morning." As always, the patrols were rotated; two scouting details went out and one always remained at the fort to cover emergencies. "Better get my things ready," he advised her.

"I will."

A hard eagerness directed him away from her. From previous experience, Hannah knew that Stephen wanted to be present while the colonel was briefed on the patrol's activities so that he would have the intelligence firsthand on the movement of any hostiles in the area. When he walked away from her without a word, she realized just how wide the schism between them had become. More and more he treated her with indifference and found reasons to be absent. When they were together, they were always on the edge of quarreling. She didn't stay to see the weary column forming up on the parade ground to await dismissal. Instead, she turned to walk the rest of the way to their quarters.

The rooms stifled her with their airless space and confining walls. Within minutes of returning, Hannah was seeking the shade of the *ramada*, from which she could view the fort's routines. She sat in a chair, crudely made of bent wood with a slatted seat and back, too many troubled thoughts running through her mind to be able to completely relax.

Most of the activity centered on the stables, where the returning troopers were busy unsaddling their horses and making sure they were watered and fed. Then Hannah recognized a familiar figure coming down Officers' Row. Her heart seemed to lift at the sight of Cutter's long-legged and lean shape. Alkali dust powdered his uniform, and he looked hot and dry, saddle-weary and trail-worn.

On an impulse, she called to him. "Captain!" She watched him hesitate in mid-stride as his head came up and his gaze swung toward the low adobe building. "I have some Sonora lemons if you're thirsty."

There was the smallest pause before he switched directions to walk toward her. "Sounds damned good."

He followed her inside and down the narrow hallway to the kitchen in the rear. The lemons were sitting out, and Hannah began slicing them while Cutter went to the washbasin to clean up. The splash of water and lathering soap was a companionable sound, accompanying the thud of the knife that released the citrusy tang of lemon scent into the air. Cutter stood for a minute drying his hands on a towel and watching Hannah as she crushed every bit of juice and pulp from the lemon halves into a small glass pitcher. When she began grinding sugar lumps into coarse granules, he fetched in an olla that was suspended from the rafters of the rear porch.

"I wish we had some snow from the mountaintops." Hannah diluted the sugared lemon juice with the tepid water in the olla.

"It's all melted." Cutter took the glass she poured for him and lifted it to her in a toast. *"Salud."* He downed half of the glass before he lowered it. He smacked his lips with relish and smiled at her. "I've found few drinks in my life that are better than whiskey, but this is one of them." Cutter sat on the edge of the table, hooking a yellow-striped leg over one corner.

Hannah sipped at her own glass, a smile acknowledging his compliment. "How was the scouting patrol?"

"Same as always—a lot of hard riding, the horizon dotted with smoke signals, and meals of hardtack fried in bacon grease." In a few words, Cutter sketched a fairly accurate picture of the tedium and hardship of a patrol into the Apacheria country.

"You must be exhausted." Belatedly she noticed the

deep creases around his eyes and the beard-shadowed hollows in his cheeks. Yet the overall impression he gave remained one of tough resilience.

Cutter shrugged and rubbed thoughtfully at the bristle on his face, the motion making an abrasive, scraping sound. "Guess I look pretty bad."

"You look fine," Hannah assured him, a wide, warm smile spreading over her face.

For a moment, Cutter paid close attention to her smiling mouth, then averted his glance to gaze into the lemonade glass. "What have you been doing with yourself lately?"

"Keeping the gossips busy," she admitted with a certain wryness.

"How?"

"I went to the guardhouse today to see Lutero. I thought . . . I wanted the satisfaction of seeing him locked up, imprisoned the way I had been, even though my bars were invisible. But I couldn't hate him for that anymore." She looked at the lemony pale juice in her glass. "I can't blame him for the small and petty attitudes of other people."

"No, you can't." Neither of them named names.

"It's been suggested that I should go east for a while."

"Are you going?"

"I don't know." Agitation pushed her away from the table, restlessness and indecision pressing on her. At the window, Hannah swung back to look at Cutter. "What do you think?" She had come to value his opinion and his judgment.

He seemed to be taking care with his words. "I think that we would miss you. We don't have that many young, beautiful women on the post."

"That's an evasion, not an answer," she retorted.

"I can't help you make that decision." Cutter un-hooked his leg from the table's corner and straightened, his thick brows pulling together in a single line. He came to the window and looked out for a moment, then turned to look at Hannah, conscious of the rawness of his emotions. "Do you want to leave?" he asked, too casually.

"No," she admitted, and thought that he breathed easier, but it was difficult to tell with Cutter. He was too frequently poker-faced.

"You have to do what you think is right, Hannah—not what somebody else says." Cutter swirled the liquid in his glass, then gulped down another swallow of it.

"Hannah." Stephen's voice came from the front parlor.

"I'm in the kitchen," she answered him as Cutter moved away from the window and put the table between them. When Stephen entered and saw Cutter, he stiffened, displeased at finding the other officer in his quarters. Suddenly the room seemed very small to Hannah, with the two men filling it. "Some lemonade, Stephen?" She reached for the pitcher and poured some into a glass.

Stephen took it and sipped at the juice while watching Cutter finish his and set the empty glass on the table. "Thanks," he said to Hannah. "It's a guaranteed quencher for a thirsty man." Then to Stephen, "Good hunting to you, Major."

After Cutter had left, Stephen looked at her with grim disapproval. "What were you thinking, Hannah? Entertaining a man alone in our quarters. People have enough to gossip about now without you giving them more."

"If they can make something out of a glass of lemonade, then let them," she flashed. "Cutter is the only friend I have at this fort." She set her unfinished glass of lemonade on the table with a sharp click and left the room.

They barely spoke to each other for the rest of the

day. That evening Hannah sat at the vanity table and pensively brushed her long auburn hair. Tattoo call lifted into the night's stillness.

Her glance strayed to the unoccupied bed. The last time she'd seen Stephen, he was at the escritoire in the parlor. Her hand paused on a downward stroke of the hairbrush. This contention between them had to end, regardless of its source or her feeling of justification. She couldn't let him go out on patrol tomorrow without making an attempt to patch things up. For too many nights lately she'd gone to bed without touching him, without talking to him at all. Tonight was not going to be another one of them.

Putting on her robe, Hannah left the bedroom and walked on slippered feet down the narrow hallway to the parlor. Stephen glanced up from the writing desk only briefly when she entered. She glided silently across the room to stand behind him and spread her hands over the tightly corded muscles in his shoulders.

"It's getting late, Stephen," she said gently. "Shouldn't you be coming to bed?"

"Later." His shoulders were rigid under the affectionate caress of her hands.

She hesitated for an instant, then slid her fingers into the thickness of his tobacco-brown hair at the nape of his neck. "Then I'll wait up with you."

Impatiently he caught at her hand and ended its fingering of his hair by dragging it down. "I don't want you to wait up for me, Hannah. Now, please go to bed."

"No." She moved away from his chair and crossed her arms in a stubborn, determined gesture. "I'm not going to let you ride out of the fort tomorrow with this harshness between us."

Her action accidentally pulled open the front of her robe and revealed the golden-tan flesh over her collarbones. When Stephen looked at her, his glance was drawn to the exposed skin; irritation flashed across his ruggedly handsome features, thinning his mouth beneath the bushy mustache.

"Close your robe, Hannah," he ordered curtly. "I don't want to be reminded that you're as dark as an Indian all over."

"It isn't something I can change overnight." She pulled the front of her robe together and held it closed with her hand. "It will fade in time, Stephen."

He laid the ink pen on the writing desk and, for a moment, cradled his head in his hands, his elbows propped upon the desk. Then he rubbed his hands over his face as if trying to wipe something from his mind.

"When you came back to me, more than anything else I wanted Lutero caught so he could be punished. I kept telling myself that everything would be all right if only I could get my hands on him and make him pay for what he'd done to you. Now he's in the stockade." His voice was low and haunted. "And I have a face to go with the knowledge of what he did to you. I can visualize the two of you now."

"Stephen, don't do this."

"Every time I look at you, I see him. Every time I touch you, I wonder if he has touched you the same way. You say that you hated him—you hated it."

"I did!"

"No. If you had, you would have killed yourself before you let him do it." He went back to the same line of reasoning, the same belief that had punctuated all their arguments.

"Death is very final," Hannah reminded him. "And I wasn't ready to die. I still had hope. I still expected to be rescued." She paused, her mood suddenly turning bitter. "I hadn't realized that rescue would mean I would be treated with cruelty and meanness equal to any physical torture I endured at the hands of the Apaches. Because I was a victim, I'm shunned, ostracized, and condemned by everyone I once considered my friend."

"How do you expect people to react when you let yourself become some Apache's squaw? You didn't have any respect for yourself, so why should they respect you?"

"When an Apache thinks his wife has been unfaithful, he cuts off her nose. Why don't you try that, Stephen?" she challenged.

"I think you preferred being his squaw," he countered savagely. "You certainly aren't happy with me."

"No. No, I'm not," Hannah agreed. "I expected you to be happy to have me back. I thought you wanted me, that you loved me. It was a miracle that I survived, and I thought you'd be as grateful as I was that we were together again. But I honestly think you are sorry I didn't die."

"You'd be better off dead. We'd all be better off if you were dead," Stephen stated harshly. "We'd be spared all this humiliation and ugly gossip, all the scandal and recriminations. Sometimes, Hannah . . . sometimes I wish you had died. I loved you." Past tense. "Now, when I look at you I see that Apache. His handprints are all over you. Everybody can see it."

"If someone stole your horse and rode it, you'd ride it again when you got it back. Or if a thief broke into your house, you wouldn't move out of it just because someone had been in it. Why do you despise me because I was assaulted?" Hannah couldn't understand.

"You're not a horse. You're my wife. And a woman other men have used is soiled—her virtue is gone, and without it, there is nothing to respect."

"I'm a whore; is that what you're saying? You're married to an adulteress?"

"Go to bed, Hannah." Stephen abruptly ended the argument. "We will not discuss this subject again. Not ever. In time, we'll forget it. For now, we'll put it behind us and never mention it again."

Hannah felt very cold inside. She said nothing, simply turned and walked from the room. A great deal was behind them, gone and never to be retrieved, beginning with love and trust.

# CHAPTER 19

Stable call followed reveille at six o'clock the next morning. After the horses were fed and groomed, twenty of those from A Company were saddled and packed with field equipment. The newly risen sun laid soft pastel yellow and pink light on the collection of adobe buildings surrounding the parade ground as the troopers led their mounts into the rectangular area.

Along the edge of the parade ground, Hannah stood slightly apart from the other officers' wives who had gathered to see the patrol off. On the field, Sergeant Hooker's deep-toned voice issued a command, and the troopers began counting off as she watched Stephen and Lieutenant Digby approach Colonel Bettendorf and the officers standing with him.

Colonel Bettendorf issued some last-minute instructions and then the leave-taking ceremony began. Stephen and the lieutenant traveled down the line, shaking hands and accepting the well wishes of Cutter, Lieutenant Sotsworth, and the others remaining on post. When Stephen reached Hannah, an air of reserve cloaked him. He took her hand, holding it and managing to make her conscious of its lingering traces of roughness.

"Good-bye, Hannah," he said.

Everything except that had been said last night, and she wondered if he realized that. "Good luck, Stephen," she said with an equal lack of feeling, and watched him wheel away to join the patrol, followed by Lieutenant Digby. Her chest ached with anger and a bitter rage that was more the backlash of pain than anything else.

Sergeant Hooker reported to him. "Patrol ready, suh." At the responding nod, his voice lifted to order, "Prepare to mount. Mo-ount!"

In unison, the black soldiers swung onto their army saddles amid the sounds of legs slapping leather, horses grunting under the weight, and equipment clanking together. Amos Hill and three of his Apache scouts waited astride their horses in a formless group while the ranking corporal affixed the pole holding the company guidon into the socket of his stirrup.

"Right by twos!" Hooker sang out the call. "March!" The column rode out at a trot. They were scheduled to be back in less than a week. With the advent of hot weather on the desert, patrols were limited to a five-day stint to spare the men and horses.

The churned-up dust on the parade ground settled slowly onto the hard ground. Hannah stood in stiff resistance to the eyes she felt watching her. When she turned to go back to their quarters, the glances were quickly averted, the women's heads dipping together to exchange whispered comments. She suddenly couldn't bear the thought of reentering those dark, airless rooms. They wanted her to run and hide like some shamed child. She was suffocating under their stuffy, self-righteous moral judgments; she needed to breathe.

She changed directions, altering her course to head toward the stables. The air might reek there, but at least it would be with honest smells. She extended her muscles, feeling the stretch of her legs and the release of pent-up energy. Her heavy skirts wound about her legs and interfered with the reach of her stride, while their swishing rustle almost masked the footsteps approaching behind her.

"May I walk with you?" Cutter was beside her, matching her long stride.

"Are you quite sure you want to be seen with me, Captain?" She was conscious of the bite in her voice, and of the observing eyes along the parade ground although she refused to look in the direction of the other wives. "In case you hadn't noticed, I'm something of a pariah at this fort."

"I believe my reputation can stand it." He ranged easily alongside her, like Hannah looking neither left nor right.

She heard the smile in his voice, but her blood was running too high for it to calm her. The stable area was astir with activity. New horses, purportedly greenbroke when the army bought them, were being broken to saddle by the more experienced riders of the colored troop. Hannah swept past the dust-laden corrals where the grunts of man and animal filled the air accompanied by the reverberating thuds of stiff-legged bucking. When she came to the empty enclosure where the Apache prisoners had been held before being transferred to the agency reserve, she would have bypassed its ghostly reminders for the solitude of the high desert beyond, but Cutter stopped her.

"I can't let you go beyond the fort's perimeter. It isn't safe, even in daylight, twenty yards from here."

She offered no argument against his restriction as she swung back toward the pen of the former prison camp. Hannah crossed her arms, rubbing them with her hands in suppressed agitation. Cutter observed the turbulent sweep of emotion animating her features.

"Do you know what it is I've done that is so wrong?" She turned on him, but Cutter knew she wasn't asking for an answer. "I didn't hide my head in shame. I walked among them with my head high. I didn't grovel at Stephen's feet and beg him to take me back. I went through hell and survived. That's my sin. Now they all expect me to feel guilty because I didn't kill myself. And I won't!"

"No," he agreed quietly. Her gaze fell to the yoked front of his uniform blouse and the army insignia on the brass buttons.

"I hate that uniform," she insisted with vehemence. "I hate the duty it represents and its strict, unforgiving codes. 'Death before dishonor.' I did nothing wrong! Nothing! It isn't fair." Her raised fists pounded against his chest as her broken voice declared over and over, "It isn't fair. It isn't fair."

Impassively Cutter absorbed the force of her blows, letting her expend all the violent energy that had to lash out at something. When it was finally drained and she was left empty, he gathered her close. She stirred in brief resistance, then settled against him, burrowing her head against his shoulder. The hurt he felt in her made him ache. He gritted his teeth, damning those narrow-minded people for doing this to her.

His hands stroked her shoulders and back in comfort as her warm body pressed against him, penetrating the barriers that he usually kept between them. Bending his head, Cutter pressed his lips to the top of her head, then stayed to nuzzle the silken texture of her hair, and breathe in its fragrance.

Without thinking, he kissed the salty wetness on her cheek left by the angry tears. When she shifted, tilting her head up to look at him, Cutter gazed at the face that had lived in his mind for so long, seeing its strength and its stillness. It stirred alive his reckless urges and made him rash.

"You're beautiful, Hannah." He saw the sun-bronzed skin over her cheekbones, fully aware that the color didn't stop with her face, but it was all on the outside. It was the woman within who moved him.

Her lips were soft and unresisting in that first instant of contact. Encouraged, Cutter pressed his advantage and drove against them with warming insistence. Her hungry response jolted through him and his arms tightened aggressively around her. His feverish longings broke through, making him rough with her when he had meant to be gentle.

All sense of restraint was lost in the heat of the moment as they strained together, locked in each other's arms as their lips found the closeness each was seeking. They stood on the edge of the high desert, giving in to the temptation that was upon them.

When Hannah pulled away from him, Cutter was unprepared. Breathing hard and shaken, he saw her bow her head as she turned from him to avoid his gaze. The sensation of her was still with him, the press of her long legs, so firmly muscled, the strength of her arms, the sensation of her fingers sliding into his hair. He took a step toward her to bring her back, but a small lift of her hand stopped him.

"No." Pride made her lift her head. The deep disturbance his kiss had caused was revealed in the troubled darkness of her eyes, but there was no mistaking the determination in her denial. "I am married. Maybe it isn't much of a marriage anymore, but Stephen is my husband." She turned suddenly wary. "Or did you think that because of the Apaches I have no morals left?"

"No, dammit!" Cutter abruptly checked his rising

temper. "Maybe I stepped out of line, but what happened with the Apaches has nothing to do with it. I've wanted—"

"Don't say it." She shut her eyes, then opened them wide, in control again. "Don't say something both of us would come to regret, Cutter." Unable to argue, he turned grim and silent. She turned to leave, then paused. "Thank you, though, for giving me a sense of worth again."

A muscle worked in his jaw as Hannah left him to slowly retrace their route. He didn't want her to walk alone, but he had no right to be at her side, as she'd reminded him. All he could do was add to her problems. He'd never meant to start thinking about her; now Cutter didn't know how he was going to stop. More than once he'd told himself that he would be better off leaving the service, getting away where no talk of her would follow him, but he'd kept postponing the decision. Maybe now was the time, before more hurt was done. He turned when she was out of his sight.

"Well, if it ain't the honorable Cap'n Cutter." Cimmy Lou Hooker sauntered toward him. "I thought you was too good t'mess around with another man's wife. Or ain't you got no respect for Majuh Wade?"

His glance sliced past her to the brushy area from which she'd emerged. "How long have you been there?"

"Long enough." The catlike smile on her mouth became more marked. "You reckon she's tryin' t'pay the Majuh back fo' all the time he spent with me while she was gone?"

"My God," Cutter swore under his breath. "Does John T. know?"

"No, an' you won't tell him," she said, and laughed at the impotent anger darkening his craggy face.

"He'll find out sooner or later—I won't have to tell

him. What do you think will happen then?" he challenged.

"I can handle him." Cimmy Lou shrugged confidently.

He viewed her with utter disgust. "Who ever put the thought in your head that your body is all a man needs to make him happy?" He walked away, returning the salute of a black trooper on a clean-up detail who was coming toward him.

Cimmy Lou's smile deepened. Now Mrs. Wade couldn't make a fuss about the presents the major had given her, or she'd have to tell the major what she'd seen. It would serve that high and mighty Captain Cutter right if she did. She took a step in the direction of the enlisted men's housing, where she'd been going when she'd heard Mrs. Wade's voice raised in anger and gone to investigate. But Leroy Bitterman's approach caused her to pause.

"Workin' hard?" She saw the wheelbarrow he'd left beside the manure pile.

"You shore ain't," he accused.

"I got the day's wash all hung out on the bushes t'dry," Cimmy Lou informed him.

"Don't give me that. I seen ya with the cap'n. How come you won't leave them white officers alone?"

"Why don't you jest mind yore own business?"

He caught her wrist, ignoring the twists of her arm that attempted to free it. "Yore my business."

"Yore no good," Cimmy Lou hissed angrily. "Everybody says you got a rotten core. You even cheat yore own kind."

"Then make me good. Takes a woman t'make a man good. It's a woman what makes a man settle down an' make somethin' of hisself. Settle me down, Cimmy Lou." He moved backward toward the thick brush, pulling her with him.

321

"No." Her struggles were as weak as her protest as she let herself be dragged into the desert brush. "I don't want to."

"I waited long enough." Bitterman shoved her to the ground and held her down with the weight of his body, pinning her wrists against the sand above her head. She thrashed wildly under him, and he struck her with the flat of his hand. "Why do you make me hurt you? You want what I got t'give." As she lay panting and still, her cheek throbbing from the slap, his hand grasped the cotton material of her drawers and tore it away from her skin. The ripping sound drew a groan from her. He cupped her face in his hand and turned it to him. "I'll make you cry out fo' me before I'm through." One-handed, he loosened his pants. "It's time you found out there's only me."

She gave a little moan. "Yes." The assent was reluctantly drawn from her as she gave in to the eagerness growing inside. "Do it, Leroy," Cimmy urged in aching agreement. "Do it to me."

He released her hands and they went around his neck to bring him down to her as she wrapped her legs around his waist to lock and hold his hard-driving hips. More than once she called his name, finding primal wonder where before she'd known only calculated pleasure.

"Bitterman? Hey, Bitterman!" a searching voice shouted.

Still panting, he straightened to tuck in his gray uniform blouse and fasten his pants, throwing a glance over his shoulder before bringing his attention back to her love-heavy features. Her slack lips were swollen from his kisses and her black eyes were heavy-lidded and dreamy soft. Behind them, Bitterman could hear someone moving along the edge of the brush looking for him.

"You wanna see me again, don't you?" he said, low and confident of how completely he'd gotten to her.

"Yes." Cimmy was slow to rearrange her skirts over her legs.

"We're gonna get outta here, you an' me, an' make us some real money offa these miners. Soon, baby. Real soon," he promised, and moved away quickly as his name was called again. The rattle of dry brush marked his passage. A moment later, she heard him speak. "You lookin' fo' me, Corp'ral?"

"Where the hell have you been, Bitterman? I was about t'figure yore scalp was hanging from some 'pache's belt." Then the voices faded as they moved away and Cimmy didn't hear Bitterman's reply. She dawdled a little longer, her body still tingling from its thorough satisfaction, before going back.

The Silver City *Gazette* ran a sensationalized account of Lutero's capture and imprisonment at the fort, never stating that he'd come to reclaim his white squaw, but covertly raising the question. After two days of more looks and whispers, Hannah came to realize that it didn't matter whether there was any truth in it; it was what people wanted to believe.

An orderly was lounging in a chair by the door to the post commander's office when Hannah entered. The tipped-back chair thumped down onto all four legs as he came smartly to attention. But she saw the way he looked at her and knew that the speculation had spread to the colored ranks.

"I'd like to see Colonel Bettendorf, please." Dust particles danced in the sunlit air by the window, where the morning heat invaded the shadowed interior.

"Yes, ma'am." For a second longer he eyed her with curious interest, then disappeared into the next room. She heard the low murmur of voices from within and the returning footsteps as the orderly reappeared. "The colonel will see you, ma'am." He stepped aside to admit her.

The mutton-chop-whiskered commander stood behind his desk, stern and imposing in front of the map of territorial New Mexico. "What can I do for you, Mrs. Wade?" He was stiff with her.

"I would like your permission to ride one of the calvary mounts."

"I'm sorry. I can't allow any pleasure rides to leave this fort. You understand that it's for your own safety."

"I am aware of the restriction, Colonel," Hannah conceded. "I would be content to confine my riding to within the boundaries of the fort. It is the exercise I seek, not the change of scenery."

"Be that as it may . . ." He faltered slightly. "These are rough horses. We don't have any mounts suitable for a lady to ride."

"Excuse me, sir, but Sergeant Hooker pointed out a blue roan with a gentle disposition. I'm sure the horse would be quite satisfactory." She didn't bother to remind him that she had ridden rougher horses when she lived with the Apaches—without the benefit of a saddle and curb bit. "Perhaps you could have your orderly accompany me to the stables. If not, I am capable of catching and saddling my own horse."

Decidedly displeased, he gave in to her request. "Henry!" he summoned, and his orderly came into the room. "Go with Mrs. Wade and saddle a horse for her to ride. She knows which one."

"Yes, suh." He saluted, then paused. "Suh, Cap'n Cutter's outside." The mention of his name brought an immediate tensing of Hannah's nerves, a lifting of her guard.

"Show him in." The colonel hitched up his pantlegs to sit down as Hannah left his office.

In the outer room, she saw Cutter perched on a desk

corner, his long body loose and lanky. The keen blue of his eyes met her glance and held it. She sensed the remembrance of their last meeting turning over in his mind and felt the heated disturbance that the recollection caused. She recognized the danger of such feelings.

"Captain." She nodded smoothly to him.

"Mrs. Wade." The acknowledgment was returned with a touch of his hat.

"The colonel said fo' you to go in, Cap'n." The orderly relayed the message as Hannah walked past Cutter.

"Thanks." Cutter pushed off the desk, his gaze following her out the door. There was a heaviness in his chest at the deep reserve she'd shown him. It weighed on him as he went into the adjoining office.

"Good morning, Captain." Bettendorf looked up from the sheaf of reports and returned the salute Cutter gave him. "I've just been advised that C Company will rendezvous with seven other companies of the Ninth along with Agent Clum from the San Carlos reservation and his Apache police on the twenty-first of April. Geronimo and his renegades have been operating out of Ojo Caliente, and the plan is to arrest them and remove them to San Carlos. That's likely to be a major task for your men. I can't imagine Geronimo surrendering peaceably."

"Neither can I, but I won't be there." Cutter reached inside his shirt and removed his letter of resignation. "I'm resigning my commission as of the end of March."

The announcement accompanied by the formal notice stunned the commander. "But we need good officers like you, Cutter."

"But you don't need me, Colonel." Cutter smiled ironically as he automatically rebuttoned the yoked closing of his shirt. "I've had it in my mind a long time to get myself some land and run horses and cattle on it. There's a valley northeast of here with good graze and water. I've saved up some money, and that's where I'm bound."

"You're making a mistake. The army's in your blood."

"No, it isn't." He slowly shook his head. "After the war, I stayed in out of stubbornness—because somebody wanted me to quit for the wrong reasons," Cutter said, recalling the southern-bred girl whose face had long ago faded into a blur in his memory. "I'm tired of a lot of things, Colonel, but mostly I'm tired of the hate—and what it does to people. I guess when I was young I thought I could change it. Now I know better. It's time for me to get out."

"Well, if that's the way you feel . . ." Bettendorf didn't understand any of what he'd said.

"That's the way I feel."

Outside the building, Cutter stopped under the thatched *ramada* and raked a match-head across a rough post to light his cigar. Hannah was riding a white-legged roan around the parade ground. For a long time, he stood and watched her put the horse through its paces. Hungry impulses stirred inside him. The thought was in his mind to tell her of his decision to resign. He took half a dozen steps in her direction before he realized that it changed nothing for them. Instead, he turned away.

When she saw him turn away, Hannah pulled the roan up and absently patted its arched neck. Cutter had the loose, rolling walk of a man accustomed to the saddle, his long arms swinging freely at his sides. Tall and lean, he wasn't a handsome man, yet he drew her interest almost magnetically. She sat astride the horse, her legs hidden in the voluminous folds of the split skirt she'd made, aware that Cutter at least wouldn't disapprove of the costume. His easygoing ways and steady patience always gave her a kind of reassurance. But there was nothing about him that explained the restless pitch of her feelings and the yearning that tugged so wistfully at her heart. It was much too easy to recall the pressure of his arms around her, that release of a temper and a will too long held in check that had broken through his kiss to move her. Cutter had a man's needs and a man's hunger—and a man's inability to resist temptation. It undoubtedly had been a long time since he was with a woman, and she had tempted him, no more than that. Hannah touched her heels to the roan, urging it forward.

Stephen's uniform was stiff with dried sweat and caked with layers of dust from five days of scouting patrol. The guard on duty outside the barred door of the adobe-block guardhouse came smartly to attention and held a rigid salute until Stephen returned it. He tapped the four-day-old newspaper against his leg as he glared through the iron grate at the Apache prisoner.

This murdering savage had defiled his wife, ruined his name, and tainted his career with scandal. Everyone in the whole territory and beyond knew of his shame and his failure to avenge the wrong. The stories would never stop as long as this Apache lived. He swatted the rolled newspaper against his leg with increasing force, the thwacking sound eventually penetrating his consciousness even though the stinging slap of it did not. Stephen ceased the motion and eyed the guard.

"Why hasn't the territorial marshal arrived to take this prisoner away? We are not operating a prison here." He wanted the Indian out of his sight, removed to some distant point where his presence would not be a constant reminder of the degradation to which Hannah had submitted.

"I don't know, suh," the guard answered uneasily.

"Has he had any visitors?" Stephen again directed his gaze at the shadowy figure squatting on his heels against the back wall of the cell, leaning his shoulders against it, as silent and as motionless as a coiled rattlesnake, but without the warning rattles.

"A few's come by t'look at him, suh—the ladies mos'ly."

"My wife?"

"Yes, suh." The tap-tapping of Stephen's newspaper started again. "She been here."

"If he makes any attempt to escape, Private, you shoot—and you shoot to kill. I don't want his kind loose among our women again." Stephen warned.

"He jes' sit there, suh. We bring him his food, he don't move, an' don't say nothin'."

"Just remember your orders." Stephen wheeled away, driven by the raw anger that pulsed through him.

When he found himself turning onto Suds Row, he stopped for an instant, breathing in the lye-strong air. He knew of only two releases for the wild energy he felt: violence or passionate sex. The latter could be found here. He set out again, ignoring the ragtag children who stopped their play to stare at the white officer in their midst.

At the canvas dwelling where Cimmy Lou lived, he ducked through the opening, and felt the rush of blood in his system. All of his urges were intensified by the sight of the full-breasted woman stacking bundles of neatly folded laundry. She barely paused in her work, her profile a black cameo for him to admire.

"What're you doin' here, Majuh Wade?"

"It's been a long time since I've seen you, Cimmy." He crossed the tamped-earth floor to the table where she was separating the laundry into piles.

"It's Miz Hooker to you."

"That isn't what you want." He smiled with certainty.

"You don't know what I want." She whirled around to face him, her arms akimbo, and his glance was immediately drawn to the thin blouse stretching tautly across her breasts.

"Then tell me what it is you want and I'll get it for you." He began unbuttoning the front of her blouse, undeterred by the slap of her hands in an attempt to stop him. "A new dress, a new gown, jewelry, a hat—just ask for it and it's yours. I need you." Stephen didn't bother to unfasten the garment all the way, just enough to get his hands inside and feel those firm, round breasts. When she tried to pull away, he slid an arm around her waist. "I lie awake nights remembering what you used to do to me, and wanting it again."

"Let me go." She clawed at his hand. "You can't buy me."

"I did before—with all those gifts of Hannah's old things." Stephen denied her protest. "Now I'm offering you something new, something all your own."

"No. I don't want it." She struggled wildly against his tightening arm, pushing and twisting to break free.

But Stephen laughed in his throat, aroused by the motion of her body writhing against him. "I like it when you fight me." The roughness provided an outlet for the turbulent forces inside him. Gripping her under the jaw, he held her head still as he devoured her lips with a brutal hunger. "Meet me somewhere. Anywhere," he breathed into her mouth as he felt some of the fight going out of her. "I'll buy you anything."

"I . . . don't think I can. John T.—" Cimmy turned her head. The sentence remained unfinished as her dark eyes widened with alarm, focusing on a point behind him. "John T."

At the recognition in her voice, Stephen jerked his head around and found himself staring at the sergeant standing just inside the tent's opening, a rigid figure with a rifle tightly gripped in his hand.

# CHAPTER 20

"Sergeant—" Wade took a step toward him.

"You better leave, suh." John T.'s teeth were bared against the pain tearing apart his insides. He thought with odd clarity that now he knew how a mortally wounded animal felt before it went on a rampage. "You better leave, suh, before I kill you."

After a split-second hesitation, Wade walked quickly past him and out of the tent. The moment he was gone, Cimmy Lou rushed to her husband. "It ain't what yore thinkin', John T."

"I'm thinkin' that all those things the major gave you, they weren't for helpin' him, were they?" His eyes felt raw, like the rest of him. "I heard what he said. You bedded him."

"It wasn't like that. He—he forced me," she insisted, and John T. turned away with a groan, fighting the desire to believe another lie.

"I'm a big enough fool, Cimmy Lou. Don't make me

a bigger one," he begged. "I think I knew all along what you were doin', but I didn't want to see."

"John T., you gotta listen t'me." She came around him so that she could see his face. He felt again the pull of her beauty; it was so magnetic that he could hardly blame anyone else for being entranced by it.

"A white officer. How could you do it?" he demanded brokenly. "I'm top sergeant. I could walk with my head up and be proud of who I was. They respected me. I've got an education, I'm supposed to be smart. But look at the fool you've made of me. Don't you care what people think, what they say about you? Haven't you got any pride?"

"It won't happen again, I swear it. I'll make it up to you." She pressed herself against his length, her hands moving over his neck and shoulders in supplicant caresses. He felt the insidious heat of her body enveloping him in its age-old message. "Everything will be all right. You'll see."

The rifle slipped from the loosening grasp of his fingers and fell against the side of his leg, then onto the earthen floor. The minor distraction was enough to make him realize what was happening. He gripped her arms and held her away from him.

"Did you love him?" John T. demanded.

"No." She strained toward him, but his arms were rigidly locked to keep her at a distance.

"Then why? Why did you do it?" He shook her, angered that she could be with another man without even having feelings for him.

"Because he gave me things!" Cimmy regretted the truth the instant it came out. John T.'s rough push shoved her backward.

"You suck a man dry, then move on, don't you? You got all you could get from me and the major. Who's next? There'll be somebody 'cause that's the kind you are." John T. was trembling with the hurt raging inside him. "One of us needs to be put out of his misery. I just can't figure out whether it should be you or me. As much as I've loved you, I swear that right now I could kill you, Cimmy," he declared in an emotion-thick voice, and reeled out of the canvas dwelling, half-blinded by the tears he couldn't cry.

She believed him. The panic of it raced through her nerves: she had lost control of him. She had to get away before he carried out his threat. Cimmy knew of only one person who could take her from this place. She ran from the tent shanty in search of Leroy Bitterman.

Out of breath and scared senseless, she finally found him scrubbing pots and pans in the company mess. She grabbed his arm and pulled him aside as she gulped in air. His wet, soapy hands gripped her sagging shoulders as she swayed against him.

"What is it? What's wrong?" He sensed the panic in her.

"It's John T. He's gone crazy," she declared wildly. "He said he was gonna kill me. He will. I know it."

"Is he after you?" Bitterman glanced toward the door as if expecting Hooker to come charging through it. "Where is he now? Do you know?"

Her head moved from side to side in a vague response. "I don't know. The last time I saw him he was outside the trader's store. I hid behind a building so he couldn't see me. I don't know where he went."

"Did he have a gun?"

"No. Yes, his pistol." Her hands clutched his shirt-front, twisting into the material. "You said we'd go away. Let's leave now."

"In broad daylight? We can't. Don't fo'get I can be shot fo' a deserter." His cunning mind was working fast as he considered the alternatives. "Is he after me?"

"No." She shook her bowed head. "He don't know 'bout you. It was the majuh. He was tryin' to get me back when John T. walked in."

"Maybe we'll get lucky an' he'll shoot hisself an officer," he suggested in a wry attempt at humor.

"What're we gonna do?" It was not his light remark that began to calm her; it was a sense of returning power. She was regaining control of the situation. She had drawn Bitterman into it, involved him to the point where the problem wasn't hers, but his.

"First I'm gonna find out where he is and what he's doin'. You wait here till I come back." He pressed her backward against the rough adobe-brick wall and gestured for her to stay there.

The moment she was alone, Cimmy began plotting where she would have Bitterman take her and what she would do. The thought kept coming back to her that miners in Silver City were paying seven dollars for a clean shirt. She could wash a lot of shirts in a day's time. It would really be something to be able to buy her own fancy dresses and not be beholden to any man for them. Instead, the men could buy her jewels. She held out her hands, visualizing the sparkling rings she would wear.

The door opened and Bitterman slipped inside. "I found him. He's at the trader's, sittin' at a table with a bottle of whiskey an' workin' on gettin' drunk. Like as not, he'll pass out. That gives us time. You go home, pack all yore things, an' meet me behind the stables right after the midnight call."

"What if John T. comes home an' catches me?"

Bitterman grinned, the action stretching out his thin mustache. "You can handle a drunk. Git goin'." A slap on the rump sent Cimmy Lou on her way.

Two soldiers with rifles at the ready followed Cutter inside the Suds Row shanty. A momentary pause allowed his eyes to adjust to the change from brilliant sunlight to the interior shade; then his glance settled on the uniformed figure sprawled across the bed. A vague sense of relief filtered through him as Cutter crossed the one-room shack. His boot knocked over a whiskey bottle standing on the earthen floor by the bed. It fell with a dull clunk and rolled underneath the bed frame.

The reek of alcohol was strong as he stared at the slack-mouthed sergeant, a heavy beard stubble adding its black shadow to the already dark skin. Hooker's uniform was ringed with salty sweat stains and trail grime, unchanged from the day before. Cutter gripped his limp shoulder and shook it hard.

"Hooker! Hooker, wake up!" A low groan was the only response. "Come on, John T. You missed roll call." Cutter straightened, his mouth tightening with grim impatience, and motioned to one of the black troopers. "Get me that bucket of water."

It was half full, and he poured it all on Hooker's face and handed the empty bucket back to the soldier as Hooker came sputtering to life, sitting bolt upright. Almost immediately, he groaned and leaned forward to cradle his head in his hands.

"My head." The heavy dullness of a hangover was in his voice. "What time is it?"

"Bitterman didn't answer at roll call this morning," Cutter informed him. "And two horses are missing from the stable."

"Roll call?" John T. frowned and focused his bloodshot eyes on the sunlight coming through the door of the tent. "Why didn't Cimmy Lou wake me?" He looked around. "Where is she?"

"I haven't seen her."

"Oh, God, I remember." John T. buried his face in his hands, his head moving from side to side in mute pain.

"What the hell's the matter with you?"

"Cimmy?" He lifted his head to look around again. "Where'd she go?" Something akin to fear was in

Hooker's expression as he staggered from the bed to stumble to the door. "Cimmy Lou?!"

"Find some hot coffee, Grover." Cutter snapped the order to the private, troubled by Hooker's odd behavior and more than a little impatient that a woman like Cimmy Lou was the source of it, and went after him.

No clothes boiled in the iron kettle and no fire burned beneath it. All up and down the line, the enlisted men's wives were busy with the day's wash—except here. John T. reeled around, looking lost. He grabbed the arm of a large-boned woman at the next fire.

"Bess, have you seen my Cimmy?"

"Ain't seen hide nor hair of her this mornin'."

He came back to the tent shack and Cutter stepped aside to let him in, then followed to watch John T. search the place wildly, throwing clothes in every direction. Private Grover came back with the cup of hot coffee. As John T. sank onto a crude bench in silent despair, Cutter took it to him.

"Drink this." He fitted John T.'s limp hands around the tin mug.

"None of her things are here," he said brokenly. "She's gone."

"So's Bitterman," Cutter said.

"What?" John T. gave him a blank look.

"Bitterman was missing at roll call this morning. And two horses were taken from the stable last night."

And two and two were beginning to make four, even to John T.'s liquor-dulled brain. "Not him, too." He hung his head in utter dejection.

"Then she's with him."

"She promised me she wouldn't do it again. I was gonna forgive her." He drew in a sniffling breath and furtively wiped at his eyes, trying to hide his broken emotions.

"With a woman along, Bitterman won't be able to travel very far very fast. I'll send a detachment after them." Cutter started to turn away, but John T. caught his forearm.

"I wanta go after them." His red-rimmed eyes were shiny with tears, his black cheeks wet with them.

"You're in no condition to go," Cutter denied quietly. "Corporal Haines can take them."

"No." John T. came to his feet. "She's my wife. I can't let someone else go after her and bring her back. How would that look?"

Cutter saw the desperate attempt to hold onto what was left of his pride, and slowly nodded, silently damning Cimmy Lou for what she'd done to Hooker. "All right. Take six men and a tracker. Leave whenever you're ready." He knew Hooker would be better off if he never got her back, but it wasn't his place to say it.

"Yes, suh."

Within an hour, the small detail was mounted and the Apache tracker had located the trail of the two horses heading away from the stables toward the rough canyon country. Cutter watched them disappear into the chaparral, then went back to checking horses and equipment in preparation for the departure of his routine patrol the next morning, the last one he'd lead. He saw the blue roan being saddled and guessed that Hannah would be taking her ride before the midday heat turned the parade ground into a furnace. He felt the rise of an old recklessness, and knew that it was a good thing he'd soon be far away from her.

"I'll wager that the Ninth didn't have more than a handful of desertions this past year," Colonel Bettendorf commented to Stephen as they stood in the olla-cooled shade of the headquarters *ramada*. "From what I've heard, the Fifth had more than two hundred. One thing you can say about these coloreds, they're not only good fighting soldiers, but they take pride in the uniform they wear. They serve it well and honorably."

"Indeed." Stephen stood at ease, his hands clasped behind his back, yet he was anything but relaxed.

"You heard that Hooker's wife is missing, too, that Cimmy Lou girl? It's unfortunate when a man can't control his own wife."

Wade stiffened, unsure whether that remark had been meant to reflect on him as well. Hannah came out of their quarters at that moment, walking with a free-swinging stride he had come to regard as masculine. He noted the leather riding gloves she wore and the small blue hat on her head. A soldier waited for her, holding the reins to a blue roan—with a regulation saddle on its back.

"Your wife has taken up riding again while you were on patrol," the colonel informed him, obviously noting the direction of Stephen's gaze.

"We'll see about that," Stephen said tightly, and swung away from Bettendorf.

All of his focus was on Hannah as she fed sugar lumps to the horse. The fury in him blocked out everything else. That she should do this without his permission was provocation enough, but to ride astride like an Apache squaw was the ultimate defiance. He was so intent that the first flurry of movement from near the guardhouse and the sudden shout of alarm failed to attract his notice.

The second cry succeeded. "Corp'ral of the guard! Prisoner's escaped!"

He whirled in the direction of the guardhouse and reached down quickly to unfasten his holster flap. By then Lutero was racing across the parade ground toward the roan horse Hannah held. The tramp of running feet came from all directions, but before the first shot was fired, Lutero was on the horse's back, kicking it into a gallop. In a cold rage, Stephen drew his pistol and took steady aim at the low-crouched rider coming straight for him. All he could see of his target was the black hair flying and part of a bronze shoulder. He squeezed the trigger.

The impact of the bullet tumbled the Apache from the saddle and rolled him into the boiling dust. Stephen started walking toward him, oblivious to the riderless horse running by him, never taking his eyes off the Apache on the ground. He heard the click of the hammer revolving the cylinder to bring another bullet into position, and felt again the buck of the gun in his hand as the hammer fell. But he didn't hear the explosions as he watched the jerking of the Apache's body as the bullets tore into his flesh.

The hammer struck on three empty chambers before Stephen finally realized that there were no more shells in the gun. He lowered the muzzle, letting it point at the ground as he stood over the body. He'd wanted to kill Lutero for a long time and, now that the deed was done, a hard satisfaction claimed him.

Hannah saw the look of vengeful pleasure on his face and felt her blood run cold through her veins. No matter what Lutero had done, murder did not condone murder, and that's what this had been. It sickened her.

"Are you all right?" Cutter was beside her.

"Yes." The horse had knocked her to the ground, but she hadn't been hurt. Dust and dirt smudges marked her split riding skirt, but the damage was slight. Hannah was conscious of the steadying influence of Cutter's presence as Stephen approached her, the killing lust not fully gone from his eyes. When he stopped before her, she knew that many things were dead. Most importantly to Hannah, he had killed their past. She no longer felt bound to him because of the feelings they had once shared.

"Your plan to help your Apache lover get away didn't work."

His harsh accusation broke the self-imposed silence that had previously kept her from voicing her opinion of him in front of others. "You are *hesh-ke*, Stephen, one of the crazies—the unreasonable haters." She saw his stiffness, his righteous rejection of her claim, and walked away, finding a path through the soldiers crowding around the scene.

"What happened?" somebody asked.

"How'd he git out?"

"The guard took him a fresh pail of water. When he turned his back on him, the Indian jumped 'im. His back's broke, the doc says."

Cutter glared at Wade. His teeth were gritted. "You fool. You don't deserve her." He roughly shoved him aside, almost hoping for some physical provocation that would lead to a fight, but Wade didn't oblige him.

The commotion had drawn their striker outside. When he saw Hannah coming up the path, Delancy opened the door for her. "Did the majuh kill that Indian, Miz Wade?"

"Fetch my trunks, Delancy." She brushed past him.

"Yore trunks, ma'am?"

"Yes, my trunks. And bring them to the bedroom." Without a break in stride, Hannah continued down the hallway, tugging off her gloves as she went.

She entered the bedroom and began emptying the wardrobe and throwing the clothes on the bed, separating her things from Stephen's. Delancy carted a trunk in a few minutes later, looking with dismay at the scene.

"I'll need something to wrap my mother's china in when I'm through here. See what you can find," Hannah ordered.

"Yes, ma'am." There were a thousand questions he wanted to ask, but he knew she wouldn't be inclined to satisfy his curiosity.

Delancy brought the second trunk into the room and Hannah set to work folding and packing her things, a tedious and time-consuming task. When Stephen walked in shortly after noon mess was called, she didn't even pause.

"What's going on here?" He stood beside the first trunk, which was already packed and locked.

"I'm leaving." She carefully folded the long skirt of a gown in order to minimize the creases.

It was an instant before he responded. "Well, I'm glad you finally came to your senses. I have been urging you to go back east for a visit for more than a week now. If you had listened to me sooner instead—"

"You misunderstand me." Hannah turned around to face him, calm and prepared for this confrontation. "I didn't say anything about going east. I said I was leaving. I'm leaving *you*, Stephen."

"You can't do that." He was stunned.

"Not as easily as the Apaches, perhaps. Do you know how they dissolve a marriage when one of the partners becomes dissatisfied? One of them moves out. Well, that's what I'm doing." She turned to continue folding the gown, but he shoved it away.

"I'm not going to let you go." The cords in his neck stood out, betraying his tautly checked anger.

"Why, Stephen? You don't want me anymore. You can't even bear to touch me."

"Because *he* was always between us. I couldn't stand knowing he was alive. But he's dead now."

"Do you think that makes a difference? Do you believe killing him changed anything? You didn't kill him—you murdered him."

"I shot a prisoner who was trying to escape," Stephen insisted.

"Yes, it was all in the line of duty, wasn't it? But what does it matter anyway? No officer would ever be court-martialed for killing an Indian. You knew that. That's why you shot him again and again and again." She trembled with the force of her anger. "What were you trying to kill, Stephen?"

"You don't understand." His fingers bit into her shoulders. "Now that he's dead, all the stories will stop. There won't be any trial for the papers to print stories about—there won't be any reason for them to rake up the past."

"Is that what you wanted to stop? The stories?" Hannah challenged. "And what if it doesn't end? What will you do? Kill Mr. Boler? You can't make people stop talking about me."

"They'll forget—in time."

"Will they?" Just for an instant a note of self-pity crept into her voice, the unfairness of the situation stinging her and bringing tears to her eyes. "Oh, the story may get old after a while," she conceded. "But if I say or do anything that is out of the ordinary, you can bet they'll look at each other and explain it away by saying, 'She lived with the Apaches for almost a year.' And when they do, they'll always wonder. That's what it's going to be like, Stephen, for the rest of my life. Even if I wanted to forget it, people won't let me. Will you?"

He drew back from her biting cynicism. "You've changed, Hannah. You've grown hard."

"I suppose I have." She grew quiet, her outburst cleansing her of much of the bitterness. She picked up the gown and once more laid it out flat on the bed to fold it. "Even if I could go back to being the woman you remember, you won't let me. Today your first thought was that I had the horse waiting there for Lutero—"

"That's how it looked." He turned from her and raked a hand through his hair, then rubbed at the tension knotting the muscles at the back of his neck. "I admit I was wrong. But I knew you'd been to see him. What was I supposed to think?"

"It doesn't matter anymore." She knew the futility of this discussion. All of it had been said too many times before with the same results—more accusations and arguments. "I can't live like this, Stephen. Always treated as if I'm unclean, as if I should be ashamed because I didn't die. I won't live like this."

"You're my wife," he protested.

"But that's all I am," Hannah flared briefly, hearing the possessive ring in his voice. "And only when you choose to remember it. All that's left of our marriage is a piece of paper. The rest has gone—love, trust, respect. I don't even like you anymore, Stephen. So let's admit that it's over. If you don't seek a divorce, I will."

When she turned to lay the folded gown in the trunk, Stephen blocked her movement. "You aren't leaving me, Hannah."

"That's what really galls you, isn't it? That I would leave you," she realized. "If it bothers you so much, tell people that you threw me out. Tell them how ungrateful I was when you so generously took me back after I had lived with the Apaches—and married one of them. Tell them anything you like, Stephen. Sooner or later you'll convince yourself that it's the truth."

He didn't try to stop her as she walked around him. Hannah could feel his brooding gaze on her, watching as she arranged the gown atop the clothes in the trunk.

"Where will you go? Back to the Apaches?"

She almost laughed. "You never stop, do you? You still persist in believing that I must have liked it." A sigh trailed from her as she paused thoughtfully. "I don't know, Stephen. But I am discovering that the Apaches were more willing to accept me than my own people are. However, to answer your question"—

Hannah straightened with a small push and swung around to face him, her head up—"no, I'm not going back to live with the Apaches."

"Then where are you going?" His frown almost made her believe that he cared, but she knew it was a selfish interest.

"I don't know yet." The decision had been made too abruptly for Hannah to plan much beyond the moment. "I'll go into Silver City and decide from there."

"This is insane, Hannah." The sweep of his hand indicated that all of the packing and her intention to leave were included in his disgusted assessment. "What will you do? How will you live?"

"I'll find work. I could teach or work in a restaurant —or hire out as a lady's maid. After all, I do know the life," she reminded him dryly.

"If you leave, you'll regret it," Stephen warned.

"No, I don't think I will."

"The West is no place for a woman alone. You'll be unprotected, with no one to look after you."

"You have forgotten, I was alone before—and I survived." She took courage from that knowledge. It was something Stephen couldn't understand about her.

A knock at the bedroom door broke into their conversation. "Come in," Hannah called, as Stephen turned away in agitation.

Delancy stepped inside, plainly ill at ease with the situation. "I've found some ole rags to pack 'round yore china."

"Thank you, Delancy. Just leave them in the kitchen. I'll see to the packing of it myself." She dismissed him, and the striker left gratefully.

"The china?" Stephen exploded the instant the door closed. "You're taking the china?"

"It belonged to my mother. I'm taking it and everything else that's mine." She had no intention of ever coming back. "Unfortunately, I won't be able to have it all packed in order to leave before nightfall. Therefore, I would appreciate it if you would arrange for some kind of transportation to take me into Silver City first thing in the morning. Or shall I do it?"

A grim anger darkened his features. "I will." He stalked to the door and left.

Hannah felt no sense of victory. Her marriage was over. Six years of her life were gone. In their place came a creeping loneliness; but she had endured that before, too.

# CHAPTER 21

THE ARMY AMBULANCE CLATTERED TO A STOP IN FRONT OF the low adobe building. Hannah cast one last glance over the two trunks, two crates, and satchel to make sure all of her luggage was there and ready to be loaded, then walked to the door. As she stepped outside, she heard a bellowed order: "Column left! By twos!"

In unison, the mounted riders on the parade ground wheeled their horses to the left, pairing up with precision while the company guidon fluttered with the motion. A patrol was leaving on a routine scout, a sight she wouldn't see anymore. Jake Cutter was at the head of it. She recognized his long body sitting deep in the saddle, and Hannah realized how automatically she looked for him. No more. The heart-lift she'd felt when she saw him became a tugging twinge of regret.

His head turned in her direction and she lifted a hand, waving it slightly. Although she was too far away to see, she was almost certain that he smiled as he threw her an acknowledging salute. It briefly warmed and reassured her. She watched the column ride to the main gate and saw Cutter turn in his saddle to look back. He held that position until he disappeared from her sight. Only then did Hannah feel the straining of something inside, and the ache it left. She knew the route the patrol would take away from the fort: along the Silver City road, then north into the rough breaks in the mountains. In her mind, she rode with them for a little of the way until someone cleared his throat to gain her attention and she noticed the two enlisted men standing a few feet away, waiting for instructions.

"My things are inside—five pieces." She started for the ambulance, then stopped as she saw Stephen walking toward her. She adjusted the strings of her reticule and waited for him to speak. She had nothing more to say.

"Hannah, I'll ask you one last time to stay."

She smiled wanly. "That's very generous of you, Stephen." She moved past him toward the ambulance.

His warning voice called after her. "If you leave now, I won't take you back again."

Unassisted, she climbed onto the seat. "Good luck to you, Stephen." She couldn't hate him for being what he was, anymore than she had been able to hate Lutero for what he'd been. She was saddened when he wheeled away, too proud to face her rejection of him.

As her luggage and boxes were loaded into the rear, she sensed the eyes watching from the windows along Officers' Row, but no one came out to ask where she was going. She no longer felt any obligation to go to the trouble of telling them.

When the army vehicle rolled out of the fort twenty minutes later, it was flanked by an escort of four troopers. The stretch of road between Fort Bayard and

Silver City was a favorite ambush site of the Apaches, so a state of alertness reigned among the riders as they traveled down the road.

The sun was making its morning climb into the high blue sky, throwing its heat onto the parched Southwest. The tight coat of Hannah's traveling suit was hot and confining, and the dust boiling up from the double hitch of mules swirled into the military wagon to sting her eyes and occasionally choke her. Absently, Hannah held onto the seat of the bouncing ambulance, indifferent to the jolting discomfort of the ride.

With her eyes narrowed to screen out the rolling dust and the glaring sun, she looked north at the line of rising mountains thrusting into the sky, the Pinos Altos range—the mountains of the Tall Pines and the southern extension of the Mogollons. The patrol was somewhere in them—and so was Jake Cutter. Hannah examined her decision, and knew that if she had any regrets about leaving, they centered on him. She shut her mind to the memory of the wild run of feeling she'd known in his arms, its depth and power, and shifted to a more comfortable position on the seat, bracing her feet against the bouncing jar of the wagon.

She felt no sense of elation at being free at last, only a kind of relief. She was undaunted by the prospect of being on her own; if anything, she looked forward to the challenge of it.

Silver City was a bustling mining town high in the foothills of the Pinos Altos Mountains. At the beginning of the decade, a small Spanish village had been built on the site and called San Vicente de la Ciénaga, St. Vincent of the Marsh. Then silver was discovered in the Mogollons, and the town boomed and became the seat of Grant County, New Mexico Territory.

The main street was alive with activity, teams of horses pulling wagons, horses and riders, and people walking. The rank odor of manure polluted the air, its smell intensified by the hot sun. It was a noisy place, with its rattle of harness and chain, cracking whips, and cursing voices. Hastily constructed wood-fronted buildings lined the street, and the businesses they contained catered heavily to the mining trade, with the emphasis on pleasure. Gambling halls and saloons outnumbered such legitimate business establishments as banks, general stores, and freight offices.

The mulatto driver turned to ask, "Where'd you like us to take you, ma'am?"

"The Silver City Hotel."

The two-story structure had initially been given a coat of whitewash, but the constant dust had already dulled it. The soldier hauled back on the reins, stopping the mule team in front of it and setting the brake before he hopped down to give her a hand out of the ambulance. Hannah paused for a moment, sensing the town's fevered character, the excitement of the silver boom. Few women could be seen on the street, and she was conscious of the attention she attracted. Two of the soldiers dismounted to unload her belongings as she walked into the hotel.

A thin young man wearing wire-rimmed glasses straightened attentively when she approached the desk. "May I help you?" he inquired with studied formality.

"I'd like a room, please." She pulled on the fingers of her glove to remove it.

"If you'll sign the register, I'll see what we have available." He pushed the open book toward her and handed her a pen, then turned to the row of boxes behind the desk. "How long will you be staying with us?"

"I'm not sure." Hannah dipped the pen in the inkwell and signed her name. "I'll let you know."

"Your room will be the second one on the right at the

top of the stairs." With practiced ease, he turned the register book around so that he could covertly glance at her name as he handed her the key. "Here's your room key . . . Mrs. Wade." The desk clerk noticed the two soldiers carrying one of her trunks into the lobby. A startled expression came over his face as he looked again at her; she could almost see the click of recognition. "Mrs. Wade?" He appeared flustered and uncertain. "Your husband is Major Wade . . . at Fort Bayard?"

"Yes." Hannah folded her fingers around the room key.

"Ma'am," he began awkwardly, "this is a respectable hotel—"

"I am relieved to know that." She smiled across his attempted protest. "There aren't many decent places a lady can stay in this town. It's good of you to reassure me."

His mouth was open, but he seemed incapable of speech. Before he could recover, Hannah moved away from the desk and walked to the stairs. Raising the hem of her skirt a few inches, she climbed the steps, followed by the soldiers with her trunk.

An hour later, Hannah poured water from the pitcher into the basin and rinsed the dust from her face and hands. As she patted her skin dry, she thought about her next step. She had some cash, monies left from her aunt's legacy, but it would only be enough for room and board for a week and stage fare to another town. Even if she had wanted to ask Stephen for money, there had been none to give her. No army payroll had been sent to the fort in more than three months, and with all the entertaining, household expenses, servants' wages, and the moving costs each time Stephen was transferred, they had never been able to save very much. So first of all, she had to raise some more money. She removed a pouch from her satchel and looped the strings of her reticule over her wrist, then left the room to venture out into the streets.

The general store was jammed with the assorted tools and equipment of the mining trade—picks and shovels, canteens, pack saddles, and a variety of other items, plus the usual cloth goods and food supplies. Her bustled skirt swept against them as Hannah threaded her way through the jumble of goods to the counter. Half a dozen men lounged about the store, all of them roughly dressed, most of them unshaven, and two of them wearing the heeled boots of the cowboy.

It was busy behind the counter. A thatch-haired boy of not more than fifteen with protruding buck teeth was darting back and forth from shelf to counter, filling an order. An older man was painstakingly rechecking the total of a bill. The man had a full head of dark hair, but his muttonchop whiskers were hoary white, accenting his florid, apple-red cheeks.

"I'll take these peaches, Homer." A dirty slouch hat shaded the face of the unkempt man who spoke and plucked a tin from the shelf. The flushed and harried proprietor nodded and added the figures again, including the price of the peaches in the total. The customer cut open the tin with his knife, stabbed a peach with the point of the blade, and jammed it whole into his mouth. Hannah stood patiently waiting her turn.

"Be with you in a minute, ma'am," the man promised after a hasty glance at her fashionable attire.

"Thank you."

After a brief haggle over the amount owed by the peach-eater, the account was paid, and Homer, the proprietor, turned to Hannah. "I'm sorry to have kept you waiting. May I help you?"

"I hope you can." She opened the pouch and spilled its contents onto the counter. A strand of matched pearls, ruby earbobs, a topaz brooch, and a gold locket lay in a tangle with others of her better pieces. "I have some jewelry I'd like to sell. How much would you offer for it?"

The corners of his mouth were pulled grimly down and his hands stayed on the edge of the counter, not reaching to inspect any of it, not even the pearls. "I'll give you fifteen—make it twenty dollars for it."

"For what?" Stunned by the low amount, Hannah tried to guess which piece he meant.

"For all of it." His hand made an uninterested sweep over the pile of jewelry.

"You can't be serious. It's worth at least twenty times that." She picked up the pearls that had belonged to her mother. "These alone are—"

"—very expensive. Yes, I know." He waved his hand in a dismissive gesture, silencing her protest. "What would I do with them?"

"Sell them, of course. The silver strike has made this town rich. Outside the freight office, I saw bars of silver stacked on the sidewalk."

"There's more poor than rich. And even the ones with money aren't spending it on gewgaws and fripperies. Now, I'd buy all the tools and equipment you could bring me."

"But surely—"

"Lady." He stopped her again. "They aren't buying gold and silver around here. They're looking for it. As fine as those pieces are, there's no market for them. I oughtta know." He reached under the counter and lifted out a strongbox. Inside there was a glittering mound of jewelry. "Prospectors are always trying to sell me something to get a grubstake. I've got gold watches, silver watches, chains, wedding rings, watch fobs, lockets—and here's a diamond stud pin some gambler gave me for a poker stake." He showed her the sparkling gem, then closed the strongbox and set it back under the counter. "I'm sorry, ma'am, but twenty dollars is the best I can do."

"No, thank you." Hannah refused firmly even though she believed him. "I want to sell it, not give it away." She began gathering up the jewelry and putting it back in the velvet pouch. The gold locket slipped from her fingers and fell on the counter, snapping open to reveal oval pictures of herself and Stephen.

"That's a nice locket." The proprietor picked it up and glanced at the pictures. "Your husband?"

"Yes," she replied, and reached for the locket.

"He looks familiar to me." He studied the picture thoughtfully; then a smile broke across his ruddy face. "Of course, it's Major Wade from Fort Bayard. I've seen him in town a time or two. Last year it was when his wife—" He caught himself and stared at her. "You're Mrs. Wade."

"Yes." Hannah took the locket and dropped it into the pouch with the rest. "Since you aren't interested in purchasing my jewelry, perhaps you could use more help to work in your store. I am quite strong, so lifting heavy things wouldn't be a problem. My writing is very legible, and my skills with sums are good if you require help keeping the account books."

"I don't have any openings at the present."

After his reaction upon learning her identity, she had anticipated his answer. It was the stigma of the Apache again. She smiled with cool politeness. "Thank you for your time."

As she turned to leave, Hannah caught a glimpse of a dark-skinned woman over by the ready-made clothes. For an instant, she thought it was Cimmy Lou even though she couldn't see her face, but too many things were on her mind to wonder what Cimmy might be doing here. The passing distraction was forgotten the minute she walked out of the store.

From there, Hannah made the rounds, stopping at every place of business that might be interested in buying her jewelry. The result was more of the same ludicrous offers, which she chose to reject. At this point, her circumstances were not so dire that she felt forced to accept less than what was fair.

Late in the afternoon she returned to the hotel, hot, tired, and frustrated. She went to the desk to get her key. The young clerk didn't see her walk up, too engrossed in the newspaper he was reading: "Husband Slays Apache Rival" announced the headline. She pressed her lips together in a tight, angry line.

The pages rustled together. "Mrs. Wade!" The newspaper was quickly shut and folded to conceal the headline. "Would—would you like your key?"

"Where's the newspaper office?" Her hands had a stranglehold on her drawstring reticule and the pouch.

"The newspaper office?" His voice cracked on a squeaky note. "Just down the street."

She thanked him and left the airless hotel, venturing again into the broiling heat of the dusty and rank-smelling street. Dodging horses and assorted drawn vehicles as well as the piles and puddles of animal excrement, Hannah crossed to the other side.

Hy Boler was sitting at his desk, his jacket on the chair back and his shirt-sleeves rolled up. The buttons of his vest were nearly pulled apart by the way the material was stretched to fit around his solid paunch. Perspiration glistened on the bald spot on top of his head, ringed like an open horseshoe with thick hair that grew into his Dundrearies.

A stack of newspapers sat on a table just inside the door. Hannah grabbed one from the top of the pile as she walked by it and went straight to his desk. Belatedly he heard the sharp sound of her footsteps and turned. He stood up to greet her, rolling down his sleeves.

"Did you wish to buy that, Mrs. Wade?" He wryly indicated the newspaper in her hand.

Hannah tossed it on his desk. "I don't even have to read that story to know that you distorted the facts!" Her low voice vibrated with the anger she felt.

"Well, well, I see you do have a temper to go with that red hair." He picked up his jacket and put it on, shrugging his bulk into it.

"How can you write this kind of tripe? Don't you realize what this can do to people? Let's forget the way my reputation has been ruined and the outcast I've become. All this notoriety has damaged Stephen's career. It's destroyed our marriage—"

"Have you left him?" he asked quietly.

"Yes." Hannah stopped abruptly, checking her outburst of temper. "I suppose you'll write about that next," she accused in a steadier voice. "How will the headlines read? 'Wife Leaves Husband After Slaying of Apache Lover,' perhaps."

"Too long."

"Doesn't it bother you that what you write can hurt someone? Surely you know it's true that the pen is mightier than the sword. Your stories can bias people's opinions. Don't you care?"

"Come with me." Hy Boler took her arm and led her to the door. "Look out there. The Silver Slipper, Andy's Saloon and Gambling Hall, Lucky's Place, the Hard Rock Saloon, Old Blue's . . ." He read the names of the many saloons and sporting establishments that lined the street, not even bothering with the little signs that sported only the simple words "Beer," "Whiskey," and "Girls." "Most of the people in this town can't read. And those who can don't want to read about what goes on in Congress—unless it has to do with mining, cattle, or Apaches. They want to rub elbows with danger and excitement. That's why they're here. My business is to sell newspapers, so I give them what they want."

"What about me, Mr. Boler? After what you've printed, how am I supposed to find a decent job so that I can work and support myself?" she demanded.

"Why don't you go back to your husband where you belong?" he suggested.

"But I don't belong there. Maybe I don't belong anywhere, but I'll have to find that out." Her determination was stronger than ever as she turned and left the office to return to the hotel.

Cimmy Lou clutched the bundle of store-bought clothes tightly to her middle as she skirted the houses on the edge of town and drifted close to the mesquite and creosote brush. When she reached the faint trail leading into it, she stopped and checked to make sure no one was watching her, then slipped down the path, running a few yards until she was out of sight of anyone passing by.

She hurried along it, not liking the scurrying sounds she could hear on either side of her. In her haste, she missed the brush-covered entrance to the high-walled gully and had to double back. A faint smell of smoke was in the air, which worried her. She wiggled past the thorny branches that hid the camp. Bitterman stood well back in the gully, his hands clamped over the noses of their horses to silence any whicker.

"Any trouble?" He quickly came to her and took the bundle from her arms, carrying it to the small circle of dying embers and ash.

"No." Cimmy Lou followed him, eyeing the fire with misgiving. "I thought we weren't gonna build a fire in case the Apaches saw the smoke."

"I kept it small an' used only dry wood so it wouldn't make much smoke. Apache trick." He gave her a sly smile. "'Sides, I had to fix the brands on the horses. We couldn't go ridin' with that 'US' mark on their flanks. Anybody'd know fo' shore they was army horses. I changed it to 'O8.'"

"How'd you do that?" She was impressed by his cleverness.

"Heated the cinch ring off a saddle. It was easy. Now, if I can jes' git shed of this uniform . . ." Bitterman opened the bundle and shook out the pants and shirt she'd bought for him. Satisfied, he began stripping off the blue pants with their telltale yellow stripe. "Did anybody see ya?"

"No." At least she didn't think so. "I saw Miz Wade in the gen'ral store. I ducked into a corner real quick. What d'you s'pose she was doin' there?" Cimmy Lou sat on the ground and hugged her knees to her chest as she eyed his wiry body, so thin and narrow—and scarred up just like an alley cat.

"Nothin' was said? No talk 'bout anybody out lookin' for us?" He pulled on the pants and hitched them high around his waist.

"No. All the talk is 'bout that Apache. He tried to escape yestiday an' the majuh killed him."

"Maybe it took their minds off'n us." With his pants fastened, he stuck the muzzle of his revolver in the waistband.

"When are we gonna leave here?" Cimmy swatted at a fly that was buzzing around her head. "You said we was goin' to Colorado."

"Not fo' a couple days," Bitterman told her. "I wanna give those brands a chance t'heal up."

"But what if they did send a patrol after us?" She sighed her impatience at the delay and the unnecessary risks they were running. "We're so close to the fort—they might find us. We could be miles away by now."

"That's what they're figurin'. They'll never think to look fo' us this close. An' that herd of cattle we passed wiped out all our tracks. If we don't move fo' a spell, we won't leave any sign fo' them to find. This is the safest place we can be fo' a few days. By then, they'll figure we're long gone an' quit lookin'." He chuckled. "And ain't it a laugh that we been sittin' right here under their noses all the time."

"I guess it is." She smiled, then stretched out her arms, arching her back in a tired gesture. "I never thought I'd git so tired of doin' nothin'."

"You want somethin' t'do? Come here." He motioned her toward him and sat on the hard ground as she scooted over to be wrapped in his arms.

"Tell me what it's gonna be like in Colorado again." Cimmy walked her fingers across his chest with idle interest.

"It's dreams yore wantin'. I thought it was me," Bitterman chided, but he obliged. "We'll find us a minin' camp that's really boomin'—"

"An' you'll get a job dealin' faro in one of the gamblin' houses an' I'll charge ten dollars fo' every shirt I wash," Cimmy declared. "I won't throw the water out till I run it through a sluice an' get the gold dust. Maybe even find a nugget."

"An' you'll meet a rich prospector an' git him to give you all his gold." He smiled against her soft hair. "You'd be good at that."

"What you think I oughtta buy first? A satin gown, maybe—or a fancy dress." She snuggled against him, burrowing against his narrow chest. "I want a house someday—made outta wood an' painted white—where people'd come callin' on Sunday."

"Things. Is that all you want, Cimmy?" Bitterman craned his head around to look at her.

"No. I can git them. There are ways a body can do it." It wasn't often that she thought deeply about anything. She flattened her hand against the warm, hard flesh of his chest, feeling the beat of his heart.

"It's this man an' woman thing, that's what this world is all about. When it wears off, there ain't nothin' left. You might as well be dead."

"Do you think any one man can wear you out?" he asked, half-serious and half-teasing.

Cimmy tilted her head back, bringing her lips close to his. "You can try," she urged.

Laughter rumbled in his chest as he shifted to lay her on the ground. When he rolled his body onto her, Bitterman felt the power in those twisting, playful hips. "I'm gonna show you a time these next few days," he promised.

She laughed and wrapped her arms around his neck to pull him the rest of the way down. This man and woman thing was a power struggle she always won.

# CHAPTER 22

HANNAH PAUSED IN THE DOORWAY OF THE HOTEL'S
dining room and looked for an empty table. There were
few in the crowded room. Hy Boler was at his usual
corner table; he was a nightly customer of the establishment, as Hannah had learned over the last three days.
She made a point of ignoring him as she crossed in front
of him to sit at a nearby table.

"Stew, please, and hot tea," she requested when the
waitress stopped. The selection was easily made: the
stew was the cheapest item on the menu. Considering
that this was a mining town and all the prices were
steeply inflated, that wasn't saying much.

The clatter of dishes and silverware combined with
the loud talking in the room made it difficult for her to
think. It seemed that she had tried everywhere, exhausted every possibility, and no one wanted to hire
her. The town already had a schoolmaster, but they had
made it plain anyway that they didn't consider her

suitable. The local seamstress insisted that she had all the help she needed, and none of the restaurants wanted her waiting on the customers. All the stores turned her down—nothing was available anywhere. She sighed in frustration, not bothering to look up when the waitress set the bowl of stew in front of her. She had no appetite, but she forced herself to eat it anyway.

Her chair faced the doorway, and as a man walked in and took off his wide-brimmed black hat, her glance idly fell on him. His frock coat and showy cravat were the trademarks of a professional gambler. His gaze searched the room; obviously he was looking for someone. Hannah picked up her teacup. Over its rim, she saw his gaze stop on her. Immediately he started forward, wending his way past the tables and chairs straight toward her. After a momentary uncertainty, she decided it must be someone behind her he was meeting, and took a drink of the tea.

"Excuse me." He stopped before her chair. "It's Mrs. Wade, isn't it?"

"Yes." She frowned in wary confusion.

"You were described to me, but the party failed to relate how very beautiful you are. Permit me to introduce myself," he drawled. "I'm Ace Bannon."

"Mr. Bannon." She placed her hand in the one he offered and he bowed over it with courtly ease. The southern drawl, the smooth gallantry—it all went with the silver wings in his dark hair and the touch of aristocratic arrogance in his features.

"I have heard that you have been looking for work." He flashed her a smile.

"Yes, I have."

"I have a proposition for you which I'm sure will be financially rewarding for both of us. I own the Ace High Saloon and Gambling Hall. I run an honest game, but you must have noticed how much competition I have from other less scrupulous houses on the street. I need something that will attract the trade. You would make the perfect drawing card, Mrs. Wade. We'll fix you up with a white buckskin outfit with lots of fringe and beads—why, we'll turn you into a genuine Apache princess. Those miners will pay plenty for the chance to dance with you. Naturally, I'll waive my percentage, and you can keep all the money from the dance tickets."

"No, thank you." She was curt and cold.

"I beg your pardon." He showed his surprise. "I assure you that you'll find it a very profitable venture."

"No." The dining room seemed unnaturally quiet, its customary clatter of dishes and voices suspended. Hannah didn't have to look to know that everyone in the room was watching and listening to their conversation. She didn't know which made her angrier—that he thought she would consider such a proposal, or that he made it in public.

"If you don't think it's enough money, we could possibly arrange for you to receive some percentage of the drinks. I am prepared to be generous," he assured her with a faint stiffness.

Hannah set her teacup in its saucer with such force that it rattled. "Mr. Bannon, I have no intention of working for you no matter how much you offer to pay me." She spoke clearly and concisely so that everyone in the room could hear. "Nothing would ever persuade me to work for you."

He straightened, offended; then his mouth curved into a smile under his full mustache. "That's what you say now, Mrs. Wade, but the day will come when you'll be hungry—so hungry you'll do anything. When it does, you will seek me out."

She rose to her feet. "You have forgotten something, Mr. Bannon. I lived with the Apaches. A week in the desert, and you would starve to death or die of thirst, while I would find all the food and water I need. I will never go hungry, Mr. Bannon, and I certainly will never be so desperate that I'd work for you!"

His face turned red, the veins in his temples bulging with the hot blood pumping through them. He pivoted sharply and walked with rigid strides from the dining room.

After that confrontation, she had no appetite left, and the tea was cold anyway. The silence in the room was deafening. She opened her reticule to take out some money and caught a glimpse of movement out of the corner of her eye. She turned as Hy Boler walked up.

"My congratulations, Mrs. Wade. I have always admired you, and now I know why." He gave a deep chuckle. "I never enjoyed anything half as much as the way you told him off."

"I'm glad you found it so entertaining." She was still smarting from the scene, and the sting of it was in her voice.

"Put your money away. I'm buying your dinner tonight."

"I will pay for my own, thank you."

He wagged a finger at her, still smiling. "Don't let your pride get in the way of practicality." He sifted through the coins in his pocket and gave the exact amount to the waitress. Hannah moved away, but he was quick to follow her. "The sun's gone down and it should be getting cool about now. Would you care to take an evening stroll with me? There's something I'd like to talk to you about."

"If it's a proposition similar to Mr. Bannon's, you're wasting your time and mine."

"It isn't." His hand cupped her elbow to steer her outside. "Let's walk."

The Silver City nightlife was just beginning to hum as they wandered along the twilight-shadowed boardwalk.

Several riders galloped their horses up the street, and raucous voices came from the open doors of the saloons and gaming houses. Up the street, someone was banging a tune on a piano. Late at night, the shooting usually started, but it was still too early for that.

"What is it that you wanted to talk to me about, Mr. Boler?" Hannah prodded, on guard with him.

"Your story."

"I beg your pardon?"

"Your story. A few minutes ago in the dining room, I realized that there was a great deal more to it than what I wrote about."

"And?" Hannah knew there was more coming.

"And—I would like to buy the exclusive rights to it. All you have to do is sit down and tell me everything that happened, and I'll write the book. I know it will sell."

"Your version of my story would likely have me dying of a broken heart over Lutero's death. No, thank you, Mr. Boler."

Somewhere a bottle crashed, and the sound of splintering glass broke through the night.

"You've been through a lot, Mrs. Wade, and I don't mean just being captured and living with the Apaches, but also coming back and all that's happened since. It's an experience people would like to know about. I know I could sell it to a publisher in the East. We could split the proceeds. You want to earn a living," he reminded her. "With a true story of your life published, you could travel around the country lecturing to different groups."

"I see. Now I'm simply a social outcast, and you're suggesting that I turn myself into a freak for profit. You are beginning to sound like Mr. Bannon. Earlier you wanted to buy the rights, and now you want to split with me."

He chuckled. "You have a quick mind, Mrs. Wade.

Not much escapes you, does it?" Their footsteps sounded with a rhythmic tempo on the plank sidewalk. "You're intelligent and educated. Why don't you write the book, and I'll represent you—for a small percentage, of course."

"Are you serious?"

"Of course."

"Then why don't you give me a job at your newspaper? You're the only person in town I haven't asked."

Boler stopped and Hannah paused with him. "When I suggested that you were capable of writing about your own experiences, I didn't mean to imply that you had the qualifications to become a reporter."

"I didn't mean to suggest that you should hire me to write for your paper. I can do anything—clean, fold papers, keep your accounts. As you said, Mr. Boler, I am intelligent and educated, and I need the work."

"How are you at setting type?"

"I could learn." Hannah felt a lifting of her spirits, the determined rise of hope.

He reached for her hand and studied her long, slim fingers. "Women are very dexterous. Half the time my typesetter is drunk. I could use somebody who is steady and dependable."

"You've found her," she stated.

"So I have." They shook hands to confirm the agreement, and Hannah found that she had something to smile about for the first time in days.

"How much are you paying your typesetter now?" she asked.

"The man's experienced—"

"He's also a drunkard, you said." The sky was purpling into night, the darkening shadows making an indistinct shape of his features.

He shook his head mildly. "All right. I'll pay you the same wages I'm giving him. I have the feeling it's going to be a new experience working with you, Mrs. Wade. You're going to keep me on my toes."

"Indeed, Mr. Boler." They started walking again.


A high morning sun made an oven out of the steep-walled arroyo, the scant breezes passing over rather than through it. The Apache tracker squatted on his heels and poked through the accumulated piles of horse dung. After testing its smell and crumbling some between his fingers, he straightened and looked at the gaunt, hollow-eyed sergeant.

"Long time here. Maybe four days," the tracker concluded. "One dung still warm inside. Maybe two, three hours."

"See which way they headed when they left," John T. ordered, and jerked his hand toward the brush-blocked mouth of the gully. The Apache scout trotted past him, his moccasins making faint scuffing sounds on the sand.

"Sergeant! Look what I found." Hooker turned toward the voice. Grover's search of the hidden camp had unearthed a uniform, half-buried under a tumble of large rocks. He carried it over to John T., sweat streaming down his face and plastering his gray shirt to his back, and remarked, "It's Bitterman's, all right. Hell, I thought he'd be halfway to California by now."

"He's clever, but not clever enough to brush out the tracks leading into here," Hooker said absently, and turned to issue an order to the other troopers. "All right, let's mount up."

No one mentioned Cimmy Lou or the way Hooker had pushed them during the last week, refusing to admit that they'd lost the trail and searching ceaselessly until they found it again. They hadn't seen him sleep at all, and all of them had noticed the glazed, distant look about him. This wasn't like their sergeant. Something was going on inside him that made them all uneasy.

The Apache scout had found fresh tracks leading away from the gully hideout, and they pointed to town. Another trooper muttered to Grover as he swung into the saddle, "Bitterman shoulda kept runnin'."

"I got a feelin' he could never've run far enough," Grover murmured, and dug his heels into his horse as the sergeant gave a hand signal to move out.

Cutter rode up to the hotel and dismounted, looping the reins around the hitching rail in front. The heavy tread of his boots echoed loudly as he walked across the raised board sidewalk to the hotel entrance. Inside the lobby he hesitated, then crossed to the desk.

"I'm looking for Mrs. Hannah Wade. I was told she came here a few days ago," he informed the young clerk behind the counter. "Could you tell me where I could find her?"

"Mrs. Wade? She's at the newspaper office down the street."

Faintly surprised by the answer, Cutter pushed away from the hotel desk and retraced his steps across the lobby to the door. Outside, he swung himself into the saddle and rode down the congested street to the building housing the newspaper. When he walked in, he automatically took off his hat and smoothed his shaggy black hair.

"Captain Cutter, isn't it?" The newspaper publisher came forward to greet him.

As of this morning, the rank was no longer his to claim, but Cutter didn't bother to go into that. "I was told at the hotel that Hannah Wade was here."

Boler's look instantly turned speculative and curious. "She's in back setting type for tomorrow's edition of the paper. Go on through if you'd like."

"Thank you." The absent response was given as Cutter walked by him, his attention already shifting to the back.

The cumbersome machinery of the printing press blocked his view of the rear area. The smell of oil and ink was strong as he moved by it. Sunlight streamed through a back window, shining on the wide, slanted table where Hannah was at work. A warm rush of feeling went through him when he saw her.

Her concentration was focused on the copy she was setting, and she remained unaware of his presence. Cutter paused for a minute to watch her. Stray wisps of auburn hair had escaped the bun at the back of her neck, softening its prim style, and there was something vital and strong in the deep tan of her skin. The long, bibbed apron she wore was smudged with ink, and her fingers were stained with it, too.

"Hannah."

When she turned around, the rush of pleasure lighting her face was a heady sight. "Cutter." She quickly checked her reaction. "It's good to see you."

"I just came back from patrol this morning and learned that you were gone." Her withdrawal puzzled him, and he fiddled with his hat, fingering the creases in the crown and rolling the brim. "I wasn't sure where you had gone."

"I didn't go far." She fitted a slug between some words to space out the line to the end of the column. "I had to find work."

An awkwardness stretched between them, and Cutter couldn't seem to find the words to break it. "Will you be staying here, then?"

"Long enough to learn the trade. With a recommendation from Mr. Boler, I should be able to find a job at a newspaper in some other town."

"Where will you go?"

"Maybe Prescott or Denver." Her shoulders lifted in a vague shrug.

"What about Santa Fe?" It was closer to the valley where he planned to settle.

"Regimental headquarters for the Ninth? No, I don't think so." She shook her head wryly at the suggestion.

Cutter breathed in deeply. He wasn't thinking of it in that way. He had so many things to say to her, but he could find no sign that she wanted to hear them. Maybe he had only imagined that she cared about him. Maybe when she had waved to him it had been only a casual gesture, and not some silent promise to wait for him. Lord knows, he'd built up enough visions in his head from it, and from the kiss she'd given him. She was his daydream and nightdream. But it was all locked up inside him, and he didn't know how to get it out—or if it would be welcome.

The tracks were lost where they joined the main road into Silver City, the hoofprints obliterated by the horses and wagons that had come afterward. John T. halted the detail on the roadside and looked toward the town.

"Could be he's tryin' to lose us again like he done with the cattle." Private Grover ventured the thought. "No tellin' which way he went."

"He doesn't know we're on his trail." John T. collected the reins, slapping them against the horse's neck to stir it forward. "He went into town. He'd be that brassy."

A wave of his hand ordered the troopers to follow him as John T. rode alongside the Apache scout. They entered town in a straggly column of twos, walking their horses down the busy main street. Hooker's staring eyes searched the faces they passed and scanned the brands of the horses tied at the hitching rails. One of them jarred him to attention, and John T. pulled his horse up and rode over for a closer look, sidling his horse up to the flank of the chestnut gelding. He ran his fingers over the 08 mark burned into the hide and flicked off a scab. The older US brand was barely visible. The Apache slid off his horse and checked the gelding's shoes and those of the horse tied next to it.

"Same horses," the scout announced.

At the confirmation, Hooker's attention swung to the building directly in front of the hitching rail. Tall letters painted on the false front of the second story identified the establishment as the Ace High Saloon and Gambling Hall.

"Bitterman used t'brag that he dealt faro in N'Orleans," Grover said.

John T. dismounted and passed his horse's reins to the private. When he unholstered his gun and started for the saloon's door, the troopers quickly swung out of their saddles to follow him, sensing that no order would be given.

His gun was leveled when he walked through the door. He had no conscious thought of what he was doing or of the soldiers behind him as he paused to look around the nearly empty gaming room. The click-click-clicking of a spinning roulette wheel made its sound against the background of muted voices.

Cimmy Lou laughed, and he turned and strode in the direction of the laughter. She stood beside Bitterman's chair at a poker table in back, watching while he raked in the winnings from a poker hand and added them to the small pile beside him. John T. leveled the gun at the narrow chest of his target. In some distant part of his brain, he heard Cimmy scream a warning to Bitterman.

"Leroy! Look out!!"

He adjusted his aim as his target pushed back from the table to stand and grab at something tucked in the waistband of his pants. Unblinking, he pulled the trigger twice in rapid succession, and watched Bitterman slam against the back wall, then slide to the floor, a red stain spreading down his shirtfront. Cimmy Lou was still screaming, and John T. shifted the gun muzzle and pointed it at her. The explosions reverberated through the hall. Then silence—that awful, killing silence and the blue powder smoke drifting in the air, that's all he knew when he lowered his gun.

"Sweet Jeezus," someone murmured.

At the sound of gunfire, Cutter lifted his head, instinctively attempting to determine distance and direction. The call was one he'd answered for too long to break the habit of investigating it now. He broke for the door, aware that Hannah was following him, and met Boler on his way out, jamming the derby hat on his head. Outside the newspaper office, Cutter paused to locate the source before he plunged into the trouble.

"Where did it come from?" he asked. Boler had been closer to the door than he had.

"Up the street, I think."

There was a stir of activity outside one of the saloons as others were drawn by the sound of shooting. Cutter headed in that direction. A freckle-faced boy ran toward him, wide-eyed with the excitement of danger.

"One o' them colored soldiers just shot somebody at the Ace saloon!" the boy shouted eagerly, wanting to be the first to spread the news.

Cutter broke into a lope. When he reached the crowd gathering outside the Ace High, he shoved his way through to where the cavalry horses were standing at the rail. Two of the black troopers stood at the door, uncertainly facing the crowd and holding their rifles diagonally across their bodies.

"Captain, suh!" An agitated Private Grover came out of the saloon to meet him. "Am I glad t'see you, suh."

"What happened here?" All was silent within the gaming hall.

"It's Sergeant Hooker, suh. He jest went in there an' shot 'em. Never said a word."

Swearing, Cutter took a step toward the door just as John T. walked out with Cimmy Lou's limp body cradled in his arms. His face was like stone, black marble with vacant, staring eyes. Nothing lived inside anymore. Another string of swear words came from Cutter, this time cursing the injustice of life, and the sense of inevitability of some things.

"Hooker." He planted himself in John T.'s path.

"Captain." Hooker's voice was devoid of emotion, flat in its delivery. He looked down at the body in his arms and the smooth, dark-skinned face, beautiful even in death. "I had to do it. There was no other way."

"Let me have her, John T." Cutter reached out to remove the burden from him. "She's dead now. It's over." Hooker offered no resistance as Cutter took the death-heavy body into his arms. The front of Hooker's shirt was dark with her blood. Cutter turned and gave Cimmy's body to Private Grover. "Find the undertaker," he instructed quietly. When he turned back, John T. was slumped against the wall of the building, his body slack. Cutter sighed heavily, unable to look at him. "Where's Bitterman?"

"Inside."

"You killed him, too, I suppose," he said grimly, and watched the slow, affirmative nod. "Why, Hooker? Why did you do it?"

"I had to stop her. She couldn't do it herself, so I did it for her. I guess she couldn't help bein' what she was. She had no feelings, not the good kind that make you want someone else to be happy. She used people an' she was gonna keep on usin' people—an' hurtin' 'em. She can't do that anymore."

"Damn," Cutter muttered with savage impotence.

"What's going on here?" a voice demanded, and Cutter swung around to face the man wearing a marshal's badge.

"It's army business," he said. "We'll handle it."

"What happened?" The town marshal glanced at the body being carried out of the saloon by two of the soldiers.

"My sergeant shot a deserter, and the woman was killed in the cross fire," Cutter snapped.

"No, suh." John T. shook his head at the answer.

"Shut up, sergeant!"

"I can't, suh."

"Dammit, Hooker, I'm trying to save your neck." Cutter growled the low warning.

"But I killed her, suh."

Fighting down his temper, Cutter faced the marshal. "This is an army matter. We won't be requiring your assistance."

After a small hesitation, the man nodded. "Very well. I'll leave you to it."

Cutter waited until he had disappeared into the milling throng of curious onlookers before he turned back to Hooker. He leaned toward him, bracing an arm against the side of the building. "Listen to me, John T.," he ordered. "I want you to walk over there and get on one of those horses and ride out of town and keep riding. No one will stop you; I'll see to that."

"No, suh." Dully Hooker shook his head.

"Dammit, John T., will you get the hell out of here! All right, so she's dead. Don't let her destroy you—she isn't worth it. Run while you've got the chance," he insisted angrily.

"I can't run, Captain. I'm a soldier. They said I was a hero at the battle near Kickapoo Springs, and they gave me the Medal of Honor. I was top sergeant. If all that's gonna mean somethin', I have to stay."

"Damn." Cutter's hand pounded the building as he pushed away from it. The tightness in his throat hurt as he turned away. He saw the two soldiers silently looking on. "He'll have to face charges," he told them. "Consider him under arrest."

From the outer edge of the crowd, Hannah caught glimpses of Cutter by the entrance to the saloon. Even from this distance, the grim set of his features was evident. She made no attempt to get closer. Word had passed through the crowd, so she had a general idea of what had happened inside, and she'd seen the soldiers carrying the bodies of Bitterman and Cimmy Lou to the undertaker's.

Nothing could be gained by waiting for Cutter, so Hannah drew back to leave. As she turned, a horse and rider approached the crowd, attracted by the assembly in front of the saloon. It was Stephen. Hannah stiffened at the sight of that erect figure in the saddle, so unbendable, like his codes of right and wrong. When he saw her, he reined in his horse.

"I was just coming to see you." He dismounted and walked toward her as if he expected her to be glad to see him.

"Were you?" Hannah murmured coolly.

"Yes. What's going on here?" He gestured at the crowd. "I noticed a couple of our troopers by the door of that saloon."

"The detail caught up with that deserter. There was some shooting. He and Cimmy Lou Hooker were killed." Hannah watched his face, wondering if he'd show any reaction to the news of the woman's death. She suspected that Cimmy and Stephen had been lovers, but she didn't bother to ask. She really didn't care.

"This is no place for you." Stephen took her by the arm and led her across to the empty side of the street. The wind churned up a spinning dust devil and it danced by them, whipping at the hem of her skirt.

"You said you came to see me." Hannah brushed back a strand of hair that the wind blew into her face.

"Look at your hands." Stephen caught her ink-blackened fingers and turned them up for his inspection. "What have you been doing?"

"Working." She calmly pulled her hand away.

"Where?"

"At the newspaper, setting type for Mr. Boler. Were you hoping to find me working in some dance hall being mauled by a rowdy bunch of men, so desperate that I would run into your arms?" She tipped her head to one side, knowing him too well.

"I was hoping that by now you would have realized how foolish and ill-conceived your actions are and would be ready to come back with me," he admitted with harsh impatience. "It's time you came to your senses."

"But I have." Hannah smiled coolly. "I have spoken with an attorney, Stephen. It appears that it will be relatively easy to obtain a divorce. I believe it has something to do with the shortage of women in the territory."

His face was white with fury beneath his tanned complexion. "Then you intend to go through with this notion of yours?"

"Yes."

"I have tried to be patient with you, Hannah, but there is a limit to how far I'll go. Now, either you stop this nonsense and come home, or—"

"Or what, Stephen?" she demanded.

"Don't be a fool, Hannah." His voice was thick with anger. "No one else will want you."

His words stung and resentment flared through her. Stephen saw the maintenance of their marriage as his duty, and she was supposed to be grateful for the favor he was doing her. She was supposed to be grateful that he was willing to provide a roof over her head and food

374

on her table; she wasn't supposed to expect more. But that was a step backward to mere existence.

"Good-bye, Stephen. I see no necessity to ever see you again."

That stiff-necked reserve hardened him, and Stephen's chin lifted with offended arrogance. He didn't rage at her or plead for her to reconsider. He expressed neither grief nor regret; all his thoughts were for himself. His self-centered ego did not admit anything except his own image of himself. When he turned on his heel and walked crisply away from her, Hannah knew that it was truly over. As long as she had fed his dream of himself, things had worked between them. When she had stopped, there had been nothing left. Now, he would play the role of the maligned husband.

Cutter watched Wade coming across the street, but it was the expression on Hannah's face, so grim and saddened, that prodded him to rashness. He met Wade halfway. Stephen hesitated in mid-stride and threw a frowning look over his shoulder at Hannah before bringing his hard, questioning gaze back to Cutter.

"What are you doing here?" he demanded.

"None of your damned business," Cutter snarled in reply, his temper breaking through the harsh restraints he usually placed on it.

"I do not care for your insolence, Captain." Stephen stood stiffly, the brass buttons on his uniform shining brightly in the sunlight. Everything about him was precisely "by the book," following strict regulation. "You will retract that remark."

"Like hell!" Cutter's stomach muscles tightened into a solid wall as his every nerve tensed in readiness. He felt the throb of blood through his veins, his pulse quickening. The smells were sharper—dust, sweat, horses—and the sounds around him were clearer. Yet everything seemed more distant, outside the arena in which he stood.

"May I remind you that insubordination and failure to salute are punishable offenses, Captain?" Wade frowned, sensing trouble and puzzled by it.

"The hell you say." Cutter had never been a talker. His right arm cocked and swung with lightning precision, his doubled fist connecting solidly with Wade's jaw. All his weight went into the swing and it drove Wade backward, snapping his head to the side and sprawling him across the ground. Cutter stood crouched and ready, his fists up, waiting for Wade to come at him. But the major merely propped himself up on his elbow and rubbed at his jaw, glaring his dislike at his attacker.

"I'm bringing charges against you for assaulting a superior officer, Cutter. I'll break you," he threatened.

"No, you won't. Not that way." Cutter ripped the captain's bars off one shoulder, then the other, and threw them on the ground beside Wade. "My resignation went into effect this morning. That was civilian to soldier. So if you want to break me, you either have to stand up or have me arrested. And I wish to hell you'd stand up."

But he didn't, and Cutter slowly straightened, squaring his shoulders and flexing the bruised knuckles in his hand. After a last look at Wade as he got up and brushed off the dirt, he walked across the street to Hannah. Somewhat guiltily he avoided meeting her level gaze.

"I've been wanting to do that for a long time." He couldn't express regret for something that gave him a lot of satisfaction.

"So have I." The smallest smile touched her lips, lifting the corners as he finally looked at her in surprise. "I have something to thank you for again."

"I wasn't sure . . . how you felt about him." Cutter still wasn't. "Sometimes it doesn't seem to matter how badly a man treats a woman; she just keeps on loving him."

"I'm not one of those women." The milling crowd began to disperse. The glimpse of a bowler hat heading in the direction of the newspaper office offered Hannah the excuse she sought. "I have to get back to work."

"Then you are through with him?" Cutter didn't give her a chance to leave.

"Yes. Mr. Hawthorne, an attorney here in town, is drawing up a divorce document for me. We're finished. I think Stephen has finally accepted that." On the other side of the street, Stephen was issuing sharp orders to the troopers to reaffirm his authority. Hannah watched him and felt nothing, not even pity. When she brought her glance back to Cutter, it strayed to the darker blue marks on his sun-faded uniform where his rank insignias had been. "You have left the army."

"I handed in my resignation before I left on patrol. I had intended to tell you, but—" He shrugged away the rest of that sentence. "I knew I couldn't stay in."

"No, the life didn't suit you," Hannah agreed lightly, feeling the tension taking over once again as it had in the newspaper office. She tried to ignore it. "It's too restrictive. You're the kind of man who needs room; otherwise you just drift along."

"That's what I was doing—drifting—until I met you and realized how unsatisfied I was."

She didn't want to hear the implication of his words, so she shied away from reading anything into them. "What will you do now? Do you have any plans?"

"I chased some Apaches into a long valley northeast of here a few years back. It had a river running through it, and grass growing stirrup-high. There was timber in the mountains that a man could cut to build a cabin and a barn. A herd of wild horses ranged there, and some looked like good saddle prospects. With some work and riding, a man could trap them, break 'em, and sell them to the army. A herd of cattle could always be brought up from Texas and put out to grass. That's where I'm going, if somebody hasn't already beaten me to it."

She listened to the flow of his words, the conviction in his voice, and was glad for him. She could picture him in that setting, and knew that it was right for him.

"A rancher." She smiled. "You'll do well, I think."

"What about you, Hannah?" His probing gaze was difficult to meet. "How will you do?"

"I'll be fine," she assured him with forced lightness. "Don't worry about me."

"Asking me not to worry about you is like asking the sun to come up in the west. It can't be done. I'll always want to know if you're all right."

"Don't be kind to me, Jake," she warned with taut emotion. "I can't take it when you're kind."

"It isn't kindness, Hannah." Tension vibrated in his voice. "That valley is going to be a lonely place. I'd like you to come with me, help me build the cabin and barn, and give me a hand with the horses."

"If all you want is a woman, I'm not interested."

"It's a wife I want."

She shook her head. "I know what it's like to just live. A halfhearted thing kills a person inside. If you don't feel anything for me—" She couldn't finish the sentence. "I have so much to give you, I don't dare start. It would hurt me too much."

Cutter smiled. "That time I kissed you—I don't think you could call that halfhearted." He watched her eyes darken and the unconscious sway of her body toward him. His arms went around her to gather her in, the warm weight of her body pressing against him. Her upturned face was close.

"Will you never regret marrying a woman who once lived with the Apaches? Will it never bother you that I've been a squaw?"

His kiss held all his answers. There was no holding back of anything—not the pain of the past, nor comfort, nor love, nor the mysteries before them. The sun blazed down on them, but it was another heat that they felt.

"I have to go back to the fort." A small tremor shook the hand that touched her cheek. "I want to do what I can for John T. when he comes up on charges. Afterward, I'll be back to take you to that valley."

"I'll be waiting."

# A SPECIAL MESSAGE
# FROM JANET DAILEY

Dear Readers,

One of the questions people always ask me is "Where did you get the idea to write this particular book?" With the book I've just completed, *THE GREAT ALONE*, the answer is easy.

Approximately six years ago, Bill and I flew to Alaska to research the background for a small romance I planned to write with an Alaskan setting. From somewhere—either from watching Hollywood movies, or reading Jack London's *Call of the Wild*, or hearing stories about Eskimos and igloos, or seeing pictures of oil drilling on the North Slope—I had the impression that Alaska was a frozen wasteland where people went around bundled in parkas all year long.

But the Alaska I found that September six years ago was green—wildflowers grew everywhere and whole mountainsides were covered with forests of golden birch. I was absolutely stunned by the incredible, magnificent beauty of Alaska. Bill and I traveled through the whole United States, but Alaska was unquestionably the most beautiful of all the Fifty.

That trip to Alaska was an eye-opener for me—in more ways than one. While I was gawking at the scenery, Bill was gathering research material—material that I read in the evenings when I wasn't marveling at the Northern Lights. Again I was stunned. I had been let down by Hollywood, the adventure novels and television.

But worst of all, I'd been let down by my American history teacher. Oh, I knew that we had purchased Alaska from Russia. But I didn't know Russians had lived in Alaska for more than a hundred years before the purchase of 'Seward's Folly'—that the Russian capital of Sitka had been called 'the Paris of the Pacific' when San Francisco was little more than a Spanish presidio.

From the moment some six years ago, my curiousity was piqued. The more I delved into Alaska's past, the more I found a history rich in human emotions and high drama. All the stories were there—of triumph and tragedy, greed and glory, rape and revolt, boom and bust, the godly and the godless. A history constantly repeating itself with the lure of gold—whether it was the 'soft gold' of the sea otter pelts sought by the Russian fur hunters or the yellow nuggets of the numerous gold rushes or the 'black gold' of the oil strikes. A story virtually unknown. All that was left to do was to tell it.

Tackling this novel was an awesome task, requiring both mounds of research to assure historical accuracy and many months of writing. And in telling the story of seven generations of Alaskans—of over 200 years of dreams and desires, love, loss and renewal—the book took on a life of its own, growing into the longest and most ambitious novel I had ever written. *THE GREAT ALONE* is the result. And I've never loved working so hard in all my life.

I'm proud that Poseidon Press will be publishing *THE GREAT ALONE* in hardcover in June of 1986. I'm so excited about it, I wish I had it ready for you to read right now, but since I don't, I've selected one of my favorite scenes from the novel to share with you on the following pages.

I sincerely hope that you get as much enjoyment out of reading *THE GREAT ALONE* as I did in writing it, and I'll look forward to hearing from you when you get to read the entire book next year.

Sincerely,

Janet
Dailey

# SITKA, ALASKA
## *Summer, 1897*

SINCE THE STEAMER WAS EXPECTED TO BE AT DOCKSIDE FOR several hours, off-loading supplies and taking on more fuel, Justin Sinclair took advantage of the opportunity to look around the old Russian town and stretch his legs a bit. Lord knew, he'd had few chances to see much of anything in his twenty-two years. What sights could a man see from the deck of a fishing boat? He swore that when he struck it rich in the goldfields of the Klondike, he was going to eat nothing but meat. He never wanted to smell another fish again. He hated fish and he hated the sea. His father was welcome to both, but he wasn't about to spend the rest of his life stinking like a fish.

Other passengers aboard the steamer had disembarked ahead of him, obviously sharing his intentions. A group of Indians, mostly squaws, crowded around them, trying to peddle their goods, which ranged from miniature totems carved from wood to silver bracelets and Indian blankets. Justin Sinclair shouldered his way through the bodies, firmly shaking his head in refusal to every object thrust in front of him.

Once free of the throng, he paused to look around and get his bearings. A perfectly cone-shaped mountain rose in the distance. Snow still frosted the cratered peak of the extinct volcano, making it stand out that much more sharply against the blue, cloud-studded sky.

"Could you tell me where that ship is going?" The question was asked by a woman, her voice oddly accented.

Justin vaguely recalled there had been a woman standing on the fringe of the crowd at the wharf. He'd noticed her mainly because she had looked so dowdy, dressed in a drab, dark-colored dress, a dark wool shawl around her shoulders, and a dark kerchief tied under her throat, completely covering her hair. But this woman's voice sounded young. Justin turned curiously, surprised to find the voice belonged to the woman he'd noticed earlier. His interest faded sharply.

"It's headed for Mooresville."

"Have you heard they've discovered gold on the other side of White Pass in the Klondike region of Canada?" Again the voice betrayed a youthful vigor.

"Yes, I know." Justin took another look at her, but it was difficult to see her face. The scarf that covered her hair was pulled forward, obscuring her eyes as she gazed at the vessel tied up to the dock. Then she turned her head to look at him. He was startled by her face. Her complexion was smooth and shone with the lustre of an abalone shell, and her eyes were like large nuggets of shiny black coal.

"Is that where you're bound?"

"Yes." He would have stared at her much longer, but she turned away again to gaze at the steamer.

"I wish I were going." She spoke so softly that Justin knew she hadn't intended him to hear it, so he pretended he hadn't.

"Do you live here?"

"Yes." She pulled the shawl more tightly around her shoulders, and seemed to withdraw into herself.

"I have a few hours to kill before the ship sails. I thought I'd look around the town. One of the hands on the ship told me this used to be the old Russian capital of Alaska before we bought it. Maybe you could show me around."

"There isn't much to see." The shrug of her shoulders seemed to express her dislike. "Some broken-down old buildings, a church, and a cemetery. There is little else."

As he glanced toward town, he noticed the green-painted spire of a church, topped by a peculiarly shaped cross. "I've never seen a cross like that. What kind of church is it?"

"That is St. Michael's Cathedral. It is of the Russian Orthodox faith."

"Why does the cross have that slanted bar at the bottom?"

"When the Christ Jesus was put upon the cross, His feet rested on the lower bar. At the moment of His death, His weight tipped it to one side." Her dark eyes gleamed like obsidian. "You should go inside the church. All the gold ornamentation and silver icons are very beautiful."

Justin noticed the suggestion was not offered with any religious fervor. "Why don't you show me the inside of the church?"

Again she drew back. "No, I couldn't go there with you." She shook her head.

"Why?" His curiosity was aroused by this unusual young woman. She had such an extraordinary face that he wondered why she dressed in such homely attire.

"My aunt might see me with you."

"Naturally she wouldn't approve of you being seen with a strange man," he guessed. "We can correct that situation. My name is Justin Sinclair, formerly from Seattle. And you are—?"

An impish light danced in her eyes. "Marisha Gavrileyna Blackwood. And I'm afraid you don't understand."

"Marisha Gavrileyna. Are you Russian?" He wondered if that was the source of the faint accent that gave her speech its distinctive sound.

"Russian, American, Indian—I'm a little bit of everything."

He was a little surprised by the open admission of her mixed ancestry, although it certainly made the situation easier for him. At least now he knew what kind of woman he was dealing with.

"It was a pleasure meeting you, Mr. Sinclair, but I must go."

As she took a step away from him, he laid a restraining hand on her arm, feeling the coarse texture of the wool shawl. "Why? We aren't strangers anymore. I'm Justin and you're Marisha. How could your aunt possibly object now?"

"My aunt objects to all men. She says they can't be trusted, that they only bring pain. My father ran off before I was born

385

and took everything my family had. She insists that all men are tarred with the same brush."

"What happened to your mother?"

"She died when I was eleven."

"How old are you?" It was impossible to judge her age—all he could see was her face.

"Nineteen. Already I'm an old maid—like she is." Bitterness flashed across her face, hardening the set of her lips. "There aren't many bachelors in this town and she's managed to chase away the few that have come calling."

"Where is she now?"

"At St. Michael's, cleaning. I'm supposed to be working in the garden, but I slipped away to come down here." The corners of her lips twitched with a smile as she made the admission with no hint of remorse. "She'll be furious when she finds out."

"Is this where you usually come?"

"No. I just wanted to see the ship and find out where it was going." She gazed longingly at the steamer.

"Since I'm not doing anything and your aunt is already going to be mad at you, why don't you take me to the place where you usually go when you sneak off from your aunt?"

She studied him for a minute, as if assessing the degree of risk. Justin didn't doubt for an instant that this aunt of hers had practically kept Marisha under lock and key, but she obviously had a rebellious spirit.

"This way," she said and started off.

Walking swiftly, she skirted the edges of town and led him along the southern shoreline facing the Sound and its scattering of small islands. Most of the time she kept her head down, avoiding eye contact with anyone who might be watching. Only twice did he notice her glance around to see if they were being observed. They were on the outskirts of town and nearing the forest when she finally slowed down.

"They call this path the Governor's Walk," she told him. "Supposedly Baranov used to walk along here."

"Who's Baranov?"

"Alexander Andreivich Baranov was the first Russian governor of Alaska. Actually, he built Sitka. There used to be a big old mansion on that knoll we passed. It was known as Baranov's Castle, but it burned down three years ago. Do you

386

see that big rock by the shore just ahead of us? During his last days here, they say he used to spend hours sitting there, gazing out at the Pacific. Guess what it's called."

"Baranov's Rock."

"Yes." She laughed and ran ahead to the boulder.

There, she stopped to lean against it and gaze out to sea. Stare as he might, the heavy shawl and the voluminous material of her dress made it impossible for Justin to tell if she was plump or if her clothes merely made her look that way.

As he approached the rock, the beach gravel crunched underfoot. Although she didn't turn, a slight movement of her head indicated her awareness of his presence while she continued to look at the wide stretch of island-studded waters.

"In the spring, when the herring come into the bays and inlets to spawn, the Tlinget Indians wait until low tide, then spread hemlock boughs on the exposed beaches, and fasten them down. The herring deposit their eggs on the branches. You should see it," she murmured. "The boughs look like they're covered with thousands of pearls."

"It must be something." But fish was about the last subject that interested him.

"It is." She sighed and pushed away from the rock. As she turned toward him, she reached up and began tugging at the scarf knot under her throat. "I hate this *babushka*. It makes me feel like a *babushka*."

"What's a *babushka?*"

"It's a scarf old women in Russia wear. So the word means both scarf and old woman. It's also a word for grandmother—which I'm never likely to be." The knot initially defied her attempts to loosen it. Using both hands, she finally managed to free the ends and pull the scarf off her head.

"Glory be." Justin stared in surprise.

Her hair was a bright yellow-gold that glistened in the sunlight; it was neither brassy nor tarnished with dark streaks, but pure and rich. The contrast between her dark, almost black eyes and brows and her golden-blonde hair was striking and dramatic. The feeling of shock was slow to leave him even though he noticed how amused she seemed to be at his reaction.

"You're beautiful," he murmured, unable to get over it.

387

She smiled wryly and moved away from the rock, absently swinging the scarf in her hand. "Beauty is a curse. That's what Aunt Eva says." Despite her attempt at lightness, Justin detected an underlying bitterness in her tone. "A girl shouldn't be concerned about her looks. She should dress plainly. Wanting to look pretty is vain, and vanity is a sin. This is the only kind of clothes I have, but someday I'm going to have beautiful gowns to wear. Someday," she repeated with a determined lift of her chin.

"I don't care what your aunt says, she's wrong. Nobody with hair like yours should cover it up. My mother always said a woman's hair is her crowning glory."

She touched her hair, smoothing the strands back to the golden knot at the nape of her neck. "Her crowning glory. I like that," she murmured thoughtfully, then seemed to dismiss it from her mind. "Let's walk this way. There's something I want to show you." She followed a faint trail that paralleled the shoreline for a ways, then led into the woods. Justin was too intrigued by her to care where they were going.

Huge trees towered all around them, their overlapping branches shutting out any direct light from the sun. A high humidity made the air seem heavy as they walked along the path through the forest, their footsteps making hardly any sound, cushioned by the soft, composted soil.

"Have you ever seen gold? Real gold, I mean." She didn't wait for his answer. "I saw some once. Blue Pants Kelly—he's an old prospector from around here. He used to be in the army, but even after he got out, he still wore the blue pants from his uniform. That's where he got his name. One time, he showed me a piece of ore that had thin slivers of gold running through it."

"They've found gold around here?"

"Some." She nodded. "There are a couple of mines over on Silver Bay and a stamp mill, but I guess they haven't recovered any large quantities of gold." She walked a few steps farther in silence. "I'd like to find some gold."

"It's up there in the Klondike. Only there it's placer gold—loose gold. All a man has to do is pan it out of the streams. You don't have to dig tunnels or have a lot of machinery to crush it free from the rocks. You just put some gravel in your pan and pick out the nuggets. It's so easy a child could do it."

"Or a woman," she murmured as if to herself.

Through a break in the trees just ahead of them, Justin saw the shimmer of sunlight reflected off the surface of water. The towering spruce thinned out where the ground sloped down to the water's edge, the finger of land claimed by a tangle of tall brush and bushes. The graveled shoreline was strewn with huge drift logs, some almost as tall as a man. As they rounded the point of land, Justin saw the mouth of a river.

"That's the Indian River," Marisha Blackwood stated. "The Russian name was Kolosh Ryeka. See that bluff of land back in the forest?" She pointed it out to him. "The Kolosh, or Tlinget Indians, as everyone calls them today, had a large fort there. This is the site of the big battle between the Russians and the Tlingets. The Russian ships anchored in this bay to bombard the fort with their cannon. My great-great-grandfather, Zachar, was married to a Tlinget woman. Her people had attacked the first fort the Russians built on Baranov Island and killed all but a few men who managed to escape. My great-great-grandfather was one of them. He was on one of the ships in the bay when the Russians came to retake the island. He didn't know it, but my great-great-grandmother—his wife—was in the fort with their young son. They escaped into the forest before the Russians overran the fort. It was several years before she and my great-great-grandfather were reunited." She turned, looking into his face, then gazing again at the water. "I find it interesting to know that if her son had died that day—my great-grandfather —I wouldn't be here now to tell you about it."

"Are you the last of your family?"

"No. I have a cousin, Dimitri. He's a fisherman out of Wrangell. From things my aunt has said, I think he does some smuggling, too." Her faint smile seemed to indicate approval of his illicit activities, no matter what her aunt thought. "Most of my aunts and uncles left Alaska shortly after the Americans took over. Nobody's heard from them in years. I guess in the Russian days, Sitka was quite a city. When I was a little girl, my momma used to tell me about the fancy dress balls they had at the castle. And the concerts and the plays."

Pausing, she crooked her mouth in a wry slant. "My aunt says that the minute they raised the American flag over Alaska, everything here changed for the worse."

"It doesn't sound like she has a very good opinion of Americans."

"She doesn't. A few years ago someone suggested to her that she should apply for citizenship papers. I thought she was going to explode. She still considers herself to be Russian. I don't think she likes that I was born an American."

"And a very beautiful one." He still marveled over that, and he suspected that the trace of Indian in her ancestry was responsible for her incredibly dark eyes and well-defined cheekbones . . . maybe even the recklessness he sensed she felt.

"Now you're trying to flatter me." She gave him an accusing look, then quickly turned away. "I shouldn't have done that."

"What?" Justin frowned.

"A girl shouldn't look a man in the eye. My aunt says that's brazen." She cocked her head in his direction. "Is it?"

"I don't know." He was slightly taken aback. It was something he'd never really thought about. "Some might consider it bold."

"I don't see how you can talk to somebody without looking at them once," she declared, then giggled. "Of course, my aunt doesn't want me to talk to men."

"I'm glad you don't do everything as your aunt tells you."

"I know she has her reasons for feeling the way she does. She's told me some of the things that happened. But . . . sometimes I think she's just jealous because she's so homely no man would want to talk to her. She won't even let me plant flowers in the garden. Vegetables, that's all we've got. 'You can't eat flowers, so why waste the time and space growing them,' she says. Someday I'm going to have a garden and grow nothing but flowers in it. I'm so tired of everything being so ugly and drab and never being able to talk to anyone. I hate it!"

"That's the way I felt about fishing. Ever since I was eleven years old, I worked on my father's fishing boat. I got sick of the smell and the slime—of my clothes being so stiff and caked with ocean salt that they could walk without me—of working a run until you dropped, then unloading your catch at a cannery and going back out for another."

"And you left—walked out just like that?" She snapped her fingers.

"Yup. I happened to be down on the waterfront when the *Portland* docked in Seattle. I saw them unload the shipment of gold from the Klondike—seven hundred thousand dollars' worth—a ton of gold. And I knew I wanted to get some of it. Right then and there, I booked passage on the first ship I could get sailing north. Once I made up my mind, I just did it. There wasn't anything to think about. I wanted to go, so I left."

"I want to go, too," she stated. "Will you take me to the Klondike with you so I can pan for gold? I swear I'll do whatever you tell me if you'll only let me go along with you."

Justin was momentarily stunned. "Hey, you're welcome to come along, but you'll have to pay your own way. I've got a little money with me but that has to buy supplies for the trek over the pass and on to Dawson City. The trail is going to be rough." He doubted that a woman could make it—or that he wanted the burden of a female, no matter how pretty she was.

"I'm strong. I won't slow you down," she assured him as if reading his mind. "I've got a little money put by. I've been thinking about taking the mailboat to Juneau and seeing if I couldn't get a job there. But I've heard that unless you work for the Treadwell Mining Company, there aren't many jobs to be had. If all you have to do in the Klondike is pick nuggets out of a gold pan, then I shouldn't have to worry about a job." She paused, but he could see her mind was still working. "How much do you think a ticket on your ship would cost?"

"I don't know."

"I wouldn't need a place to sleep. I can take a blanket with me and sleep in a chair or some corner. And I can bring some bread and food from home so I won't have to pay for any meals. What else will I need?"

"You'll need warm clothes and a heavy coat. The Klondike's cold in the winter." Part of him was excited by the possibility of having Marisha Blackwood accompany him, even though he knew it was no place for a woman.

391

"Some sturdy shoes, too. How soon before the ship sails?"

Shielding his eyes, Justin tried to gauge the sun's angle in the sky. "A little more than an hour," he guessed.

"I have to go home and pack my things." Quickly she began tying the scarf over her hair once more. A smile broke across her face. "Only it's not going to be my home anymore. Will you wait for me at the wharf?"

"Sure."

"I'll be as quick as I can," she promised and took off running along the path back through the woods, her long skirts flying.

Justin stood at the bottom of the gangway and scanned the town's nearly deserted streets. Behind him, the steamer's whistle blasted its final call to board ship. The girl was nowhere in sight. He felt a little disappointed, although he was convinced it was for the best. From all the stories he'd been hearing, life was pretty rough in the Klondike. There was no sense adding to the problems by having a woman along. Maybe she'd had second thoughts, too. Or her aunt could have caught her. There was no telling.

"Wait!"

He heard the distant shout and turned, pausing halfway up the gangplank. He spied her running down the street toward the wharf, her arms laden with several large bundles.

"Come on, mate. We're shovin' off." One of the deckhands standing by the mooring lines motioned Justin up the ramp with an impatient wave of his hand.

"Don't cast off yet. You've got another passenger coming." Justin ran down the ramp to meet her and quickly relieved her of two cumbersome bundles.

"I thought I wasn't going to make it." She was panting, her cheeks glowing pink from the exertion of the run, but her smile was wide and shining.

"You almost didn't. Come on. Let's get aboard before they leave without us." He nodded for her to precede him up the gangway.

"I haven't paid my fare."

"They'll take your money on the ship."

\* \* \*

392

As the vessel steamed out of the harbor, Marisha stood on the stern deck and gazed at the green-painted spire of St. Michael's Cathedral. She'd left a note for her aunt, telling her that she was leaving but carefully omitting where she was going. Not that she expected her aunt to come after her. She didn't. And she knew her aunt wouldn't understand her reasons for leaving. But no matter how much she hated her aunt's strictures, she felt no hate in her heart for the woman herself. Because of that, she hadn't been able to run away without leaving a note for her.

But she was going. At last she was leaving that ugly, drab town with its monotonous rains—that dull, plodding existence—that narrow, lonely life without laughter or beauty. And she was going to have everything she ever wanted—bright satin gowns, pretty trinkets, and beautiful flowers. She was so excited she felt like shouting.

"Having any regrets?" Justin's voice broke her reverie.

Marisha turned and gazed openly at Justin Sinclair, free now from all her aunt's strict rules. Justin's hat was pushed to the back of his head, revealing the dark, curly locks of his hair. She liked his face, the strength of his heavy jaw and the way his hazel eyes crinkled at the corners when he smiled—as he was doing now. Constant exposure to the elements had browned his face and burned away much of its youthful softness, but hints of it remained in the smoothness of his cheeks and the gentleness of his lips.

Marisha was glad she'd met him today; she wondered how much longer she would have stayed in Sitka if she hadn't. It was after she had heard him express the same discontent with his former life that she felt, and his decision to abandon it to find something better, that she had made up her own mind to leave. She was not sorry she had left; she was glad.

"Not a single one," she declared unequivocally. "This is the happiest day of my life." Impulsively she kissed him on the cheek. "Thank you."

But as she drew back, his hands caught her. The scarf lay loosely about her neck, letting the sea wind blow freely through her hair. Marisha looked at him uncertainly, observing the stillness of his expression. Then he bent his head and kissed her lightly on the lips.

She said nothing when he released her, and instead faced the ship's stern. But she was very aware of his presence by her side. She'd never been kissed by a man before. She hadn't found the experience as revolting as her aunt had intimated it would be. In fact, the kiss had been very pleasant. Her lips still tingled with the warm sensation of his mouth on them.